A Note for Readers

As I mentioned in *A Seat for the Rabble*, industry printing requirements forced me to split my work into two volumes. As such, *An End to Kings* is the second half of *A Seat for the Rabble* and serves as its epic conclusion, picking up where it left off.

Like *A Seat for the Rabble*, *An End to Kings* touches on themes relevant to our own turbulent times—from radical political upheaval to democracy, despotism, classism, and climate change. The next seven books in this saga will take you through new cultures, mount you astride dragons and griffons, and beckon you beneath the waves with merpeople.

It's been satisfying to see the series receive recognition, both for its story and artwork. *A Seat for the Rabble* won *Indies Today*'s 2023 Best Epic Fantasy Award and topped *Independent Book Review*'s "The Best Books We Read in 2023." Several of this volume's chapter illustrations also took home Honorable Mention in the globally competitive Illustrators of the Future Contest. I hope you'll find this entry in the *A King Without a Crown* series equally gripping and enjoyable.

Finally, if you enjoy *An End to Kings*, and you'd like to make an impact, please consider leaving a review for it on Amazon (and Goodreads, if you're feeling charitable). Every review counts and will help me promote and finish this multi-volume epic fantasy series.

I appreciate your time. Thank you for reading!

—Ryan Schuette

INDIES TODAY
AWARD WINNER
2023 BEST
EPIC FANTASY

INDEPENDENT BOOK REVIEW
THE BEST
BOOKS
WE READ
IN
2023

What Readers Say About
A SEAT FOR THE RABBLE
and AN END TO KINGS

"From its electric first pages, Schuette's epic adult fantasy debut grips with a rich, tense, multi-perspective story of a kingdom in unrest. . . . A journalist, [he] writes crisp, compelling scenes that demonstrate an understanding of power, conflicted loyalties, and the ways that history—both ancient and recent, true and made up—powers contemporary conflicts."

—BookLife by *Publishers Weekly* (Grade: A)

"Schuette's extensive world is an enticing one. Religion, class systems, and past events play large parts in the conflict. . . . The competing interests make for a curious, highly detailed, engrossing fantasy."

—*Kirkus Reviews*

"Masterful storytelling and epic worldbuilding make this a must-read for fans of political fantasy."

—ALEXANDRIA DUCKSWORTH, *Independent Book Review*

"If you like getting marooned in a book, so far removed from real life that there's no need for rescue, then *A Seat for the Rabble* was made for you! . . . [It's] a sumptuous feast for the mind."

—NICKY FLOWERS, *Indies Today* (Rating: ★★★★★)

"[A]n unputdownable story. . . ."

—SHERRY FUNDIN, fundinmental.com

"Captivating, engaging, and thought-provoking. . . ."

—ANTHONY AVINA, authoranthonyavinablog.com (10/10)

"Not a word should be cut; not an action scene slashed for the sake of brevity or succinct reading."

—DIANE DONOVAN, *Midwest Book Review*

"Schuette seamlessly weaves centuries-old political theory with powerfully human stories, all within a world where a deeper, more ancient force is at work."

—SEAN MALLEN, a reader and fan

"Move over, George R.R. Martin—there's a new voice in epic fantasy."

—JASON NIEHAUS, a reader and fan

"Schuette's first book in this series is incredibly relevant, engrossingly fun, and hard to put down."

—CASSANDRA SHUPTAR, a reader and fan

"It's one of the best fantasy books I've ever read and a triumph for the genre."

—RYAN ENGEN, a reader and fan

"*A Seat for the Rabble* represents epic fantasy at its finest—addictive, shocking, and rich in world-building complexity."

—VICTOR MCDONALD, a reader and fan

An **END TO KINGS**

A KING WITHOUT A CROWN: BOOK TWO

RYAN SCHUETTE

BEDIVERE
PRESS

Published in the United States of America by Bedivere Press.

This book contains an excerpt from the forthcoming book *A Cavalry of Griffons* by Ryan Schuette. This excerpt may not reflect the final content of the forthcoming edition.

ISBN paperback: 979-8-9885986-3-3
ISBN hardcover: 979-8-9885986-4-0
ISBN eBook: 979-8-9885986-5-7
Library of Congress Control Number: 2023921367

Maps by Cartographybird Maps
Cover art by Ted Nasmith
Cover and interior design by Liz Schreiter
Edited and produced by Reading List Editorial
ReadingListEditorial.com

Printed in the United States of America.
www.RyanSchuette.com

For Mom and my sisters
and
for my country, which I hope will survive
this crucible and endure as a republic.

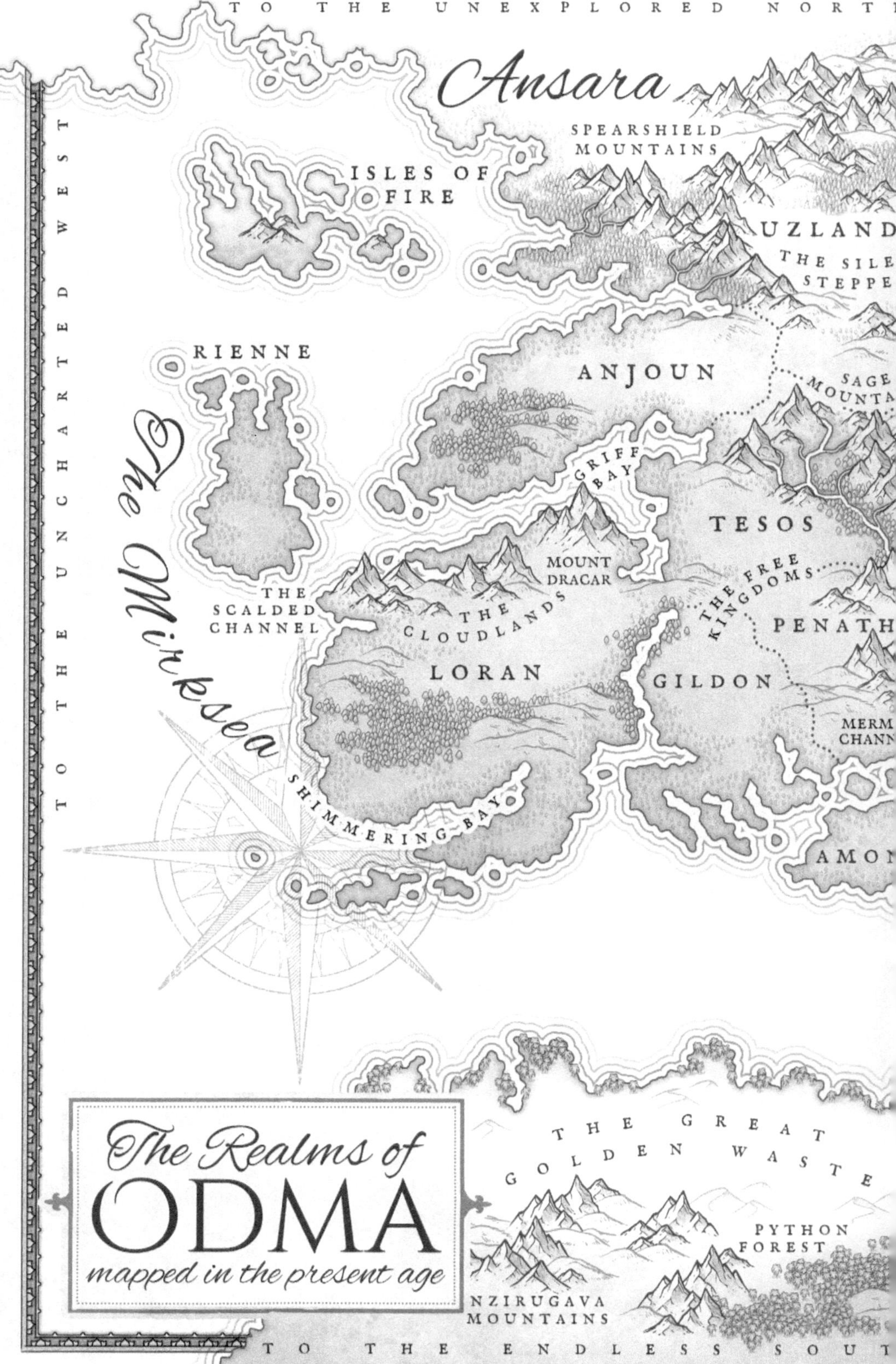

TO THE UNEXPLORED NORT
Ansara
SPEARSHIELD MOUNTAINS
ISLES OF FIRE
UZLAND
THE SILE STEPPE
RIENNE
ANJOUN
SAGE MOUNTA
TO THE UNCHARTED WEST
GRIFF BAY
TESOS
The Mirksea
MOUNT DRACAR
THE CLOUDLANDS
THE FREE KINGDOMS
PENATH
THE SCALDED CHANNEL
LORAN
GILDON
MERM CHANN
SHIMMERING BAY
AMON
The Realms of ODMA
mapped in the present age
THE GREAT GOLDEN WASTE
PYTHON FOREST
NZIRUGAVA MOUNTAINS
TO THE ENDLESS SOUT

SLEEPING GIANT
MOUNTAINS
MOUNT
ROKAR
LAKE OF
STARS
EMPEROR'S
GULF
The Stormsea
CASVIA
THE ROMARIAN
EMPIRE
THE BLACK
RIVER
ANJAN'S STRAIT
MAGNES
AMENIS
MEDECIA
THE
LONELY
ISLE
TO THE FAR EAST
DALLA'S
BAY
RIDER
MOUNTAINS
The Sea of Dracar
The Brace
The Emerald Sea
NERIMBA
SPHINX RIVER
Casaan
LAKE
ELZURA

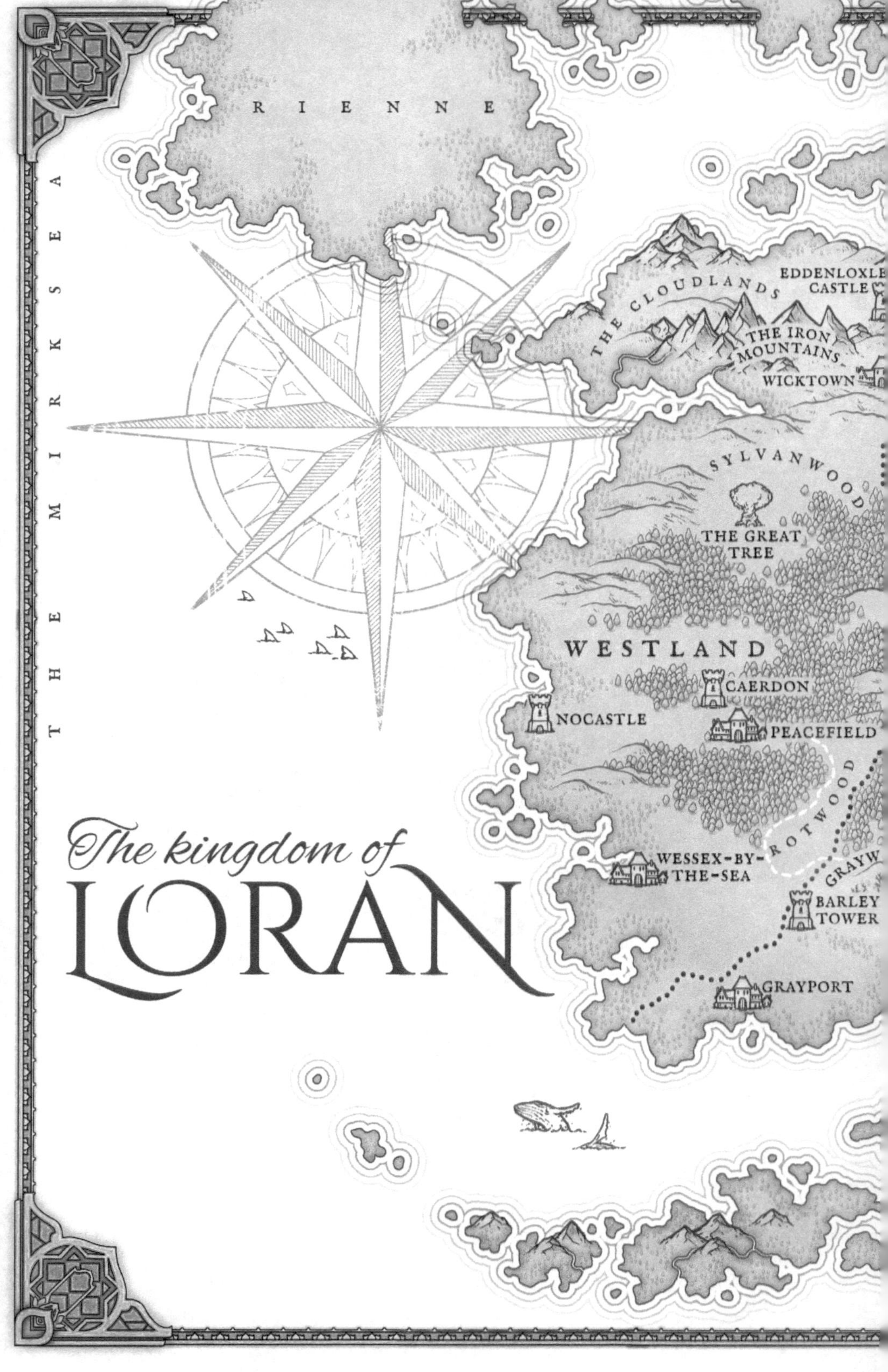

RIENNE
THE MIRK SEA
THE CLOUDLANDS
EDDENLOXLE CASTLE
THE IRON MOUNTAINS
WICKTOWN
SYLVANWOOD
THE GREAT TREE
WESTLAND
CAERDON
NOCASTLE
PEACEFIELD
ROTWOOD
WESSEX-BY-THE-SEA
GRAYW
BARLEY TOWER
GRAYPORT
The kingdom of LORAN

TESOS
THE RIVER COLOSSUS
THE COLOSSUS
MOUNT DRACAR
NORTHLAND
THE GOLDEN MEADOWS
WESSWOOD
THESSELA
WESTERLICHE
MAJOR SUNDER
SHOALTOWN
EASTLAND
SUNDER WAY
MINOR SUNDER
THE MIDLANDS
HEXWAITE
GILDON
SCYTHE ROAD
BARBARA'S GORGE
SOUTHLAND
THORN'S KEEP
ROSBURY
SOUTHPOINT
SOUTH FARCOMBE
THE WEEPING RIVER
THE SHIMMERING BAY
SAXHOLD
RAMSPORT
THE SEA OF DRACAR
THE FREE KINGDOMS
Legend
CITIES AND TOWNS
CASTLES AND FORTS
MAJOR ROADWAYS
BORDERS

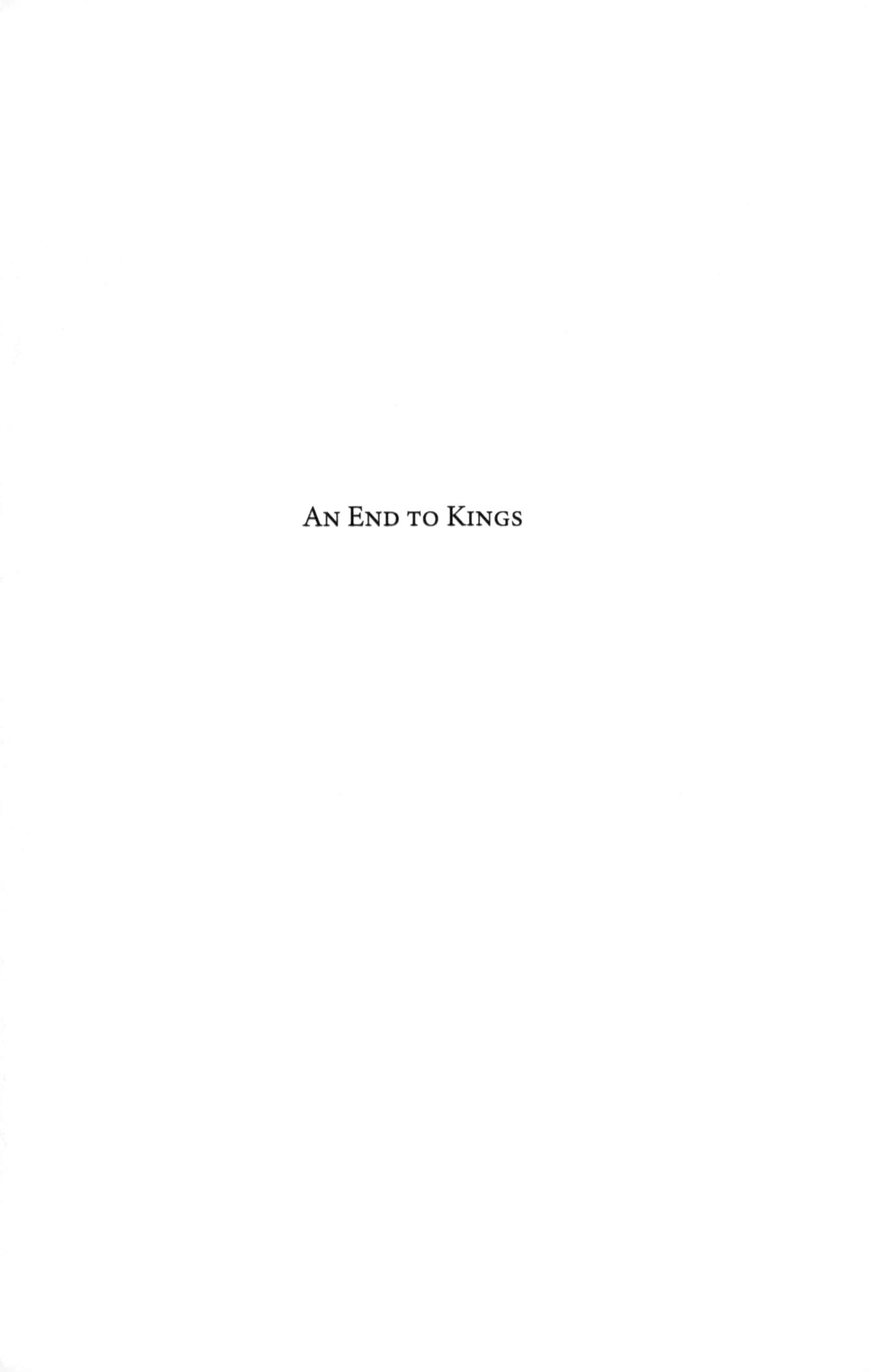

AN END TO KINGS

Go and tell the kings who were:
A tattered cloth shall be mended
With a thread of silver pure,
And the withered vine tended
By hands once and ever sure.

Go and tell the realms of men:
The lame shall rise, the blind see,
And the deaf hear the herald's din
When a king wades through sea
And comes to reign again.

Go and tell those with ears to hear:
He shall shield the few, the fearful last,
Unbowed as shadows circle and sneer,
For o'er man, beast, and blade of grass
The king shall rule far and near.

Go and warn your kings of gilt worth:
Your borders will burn with your keeps
Whilst your paper crowns soil the earth,
For terrors you've sown shall be reaped
Before him, ascendant at birth.
> —"The Ascendant King," a prophecy

Three Trials, three Wings:
Only the Worthy crown kings.
> —A Common rhyme about the Kingstrials

CHAPTER 1

The Storm

bove an inn on a hill, the sky lit up blue, as brightly as if it were day. Illuminated walls of rain rolled across the forest. Thunder reverberated through the ground like the footsteps of giants.

Standing in the hill's cavern entrance, Rathos watched the reflection of his torchflame in a puddle. He thought of the night he swore his oath to the Loyal Company in this cavern. "We are the star of reason over a troubled realm," he remembered Evan Sinclair telling him. The attainted lord had lifted a candle in one hand and raised his other palm. "Do you, Rathos Robswell, swear to safeguard that light? To keep secrets in service to the Common cause, at cost to your life if you do not?"

A gust lashed his face with rain. Rathos pulled at his hood as lightning webbed the sky. *How easily I said the words then,* he pondered. What boy of sixteen wouldn't have? He'd grown up on Evan's teachings—had watched him vanish into castle crypts to leave on secret errands. Evan, his father in so many ways, had seemed as knightly in his own way as Sir Matthus Robswell.

As Rathos endured the cold night air, flexing his toes in sodden boots, he second-guessed himself. This path. How he yearned to be with his wife. He remembered something Evan once asked him: "Who are the men who see a storm coming, and yet do nothing to warn their neighbors?"

"Complicit," Rathos said aloud, his voice lost in a growl of thunder. *I survived the Red Tower and an attack by our Pigeons,* he assured himself. *I'll survive this storm as well. I must survive it. I'm to be a father, now, after all . . .*

More than a fortnight ago, he'd dispatched Karl Redmore to find Rezlan Ambrose. A week ago, he'd received a scroll with a secret message from the Reubenite, penned in lemon juice. A gathering was to take place on familiar grounds, he'd read by candlelight, accessible through the same place he'd sworn his life to the Common cause.

Those were Rezlan's words coming through Karl, Rathos knew. The Company's co-founder had been present with Evan the night Rathos pledged himself to the Wing of the Commons. Now, he waited with their fellow traitors in this cavern, one of many underground tunnels that tentacled Westland.

Rathos knew how to find the door within, knew how to gain entry. But he wouldn't go alone. Fate had a sweet tooth for irony, it seemed. Of all people, Karl Redmore had become the one Companyman he trusted nearly as much as his warder. He needed Karl by his side tonight.

Where are you, my ally, my friend? He probed a few feet outside the cave with his torch, saw nothing beyond the gray veil of rain. Deciding firelight was a convenience he could no longer afford, he snuffed his torch.

Another hour passed in the dark before Rathos discerned movement in the forest. Some thirty yards out, a figure strode past a tree, his horse in tow, cloak flapping in the downpour. He headed toward the cave. Rathos gripped his sword pommel.

Rider and horse splashed into the cave, soaking wet. Rathos kept close to the wall until a flash of lightning blued Karl Redmore's hooked nose and shaggy blond hair.

"You're late," Rathos announced himself, a foot away.

Karl staggered back, wide-eyed, reaching for his sword pommel three seconds after the fact. "Bloody hell, you know how to sneak. Are you a Pigeon?"

"If I were, you'd be dead. You need to work on your reaction time." Rathos swept forward and hugged his ally, patting his drenched backside. "What took you so long?"

Karl scoffed. "I've seen three—count them, *three*"—he held up his fingers—"griffons today. They flew so low over the forest, I could see the fur on their bellies. Had to shelter for hours, pray they didn't catch my horse's scent. And try finding this cave in a storm! Wessex-by-the-Sea may be on the other side of this hill, but these caverns are never easy to find. Next time, find the Reubenite bastard yourself." He hesitated, as if it'd just occurred to him that someone might be listening. "Is Rezlan here . . . with the others?"

Rathos struck flint until his torch quickened again. "We're about to find out."

Karl rubbed down his horse, fed him an oat, and hobbled him inside the cave, far enough from the rain. Staying close to each other, the Companymen forged ahead through a cavern toothed with stalagmites. Shadows ran from Rathos's torch. Occasionally, torchlight revealed a scrawl of white chalk graffiti on the walls, a sign that Barefoot Knights fleeing westward had once sheltered here. A different storm, a different time.

The thunder grew muffled by the time they arrived at a familiar divergence. Here, the cave split into two stalagmited tunnels echoing with the patter of water.

Handing off his torch, Rathos pawed about a wide column of cave wall that separated the tunnels. He brushed his fingers against rough, craggy rock until he touched something else, something smooth and oaken. He rapped his knuckles on the surface for three hollow knocks.

Three dull knocks answered from the other side of the wall that wasn't a wall. Rathos glanced at Karl. He timed his next six knocks perfectly.

The false door shuddered open. Torchlight glimmered in the blades pointed at their faces.

Karl fumbled for his sword and nearly dropped the torch. Rathos held up his hands. "In," came a harsh voice. "*Now.*"

Long before Evan Sinclair and Rezlan Ambrose founded the Loyal Company, a merchant by the name of Mason Grexon had built the Last Elflord Inn on a hillside in Wessex-by-the-Sea, the westernmost town in Loran. The inn had been a poor investment on Mason's part and attracted few visitors, but its undercroft fed into caverns below the hill that men avoided on account of their history with the Barefoot Knights. Which had made the Last Elflord's undercroft the perfect gathering place for Evan, Rezlan, and a band of men dedicated to ending the way things worked in Loran.

Rathos pondered this as he gazed about presently, at the brick-lined walls, wooden rafters, and torches aflicker in their iron braziers. *Are we still safe here?* he wondered. He sat with Karl at one of the undercroft's trestle tables, patiently fielding questions posed by dozens of grim-faced traitors surrounding them.

These were the men of the Loyal Company, the merchants and readers and lords who'd long made themselves a thorn in the side of Gram Sothos and the priestking's allies by working as a united bloc in the Worthy Assembly. Not all the Company was present, as it only ever gathered its strength in the north, but the room felt cramped.

Everyone was furious. *And why not?* King Hexar was dead, Evan Sinclair was missing, and the Pigeons—their swords and shields in a realm ruled by lords who yearned to see them all flayed and headless—had betrayed them. *Yet I must win them to Jason Warchild's cause,* thought Rathos. *I hope I can.*

The two factions piled on their inquiries.

"How many were they?" asked a Reubenite. Apart from Evan and Rezlan, no one in the Loyal Company knew anyone's names. If by chance a man came aware of another's identity, by virtue of meeting in the Worthy Assembly, at court, or on the road, he kept the secret—and his oath—or risked dying from a well-placed arrow somewhere.

"Five," Rathos responded calmly. "Just five."

"They called themselves the Soothsayers?" demanded a Petitioner, a wattle-throated Southlander. "Should've known better. The Waterfowl patrol the Rotwood."

"That's what I said," Karl said defensively, arms crossed.

"Silvertongue led you astray, then," said the Reubenite who stood leaning over them. He had flaxen hair, a hooked nose, a black mole wedged into the corner of his lips.

Karl cast Rathos a sidelong glance. He could blame Rathos easily if he wished to betray him. But he didn't. "No," he sighed. "It wasn't like that. The Pigeons baited us into the swordwood with Rezlan's name."

"Now *there's* a question," said a Petitioner, a lean man with black bangs fringing his forehead. Despite calling himself a Petitioner, this one had a habit of siding against Evan. Rathos suspected he was Tristan Lox, one of the kingdom's wealthiest fur traders. Like a number of other Petitioners, he pressed for reform only to lower his tax burden, not to empower peasants. "How was Rezlan's name even known?"

"The whole kingdom knows his and Sinclair's names," the flaxen-haired Reubenite retorted. "Don't foist Sinclair's failure on Companymen who know the worth of petitions."

"The Petitioners fucked this all up," another Reubenite spat. "Evan failed us in his petition for the Fourth Wing. Then Hexar died. *And the three of them were thrown into the fucking Tower!* Who knows what they told Charles Burke? I say expel them—Sinclair, Silvertongue, and the Reubenite who went with them."

Expulsion. Another word for murder.

Karl rose defiantly for a heated exchange with the Reubenite. The undercroft plunged into turmoil. Fists flew. Finally, several Companymen intervened, forcing them apart.

Rathos massaged his temples. *Evan, how am I supposed to win the Company over to Jason's claim when the false Pigeons focus all the attention on us?*

A tall, grizzled Reubenite navigated the press of men to tower over Rathos. "I think it's all a ruse," he said with a deep baritone. "Sinclair failed us, and I wouldn't put it past him or Silvertongue to feign a Pigeon betrayal to distract us, lest we elect Rezlan speaker. Fucking cowards."

Finally, an opening. Rathos surged to his feet. He ripped his sleeve up to the shoulder, then curtained Karl's tunic open at the belly. Fidgeting torchlight displayed the puzzlework of scars they'd bear for life, a long leathery one up Rathos's arm and ugly grooves across Karl's abdomen left by metal leaves.

Rathos showed his scar proudly as he stalked around the table, locking eyes with Companymen. *"DOES THIS LOOK LIKE A RUSE?"* he demanded. "WELL? Why in hell would we risk our lives, just to win some damn election in a Company defended by disloyal fighting men? THEY NEARLY KILLED US." He came within inches of the tall Reubenite's face. "We threw the dice—aye, you can say that. We all knew the King's Crow's invitation was a risk. But cowards?"

The sound of applause echoed from across the undercroft. The Reubenites parted for a line to the stairwell tucked into the room's corner, where the Lord of Shoaltown leaned against earthen wall, clapping half-heartedly.

Rezlan Ambrose was not a handsome man. The Loyal Company's other parent cut a stocky, rugged figure as bleak as his coalfields. Coarse, ash-gray hair draped his shoulders. His nose and chin jutted off his face like hard slabs of rock. He had a travel-stained cape over his green doublet, a flick of the nose at the sumptuary laws against Commoners, of which Rezlan counted himself one, proudly.

Only fools would underestimate Rezlan Ambrose. In many ways he was like the Little King, a man with thousands of eyes and ears in his service . . . and just as dangerous. Like Evan, his mind held secrets more precious than gold—the actual name of every Companyman, present or not.

For the last half hour, Rezlan had sat in silence, content to let his lackeys do the questioning. Now he joined the fray.

"'Let Silvertongue speak,'" Rezlan said on approach, "'and he'll put a spell on us as surely as the King's Crow.' That's what we said of you when you spoke so convincingly of this mission to the Silver Walls. It failed. You failed. Evan failed. And we are no closer to returning peasants to the Worthy Assembly. Why should any of us listen to you now, regardless"—he gestured blithely at Rathos and Karl—"of your scratches?"

Yes, mere scratches, Rezlan. "Because our mission to the Silver Walls did some good. Gram Sothos and his handless son rot in the Red Tower because of us." He ignored Karl's sidelong look. If the steward was as cunning as she seemed, she'd agree with them taking credit for Sothos's imprisonment.

Rezlan had a smirk in his amber eyes. "Hexar's death did that, not you. And for all the good it's done us. You do realize that Sothos bought our Pigeons?"

"Before Remembrance Day, no doubt."

"Before the steward gaoled him or after, it matters not," the flaxen-haired Reubenite interjected. "He bought *Pigeons.*"

"If the Hammer of the Commons could buy or influence one Pigeon unit, he could do the same to others," Rezlan said, as if translating. "Leaving Loran's Loyal Company blind, deaf, and disarmed. And *still* without a Wing of the Commons."

"We *are* blind, deaf, and disarmed," Rathos said. "And if Sothos infiltrated our fighting men, I know who in our 'Loyal' Company betrayed us to him."

Reubenites stiffened indignantly, preparing no doubt for Rathos to blame the easiest culprit—the one man who could challenge Evan for his speakership and deny Jason his crown. Rezlan's smile almost dared Rathos to try.

"It's not Rezlan, to be sure," Rathos said. "Why would the Company's other parent betray us—and so obviously?"

"I'm glad we agree," Rezlan said to grim chuckles.

"But it *is* a Reubenite who betrayed us. When the three of us were in Southpoint, we saw him preaching to the Commons. He openly challenged the Grand Inquisitor. Now there's word that a temple burned in South Farcombe. Not far from Rosbury, where he's known to stoke anger in tavern halls."

"And name the man among us who isn't glad to hear that a temple burns," a portly, red-cheeked Reubenite chimed from the rear.

"The High Bishop steals peasant children from their parents like an egg-sucking snake every day. A temple hasn't burned in Loran since the Interregnum. Maybe it's time one fucking did." He was met with deep-throated ayes.

Rathos had expected that. Whereas Evan's Petitioners consisted of rich merchants and freeholders, Reubenites by and large counted themselves parish readers and proud Free Believers. There were no priests in the Loyal Company, of course, no one sworn to the priestking and his untouchable temples . . . at least openly.

"You'd blame Firemouth for a temple burning *as well as* the Pigeons' betrayal?" scoffed a Reubenite, his head a shiny dome. "I suppose Jon Watley poisoned the king as well."

"Not Hexar, no," Rathos said. "Nor would I go so far as to say that Firemouth deliberately betrayed us. But his passions cloud his star of reason. He parades his membership in this Company as if it were his house sigil. He's reckless and stupid, and thinks a friendship with Tomas Fawkes is armor. If he met with Pigeons—if anyone followed him and overheard the codes we use to identify ourselves to our fighting men—he would've exposed them—*us*—to sabotage."

A Petitioner rustled up from his bench. Thick strips of red hair bushed his jowls. "Silvertongue isn't blaming that moron for anything he hasn't urged peasants to do themselves," he said. "That we all know his name is proof enough that Watley endangers us. We *should* expel him. Hear hear, Silvertongue!"

Seated at their tables, Petitioners rapped their knuckles in solidarity. The racket left Watley's fellow Reubenites looking defeated. *Would you feel proud of me, Lord Evan? In one stroke I deflected questions about Karl and me and hung the noose of this Pigeon predicament around that loudmouth's neck. And justly so.*

"Agreed," said a Reubenite. He seemed rattled by the disapproving looks from his faction members. "Oh fine, fine! Call me a traitor to the Reubenites. But we all swore an oath, did we not?" *We did*, thought Rathos, remembering his. "Jon Watley is a leak in this vessel we can't afford. Who else would be so bold to burn a temple, save for the mad dog Firemouth and the packs that run with him?"

The flaxen-haired Reubenite harrumphed. "Do you see our kingdom as it is, or have you bought the idea that we can ask politely for justice in Loran? Look where that's gotten us." Men applauded and jeered him.

The big-bellied Reubenite slammed his table with his fist, gaining silence. "*Enough!* I risk my neck for the Common cause. I won't risk it so this Watley can have more songs sung about himself. We must silence this dog, or he will lead the enemy to us. Expel him." And he sat down.

After that, more Companymen fell in line, the bickering subsiding as a consensus emerged. Rezlan acquiesced to the drumming knuckles and muttered ayes with a call for a vote. Scanning a room of raised arms, Rathos saw the motion carry.

Let's see how much longer you breathe fire, Watley. In the absence of their trustworthy Pigeons, several men with means pledged to find the renegade. *One less leak in the Company, and one less Reubenite to oppose us, Evan.*

"Well done, Silvertongue," Rezlan said. "Sinclair was wise to name you his deputy speaker." He sat on the edge of a table. "But are the spells you cast enough to sway us for the nephew he'd crown through the Kingstrials?"

Of course he told them, Rathos thought with a glimpse of the expressionless Companymen. *Of course Rezlan knew.* Karl gave a slight headshake, as if protesting his innocence in the matter.

The Petitioner whom he believed was Tristan Lox stood. "Tell us this isn't true, Silvertongue," he said. "Tell us Sinclair doesn't pitch us into this viper's pit for Sarah's son!"

"He does," Rathos said, to sighs, asides, and aspersions.

"He sends you to us seeking our support for the bastard's claim, after his failure at the Walls," Lox said, exasperated.

And you're supposed to be with us, Lox. "He does." Sounds of disagreement loudened. Someone urged an election.

"To enthrone his own blood. We may call ourselves the Loyal

Company, but that doesn't mean we're loyal to Sinclair. We shan't be used like this, to enthrone another Hexar. One was bad enough, with the wars and debt . . ."

Rathos hastened forward, quieting the Petitioner with the sternness in his expression. "That's where you're wrong. Jason Warchild is not his father."

"Start with Hexar *was* his father," quipped the wattle-throated Petitioner.

Rathos well knew the undercurrent of rumor beneath that quip, and didn't engage it. He waited for the laughter to fade. "How often have we met in this dark, dusty chamber?" He pointed at the cavern door. "How many times have we played our games—skittering through caverns like rats, hoping no one sees us? Timing secret knocks like children?" He fingered the rut of his scar. "Working through spies to stay one step ahead of death?"

"Get to the point, lad," Rezlan said wryly.

"Warchild *is* the point. The point of it all. The reason why we're here. Rezlan—you and Evan brought us together because you saw the rulers of Loran had broken the First King's Great Covenant with his subjects. What Romarians gave us in service to that Covenant—a seat for everyone, and peace through it—the lords and priests stole from the Commoners like cutpurses. Over centuries, they've taken more, more, and more"—Rathos grabbed at the air, drawing his fists toward his chest—"and contributed less, less, and less, forcing the merchants to give up fortunes while the peasants suffer and perish in desperation." Ayes seconded him. "You brought us together, Rezlan—you and Evan—because you wisely saw disaster coming. Peasant revolts. A new Interregnum. War." *Only Evan wishes to prevent a war,* he thought, but adding that wouldn't help Jason.

"*Hexar made things worse!*" a Reubenite shouted.

"Aye, he did, he and Sothos both," Rathos went on. "And I tell you, *Jason is not Hexar.* He's the king we've prayed for. A man who fought the Muhregites and lost a sibling in the Brace knows enough of war to keep us out of more. A man whom the Assembly forced Hexar to name Warchild knows what it's like to suffer under the Worthy's yoke, and will unfasten it from our necks. And when he sits the Silver Walls"—he lifted a hand, as if to grasp something elusive, and lowered it clenched—"he'll seat a Wing of the Commons where it belongs. *King Jason will make the Worthy Assembly whole.*"

Rathos relished a respectful silence.

A Reubenite with a shock of carrot-orange hair asked why the Company should back the Warchild and not Tomas Fawkes, a Free Believer tried and true. He waved off complaints about the Lord of Westerliche's friendship with the expelled Watley.

Karl stepped forward. "The Warchild defended a peasant girl with his own flesh when Tomas wouldn't," he said, turning heads. "It happened on Remembrance Day. Sothos's son played Lily's Apple with Jason and Tomas, placing fruit on her head. While his king father lay dying, Jason made himself a shield for her—against Sinclair's own wishes."

Rathos watched his ally admiringly.

After that, the arguments against Evan's ploy grew fewer. With his voice rising and falling at dramatic moments, Rathos commanded the hall's attention like a gifted minstrel weaving a tale on his harp. It was an exhilarating rush he felt from head to feet. *I missed this,* he realized.

"The time is ripe," Rathos added. "Hexar is dead. Sothos languishes in the Tower. If Lord Jason fails to win all his Trials, we must use our seats in the Assembly to vote him king. *This* is how we'll seat peasants."

"One thing," Rezlan said. "The Warchild is a bastard in the Worthy's eyes. How does Sinclair plan on getting him past laws of bastardy? Sothos's minions still control half the Assembly."

This was the hard part, Rathos knew. He steeled himself. "Sinclair is away because he seeks to renew a friendship with Trevor Wexley, whose good name would champion Warchild."

The flaxen-haired Reubenite balked. "The Cloudlanders despise their peasants as much as Sothos does. They call them shit beneath their boots. Why would Trevor Wexley agree to end the Silent Friendship for a king who would seat the rabble in their Assembly again?"

There's the question. And I have the answer. Rathos felt as if he teetered on the brink of a precipice, as if one false step—one ill-spoken word—would send him, Karl, Evan, and Jason Warchild flailing to their doom. He inhaled softly, and made a leap of faith.

All at once, the Loyal Company plunged into disarray, the Reubenites on their feet, the Petitioners looking as if the floor had opened up beneath them. A smile teased at Rezlan's lips.

The baldheaded Reubenite staggered off his bench. "*AN UNHOLY ALLIANCE!*" he bellowed.

Rathos had prepared for this moment on his journey west from Caerdon, but he'd never been on the receiving end of this uproar, as Evan often had. It tested him. "We must try to see the star of reason," he urged Companymen.

The Reubenite, his cheeks a pomegranate red, trembled as he listed on his table. "*STAR OF REASON!* You'd marry us to the Cloudlanders, for Sinclair's nephew, and give us the Fourth Wing, unwhole, defanged?"

"It's not like that," Rathos said forcefully. "Under Sinclair's arrangement, King Jason would seat the peasants again in their Worthy Assembly. Their votes—their voices—would bind the land with the same power as any lord, clergyman, or merchant. Just for a time"—he ignored mocking laughter—"the Wing of the Commons would have no power over the Cloudlands."

"And no Cloudlander would sit in the Fourth Wing?"

"For a time."

"Then the Silent Friendship continues, and we betray the Cloudlands' peasants. Do you really think the Bull would hand Hexar's bastard the crown if he thought he'd give peasants *any* power over his lands? We cannot seat some peasants and not others. The Wing of the Commons is no wing if its power ends at a tract of land on which a fourth of our peasants sweat, toil, and die."

"Griffons," Rathos said. "Gram Reuben wrote that griffons mark vast swaths of land as their territory, never overnight. To claim land takes years, piece by piece. Progress takes time. It takes—" A small stone struck his cheek, dazing him.

He glared at the stone-thrower, a Reubenite with teeth rouged by pinkbud. "A farce!" he shouted. "You sell us poisoned meat, Silvertongue!"

"*We've already been sold,*" cried another. "Evan Sinclair's wedded us to this hideous bride without our consent, and the dowry's a Fourth Wing in name only."

"You throw away the good for the ideal, you fools," Karl scolded them. Reubenites threw pebbles at him.

These are the inheritors of the Awakening, Rathos thought with contempt, *and yet still our only salvation in the Assembly if Jason fails to win outright. Fools they are, but fools we need.*

The rancor raged on as the storm loudened outside. A Reubenite suggested that they revoke Watley's expulsion and join with him to burn *all* the temples. Karl stepped in front of Rathos protectively when a Reubenite tried to strike him; the Petitioners banged on their tables for censure.

Out of the storm of voices, the tall, grizzled Reubenite's thundered loudest. "*Evan Sinclair's betrayed us!* He perverts our Company's noble aims by making common cause with the Bull, a tyrant over his folk . . . *all to crown his own blood king!*"

I warned you, Father. With every second, Rathos felt his tenuous hold on the Company slipping. *I am not enough.*

The tall one raised his hands and spun to address Rezlan's faction. "Brothers! Follow your star of reason. We have but one path now. The Pigeons can't be relied upon; Sinclair's petitions fail us; and we've been betrayed for personal gain in the Trials. I say we expel Sinclair and elect Rezlan Ambrose speaker. We'll seat peasants in the Assembly . . . *BY FORCE!*"

At the sound of a single word, the Reubenites' deafening cheers collapsed. Rathos looked as incredulous as anyone else.

"No," Rezlan repeated himself. "No, no, no. Much as I do appreciate your support, I cannot accept the speakership."

Rathos made his face a mask. *What is this game, Rezlan?* The so-called Lord of Shoaltown, merely the son of a poor coal trader hanged by Stoddard Trambar, had toiled all his life for historical significance. If the Worthy Assembly still seated the Commons, Rezlan would be its speaker. Evan Sinclair always feared this moment, when the Loyal Company was but laurels for the warmonger Rezlan to don—when all he needed do was stretch out his hand, take them, and call for violence.

But the Pigeons' loyalties were questionable, as a fierce throb in Rathos's arm reminded him. And Rezlan Ambrose was declining the speakership, insistently. *Does the first mate flee the sinking ship, rather than go down as captain?*

Like fire beneath the cauldron, Rezlan's refusal brought his supporters to boil. The tall Reubenite offered a hand to his leader, as if he held the speakership. "Your men call on you to take control, Rezlan. Sinclair wasn't alone at the birth of this Company. We need you. *Loran* does! What say you, old friend?"

You bloodthirsty fools, you'd give us a second Long Summer Rebellion when we have a chance—one good chance—to seat the peasants by writ, through an honorable man. Rathos and the Petitioners watched the Lord of Shoaltown, riveted and confused.

Rezlan laid a solemn hand over his breast. "I am honored, friend. You all"—he gazed at several Reubenites each in turn—"do me a great honor. Under any other circumstance I'd accept it." He lingered on Rathos. "Even with noble intentions, Sinclair *has* wronged us. He failed us. We dispatched him to the Silver Walls to show us the value of petitions, and he did."

"Then why not lead us in this dark hour?"

"What would we do?" Rezlan rejoined. "We're blind. Deaf. Disarmed. Silvertongue and his Reubenite showed us their scars. A unit of our fighting men betrayed two of our members, so we must hold as suspect all of them. Inquiries will take time. But time is not with us, or with Loran's peasants."

"The lords with us could summon their men-at-arms."

Rezlan shook his head. "Many of their men *were* Pigeons. *Are.* And to be honest, I don't fully trust every lord in this Loyal Company." Reubenites muttered their agreement. "Still, I say no to this generous offer. We are in despicable circumstances. I despise the Kingstrials. And Sinclair . . . he has much to answer for. But at this moment, swaying the Worthy of Loran for a king is the unquestionable strength left to us. The Company lives or dies in these Kingstrials, and with it the flame of the Common cause. *Turel e'sartha.*"

"*Turan e'sparta,*" replied most, including Rathos, hands over their chests.

He couldn't believe his ears. Karl looked as baffled. *You sent me, Father, but it's the warmonger who points your Loyal Company to its star of reason. And he took the words off my silver tongue.*

A scrawny Reubenite rose. "Rezlan, we should stand with Tomas Fawkes."

"We'd have to," Rezlan said, "if Warchild perishes. But to wrest the Company from Sinclair now would plunge us into turmoil and undermine him when the peasants of this realm need us united. We are the light in the darkness, and I will not risk snuffing it out. Whether we like it or not, we are on the road to the Golden Meadows, all of us, in an alliance with the Walls and Cloudlands. Loath as I am to tolerate it, that's more than what we can offer this kingdom with our fickle Pigeons." He pivoted to Rathos. "And I am, shall we say . . . spellbound by what Silvertongue has said about this bastard the Assembly detests. Perhaps it's King Warchild who will make the peasants Worthy again."

Rathos inclined his head deferentially. "Rezlan, you show your finest colors in this hour. I am heartened you've joined us to see Jason king."

Rezlan gave a withering laugh. "Joined you? No. If we had another way, I'd gladly take it." He leveled a finger at Rathos and Karl. "But you are in bed with Evan and his nephew, and now, so are we . . . *if* the Company approves. But understand this: if Warchild falls, or betrays our cause, it will be on your heads. God help you if he does, Silvertongue."

Thunder clapped aboveground as Rathos extended his arms. "Then let's put it to a vote," he said.

Rathos cast his vote and left promptly, deciding he could use a cup of mead after all the contentiousness, and even more, the absence of quarrelsome Companymen. Mason Grexon closed his inn for their gatherings, allowing Companymen like Rathos to migrate upstairs without fear of unwanted attention. Karl remained below to ensure fair proceedings.

Climbing up a narrow stairwell, elbows brushing against dirt wall, Rathos entered a long, rustic, and refreshingly empty tavern hall. The Last Elflord Inn hosted only trestle tables and benches tonight. The front door was barricaded. Rain pattered shuttered windows. A cozy hearth fire lit the room.

The innkeep busied himself wiping down tables. Plump and bearded, with a face seamed from laughter, Mason had a guileless, grandfatherly air, which made him an essential co-conspirator. He had a talent for sensing when men required space, and so poured Rathos a frothy cup of mead, pocketed a sylven, and trudged upstairs, unspeaking.

It was only when Rezlan emerged from the stairwell that Rathos realized Mason had an ear for the coal hand's footsteps, too.

Pretending obliviousness, Rathos nursed his mead. In the periphery of his vision, he saw Rezlan fill a cup and set a loren on the bar. Holding two frothy drinks, he headed for Rathos.

"May I join you?" asked the Lord of Shoaltown, in a tone that suggested refusal wasn't recommended.

Rathos feigned a smile. "To each a chair." Rezlan eased himself onto the bench across the table. Up close, he looked his age. Silvery stubble filmed his face; lost sleep bagged his deep-set eyes. "You paid with gold. How's the coal trade these days?"

It was a jab. Rezlan Ambrose hadn't been in coal for years, or even in Shoaltown. Years before, a careless error had led Charles Burke to learn his name. To this day, Rezlan continued to pay the price with interest, forced to stay a step ahead of Burke and Sothos by lodging with the faceless lords of their Company, or fleeing Loran altogether when spies hounded his trail. Evan suspected that Rezlan, like Firemouth, had a lordly benefactor in Tomas Fawkes—perhaps even in one of the kings of the Free Kingdoms. It still astonished Rathos that Karl had known where to find Rezlan at all.

Rezlan smiled with false warmth. "To all a piece," he replied. He sipped his mead. "Mason is our friend, but we should help with upkeep, like any good guest."

"Of course. What was the tally?" Glad of Rezlan's support as he was, he didn't relish his presence, and yearned for sleep.

"Why, you won the day. Our Companymen in the Worthy Assembly will cast their weight behind Warchild, if he fails to win three Trials. No small victory for Evan's nephew."

"Thanks to you."

"The uproar wasn't your fault, you know," Rezlan said, speaking over him before he could finish. "Evan was right to send you to persuade us." He wagged a finger playfully. "It was Lorana's gamble that forced Evan to make his deal with a beast like the Bull. That deal forced my hand."

He knows it was the steward's scheme. "I thank you for it."

"One caveat. Not everyone goes to the Colossus. We will keep enough men behind for quorum."

Rathos's composure cracked. "Are you blind? We need every man in Northland by the Meet for this to work, you fool."

The Loyal Company's other founder tightened his lips in warning. "This is the work of both factions. If Evan fails again, we will seat the peasants ourselves—by force. That's the deal."

There was nothing Rathos could do. *The Company's support will mean something, Evan, but Jason must risk no offense to undecided Assemblymen.*

He studied the rebel. "Rezlan, the speakership was yours for the taking. Why did you support the Petitioners by refusing it?"

Light from the fire fidgeted in Rezlan Ambrose's amber eyes. "There's a difference between us, Silvertongue. Do you know what it is?"

"Aye." Rathos sipped his mead. "I'm no warmonger."

"I'm a peasant." Rezlan pointed at him. "You're highborn."

"My father was a Commoner, same as yours. Poorer, I figure. He stole in the streets just to eat—"

Rezlan snatched his hand. Before Rathos could blink, he dragged him across the table, crushing his hand in his grip. The older man smirked as Rathos fought in vain to pull free.

"A man's hands tell his story," Rezlan said. His breath reeked of onion. "Take you. Even if I were blind, these palms would tell me about your good birth. How you spend your time. I feel leisure: reading, writing, horse-riding, swordplay with a master-of-arms." He waxed a thumb over Rathos's palm. "Light callusing. No scars."

With a start Rathos freed himself, knocking over his cup. Spilt mead trickled through the table's planks, *splatting* floor. "Shall I show you my scars again?" he snarled. "Mayhap the blade I put in a Pigeon's chest."

Rezlan lifted palms cauliflowered with callus, scabrous and cracked. "These are a peasant's hands. The hands of a coal miner." He traced a scar down the center of his left palm. "This I took from Lord Stoddard Trambar's knight the day he had my father hanged. My father's killer wouldn't dirty his hands with me, a peasant, even to teach me a lesson. He set his dog on me."

"Get to the point, lad."

The smirk faded. "You're not one of us," Rezlan said. "You lack titles, but in every way that counts, you're highborn. Like *Lord* Evan Sinclair, you first saw the world from atop tall castle walls. Like him, you're blind in one eye. And your blindness has hurt the Common cause."

"Says the man who'd shatter our peace for his ambition."

The Petitioner knew he was wrong the moment he said *ambition*. The Company's other parent righted Rathos's cup, flicking froth off its rim as if it were the last shred of respect he had for him, for Evan, for all Petitioners.

"My point, made." Rezlan eased forward. "You Petitioners believe there's a peace worth saving. There isn't. Tonight, some poor farmer rots in his lord's dungeon because he can't pay his rents and taxes. His wife cries into her pillow because one of the steward's justices gave their daughter to a priest. Peace for you. Not for us."

"What's the alternative? Violence. Bloodshed. Anarchy. This is what you'd prefer, to a Wing of the Commons seated peacefully by a king crowned without war."

Rezlan snorted. "Justices. Princesses. Lords and wards. You're all the same. You see only what you could lose if the house of this realm collapses. If you lose the roof, the storms will batter you same as it does any wretch. A terrifying notion to the castle-born. So you place faith in what you know—in process, petitions, and Kingstrials. Crown a good man, and he'll thatch the leaking roof. But you're staring up, and can't see truth." He stamped the floor. "The floor rotted away long ago. An abyss awaits. You're plunging into it . . . along with the house and everyone else in this unjust kingdom."

"I still feel solid floor, Rezlan."

Rezlan shook his head wearily. "You, Evan, and your Petitioners fight in a contest rigged against you—against everyone. The Kingstrials symbolize everything about this realm that is wrong, corrupt, and evil. I'll be there when you understand that, Silvertongue."

Rathos tired of this back-and-forth . . . more so because Rezlan knew something, and he wasn't telling him. He leaned forward. "Tell me the truth. You could've been made speaker tonight. Denied Jason our support. Thwarted Sinclair. Armed your cause. We don't know whether all the Pigeons are suspect. The position was yours. *So why didn't you take it?*"

Something between resignation and disgust lurked in the coal hand's eyes. "There it is. *Position.* It's all you highborn care for. Why Evan fought for the Fourth Wing with one hand tied behind his back all these years." He refilled Rathos's cup with mead from his, to the last drop. "Fuck position. I helped you so that we'll finally have what this kingdom needs."

"War," Rathos finished for the warmonger.

"*War is already upon everyone not a lord or priest,*" Rezlan spat. "It just hasn't been declared. Helping you will prove the folly of these Kingstrials and get us to that declaration. It'll give us a spike to mount every greedy lord's head, and wood and oil for every perverted priest."

Giving up, Rathos chuckled with disdain. "Then you made a foolish wager. But it's one that will save this realm. I may not live under the Worthy's boot, but the Warchild does. The peasants love him for it. They'll suffer more than calluses to see him king if the Assembly—or this Company—fails him."

Rezlan shrugged. "We'll see. I allowed Watley's expulsion, but if he burned the temple, he didn't act alone. Soon, someone with authority will do something stupid—a priest, or maybe a justice. War will follow, regardless of who's king. The question isn't whether, but when . . . and how we'll win that war."

So, the truth. Blackpowder. He knows I'm the key. That's what this is all about. "We'll win before war even begins. With our power mustered at the Colossus. To make Jason king. To seat the Fourth Wing."

"We'll win it with blackpowder. I know Hexar kept some on hand."

"Sorry to disappoint. The king told Evan he sold the last caches." Rathos stood. "If you'll excuse me, I need the truth of this vote. Be a good fellow and clean up the mead, will you? I'd do it myself, but"—he flashed his palms—"I'm highborn."

Rezlan's lips quivered with anger. "Evan couldn't see the star of reason, either. He thinks that if he can crown his sister's son and seat the Commons, it'll all have been worth it. Sarah's death. Your father's."

"Isn't that what your war is for—to find meaning in your papa's broken neck?"

Rathos immediately regretted his unkindness.

Rezlan smiled poignantly. "I pray you'll never suffer the mercy of lords and priests, Silvertongue. When they come, they come for people you love."

"Forgive me." Rathos headed for the stairwell.

Rezlan bolted up and caught Rathos by his sleeve. "I didn't come to spar. I have news." He pulled him close. "The Old Oak and his sons were ambushed on a hunt. *Lord Greg Thorngale is dead.* His sons are blaming the Pigeons, the Loyal Company—and Evan. It's rumored the Stormsword will swear his blade to Jason, if he gives him Evan's head. If not, he'll kill them both."

The Stormsword. He pictured the dead-eyed swordsman at his table on Remembrance Day. "Why didn't you share this before we voted?" Rathos asked.

But Rezlan had already confessed his reasons.

"The Loyal Company wouldn't have backed this venture if it became known that the deadliest swordsman in the realm was coming for Evan." Rezlan smiled. "I told you—I wanted the vote to succeed. The Assembly will corrupt these Kingstrials, as they corrupt everything. Sinclair's failure will disillusion this entire kingdom—including you. Then, you'll see the star of reason."

Fear knotted up his stomach. *I hope our horses carry you fast enough, Leah,* Rathos thought. *Evan's life depends on it. As does mine.*

Sara's Prayer

he road to Rosbury was long, bumpy, and tense from everything unsaid. Hooves drummed soil, cicadas sang lustily, the wagon's axles creaked with every spin, and none of it was loud enough to muffle her conscience.

Huddled in a rear corner of Willard Rittman's wagonbed, her wimple cinched tight, Sara suffered lashes from her guilty inner voice, again and again, as surely as if she were one of the justice's poor mules. *Sacrilege and treason, I'm guilty of both,* the peasant girl wanted to scream aloud, to her twelve-faced god, to the twelve gods of Saint Eric's, to the sun and sky. *I'm guilty of burning the temple. It was me, and I can't unburn it.*

The stain of guilt upon her seemed as stubborn as the ash and soot that blackened Saint Eric's rubble. Sara couldn't purge the sounds of that night, not the crash of glass or the groans of scorched beams collapsing. The day after the burning, after the hue and cry by Rittman and Elvarenist villagers, they'd gone to survey the ruins, sift through charred stone among the smoke. The scowls of toppled grotesques had seemed to follow Sara, as if they'd witnessed her crime.

Yet one memory eased her burden, somewhat. Save for a handful of Elvarenists, most of the village's other peasants had gathered with stony faces and distant eyes. No one seemed to share the outrage of Rittman and South Farcombe's own justice of the peace.

She recalled Connor Bagman's words to her two nights past: "Commoners aren't like their kings and lords. They're honest folk who respect fair play."

I'll respect fair play, Connor, like my father, Sara thought, *but it hurts to keep this secret.* She ran a finger along her gown, tracing the uneven surface of Dray's knife hidden inside. Its edges were fearsomely sharp. *But Father is worth it.*

Rittman smoldered at the wagon's front with her mother, cracking his braided whip at the mules. "It may be time for you to return to Thorn's Keep, Rose." For the first time, Sara heard fear in his voice. "I worry for your safety. Devils walk among us, killing officers and desecrating the temples that house their remains."

Her mother shared his burden with a long look. Sara's own guilt surrendered to unease. *We can't return to Thorn's Keep,* she thought. *Dray expects me at the next moon.*

Geffrey sat up, staring past Rittman and her mother. He pointed ahead. "That's Farmer Grey."

Up the road lumbered the bent-backed peasant, guiding a mule saddled with bundled oats and hay. He wore a long tunic, gray bonnet, and shoes of cloth felt. Recognizing them, Farmer Grey stopped to wait beneath the shade of a tree, rubbing the small of his back.

The sight of a familiar face was heartening for Sara. Grey hadn't been a friend to her family like Caleb, but his presence kindled memories of home, of a time before Sir Damien went missing, before dead kings, Red Towers, and torched temples.

Rittman eased the mules to a halt. "What's your business on this road, Grey?" he growled.

The justice's harsh tone of voice startled Sara, but Farmer Grey looked like he was somewhere else entirely. "I was on me way to Southfar, Sir Will," he admitted. "Got barley to sell, need to sell it whilst I can on the Day of Felos, outside Saint Eric's."

Rittman sobered. "Then it will pain you to learn that Saint Eric's was destroyed. Two days ago. Outlaws did as no one has since the Interregnum and burned a house of the twelve gods." He signed the diamond, his thumb to forehead, shoulders, and heart.

The farmer looked down, then back up. Something was off. "Then I fear we know evil days, Sir Will. Donna . . . donna you know?" When the justice made no reply, Farmer Grey pulled off his stringed bonnet. "Lord Uthron is dead."

A cry of anguish went up from Rose. She covered her mouth with both hands, her shoulders shaking. The justice stared off numbly.

Was the world ending? Sara pictured Uthron Morley the last time she saw him, in Elf's Grove. *Was it Uthron who died,* she wondered, *or the shadow I saw?*

Geffrey flew to the wagonside, leaning over. "*How,* damn you?" he demanded. "Was it outlaws? Connor Bagman?"

Farmer Grey clutched his bonnet to his chest, as if falsely accused. "N-n-no, Geffrey. Wasna like that t'all. Lady Cathreen, she had the village go to Ol' Sturdyroot. Brother Elfred made Sam Morley the new Lord Warden of Rosbury. They accused the King's Crow—"

Rittman leapt down from his box. Uncoiling his whip, he flogged the farmer repeatedly, viciously. Grey shielded his face with his arms, crying for mercy. Protests from Rose, Sara, and Geffrey fell deaf on the justice, who didn't stop lashing the old man until he collapsed. Skin dangled off the farmer's arms like the red flesh of a half-peeled apple.

Rittman dropped the whip. He staggered until he doubled over, hands on his knees, breathing deeply.

Sara flew to the wagonside. "Murderer, *MURDERER!*" she screamed loud as she could. "*I HATE YOU!*"

Geffrey held her by her wrists, surprisingly gently. "Easy, Sara. He's not dead. Look." He pointed at the comatose farmer. "His eyelids are twitchin'. See?"

Rittman mopped off his forehead. "Geffrey, help me, help me pick him up," he stammered. "I didn't mean, I—" He glanced at Rose, who couldn't seem to withdraw far enough on her seat. "Help me get him in, Geffrey. We'll show Grey to Lord Uthron's apothec—" He sighed. "To the *new* Lord Warden's apothecary."

When Farmer Grey's scarred, convulsing body was in the wagonbed, Rose asked Sara to help her pray over him.

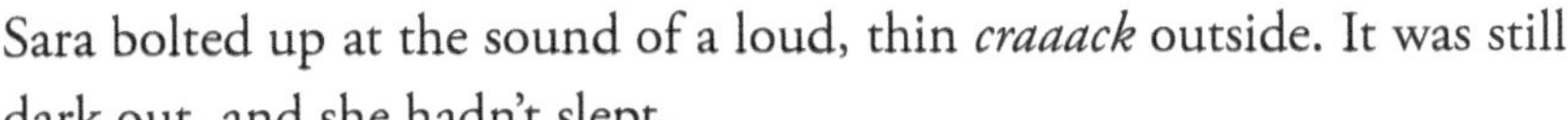

Sara bolted up at the sound of a loud, thin *craaack* outside. It was still dark out, and she hadn't slept.

Her mother was already awake, or perhaps hadn't slept at all, either. She stood at their front wall, peering through cracks in daub and wattle. Sara found a crack to look through.

Outside, faint shapes gave chase in the predawn gloom. Shapes of armored men. They shouted orders and ran up and down the village main. Her skin grew clammy all over as she listened to children wailing. Daub and wattle snapped apart. Pigs squealed as they rumbled past their house, loud as horses.

A knock at their door startled mother and daughter. Rose clutched at her wrist, and it wasn't in reprimand. Sara realized that she was afraid. That made her afraid.

They've come for me, Sara thought frantically. *They know I was there at Saint Eric's. They've come!* She ran to her straw matte, pawing about for Dray's knife until a fierce edge pricked her finger.

Rose opened the door. There stood Rittman. He'd shaven since they'd delivered Farmer Grey to Thorn's Keep. He looked a mess in his armor, his breastplate raised off his fat chest, his kettle helm askew.

Behind Rittman, a man in deputy's clothing stalked after Frogface Jenny's father, menacing him with a club. "Rose." The justice flickered at Sara. "I've come to collect you. Rosbury isn't safe anymore. For either of you. Lord Sam commands you to Thorn's Keep. Yes he does."

Relief that Rittman hadn't come to arrest her gave way to fear of something else. Still in her night linen, Sara balled her fists.

"Mother, we can't go," she said. *I need to see Dray again, and I can only do that in Elf's Grove.* "We can't—"

Rose twisted her earlobe between fingers of iron. "You'll do as your noble lord commands you," she said in a growling whisper. "Dress up." She shoved her on. "*NOW, GIRL.*"

She had half a mind to refuse her again, but she realized it would only delay her concealing the blade. Dray's knife was the key to everything, and she'd paid for it with treason. She did as she was bidden, retreating into the shed's shade to throw on a gown and wimple. She folded the blade inside her dress several times over, then tied a makeshift knot, considering her options.

What could she say? What could she do? Lord Sam Morley (and she wasn't sure she'd *ever* get used to calling the boy her lord) had summoned them to his castle. *Be with me, Dray.* A bee whirred past her ear.

Glimmers of morning sunlight peeked over the rooftops. Two huge garrons waited outside their house, hoofing dirt. Her mother helped her onto the smaller of the two, then joined her; the justice threw a leg over the other horse.

Sara whipped around for a look at her father's stables. "What of Little Lady?" she said insistently. "We can't *leave her unlooked-after.*"

"She's a half-mad horse your father wanted to sell," Rose said bluntly.

The justice looked at the horse, then Sara. "I'll send Geffrey to feed her," he said with more gentleness, only irritating her.

Sara twisted in her saddle to linger on the poor horse, tears in her eyes. *I'll return, Little Lady. I promise.*

They rode off to Thorn's Keep at a canter, passing by a village in distress. Up and down the main, deputies in the red and black of House Morley stormed houses, thumping on wicker doors, dragging out bawling children by their arms and wrists. "Justice's orders," deputies told bewildered and furious Commoners emerging from their residences, and if any man refused or made threats, they surrounded him and beat him.

They passed deputies carrying armfuls of goods like big wooden chests, sheepskin quilts, and brass pots. In the middle of the road, Rittman's underlings piled the seized loot: plows, bales of hay, fetters, bundles of horsehair, barrels, satchels. Beside the loot sat a scrawny, pinched-faced man at a table laden with towers of plundered coin, quill bobbing diligently as he recorded sums on calfskin.

He counted more than goods and coin. A rope tethered a line of confiscated mules to an oak. Nearby, a deputy pounded wooden stakes into the soil, finishing a pen packed so tightly with pigs scarcely any within could move. *They've taken all Rosbury's things, even the animals, even . . .*

Sara felt her heart sink. Beside the pen, a pair of deputies sorted dozens of Rosbury's tousled-headed sons and daughters like cattle. Many were around Sara's age, some younger. Rose lingered on a ten-year-old girl they knew struggling to soothe a squealing babe she held. Upon seeing the justice ahorse, most children looked away.

Frogface Jenny didn't. Her gaze arrested Sara as they rode by. *Her mum and dad hid her,* she realized. She'd never seen so many children taken, not all at once. Not like this.

Rittman urged a halt to his garron by Griff's Bridge on the village's outskirts. He removed his helm to smooth his greasy curls. "I'm sorry you have to see such unpleasantness," he said. "They say it's my orders, but it's not. The steward commanded me in this reckoning. The fire in Southfar gave the Silver Walls the reason it needed to overturn Rosbury for not just Connor Bagman and his conspirators, but unpaid poll taxes also. The Kingstrials cost a pretty coin, yes they do, and this village has denied the crown its due for too long. Now Rosbury pays."

Her mother had a paleness to her that Sara hadn't seen since the Tower. "What of . . . of all the children, Sir Willard?" Rose asked softly.

"You know the law, Rose. Peasants who cannot afford their rents and taxes cannot keep their children. It's for the best. They'll get a sought-after education under High Bishop Peshar. I'll keep an eye on them to make sure they're safe. I promise."

Sara circled about to face Rosbury. She remembered how her mother had told her to pray for Farmer Grey. *I pray for fire,* she thought, *a fire that stirs us all awake.*

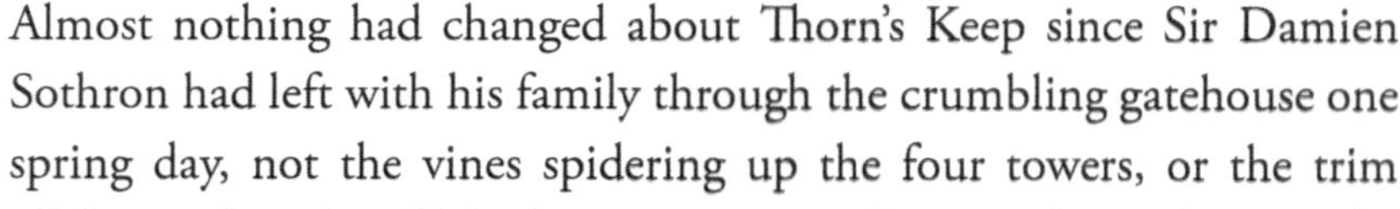

Almost nothing had changed about Thorn's Keep since Sir Damien Sothron had left with his family through the crumbling gatehouse one spring day, not the vines spidering up the four towers, or the trim of the garden chapel's hedge entrance, or the rusted iron bars in the sunken dungeon's windows.

What *had* changed was the family that called the castle their home. Uthron Morley's absence was felt as his successor and son received Sara, her mother, and Rittman at the dais in Hardigan's Hall, a chamber covered in tapestries displaying House Morley's red oak tree against black.

Sam Morley sat on the black cushions of his father's chair, a throne of solid oak engraved with linenfold carvings at least two feet taller than he was. Thin and pale, with a clinging bowl of hair and big fishy eyes, the new Lord Warden was not even in his father's shadow. He fidgeted with a wooden toy knight in his lap while his lady mother received them on his behalf.

"In this dark hour we welcome you again, Rose and Sara Sothron," Cathreen Morley said with a faint accent and perfect poise from where she stood by her son. "Please be warm at our hearth and let no more trouble you, away from Rosbury."

Uthron's widow had been said to be a comelier girl in her youth, but fifty-one years had paled her skin and turned her hair white as snow. She had on a tight gown that accentuated the veins snaking up her arms. Lined up beside her were her somber daughters, Harriett, Maeda, and Barbara, all in bliauts, their eyes puffy with grief.

Rose walked up the dais, keeping her face deferentially low. She knelt before Sam Morley and kissed the sapphire of his pinkie ring. A strange thing it was, seeing her mother pay homage to the boy whose bedwetting had so often sent her riverward to clean his soiled sheets.

"Thank you, my lord," Rose said reverently. "We grieve for your loss. We pray that justice be done for our Lord Uthron."

Sam Morley asked his mother for approval with a big-eyed look. "I thank you," he responded with rehearsed formality. "To lose our king and lord father in months has left my house shaken." He clutched at his toy knight. "The steward has named Lord Drexan Lorrain my father's murderer. Should you learn of the King's Crow's whereabouts, you shall tell me without delay. He is a traitor. He must die for his crimes against our house."

Sara heard the river gurgling as Uthron Morley addressed the night air at Elf's Grove. "And what of the Crow?" he'd asked nothing and no one that night.

Rose agreed so solemnly, so dutifully, one would think she'd armor up and depart that second to arrest Lord Drexan herself. "Yes, milord. I will report his whereabouts if I learn of them. I pray the King's Crow pays for his crimes."

What of other men's crimes? Rittman paid Sara a sidelong look as she watched him. It seemed a wrong and untrue thing, for the sheriff to be called a justice of the peace. Farmer Grey had been innocent, and he'd gotten neither justice nor peace.

Cathreen's green eyes followed Rose as she stepped off the dais, curtsying. "Prayer is powerful," she said. "Now that you've returned to Thorn's Keep, we will expect you and Sara to join us at chapel and pray with us eastward, to the White Citadel. They say Prieslenne Edenia sails to Loran. We'll have nothing else while Her Blessedness is on our soil."

Rose acquiesced with a bow. Sara suppressed the urge to say something. They'd ostracized the Sothrons over Damien's reluctance to give up his Free Beliefs. Her father hadn't wanted Sara to pray like an Elvarenist.

Especially not in the gardens.

"Where is Farmer Grey?" Sara blurted abruptly, to echoes through Hardigan's Hall. Rose glared at her for silence. "We brought him here yesterday. Is he okay?"

Rittman shifted uncomfortably. Lord Sam didn't seem to know how to react to Sara's outburst. Cathreen merely smiled.

"Grey continues to recover under care of our apothecary." Cathreen clapped her hands, and the servant Manni rounded a corner into the hall. The Morleys were one of the few highborn families to refuse to hostage Casaanites. "Let us eat the dinner we prepared for your welcome home. You will be seen to your chambers afterward."

"But how long will we be here?" Sara persisted.

Rittman's stare brought her into line. "You have suffered without the father's hand, child, it's plain to see," he chided her. "You will remain for as long as it pleases your lord. And you'll speak to his lordship and his noble family *with courtesy.*"

Dinner was wonderful, at least. They dined on salted cod, honeyed nuts, and buttered rye bread. After that, Manni parted her from Rose, a thing that unexpectedly caused Sara a cold sweat.

She couldn't forget Frogface Jenny's watery gaze, not for the rest of her life. Being separated from her mother made her fret that they knew. They wished to punish her. Sara feared a dungeon cell.

Instead, Manni showed her to Barbara Morley's solar, a spacious room decorated with the trappings of nobility: two soft featherbeds, pillows stuffed with goose down, a rosewood wardrobe, a foliated mir-ror, and an iron-hinged wooden chest that smelled richly of cedar. Sara thanked Manni, and he shut the door gently.

No one would dare take Barbara's things to pay for any Kingstrials, Sara thought as she admired the noblewoman's treasures.

Barbara came and went throughout the afternoon, telling Sara only to keep her grimy hands out of her wardrobe and off her chest. Manni returned a time later to light the fireplace.

Sunset washed over the ramparts outside. Sara looked out the win-dow, watching as deputies poured into the bailey with all the plunder from Rosbury. Some were swapping jokes about peasants.

She couldn't see any of Rosbury's children with them.

After nightfall, Sara plotted her escape. From her window, she stared at the gatehouse portcullis.

There were ways out of Thorn's Keep apart from the gatehouse; that much she knew. Her father had told her of secret passageways the Morleys could use in case of siege, through an undercroft or the castle gardens.

She stared up at the pale sickle of a half-moon. *You know I've been taken, Dray. Surely you know. Wait for me. We need to make the Gift that returns Father to us.*

Sara was starting to test a climb down from the window, searching for toeholds, when the doorknob jiggled. She barely had enough time to hide the blade beneath her pillow. In swept a woman she almost didn't know, attired in a gray gown over a sleeveless tunic. With her skin scrubbed to a shine, she looked radiant. Positively happy.

"Mother." Sara frowned. "Your hair."

Her rich, brown hair flowed down her shoulders. She was so pretty without her wimple.

"Do you like it?" Rose twirled about, giddy as a girl. She curled a strand of hair about her finger. "I've not worn it so *in years*. The Lady Cathreen urged me to remove my wimple. She won't allow this always, but she called tonight special."

I wish I'd known, Mother, Sara thought as she unfastened the strings of her wimple, letting her itchy scalp breathe freely.

"Where were they keeping you?" she asked.

"*Keeping* me? Nowhere. I'm sharing Harriett's solar with her and you, Barbara's, until they find chambers for us again."

Again? "How long will we be here, Mother?"

"For as long as it pleases our noble lord." Rose sat beside her on her bed. She took her hands in hers. "Listen to me, child. Lord Sam has been corresponding with the Silver Walls about your father's disappearance with Uther Brune, Jacob Weeslaw, and their men. After hearing their case, the Walls—they have declared mine husband—your—" She wiped her nose. "They've declared your father—"

"Dead," Sara finished matter-of-factly.

An ease and a relief washed over her mother. Tears clustered in her eyes. "Sara . . ." She came close for a hug.

Sara pulled away. *She needs to know.* "Father isn't *gone*, Mother," she said. "Not forever. He'll come back soon."

A line creased her mother's brow. "Sara, listen to me."

"He's dead, but not gone. Father's in the Evergreen Isles with King Anjan and the elves. And he can *come back*."

"My love—"

"I tried telling you before, but you wouldn't listen. At the Silver Walls, when we were with Caleb. I told you, I saw Father in the hedge maze. He appeared to me. He led me to you."

"Sara, Princess Lorana has declared your father dead."

"He is, but *he's not*. Do you remember the Gift that Caleb made?"

Rose pressed a shaking finger to her lips. "Never speak of it. You never should've seen that."

"But Mother. *It worked*." Sara inched closer. "Caleb's Gift. An elf showed himself to me in Elf's Grove. That's how Little Lady came back; he gave her to me. He told me he could bring Father back, too. He turned a leaf into a flower, and then made it a leaf again, just by touching it!"

Rose watched her as if she were speaking in First Tongue. She shook her head tiredly.

"Dray can find and return him to us from the Evergreen Isles, as whole as Little Lady," Sara continued. "We have to find a hare and make a second Gift. His old gods will help us. But I have to go to Elf's Grove. Tonight."

"Who . . . who is Dray?"

"*Caleb's elf.* I first saw Dray in my dreams at the Tower. He sent me to South Farcombe for a purpose." Sara crawled across her bed, to the pillow that concealed Dray's blade. "I have what he needs, but we have to go tonight, Mother, we have to go to Elf's Grove and meet Dray."

As she said *go tonight,* her mother shot up from her bed, voice tremulous until it steadied and she was shouting a single word at the top of her lungs for anyone down the hall or in the bailey outside to hear: "Enough, *enough,* ENOUGH!"

Sara stopped short of pulling out the blade. "Mother—"

"NO, THAT'S ENOUGH." Rose had her hands over her face. "Willard is right! You need a father's hand, Sara, or you'll keep descending into, into this devilry. Elves. *Elves?!*"

The scorn in her mother's laughter drove Sara to tears. Rose let her hands fall to her sides.

"There are no elves, Sara, because they left long ago," she told her. Sara sucked in snot, chest heaving as tears streamed down her cheeks. "It was Lord Uthron who saved us from the Tower, he and Sir Willard, but now our lord is gone. Caleb saved us from rents I owe, but he's dead. And yes, my love—I wish he'd never left westward, I prayed to god every night for months—but *he's* dead, too. *He's not coming back.* The steward herself declared this and she is the crown."

Sara retreated to the one unassailable place inside her, a fortress of hope as strong as a castle of silverstone. She stood on Barbara's bed, a little taller than her mother. "The steward is wrong," she said flatly.

"And in my grief, in my fear for you, I've found love again."

Found love. Her words cut more deeply than Dray's blade. "Your husband is Sir Damien Sothron. You love *him.*"

Her mother's eyes darted here and there. "Sir Willard has proposed marriage to me. He can be hard sometimes—"

"He whipped Farmer Grey worse than a mule!"

"He was upset. The temple burning. Lord Uthron's death. It was like the Awakening's sages say—he lost sight of the star of reason. I haven't, Sara. For your sake—to keep you safe—I have pledged myself to him in marriage."

Sara shoved her. "*WHORE!*"

The blur of her mother's hand sent Sara tumbling into the feathered bed, her cheek flushed and stinging.

"A silly girl, yes you are, a silly one," said Rose, her voice soft and shaking. "You survived the Red Tower, you saw children like Jenny out there, rounded up like swine, and still, you don't get it. *You. Don't. Get. It.*" Tears streamed down her face. "This is a highborn's world. It's a dragon that swallows whole the unsuspecting and engulfs the meek in flame. Especially peasants. Especially husbandless mothers with little girls."

A fire as fierce as the one that had destroyed the temple stirred in her heart. "The peasants slumber, but soon, they'll wake," Sara seethed through tears.

"Oh, Sara." Rose tried to caress the cheek she'd slapped, but the girl recoiled. "Willard is the shield I will use to protect you from the dragon. I will wed him, and in time, you will call him Father. And we'll be safe together at Thorn's Keep."

Her mother opened the door and shut it softly.

Sara flung herself into her pillow. After a good sob, she pulled out the blade, turning it over in her hands. Tears pelted its uneven mirror surface. *Soon you'll wake, too, Father.*

In the blade's mirror surface, she saw Dray, staring at her from behind her shoulder.

Sara whirled about, overjoyed to see him, but he wasn't there.

CHAPTER 3

Rose Vines

or the second time in three months, death hung over a man with the surname Sothos. Lorana stood in the doorway, watching as Andrew Windkin steadied his sword over Gram Sothos's exposed neck.

Deprived of regular sunlight and fresh air, the realm's greatest lord poetically looked more a peasant—pale, haggard, and shabbily dressed. Nearby lay a plate dotted with crumbs, a filthy chamber pot, and the rags of a wool blanket. His silver beard made him look a stranger. Along with his son's maiming and the destruction of his reputation, any other man might've caved at the sight of a headsman.

But the father wasn't the son.

Gram Sothos knelt on the floor, rigid and unwavering, unbreakable as packed winter ice. She almost admired the kingkiller's bravery.

"Look about you, Your Highness," Sothos responded to her question with a bored lilt, as if a blade weren't inches above his neck. "I'm in the Red Tower, at least five stories aboveground." He stretched his wrists as far as his clinking manacles allowed. "I'm bound. I'm not allowed visits, even by my son. How could I have had a hand in this new evil you accuse me of?"

Lorana dwelled on the scalded hands behind his back. "I underestimated you. Your resourcefulness. I should've known better, after you were willing to risk your own flesh and blood to kill a king—"

That prompted a fiery look. "Lies—"

"—all for your wretched religion."

"It was your mother's religion."

"A religion of traitors. Now you've had others murder Greg Thorngale, your successor." *The speaker I elected.* "The man who once saved traitors like you with his peace." She grimaced. "Tell me who carried this out for you. Tell me how you got letters out. Perhaps I'll leave you a pink hand."

The most insolent smile curved across Sothos's face. "Go on, then," he goaded her. "Take my head. Or take my hands, as you did my poor son's." He straightened up, raising his bald head until it touched the edge of Andrew's blade. "I do not fear death. But I think you *do* fear something. An armada, perhaps. Elsewise, *why am I alive?*"

"Yes, I thought you'd say something like that, my lord." At her signal, Andrew sheathed his blade. "As you say, I can't kill you, lest Parlisis rally half a continent against us. Sir Andrew."

The young knight took his leave reluctantly, even with the door open and guards posted outside. The nobleman watched her with a slight trace of apprehension.

"Whatever game you think you're playing, Your Highness, know this," he said. "Jason Warchild will never sit on the Silver Throne. And if by some chance he did, it wouldn't be for long. When you give peasants power, they rob us of ours. That which befell the king shall befall Sarah Sinclair's bastard son."

Lorana acted the stone maiden. "I know you had Greg Thorngale slain. Just as you had my father killed. There are consequences to crossing a griffon, Lord Sothos." She took a step closer. "Even for the priestking's favorite lord . . . but I've realized something. Your son helped me reach this conclusion after I took his hands." She bent low to his ear, almost to impart a secret. "*Parlisis doesn't care about the other Sothos men.*"

With perfect timing, Andrew returned and tossed his grisly prize into Sothos's lap.

Watching Sothos, Lorana remembered her Gram Reuben. The Awakening's first philosopher had once written that man, born naked, spent every waking hour of his existence bundling himself up in layers of self: memories, passions, beliefs, slights unforgiven. Reasons to rise every morning, to live, to be.

Lorana was witnessing a man shed these layers in real time. The lord feared by Loran's other lords breathed briskly, huskily. Tears slid off his cheeks, wetting the floor

"I expected worse to come after I removed his hands," she said. "But it didn't. Seven kings wrote me pleading for you, but not your son. There were ships sent to accompany Shaddon, a paltry band of Intercessors." *And a prieslenne . . .* "But no war declarations. Not even the expulsion of a single emissary."

Sothos stared down at his son's head.

"You live only because Loran can't yet defend herself," she told him. "It doesn't end with Justen. I have your wife and your daughters under house arrest. I'll bring them to you, Gram. One after another. They'll be your company in this cell, where you'll live forever, if that's—"

"*Go and warn your kings of gilt worth,*" Sothos said. Not to her. Not to Andrew. His eyes clenched shut, it was almost as if he prayed aloud. "*Your borders will burn with your keeps whilst your paper crowns soil the earth, for terrors you've sown shall be reaped.*" His quivering eyes opened and met hers. "*Before him, ascendant at birth.*"

It was a long walk up the Red Tower's spiraling stairs.

The princess found him in his chamber, dismally quiet behind the ornate desk that'd been her father's gift to him. His papery hands he folded one over another, on his desk, as if he expected her to cane his knuckles.

Lorana posted Andrew outside. As soon as the door shut, she vomited down the front of her gown, some of it catching in her cleavage. Charles hastened over, a wadded cloth in hand to dab the mess off her lips.

She steadied herself on the door latch and shook off his concern. Charles knew her wrath. He knew she blamed him for the recent porousness of his Tower. *As I should,* Lorana thought as she fished vomit out of her cleavage. *I'd have his head, if he weren't like family to us.*

Charles kept his eyes averted until she finished.

"Wine," she said through the wrist she held to her mouth.

Wordlessly, Charles went to his table, filled her cup with a red stream from his flagon, and handed it to her. She nursed at her cup steadily. When she was confident she wouldn't retch again, she sank into his only other chair. Still, not a word from the Grand Inquisitor.

She clutched the wine cup in her hands as if it were some treasure, breathing in and out. She chuckled. "I used to retch at more than death," she said. "It was between Sarah's death and Romara's beheading. Do you remember?"

He nodded. "As if it were yesterday. At mackerel and fritters. At onion broth and stew. Anything with a rank. Your Highness wouldn't eat. We had to settle on unseasoned peas."

Lorana rubbed under her nose and wiped off hurled-up egg white. "Father thought there was something terribly wrong with me."

"He felt responsible."

You were, Father, she thought, *and I loved you for it.* "He wanted to send me to Tesos with the idea that an apothecary there could treat me."

Seeming to sense her relaxed tone, Charles relaxed. "We had the carriage waiting for you outside the gatehouse, until Her Blessedness begged for you not to leave," he said with a small, nostalgic smile. "Prieslenne Edenia laid down in front of the horses as if she'd just died. None dared move her. We'd just taken the priestking's daughter hostage and were on pins and needles with seven enemy kingdoms."

"Some things never change." Lorana gazed down at her distorted reflection in the wine of her cup, her jaw thick as an anvil. "I wish sometimes that I'd gone to Grisholm's court. Or some foreign land. Far from the horrors the Silver Walls seem to attract."

"No, you don't."

His contradiction drew a testy look from her. It was bold for an advisor she'd threatened to remove from his post, after Gram Sothos had managed to kill her handpicked speaker from said advisor's palace.

"No," Lorana conceded with a swish of her wine.

Charles regarded her kindly. "You've a talent for ruling," he said with a sparkle in his eyes. "Your father saw it. That was why he left his kingdom in your hands so often."

Lorana sipped her wine. "Then why couldn't I save Greg Thorngale?"

The Grand Inquisitor straightened with a look of contrition that he was wearing out. "That was my fault, Highness, not yours. I am the one—"

"It *is* your fault," she said angrily. She wanted to hurl her cup at him. "Gram Sothos is your prisoner. He killed my father. Your *king*, Charles!"

He inclined his chin, thickening his wattle neck. "One of his turnkeys was an Elvarenist. That turnkey's now with his gods." He stared out his window, as if he could see the traitor's tarred head on Traitor's Gate from here.

As if that made everything right between them.

A wall of silence separated them. "But it's also my fault," she sighed. "I should've known they'd kill him. He who speaks for the Wing of Lords speaks for the Worthy Assembly, and Sothos's lackeys wouldn't allow my handpicked successor to live. And . . . I should've known better than to turn a blind eye to court after Father's murder."

"Drexan will face justice for his crimes," Charles swore. "Zuran *will* be found. No man hunts like mine. With any luck, he's already found their trail."

Zuran, Lorana thought, sick from worry. She felt like the goddess Selyssa, her belly gashed with an eternally unfillable hole. She'd slept in fits and starts since Drexan had absconded with her only little brother other than Jason. His wolfskin pelt draped the chair by her bedside, as if he sat there, still wearing it. *Where are you now, Zur? Are you alive . . .?*

It was still an indecipherable mystery, why Drexan had butchered two noble lords like meat. Her men had identified Eric Sundry only by his height and fiery red beard.

Uthron Morley was the greater riddle. A *tree* had crushed the Lord of Thorn's Keep. The sign of clean-sawed bark pointed to nothing less than swordwood, the metal that could hack good castle steel to bits.

She recalled Drexan explaining the myths of Graywood's origins on Remembrance Day, in a group that had included the slain noblemen and Zur. She spun round and round in circles trying to puzzle out what it all meant. Charles suspected a link to her father's assassination, on account that Morley had been an Elvarenist, but that didn't explain Sundry's presence, or why Drexan had murdered them. Or why Drexan had felled a damn tree with swordwood to crush Morley.

One thing was clear. Zur, as a servant of the King's Crow, had witnessed the murders. And why would Drexan keep a witness alive? *If god exists, I need him to look after him,* she thought. *We'll find you, little brother—and your abductor. Then, I'll have Andrew lob off Drexan's head like he did Justen Sothos's.*

Drexan had been family to her, to all of them, as much as Charles, Jon, and Hanor. But she loved Zur more, and Charles, she had to forgive in order to find Zur.

Sensing out permission to sit, Charles eased himself into the chair behind his desk. "The peasants of this kingdom have considered Drexan a Sylvanian, in addition to a sorcerer," he reminded her.

"Yes, I know. Why should that matter?"

He shrugged. "I've never known Drexan to be a religious man— unless you consider king-worship his faith. But Summer Solstice is nigh. Sylvanians hold that day sacred. They have an affinity for swordwood because that is where they take sheep and horses, to kill and leave them as blood offerings to gods of tree and stone. And recently, Morley's men vanished out there." He harbored a grim look. "If Drexan used swordwood to fell that tree . . ."

She made a face, disturbed by the visual of Drexan doing harm to Zur. "Drexan's a traitor. Not a pagan. But I want him found. I want no more failures, Lord Burke."

Charles nodded.

Lorana lifted her wine cup and discovered it empty; she decided not to refill it, and to change topics. "Gram committed another crime, after I had Andrew give him his son's head."

The Grand Inquisitor raised a thistly eyebrow. "Do tell. I'll find some way to punish him that doesn't risk war."

Charles was glad to find himself in her good graces again, a little *too* glad, perhaps. He'd do anything she asked of him to assure forgiveness. Yet she took succor in that self-interested loyalty. Right now, that loyalty tasted sweet as mother's milk.

"You mentioned king-worship . . . He quoted a forbidden poem to me. Looked me straight in the eyes when he said the last line."

Charles registered what she meant immediately. Rulers across Ansara had outlawed under pain of death one poem in the history of poetry. Just one.

He grunted contemptuously. "Only Gram Sothos would dare utter that verse. Perhaps he was eager to see his Justen whole again in the afterlife."

"Or perhaps he's a Barefoot Knight."

Charles gave a tilt of his head, looking away. "That would add another degree of nefariousness and conspiracy to his role in your father's assassination. Thankfully, Your Highness—"

"Thankfully," she said before he could finish, hearing the weary derision in his voice, "the Solemn Order died long ago."

Her belly turned queasily. Lorana rustled up from her chair, pressing out her gown. She glanced numbly at the stain down her front. Her Grand Inquisitor stood to show her out.

"I leave for the Meadows on the morrow, Charles, while Heather will depart with Hanor for Tesos," she said with cold dignity. "The Silver Walls I leave to you and to Jon. The Little King refuses to close his city walls, which puts our fates in Jon's hands and yours." She met his gaze. "Charles . . . he can't . . ."

Her father's loyal man wouldn't let her incriminate herself by finishing. He reached out with his liver-spotted hands, patting hers like a doting grandfather.

"Your traitor uncle will find no friends here, should the Worthy Assembly prove itself unworthy," he said firmly. "We will do what must be done. For the good of Loran."

Lorana watched the old man as he bowed to brush his lips against her knuckles. "And I'll trust that a prisoner of the Red Tower will remain just that—a prisoner," she added pointedly, staring at him.

Charles bowed his head. "I'll leave no stone unturned. Here, or in the search for Zuran of Tribe Nuur."

Out of an abundance of caution, Lorana had taken the catacombs to reach the Red Tower, and she returned to the Silver Walls the same way. Andrew faithfully escorted her in the reeking blackness, shining his torch to show the way and warding off rats.

Driving Uzmen back across the Silent Steppes had made a man of young Andrew. She'd pictured sturdy Sir Connor Tomas accompanying her, but Andrew could defend her as capably as any knight. Besides, she'd feel better knowing she left another loyal hand at the Walls. One of the king's longer-serving hands had just betrayed them, and another had failed her. Connor had served them since Hexar's own Trials. He was her failsafe.

The steward informed Andrew of her decision as soon as they climbed out of the catacombs, into the castle undercroft. "You honor me, Your Highness," he said with a formal bow. "I'll guard you with my own flesh against the Elvarenists."

Against the Elvarenists, she pondered. *Does that include Edenia?*

After seeing him off, Lorana headed straight for the baths. Steam curled invitingly off the water. She needed to disappear in the steam, wash off the vomit and the reek of sewer, enfold herself in the familiar, invisible layers, the ones not stained by blood. Her filthy gown puddled at her feet, and she immersed herself to her neck in sweltering water. Lorna Durros knelt behind her, scrubbing her skin.

When the lady grazed her nipple, by mistake, Lorana reflexively flashed her a look bordering on flirtatious. Guilt mingled with nostalgia when the look went unreciprocated. She and Eden had been that age when they first kissed.

I'd bury fear with pleasure, she thought with mild disgust for herself.

Lorna was Heather's lady now, barely a woman besides.

And she had someone already. *My fear for you misleads me, Zur. You're only the third brother I've lost recently . . .*

Layers. She found herself returning to Reuben's layers. Her father was a layer, and he was gone. Jason, another layer gone. Zur, yet another layer. *How many layers must I lose,* she thought, *until I'm nothing?*

She thanked Lorna after her bath and asked her to fetch Heather. She'd planned to spend time with her sister tonight. With Drexan's treachery, she'd had second thoughts about sending her with Hanor, but she'd go to Tesos with no shortage of other men, including Sir Blake Oxley. That gave her comfort.

But first, her love.

She couldn't locate her in familiar castle locations, and was nearly breathless, suddenly fearful, until she found her doing something unmeet by the hedge maze. The evening sky rippled with silvery light, as if it were pond water a stone had skipped across.

A dagger twirled awkwardly past the colorful whicker target used for Lily's Apple on Remembrance Day. The steward watched from the South Tower's steps as Anyasha marched to the hilt in the grass and yanked it up. The girl's brown eyes lit up when she saw Lorana.

Lorana folded her arms, pretending bafflement. "What on earth are you *doing?*" she chuckled, glad to seize on an excuse, some excuse, for laughter.

Anyasha strode back to position. "What does it look like?" She straightened her shoulders, arched her arm, and hurled the dagger again. Her throw flew feet clear of the outermost band.

"Like you're making a botch of hitting that target," Lorana said with gentle mock. "Practicing," she added when no reply came.

Squinting, Anyasha flung the dagger again. This time, it scraped the whicker's edge before *thunking* in grass.

"You know Casaanites aren't allowed to handle steel," she said teasingly.

The girl gave a fleeting eyeroll, not at Lorana, just at the world as it was. "Everyone's mind is on Zur and his abductor. Sir Connor saw me earlier and went about his business."

"Yasha, I'm touched . . . but Sir Andrew will come north with us, along with hundreds of my sworn men."

"Elvarenists conspired to kill your father, your brother, and your lord speaker," she said in a tone Lorana wasn't sure she'd heard before. "Drexan kidnapped Zuran. We're leaving home for a tournament that people liken to hell. I don't *trust* the people around you, Ana. Any of them."

She almost said it aloud. *I love you,* she thought. *I love you more than I loved Eden.* Anyasha recovered the dagger, stepped back to position, readied her throwing arm.

Lorana spotted ink-black markings on her lover's left palm. She touched Anyasha's shoulder before she made her next throw. "Is that . . . Did you get a *tattoo?*"

Drawn in charcoal, a rose vine bloomed gorgeously in the center of her palm. Thorny vines climbed from her wrist to her fingertips, budding with black flower petals. Scratches from the artist's fishbone puffed her hand. It had to have been a painful tattoo.

Anyasha watched her. "Do you like it?"

Lorana was incredulous. "You went to Fish Street?" One fisherman, a well-known Chi-Sayan, sketched his designs on flesh with a fishbone dipped in charcoal and blood. Anyasha had to have gone to him.

She smiled nervously. "I told Sir Andrew I wanted to find a flower for you sold only by a Southpoint vendor," she said. "It wasn't all a lie."

When did Andrew find time to lead her out the gates and behead my enemy's son? She almost asked Anyasha how she'd done this under her nose, but she'd barely seen her in seven days. She'd been busy finding a punishment that fit Sothos's crime, delaying the journey north, and trying to rescue Zur.

"Why a rose?" Lorana asked her.

Anyasha looked down at her feet, embarrassed. "You've been a flower to someone else," she said. "I want you to know that I'm your flower, Ana. So long as . . . you want me."

Lorana smiled rakishly. "Are you sure that dagger is meant

to protect?"

"It'll protect you."

"Come," Lorana told her, clasping her flowered hand. "We leave tomorrow, and I want to spend time with Heather." *And I feel safe with you. Safe as I can be, naked as I am.*

The Golden Meadows

ive thousand men accompanied Jason, Evan, and the Bull east to the Kingstrials. By foot or horse, kilt-clad peasants and armored knights traveled down steep mountain slopes, through Eddenwood's pine forests, past the mirrors of lakes, and over hills feathered with high grass.

The Army of the Clouds, some were calling this proud procession, until the Bull reprimanded his vassal lords and dispatched them to tell their sworn knights and *scrorn-ner-gaith* this host had but one name: the *Hathrimnyr*, which in Cloudspeech meant the King's Army.

The King's Army, Jason pondered from astride his mount, twisting to admire the long unbroken chain of men, horse, and carriage. *Can the Warchild be worthy of such commitment?*

Trevor Wexley had seemed to think so. Over the course of a fortnight, the Bull and his noble lords had mustered anointed men, peasants, and their beasts from every corner of his hermit realm. With astonishing speed, his rustic people had fashioned for Jason a respectable army.

Of course, there was no law to speak of that obligated claimants in the Kingstrials to bring an army with them. Men who valued their lives and wanted the Assembly to take them seriously did so, and camped around the Colossus until their champion died or became king. To have an army meant that you had allies, were likable enough and worth the payoff, and could feed and shelter all those bellies and heads for as long as it took to crown someone.

An army also deterred rivals from slitting your throat as you slept.

Only the suicidal staked their claims without such friends. Such men often wound up worm food before even the Meet of First Declaration, where the Worthy accepted a claimant, or didn't. This was simply the way of things, a small price to pay for an end to succession wars.

Watching his *Hathrimnyr*, Jason wondered what Garrett would think, or Erick. The crown prince had said Loran was his.

He imagined his secret wife, the prieslenne. Would *she* be proud? *Will you call me yours again when you see me, Eden?*

Jason rode at the vanguard with his uncle, Wexley, and six vassal lords. Their guide was the River Colossus, a coiling gray-blue tributary rife with game: leaping trout, fleets of duck and geese, and thirsty hare and white-tailed deer. Griffs appeared out of nowhere, plunging into the river and shooting back out with trout in their clutches.

Trouble arose when a peasant archer felled several griffs. Jason had to insist on lashes for the offender, lest he lose his head to his unforgiving lords. It was a crime to kill the sacred birds, even among Cloudlanders. "I need my men," Jason told the Bull. "I don't need griffs."

A fortnight and a day after departing Westland, the *Hathrimnyr* arrived on the outskirts of the Golden Meadows. An ocean of amber flowed west and east and north and south, as far as the eye could see. A snowcapped peak, Mount Dracar, jutted through blue sky like a white arrowhead.

At Evan's urging, they halted at the grasping skeletal hand of a chalk-white yew tree alone among the hills. "This is the Bony Yew," he told Jason. "Northerners and Midland peasants often come here to pray for a good harvest. The Colossus isn't far. Maybe a league."

Jason rode up to the sacred tree. "Send out our eyes and ears," he said. "I'll pray for my own harvest while we wait."

Returning half an hour later, scouts reported that Jason wasn't the first claimant to arrive at the Colossus with a host. Lords Tom Gelder, Sam Wuthers, and Tomas Fawkes camped with their respective forces, some more numerous than others. For now, at least, Fawkes boasted the strongest army. Evan reminded them that would change once Hexar's exiled brother anchored with his ships.

And there were Thorngale banners, the scouts said. At that, Evan bristled under unsubtle glances from other lords. *It's not your fault, uncle,* Jason thought.

Word of Greg Thorngale's death had reached them three days past. Ambushed in a clearing, Thorngale, his three sons, and their men had suffered volleys of arrows fired from tree canopies. It was a known tactic of the Pigeons, the Loyal Company's scouts and soldiers. The beloved peacemaker's murderer had wanted the realm to blame Evan.

Jason couldn't doubt his uncle's innocence. On hearing the news, Evan had cursed Sothos, Parlisis, and all the Elvarenists. "They've murdered the one true noble in this realm like swine," he'd said bitterly.

Killing the Old Oak had been a master stroke—one their enemies couldn't have played without Lordsbane's consent. On the surface, Lorana tapped Thorngale as Sothos's successor to dress the outcome of these Kingstrials in legitimacy. Yet she'd also wanted him to keep the rules from bending against Jason. With the great Thorngale gone, Parlisis's allies could fill Gram Sothos's influential role with a puppet. And by framing Pigeons, their enemies had made it easier to cast Jason as another sort of puppet—one with strings pulled by Thorngale's purported murderer.

But there was more than bent rules and tarnished causes to worry over.

Thorngale's sons had survived. And they wanted Evan's head.

The night before last, Jason had to placate lords ruffled by the thought that Evan had a hand in the treachery. "Lord Greg's murder is proof that Shaddon, Lordsbane, and their priestking fear us," he'd told them over dinner. "Our cause is that of a strong Loran, united against her foes. Our cause is just. Theirs is not. And it's why we'll win."

If I'm allowed to stake my claim in the first place, Jason thought presently.

Cresting a hill, he and his lords surveyed a vast, makeshift city of canvas and leather. Pavilions and tents sprawled across the Golden Meadows for miles, littered with smoking cookfires and bustling with tens of thousands of men-at-arms, livestock, and beasts of burden. Rutted paths quartered camps into the likeness of a giant spoked wheel, a colonnaded ruin its hub.

Jason gazed at the legendary amphitheater. "That's it?"

Ahorse, Evan clutched at his heart dramatically, as if hit by an arrow. "'*That's it*'? You wound me, dear nephew."

"Father reminisced about the sand arena constantly. I always imagined something . . . grander."

"The king fought and killed inside its walls. Swordwood and Silver Walls and Great Trees Loran is known for, but the Colossus"—Evan stretched out a hand, as if he could hold and preserve the elliptical arena for all posterity—"*there's* a symbol this kingdom deserves."

"A symbol, aye," Wexley put in. "A symbol for the oceans of blood spilt in its sands."

"And yet the Colossus remains a testament to the power of reason." Evan's boyish excitement wrung a smile from Jason. "Skilled builders, the Romarians were. The Colossus can seat a hundred thousand men. If its gates are shut, and a lever pulled, pipes will flood the arena within. Yet none of that water will seep into the bestiary cells belowground—"

Russell Wexrenn yawned emphatically. "I'd rather hear this history lesson with a cup of honey-wine, in a pavilion," he said. "My arse hurts and needs a chair. 'To each a chair,' no?"

Jason sighed. "For once, Lord Russell, your mouth finds a use. Lord Trevor, let's move the *Hathrimnyr*. It's time I staked my claim."

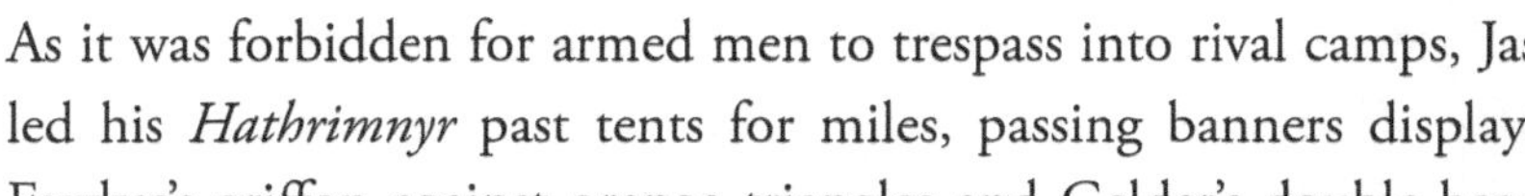

As it was forbidden for armed men to trespass into rival camps, Jason led his *Hathrimnyr* past tents for miles, passing banners displaying Fawkes's griffon against orange triangles and Gelder's double-headed dragon on crimson and jet. Men from the other camps ceased their swordplay or stood round their fires, transfixed by the procession of Cloudlanders in kilts and jacks of plate.

Inwardly, Jason smiled. *Spread the word. The son of Hexar the Bold marches with his father's Bull.*

Evan singled out a sprawl of barren earth for their lords' pavilion. Word was sent down the line, and up rolled hundreds of wagons, transporting silver-and-crimson canvas and stakes and pikes. Their camp soon came alive with the sounds of men pounding stakes, unfolding canvas, speaking in Cloudspeech.

To the disapproval of some of the Bull's lords, Jason and Evan worked alongside the *scrorn-ner-gaith*, pitching twenty pavilions, hammering stables, digging firepits. The banners of Houses Eddenhold and Wexley fluttered together, the griffon and the black mountain.

I'm in the Kingstrials, Jason marveled. *Almost . . .*

His rivals began making appearances in the afternoon.

Tomas Fawkes showed first. He wore a checkered scarlet doublet, an embroidered cape worn casually over his shoulder. With his trim goatee and feathered cavalier hat, he was worlds apart from a Cloudlander. And lest anyone mistake him for an unserious contender, forty mounted knights accompanied him.

"A pleasure to see you here, Lord Jason," he said with a doff. "With the legendary Bull, no less! Truly, I'm impressed. The priestking's allies in the Assembly will doubtless have a harder time thwarting your claim."

"They'll have an even harder time, if we work together," Jason said. "Together, we can seat the Fourth Wing."

"By 'together,' I assume you mean I'll bow out for you, no?" He leaned forward with the world's most condescending smile. "Try a little harder, Warchild. Offer me land. A chancellorship. *Anything* but Lorana." One of his men oinked like a pig, prompting laughter.

The forty men could well have not been there, the way Wexley regarded the lord. "I'll offer my fist to your moist cunt face in the arena," rumbled the Bull.

Fawkes burst with laughter. "Charming."

"I look forward to your challenge in the Colossus, Lord Tomas," Jason offered with a meant respect.

"Should you?" Westerliche returned. "I bested you once on Remembrance Day, my lord. Perhaps it would be better for you if you abandoned this folly and threw your weight behind me. Why, we could both send your zealot uncle's head back to Parlisis. In turn, I'll legitimize you once I'm king. How would you like to be *Lord* Jason Eddenhold?"

Evan beat Jason and his Bull to the punch. "More than half the Assembly follows Gram Sothos and Peshar Grathos," he said. "They won't allow an ardent Free Believer like you to sit the Walls, Tomas. Not least because of your friendship with Firemouth." He stepped closer. "Stand with my nephew. See him king! In return, we'll seat the Wing of the Commons and name you his Chancellor of the Exchequer."

Fawkes's smiling eyes cooled. "And they'll crown a bastard? One in thrall to the Old Oak's murderer?"

"That accusation is false," Jason said.

"Tell that to the Thorngale brothers," he said with a shrug. "I hear the Stormsword sharpens his steel for you, Lord Evan."

Fawkes took his leave. Other lords came by, notably Sam Wuthers, beggarly-looking with his tousled hair and unshaven stubble. He tried to court Jason but looked like to piss himself in the tall Bull's presence. Evan softened the awkwardness with easy banter and an offer to reward any alliance with the coveted Major Sunder estates in Eastland, *all* of them.

Wuthers seemed to verge on agreeing . . . up until Tom Gelder and his knights trotted by on their steeds, sneaking glances, sniggering.

Stiffening, Wuthers said, "I'll reclaim Major Sunder for my house when *I* am king," and bolted off.

Nearby, Wexrenn told his liege lord, "A man like that has no business here."

The sun was waning when the three brothers finally made their appearance, trotting into view on huge destriers. "They brought no guard," Rogir Levan reported ominously.

"That's because they have the Stormsword." Jason clasped his uncle's shoulder. "I'll talk to them alone."

Evan gave him a fiery look that said, *No, you sure as hell won't.* "The Bull goes with you."

Of the three sons, Darren Thorngale most resembled his father. They all shared their late scion's broad shoulders and chestnut hair, but the Stormsword had inherited the cleft chin, the chiseled cheekbones, the striking green eyes ladies at court spoke of excitedly. He had his hair in a tail. All three Thorngales wore surcoats emblazoned with their thrice-crowned blue hart on white. Brothers united for vengeance.

As the eldest, Gavin spoke first. "Lords Jason and Trevor, on behalf of our grieving house, we seek Evan Sinclair's head."

"Turn Sinclair over now," Darren added with a look for Jason, "and I swear to make my sword yours in the Kingstrials. If you've heard of me, you know that is no small offer."

Evan's head for Darren's sword. No surprise there.

Jason dwelled on each brother. "My lords, I have nothing but sympathy for your cause. Like me, you've lost your father and the head of your house to assassins." He placed a hand on his breast. "By Justar's face, I'll do all I can to give you justice when I wear the crown."

"Good." Darren pointed past them, at Evan. "You can start by giving up the head of the Loyal Company."

"Do so," Luc said, "and we'll drop our claim. We'll align our house with yours, fight for you in the Trials—even back your Wing of the Commons. Give us justice, and we'll give you the crown."

Jason exhaled through his nose. "I cannot. Lord Evan is guiltless in your father's slaying. We wept for Lord Greg."

Darren bared his teeth. "*Wept?* We wept in a pool of our father's blood, after Pigeons shot us full of arrows. In a pool of our blood, too." He yanked on his surcoat, revealing an angry scar on his chest. Luc flexed a hand short three fingers. "We demand justice. The Pigeons answer to Sinclair. One way or another, Sinclair will answer to us."

"You saw these Pigeons?" Jason probed skeptically.

"In hoods and cloaks colored like the forest."

"Anyone can dress like them. Your father was succeeding Gram Sothos. You don't see Lordsbane's pink hands in this?"

"Sothos is an Elvarenist like us, ever a friend to our house. His vassal lord sheltered us at his castle after the attack. Your conniving uncle undermines the Assembly through his band of traitors. Hexar should've struck off his head."

"And why would Sinclair have Lord Greg killed?"

"To profit you," Gavin said. "Our father would've put the outcome of these Kingstrials above reproach, but that's not how Sinclair will make his sister's bastard king. We thought to blame you, my lord, but we remembered how you protected that Common girl from Justen on Remembrance Day."

"You have a kind and noble heart, Lord Warchild," Darren said. "I'd rather leave it intact."

The Bull lurched forward. "Threaten my king, and I'll tear out yours. Only, I don't need steel to do it."

Darren kicked his destrier forward. Wexley put himself between Jason and Thorngale. "Shield Sinclair, and we'll treat you as party to his crime," he snarled.

With one huge hand the Bull reached for Darren's chest, grasping, as if he meant to pierce flesh with his thick sausage fingers and fish out a heart.

Gavin appeared to think the Bull could do it. Riding up, he restrained Darren with an arm across his chest. "Enough! We'll not dishonor our house by spilling blood before these Trials." He maneuvered his horse about. "We'll press our ancient claim. For justice."

The Stormsword dug his heels into his horse's flanks. "I'll see you in the sands, Lord Warchild. To you I promise a quick death, but to Evan the Traitor, I make no such offer."

The brother lords rode off at a hard gallop, carving lines through amber reeds.

"Worry not," Evan assuaged Jason after he shared their threats. "A great swordsman Darren may be, but he isn't the cleverest. Remember, the Kingstrials require more than martial skill."

Jason left him after that, deciding he could do with a stiff cup of Cloudlands mead. *And who wouldn't,* he pondered, *after receiving a death threat from the Stormsword?* The bastard prince was a tested warrior. He'd killed twenty-six men by sword or longbow.

But Darren Thorngale was better. Faster. And he'd killed thirteen more than Jason—by himself, all on the same day.

Navigating the tents of his camp, Jason stumbled upon a circle of *scrorn-ner-gaith* huddled with peasants sworn to other lords like Fawkes and Wuthers, unarmed so they could mingle freely. The sight troubled at first, but the red-cheeked peasants welcomed him at their fire with drink and roasted hare. Their banter and bawdy jokes put him at ease as nothing else could. As he ate and drank, he laughed from an authentic place, glad to enjoy good company.

Night fell. The Golden Meadows roared to life with songs and the sounds of men guffawing, fires crackling, and the low pitch of a thousand conversations on the surround. Light from thousands of fires ruddied the sky, obscuring the Lame King constellation.

There was so much singing, drinking, and laughing, you could almost forget that men were set to die the coming week.

Come morning, Jason had breakfast with Evan, Wexley, and the other nobles in their lords' pavilion, a striped canvas tent cramped with beds and barrels. Men helped themselves to sausage pork, boiled goose eggs, and blackened rye amid the sounds of a camp stirring outside.

Conversation turned to the previous night's festivities, to rumors of claimants meeting secretly with each other to broker alliances. There had been drunken brawls, but only between the peasants and knights sworn to other lords. This was because the *scrorn-ner-gaith*, Wexley said, knew their place.

Jason refused Wexrenn's offer of roasted pork. "Save it for the *Hathrimnyr*," he said. "It isn't clear how long we'll be here. I want to make sure our men eat well."

Slighting him, Wexrenn cut pork for himself. "My king, I saw a strange thing last night," he said as he bit off part of his sausage. "You, with the *scrorn-ner-gaith*. Cavorting."

The clinks of plates and cups filled the awkward silence. Wexley worked at his sausage pork, listening.

At a glance from Evan, Jason smiled. "Aye, I craved some distraction. Cloudlanders know how to sing, I'll say that."

Derek Clabbard thrummed his cup nervously. "My king, it is

considered unmeet where we're from to sup with the *scrorn-ner-gaith*. They're beneath our boots."

"And where you're from, I'll rule as king."

Wexley nodded. "As you say, my liege. So long as the will of the Wing of the Commons ends at the Cloudlands."

Jason clinked cups with Wexley. "As we agreed, my lord."

"I have news to share," Evan said when they were done drinking.

"You don't look overly glad to share it, my lord," Clabbard observed. "Has the steward failed us again?"

Jason shot Clabbard a cross look. "My sister didn't fail. Our enemies slew Greg Thorngale. Have faith in her."

The nobleman inclined his head apologetically.

"I'm a believer in reason, personally," said Evan, "but this time, god delivered. Riders came in the night to speak with Assemblymen. The ships that went to capture a dragon burned at sea. It's believed that Gordon Whitecastle and his crew were aboard."

Clabbard paled. "The work of dragonflame?"

Evan made a headshake. "The ships had just set sail from Loran. Whitecastle never even reached the Isles of Fire."

Relief swept the pavilion. Giddy as children on Winter Solstice, the lords clinked cups, sloshing mead on their hands and wrists. Wexley deflated with a long sigh, his own prayers answered. Nephew and uncle shared a knowing look.

Greg Thorngale's murder hadn't been the only news. A day before they left the Cloudlands, a messenger of Lorana's had showed at Eddenloxley with unsettling tidings: the Worthy Assembly wanted a dragonslaying for the Second Trial. That Jason could lose his life fighting a dragon was beside the point. Of any part of Loran, the Cloudlands sat closest to the Isles of Fire; dragons sometimes flew close, burning villages, melting castles. Only the Bull's stubborn honor had kept their alliance alive and marched the *Hathrimnyr* eastward.

A smile tugged at Jason's lips. *This is your doing, Lorana.* A hired hand had snuck aboard the ships and set them ablaze. He deplored sabotage as unmanly, but then, the steward wasn't a man. And one turn deserved another, after Thorngale's killing.

"There's more, and you'll rejoice less to hear," said Evan. "Our enemies in the Assembly have lost face, money, and time. They won't pursue another dragon, but they've something else in mind for the Second Trial: a *naumachia*."

Wexrenn poured himself a generous amount of mead, unmoved. "I'll take a sea battle over a dragon."

Clabbard was somber. "I'm glad the Assembly's gambit for a dragon sank, but a proper *naumachia* is no less savage."

Evan nodded. "They'll fill the Colossus with water, rickety boats, and kings with their men. We'll need Lord Derek and the Bull in the arena with Jason, if they go that way."

"It will be so," Wexley said. "What of the First Trial?"

"Most of the Assemblymen agree on a joust for the First."

"A manly test," the Bull said approvingly. "From what I've seen from our king, he'll best cunts like Fawkes easily."

"First or Second, there is still the Third Trial, and it's the most weighted," Evan said. "To be king, a claimant must mount a griffon, and stay upon it, to prove blood ties to Anjan."

"Every king whose arse the Assembly wedged onto the Silver Throne has claimed half-elven blood." Ulbridge drank mead, stifled a belch. "The Third Trial means nothing."

"Its symbolism is important," Jason said. "My own father tamed the griffon on his first try. And so will I."

Evan fingered a groove in his cup. "Hexar did, but it was a runt. Only as large as a mule." His eyes wobbled with fear—a fear for Jason. "This one sounds like a *monster*. Ten feet high it rises on all fours, black as pitch, ferocious."

"Better than a dragon, eh?" Wexrenn intoned.

"It isn't here yet," Evan said in a tone that suggested he was losing patience with Wexrenn, "and it's filled graves."

Ulbridge banged his cup on the table. "First, a dragon that could burn the land to cinders. Now—a griffon. Why would the Worthy unleash these monsters upon us?"

"Someone wishes to kill off his rivals, as many as he can," Jason offered. "Making Shaddon the Assembly's only choice." *And I expect someone will see to this griffon before it sees to me in the arena, sister . . . Move heaven and earth.*

Evan nodded. "Our king speaks truth. Gram Sothos sits in the Red Tower, but his reach is long, and still he clutches the Wings of Lords and Clergy. Soon, more game pieces will move into position for Shaddon."

Wexrenn weighed Evan with a look bordering on surly. "You have much to share with us this morning, Sinclair. Have you been speaking with your little doves?"

Evan cracked his boiled egg with a spoon. "Do you not also sit in the Wing of Lords, Russell?"

He's been speaking with his Companymen, Jason realized. They had to be at the Meadows, known by name to Evan alone. Where could he have spoken with them without drawing eyes? "He isn't the cleverest," Evan had said of Darren Thorngale. *But it appears you are, uncle,* Jason thought.

Sunlight dashed the pavilion's gloom. Lifting a tent flap, Rogir Levan walked in.

Wexrenn broke a stiff loaf of bread and dipped half in his onion broth. "In the Cloudlands, we consider it poor form for a knight to interrupt his betters at breakfast."

"I beg your pardon, my lords," Rogir said. "We've received word from scouts. Shaddon Eddenhold is here. He sailed round Loran and anchored by the shore." He gazed at Jason. "He asks for a parley."

Against his uncle's advice, Jason went to meet with his father's killer several miles out from the crowded settlements, near Loran's north shore, on a stretch of flatland pocked with shrubbery and the ruins of a steepled temple.

Jason didn't have to agree to parley. But he wanted to take the measure of the man who'd brought ruin on House Eddenhold, first on Erick, then on Hexar.

Evan and the Bull accompanied him, along with a force of fifty knights. Everyone came armed, armored, and mounted. They formed up into lines by the ruined temple, a roofless, empty shell thronged with high grass and spattered with gull droppings. This was where Shaddon wanted to meet.

They waited a half hour before a silver mirage glimmered on the horizon. A regiment of men and horse came into focus, hooves pummeling soil. In their fluttering banners, a cream-colored griffon stretched its wings against indigo sky.

Clabbard scoffed. "Shameless bastard. He took King Hexar's sigil and corrupted it with the Lonely Isle's colors."

"He has Intercessors with him," Evan intoned.

Wexley had a wild look. "He brought *Intercessors?*"

Intercessors. A band of zealot torturers, Parlisis's swift silent sword in the thirteen kingdoms. In their rippling black shrouds and scowling silver masks, they looked otherworldly, more ghouls than Medecians. Their destriers' hooves grained the air with sand and dust.

Most kings gave them freedom of movement for fear of accusation. Almost all kings. Hexar the Bold had them barred from his kingdom after the Long Summer Rebellion. Yet here they were in Loran again, torturers who impaled and burned apostates without trial. *A king lay dead, and a priestking stakes his claim,* Jason thought grimly.

"NO CLOSER, SHADDON!"

At Evan's cry, Shaddon's line slowed to a shuddering halt fifteen yards out. The man himself sat ahorse, surrounded by his ghoulish guard. Other Assemblymen were in his escort, including Dumas Sunox and Sam Gramlore.

Shaddon was a traitor, kidnapper, kingkiller, and, without doubt, an Eddenhold. He shared Hexar's manly features, from his thick anvil jaw to his flat brow. He and Lorana shared the family's stump nose. A thin brown beard coated his jowls, stuck with silvers. He wore fine filigreed armor, the best gold could buy. Rings of jade and obsidian decorated his sausage fingers. Interestingly, one ring boasted a pearl—a sign of betrothal.

Shaddon regarded Wexley. "Lord Trevor, I expected the likes of Evan the Traitor in this bunch, but not you," he said imperiously. "A man of your redoubtable reputation shouldn't slander it for a bastard beneath your heels. What would your brother say?"

Hexar's Bull looked ready to ride out and cleave Shaddon in half then and there.

"*You've trespassed into Loran under the penalty of death, Shaddon,*" Evan cried in a clarion voice. "By the orders of the steward, Princess Lorana. If you value your neck, you'll retreat to your ship forthwith, along with Parlisis's freak zealots."

One uncle of Jason's shifted to face the other. "Sinclair. My brother should've mounted your head on a spike. I'll finish his work after I win my Trials." He straightened his shoulders. "I didn't sail the Sea of Dracar to parry with you. Where is Lady Alyse's daughter, my blessed niece?"

"Have you wax in your ears? Is your hearing failing you?"

Gramlore urged his steed forward, breaking ranks. "You speak to King Hexar's only remaining successor, filth-rouser."

"Sam, *dihagaet,*" Wexley rumbled in Cloudspeech. Seeing Gramlore's reaction, Jason didn't need a translator to know the Bull had said something deeply offensive. "You assure yourself a traitor's death by accompanying a kingkiller. Hexar the Bold exiled Shaddon. His daughter affirms and enforces his exile."

"Exiled under specious charges by the Grand Inquisitor," Sunox said, "and no longer." Reaching inside his gauntlet, the portly lord unfurled a scroll that danced in the wind. "Not one *but two* Assembly speakers and more than half the Wing of Lords grant Lord Shaddon of House Eddenhold right of entry in Loran."

Jason urged his mount forward. "A shield of words and faithless lords doesn't assure your safety here, dear uncle. You, who seized your own nephew. *You,* who arranged for Erick's death—*and the death of your own brother!*"

Jason might as well have not been there. Shaddon didn't glance his way, didn't open his mouth to deny Jason's charges, didn't acknowledge him. He remained motionless as a statue.

Answer me, damn you. I want to hear you deny it. Jason lurched forward in his saddle. "*What say you,* kingkiller? Do you deny these charges?"

Shaddon stared off, unblinking. Growing impatient, the Bull growled, "You *speak* at a parley. That's what parleys are fucking for. Will you answer our king, or shall we go?"

The exiled lord coolly pivoted to Wexley. Calmly, he said, "'Lo,' said the High God, He Who Rules Unending, 'the spoilt fruit of your loins is less than a smudge of dirt in the eyes of the righteous, but still pleases me more than the rotten fruit of Eduard and Elzura. Yet the spoilt fruit speaks sin; he comes to the king's land as blight. Therefore, the faithful shall turn their heads, and hear him not, and see him not.'"

"The Head speaks," cried an Assemblyman for Shaddon.

"The Hands serve," replied Shaddon's men. Intercessors signed the diamond all at once, thumbs to the foreheads of their masks, then the edges of their shoulders and just below their chests.

Wexley rolled his eyes.

"If everyone obeyed every word in the Eighth Testament, we'd all be blind, dumb, and handless," Ulbridge remarked.

Shaddon turned to Ulbridge, careful to glaze over Jason. "This is the word of the High God, who comes before the twelve gods, elves, and the First King. He demands our respect for his prophets, Cloudlander."

"Sounds like the words of someone who doesn't wish to answer charges of regicide," Evan remarked.

Shaddon wouldn't deign to look at Jason, but he looked unhinged as he scowled at Evan Sinclair. "*How dare you,*" he fumed. "I won't defend myself to you—*you,* of all men."

Gramlore kicked his horse ahead. The maneuver brought hands to sword hilts. "Careful how you answer your next king, Sinclair, or I'll do what Hexar never finished."

The Bull matched Gramlore's provocation with his advance, unintimidated by the glint of sunlight in all their enemies' half-drawn swords. "Try, Sam," Wexley rumbled.

Whatever this was, it was unraveling. Shaddon had only one thing to offer, and he wouldn't give it up willingly. Jason urged his horse past Wexley. He was met with dark-socketed stares from the masked Intercessors.

"Tell us what you would give, Shaddon, so we can refuse and be on our way," Jason demanded.

Once more, Shaddon didn't acknowledge him, not directly at least. He extended an arm in the ruin's direction. "This was once a Romarian temple, built by King Rorin Romaris in honor of nameless pagan gods. When a brave priestking sent his men to chase Barefoot Knights across Ansara, they came across this temple. They tore down Rorin's false idols and remade a place of blood sacrifice into Saint Alban's Temple.

"Saint Alban's," his uncle continued with a faint smile of admiration. "A true temple for twelve gods. Torches lit it day and night, and the faithful prayed in its pews."

"Are you coming to your point?" Evan called out.

Shaddon glared at Evan. "Sir Bradley Durhurst and his Treasonous Twelve paid this holy temple a visit. They burned the temple—much as I understand outlaws recently burned a temple in South Farcombe. *With a state official in repose.*"

Word travels quickly, and why wouldn't it, when the first temple burns in Loran in centuries? Jason thought. Evan had predicted their enemies would wave Saint Eric's destruction about like a distress flag, to rally Elvarenists.

"The Interregnum killed a line of righteous kings, just as the Awakening stirs contempt in the hearts of a king's subjects against the one true faith," Shaddon said. "No longer. I am come to end the Interregnum that never ended. I am come to return Loran to the twelve gods! And when my betrothed and I sit the Silver—"

Russell Wexrenn passed wind so loudly the horses curled their ears.

For once, Jason smiled with the nobleman. "Sorry, my arse bleats when it hears other arses bleating," the noble said with a hapless shrug.

Shaddon pressed his wormy lips together in disgust. He signaled Sunox, and out rode the fleshy lord, slick with sweat in the sun's glare. He produced another twig of a scroll, twined in cream and purple ribbon.

"My king wishes to make you an offer, my lord," the Lord of Ramsport told Jason, making eye contact.

"Tell your 'king' the assassin that tried to kill King Jason in Southpoint confessed that Shaddon sent him," Evan interjected.

Sunox shook his head. "My king assures us he had nothing to do with that plot, nor with any that has befallen Loran or his brother's family. He wept and wore sackcloth when he learned of Prince Erick's death. He was like a son to Lord Shaddon."

Jason flexed the fingers of his right hand, his sword hand. He hadn't known Erick before war, but the man he befriended in the Brace had been stern, dutiful . . . and haunted. He never shared it with Garrett, but he often heard their estranged half-brother weeping as he prayed at night. When liquor made him brave, he'd ask Erick about what had happened after Shaddon seized him. What had befallen his half-brother?

But Erick had only ever responded with simple answers. Yes, no, yes, no—or nothing at all. Erick's silence was all Jason needed to know about Shaddon Eddenhold's hospitality.

"So he didn't kill Erick," Evan said presently, "but he *did* the king? Is that it?"

Shaddon sneered. "I'll not listen to these evil accusations. I *loved* my brother, GODS DAMN YOU, SINCLAIR." He signed the diamond with a shaking hand. "Despite his flaws—and they were many, as Lord Trevor well knows—he was my brother. No, I won't hear this, especially from *you* . . . you who slew the Lady Alyse as if you swung the axe!"

"Keep your desperate accusations to yourself, Sinclair, if you wish for Lord Jason to hear this offer," Sunox warned.

"I'm not interested in hearing it." Jason pointed at Hexar's brother. "I have terms of my own for your king, however."

He drew the barest flicker of acknowledgement from the exiled nobleman. "Confess." He stared at Shaddon. "Confess to the crimes you've perpetrated against your blood. Confess to arranging for the deaths of your king brother and the nephew you took hostage. Confess—you sent an assassin for me, like a sneak coward.

"Confess," Jason said, "and I'll assure you a quick death at Traitor's Pit, by a trained swordsman. I swear on the blood we share."

Shaddon remained staring off as he clenched his teeth, the seams of his mouth trembling. "*We share no blood, whoreson.*"

Jason felt his father's fire burn through him. A sharp look of warning from Evan stayed his sword hand. *If you could only see this, Father,* he thought. *Evan Sinclair is truer to our family than your own flesh and blood ever was.*

Shaddon narrowed his eyes at Evan. "Tell us true, Sinclair. Tell your *own nephew* the truth! The Warchild has no claim to the Silver Throne. He isn't Hexar's child, just a bastard sprung upon us from the bed of straw your sister shared with Matthus Robswell."

As if I haven't heard that one before, Jason thought.

Wexley brandished his sword and leveled it at Shaddon. "You'll watch that fucking tongue if you want to keep it, or I'll send it to the priestking myself." All his Cloudlanders drew their blades in solidarity. Wheeling his horse about, Sunox withdrew behind Shaddon's lines as Intercessors drew their swords.

Evan rode out in front of Jason and their party. "No—*do nothing!*" he warned them all. "You'll give them an excuse to throw Jason from the Kingstrials." He spun on Shaddon. "We'll see you in the sand. And if *you* do anything to harm King Jason before the Trials begin, I shall make the Worthy act, whether Sothos wills it or not. How will you dance for your priestking then, I wonder, crownless *and* headless?"

Shaddon's lips twitched. "When I am king, you will tell me the names of your Companymen, Sinclair . . . or you'll wish my brother had taken your head. In any case, Warchild is already thrown. He has been from the day he ripped open your sister's womb, as Dracar's spawn did the goddess Selyssa's."

Jason rode forward at a trot, past Evan. "You'll know my sword, Shaddon. Pray to your gods. Dine on meat, drink mulled wine, laugh and dance, if your religion permits it. Marry, if your betrothed will have you. Your last days are here."

One by one, he and his men slipped away, riding behind their host for a gallop back to the Meadows.

CHAPTER 5

Solemn Truth

ur knew the birds by their songs.

Wrens chattered excitedly. Robins piped cheerfully. The thrushes chirped in skips. Listening to birdsongs, he realized he was swaying woodenly atop something. Sunlight warmed his skin as he listened.

URRReeeeppp.

Branches and leaves thrashed apart—the sounds of a trap sprung. *A griff.* He couldn't see the king's bird, but by god *he felt it.* Felt his wings beat air. Salivated at the panic of his prey as it scrambled through the forest, trying to lose winged death in the undergrowth. *I am the griff,* he understood, somehow.

Air rushed into hearing as Zur sprang upon the little fox, rending flesh with four sets of talons. A pup, a scrawny one at that, but nourishment for the griff's cubs. He hurtled back into vast blue sky, fur and feathers rustling, shrieking with triumph. It was intoxicatingly glorious.

I'm no griff, he remembered as feeling darkness immersed him again. *Merely a hostage of the Silver Walls.* He was vaguely aware that the thing atop which he swayed was a horse. *I'm on a horse . . . but why can't I move?*

He heard himself mumbling incoherently. Whiskers raked his cheek as his rider, his captor, leaned past his shoulder. "Be silent now, my servant," Drexan whispered in his ear. His lord smelled of wilderness. "Safety is close."

Where is safety? he pondered in his delirium. *The Silver Walls.* They had to be headed there! If he could, Zur would've leapt off the horse and run all the way to the Great Gates. He swore to god's twelve faces that he'd kiss the bailey soil, and never again yearn to be a knight. *I'll take a scullion's work and be grateful for it.*

The smell of dank earth reached his nostrils. Eyes fluttering, Zur found himself on his side.

Not at the Silver Walls. He was off the horse now, and in the dark. Somewhere, water gurgled through a congestion of rocks.

I can move. His hands wandered across a ground damp with sticky leaves and rotted wood. Needles stabbed at his hand. He rushed to his feet, brushing off ants furiously.

He rubbed his itchy, pimpled hand. His mind raced. Heart thumped wildly. *How did I get here?* He remembered riding on the Kingsway with Drexan, and seeing Eric the Tall, and—

And . . .

He whimpered. Cursed himself a fool for whimpering. *A nightmare, that's all it was. But if it wasn't, am I in hell?* It was where Elzura's Children belonged for their ancestor's sin, after all.

All he could think to do was call for him. He summoned the courage. "M-my . . . my lord?" he squeaked. He listened as echoes played back. "Lord Drexan? Drex—*DREXAN?!*"

Peering up, he beheld countless bobbing, blinking stars. *Fireflies,* he realized. There had to be thousands of them. Their auras teased out a ceiling of thread-thin grooves and plunging hollows. *Not hell . . . but where, then?*

Wood scraped against wood. Sunlight erupted through darkness, sketching the inside of a tower chiseled with ruts and ceilinged in spider silk. His lord walked down rock-hewn steps, ruddied by his torch.

"Stay there, Zuran," came his voice, the most welcome sound in all the world. "I thought you'd sleep awhile longer. I assure you, a cavern is no place to lose your footing."

"A cavern." Zur fought down a feeling of unease. "Why am I . . . are we . . . in a cavern?"

A rusted brazier materialized in the torchlight, mere feet away, as Drexan approached. With his torch he dabbed needles and kindling in the pit. Embers glowed faintly. The chancellor gathered more twigs and threw them into the brazier.

"I caught hare for us to eat," Drexan said as he worked. As if this were all completely normal for them. A familiar routine.

Yet hare sounded good. *Damn* good. He felt like he hadn't eaten in weeks. He remembered the fox pup's warm essence bathing his dream talons. "I don't think that'll catch fire."

"Here, drink." The King's Crow handed him a waterskin. "You must be parched."

Uncorking the skin, Zur drank greedily, water streaming down his neck. He waited for a moment, then drank more.

Drexan knelt. "You asked me why we're in a cavern." He stripped the hare's fur in swift, ruthless motions that clapped back in echoes. "Isn't it obvious?"

"We're hiding." *But it was just a dream.*

His lord spitted one hare, propped it over the struggling fire, went to work on the other meat. "I brought our mounts with us," he said with a nod at their periphery.

Muscled shapes shifted in the dark, hoofing at the cavern floor. "Lord Drexan, *what happened?*"

"The powder you inhaled causes a brief amnesia, but I trust you remember what happened." Drexan stared at him with haunted eyes. "Don't you remember, Zuran?"

"Powder?" He rubbed his temple. "I remember only the Kingsway. And then . . ."

The nightmare. "Lord Eric." His stomach knotted up as he remembered. Remembered the ruin of the noble's face, cheeks pulpy like red, regurgitated fruit. "No, it can't be . . ."

"It is." Drexan observed him intently. "We were attacked. Lord Eric is dead. As is Uthron." That name clung to the edge of his voice.

"The powder." Anger stole over Zur, and he felt grateful for it. Anger made more sense than anything else. "You threw it at me. Made me sleep. I couldn't move. What was it you doused me with?" he demanded. "Why did you—?"

"Because you'd just seen a lord shed his skin like clothes and transform into living shadow," Drexan responded evenly. "The questions you have would've kept us. We didn't have time, so I used a sleep agent from Lord Jon's stores. I had to choose. I chose life. Life for us both."

When did you procure a sleep agent from Jon Applewood? "You told me we were investigating a matter about Jason. You *lied* to me."

Drexan frowned. "Seen from one way, I did. But seen from another—as you've seen yourself—what we saw concerns not only Jason, but all of us."

Zur ran a hand through his sweaty curls, struggling with how to even order his questions. "How long was I out?"

"Two days." Drexan peeled the second hare's fur with a savage rip, exposing pink muscle.

At the sight of raw meat, Zur retched water. Again and again, until his throat felt raw. The cold . . . He remembered how distant the summer sunlight had felt on his skin as the chill of death settled into his bones. He'd been so cold . . .

He shook involuntarily at Drexan's touch. "It was not the same for me, the first time I learned," said his lord.

"The first time you—*what in hell are you talking about?*"

At the Silver Walls, as elsewhere, a Casaanite risked grave offense, speaking thus to a person of higher station. But for the first time in his life, courtesy took a backseat.

Torchlight danced in the chancellor's eyes. "I'm sorry, Zuran. This wasn't how we wanted you to learn."

"*We?*" He felt off-balance, as if he were drunk, as he had been with Lorana and Anyasha on occasion, with Garrett and Jason. Everything felt threatening—including Drexan. "I want to leave." He surged to his feet, brushing off pine needles and vomit. "We must—"

Drexan seized his wrist. His hand had the pressure of a vise. "Stay, Zuran. You'll learn, and then you can decide your fate. Leave now and I may be unable to protect you from the next shadowking. And there *will* be another. There's power in blood, and Uthron Morley has family."

Zur breathed so shallowly he wondered if he breathed at all. He laughed at the absurdity. "Shadowkings! Mere stories. Children's stories." But he didn't believe what he said, either.

"Sit, and be still." His unrelenting grip left Zuran with few options. He doubted screaming would help; he had no idea where this place was, or how to leave safely. He'd never been in a cavern. He'd rarely even ventured outside the Silver Walls.

Hesitantly, he took a knee, thinking he could spring up if needed, run at the first sign of danger. Drexan offered him the waterskin, as an olive branch; Zur took it but didn't drink.

His lord meditated on the struggling fire. "What happened was no dream. The Lord Warden of Rosbury attacked us. Unmasked . . . as a servant of Asha-Ra and Pathazar."

"But shadowkings served the Nagarthessi, the sons of . . ."

"The God Who Rebelled and Died." Drexan snapped a rotted plank, tossed the halves into the brazier.

"But that's impossible. It's IMPOSSIBLE." Zur realized that he was shouting. "Drexan, tell me it's impossible! *Tell me! TELL ME!*" *Tell me it's impossible,* his echoes shouted back at him.

Drexan was stone-still. "Uthron Shadowking was as real as you or me, or these hares," his lord said softly, transfixed by embers in the brazier.

He's afraid, Zur realized. That scared him more than anything. *He saved us, yet he's afraid.* "It came for both of us."

"Lord Eric—the Lord Warden—"

"Are dead," Drexan finished. "I am now accused in their deaths. And that is by no accident."

It all came flooding back. The melt of the Rosbury lord's face, skin running like tallow. Spectral stars in his eye sockets, twinkling. Long black claws that burst a lord's head as if it'd been a ripe pimple.

The touch of death, seeping into his bones, colder than the fiercest winter wind . . .

"Fuck," Zur tried to say, but all that came out was *fuh,* the rest lost as he retched.

He felt numb suddenly, until the horror of what his lord said found him in the dank cavern. *Those Who Eat the Children.* Urine coursed down his leg. *Fuck, I'm such a coward.*

The chancellor didn't notice, or pretended to see nothing. "Hexar's daughter made you hers. 'Little brother,' I've heard her call you." Zur misliked his condescending tone. "Whether she ever admits it, Lorana is a child of that rubbish men falsely call the Awakening. Her skepticism became yours, eclipsing truth you first learned from the Twelve Testaments."

His wits coalesced in fragments, as if he groped about in a fog, seeing patches of air. "You speak of truth like an Elvarenist. Are you . . . are you with the priestking, then?"

The chancellor wrinkled his nose in disgust. "Never." He patted the soil. "Truth is like good, solid earth. Priestkings like Parlisis built their house of lies on that earth. Called the truth theirs alone."

"But you make light of the Awakening, so you can't be a Free Believer." The riddle was a welcome distraction. "A Sylvanian?"

Drexan glanced about, as if he saw things in the dark that Zur could not. "We're not the first people to shelter here," he said. "Do you recall what befell the Barefoot Knights centuries ago, after the Third Halfcrown War?"

Remembering that ancient conflict comforted Zur, like the pull of an old shirt over his skin. He could deal in fact.

He relayed what he remembered about the third and last war of the Barefoot Knights, the one that doomed them. After a costly battle in Medecia that failed to unite the realms behind a puppet king, the Solemn Order's last devotees and their ragged families had fled west. The priestking at the time had famously issued a decree with a leaden seal that called for the Solemn Order's extermination and the liquidation of all their holdings, down to their brass shirt buttons and the boots on their feet.

"That was how the Barefoot Knights earned their name," Zur finished. "The priestking dispatched his Intercessors and their mastiffs to track the Solemn Order's footprints across a wintered continent."

The chancellor nodded grimly. "Some survived," he said. "Starving and frostbitten, the last Barefoot Knights went where only the desperate go. As far from the east as west can go—to Loran, the land of swordwood and griffons. Into caves like this one."

The banshee screech of a wind outside made Zur tremble. In the weakening torchlight, he saw a column of ants marching past his foot.

"I don't want the torch to go out," Zur said. "I can't handle the dark, Lord Drexan. Not right now." *Perhaps not ever again.*

Drexan nodded sympathetically. "Help me find kindling."

As Zur stood, Drexan snatched his wrist. Retrieving his unsheathed staff, he steadied the steel point and sliced his arm.

The boy stumbled into cavern wall, clutching his arm with a wild-eyed look. *He means to kill me.* He bolted up, toward the cavern entrance. Drexan gripped his arm, preventing him from leaving.

"A little, that's all I needed, and no more will I take. Just watch." He released Zur. Holding the top of his staff level over the brazier, the chancellor singed its steel with his torch.

Flame exploded from the top of the staff like dragonflame. Rising slow, Drexan touched damp kindling with its tip. Fire raced through the brazier as if it contained pinewood, towering, engulfing the spitted hares.

Zur saw the cavern in bits and pieces. Tunnel mouths yawned in rugged walls. Along the periphery, a brook ran its course. Visible in the firelight, their mounts shifted nervously.

Mesmerized, Zur didn't realize that Drexan had torn cloth from his cloak and bandaged his arm until he finished. "Please don't turn me into a toad, Lord Drexan," he pled.

The King's Crow smiled. "It's not my power you fear. It's your own." He took Zur's other hand and placed it over the bandaged cut. "A small scratch. It'll heal. I just wanted you to see for yourself. Please, Zuran— no more attempts at leaving, or threats to. Not until you've heard everything."

Zur held his arm against his chest, watching the dance of a fire that *a steel-tipped staff* had kindled—*with his own blood.* "Who—or *what*—are you?" he asked softly.

"No one of great significance."

Yet as Drexan writhed his hand over the fire, he proved otherwise. Flames rose with his bobbing fingers, as if attached to invisible strings he manipulated. He swung his right hand, and out of the brazier flew a single flame shaped like a raven. Whirring around them, the raven blazed into a fireball, raced up, and exploded against the ceiling.

"I hide like my forebears." Drexan watched as embers rained down, fading. "Running from my huntsmen."

The boy eased himself to a seated position, stunned. "You . . . you *are* a sorcerer!"

"Only the ignorant would call me a sorcerer." He removed his helm, tracing the Eye of Guldan. Coppery hair thatched his balding head. "For years, the king's court, his Assembly, and all the land's peasants maligned me over my ties to the Order of Six Sights." He laughed witheringly. "The Order of Six Sights is a guild for men who'd serve Ansara's kings. I wear their insignia proudly. But because the Order is in Anjoun, a mysterious land, Loranians believe it teaches the dark arts." Noticing Zur's gaze, he donned his helm again. "I am of the Solemn Order, sworn to seat the king on his rightful throne. A knight, if you will."

"A Barefoot Knight," Zur whispered in disbelief.

Drexan blew on the fire fluttering up his staff's steel tip, and it went out like a candle.

Windriders. Protectors of the Sacred Blood. Servants of the One True King of Ansara, Casaan, the East, and All Lands. Those were the names Barefoot Knights had given themselves before they lacked footwear.

To this day, everyone else knew them by other names: heretics, sorcerers, traitors. Seditious usurpers.

Zur stared at the smoking staff. "Magic."

"Not magic. Divine power. It exists in you as much as me, Zuran of the Tribe Nuur." Drexan rolled his left sleeve up to the shoulder. His forearm looked like cracked leather, crosshatched with the lines of a hundred scars. "It has a cost. There's power in blood, and only blood summons it."

"We . . ." Zur stared at his bandage. "*I* can control fire?"

"It was your blood I drew." The flames pulsed excitedly as Drexan waved a hand over the brazier. "Control fire. Shake the earth. See as a griff sees. Much more, with guidance."

"And all for . . . which king?" He knew the answer. He just didn't want to utter it himself.

Drexan seemed to see through him, see his fears for what they were and what sustained them. "The Ascendant King."

Fascination mingled with fear. *The Ascendant King.*

A man could lose his tongue saying that—if not his life. Divided by faith, Ansara's thirteen kingdoms were united in this: they forbade subjects from uttering that name aloud. Barefoot Knights—those like Drexan, if he was one—had made the Ascendant King a rallying cry in their wars centuries ago.

On the surface, the Ascendant King sounded like a proud name for Anjan's last heir, the half-elf prophesied to return and unite the world under a banner of peace. Indeed, that was what the Ascendant King was—the last child of Eduard Linebreaker, last son of the House of Anjan Half-Elf.

But that was where similarities ended. The Ascendant King wasn't some peacemaker. He was a warlord. Barefoot Knights extolled their version of Anjan's last heir as a hero who'd liquidate the borders of kingdoms and consolidate all peoples everywhere under his rule—with or without consent. He would undo what the witch Elzura had wrought when she bewitched King Eduard into butchering his family and ending the house of god-kings charged with ruling the earth.

Drexan watched him as if this were a test, as if he were grading him. "If you know better than to air that title," he said, "surely you know the verse that inspired it?"

"In bits and pieces, I know it," Zur said warily. "It was a prophecy by the Bare—by your people."

The King's Crow held his callused hands over the brazier, seemingly just to warm them this time. "Yes, a prophecy. Of the chaos to come, and the order the First King's last heir will restore. I'll share with you what kings, lords, priests, and readers tell you repeating aloud would damn your soul."

> *Go and tell the kings who were:*
> *A tattered cloth shall be mended*
> *With a thread of silver pure,*
> *And the withered vine tended*
> *By hands once and ever sure.*
>
> *Go and tell the realms of men:*
> *The lame shall rise, the blind see,*
> *And the deaf hear the herald's din*
> *When a king wades through sea*
> *And comes to reign again.*
>
> *Go and tell those with ears to hear:*
> *He shall shield the few, the fearful last,*
> *Unbowed as shadows circle and sneer,*
> *For o'er man, beast, and blade of grass*
> *The king shall rule far and near.*
>
> *Go and warn your kings of gilt worth:*
> *Your borders will burn with your keeps*
> *Whilst your paper crowns soil the earth,*
> *For terrors you've sown shall be reaped*
> *Before him, ascendant at birth.*

It was the last lines that rulers hated most.

Finishing, Drexan pushed his sleeve down. "The power in our veins comes from Anjan, and it's his bloodline that power is meant to serve," he said. "His prophecy that we must fulfill."

"To safeguard man from demons," Zur said.

"From himself, just as importantly. Pathazar, Asha-Ra, and their vassals depend on chaos as we depend on air. And Zuran, our world is nothing *but* chaotic. Thirteen kingdoms divide Ansara, each lost in a scramble for power over class, money, religion, land, food, water, succession rights, and anything else men can find a reason to kill for. Regardless of politics, regardless of religion, men are all unsuited to the task of ruling. The world is ruled by such realms, each locked in an inevitable death spiral."

"Or ruled by tribes."

"By tribes led by chieftains, as in Casaan and Uzland, or academies of thought led by philosophers, as in the Far East. The form of rule doesn't matter. An anthill is orderly, the ant line as well, but if too many cluster together, the ants begin to fight among themselves. Men are ants." Drexan narrowed on the ants. He pinched one between his thumb and forefinger, rubbing until nothing remained but little specks. "Mere ants, constantly at war with their own and anything that crosses their path. Blind to the real enemy." He wiped off the ant bits.

"Gram Reuben's words. He compared men to ants."

Drexan shot him a look, startled. He smiled admiringly, mildly chagrinned. "Yes, I read that in Lord Reuben's *State of Nature*. I take it you found that tome in Hanor's study, not my library. Quite impressive—if a little daring, for someone who doesn't want to be a toad." He winked. "And what did even that great scholar of the Awakening conclude?"

A moment's relish from turning the tables turned to disquiet. He decided to lie with the truth, to avoid having to agree. "That the ant's saving grace is its queen."

"But more importantly, that their proclivity for infighting argued for a force stronger, wiser, and larger to rule them. To stop the death spirals." He made a fist, as if he meant to smash more insects. "This was the role elves played for us—one half-elves filled after them, saving men from their tendency to find reasons to destroy themselves. To give them something only someone with elven blood could: a real god to worship."

He remembered ripping through the fox with his talons. *That wasn't a dream, either.* "On Remembrance Day, you found me in the kitchen with a peasant girl. She asked me if I could cast spells." He gazed at his bandaged arm. "She was right. 'She cast a spell on old King Eduard.' Elzura was a witch. So am I."

Drexan sat forward with almost childlike enthusiasm. "A witchery passed to her by her mother," he said, "and to her by her maternal father, passed down from that moment millennia ago in which a cornered half-elf conferred the ultimate power on thirteen men . . . and on all their descendants."

Zur puzzled his face. "But there were twelve Windriders at the Conferral. Ansarans. Pale of skin, like you."

"So the priests tell their sheep," Drexan scoffed. "Parlisis and his predecessors erased the truth. There was a *thirteenth* Windrider. He came from Casaan, and you are his descendant." He smiled. "You're like me, Zuran, no mere hostage, but a blood relative of one of Anjan's champions. It's how you knew to sidestep that stone. Likely why the griffon let Heather alone when you approached him, brave idiot that you are."

Brave. Zur shivered with disgust from the dampness in his breeches. What Drexan described sounded inspiring, but he felt so beneath it. This had to be a joke. *How could someone with a Windrider's blood piss himself?*

"I figured I frightened the griffon with my sword."

"It'll take more than a dull blade to frighten a griffon of the Great Tree."

"Could a shadowking?"

Drexan went still. "Your guess is as good as mine. Before that day in Sarah's Forest, I'd never seen one."

"But you dispatched it as if you had before."

"Barely. Only swordwood saved us, and we have the Lady at the Tree to thank for that." Drexan pricked his finger on his notched spearhead. "The Oracle foresaw that I'd one day have need of swordwood against the enemy. Graywood's metal is a conductor for our power, in the same way that some metals transmit current from lightning strikes—"

"Something we owe to Gram Reuben," Zur chimed wryly.

"Indeed. Swordwood has power for us because Anjan and his mages created it. For that reason, it was also the First King's choice of weaponry against the Nagarthessi." He grimaced. "Yet Uthron laughed last, Zuran. I'm a sought man. We left two lords dead in that forest."

We? "But we can go back. Lorana will listen, surely."

Drexan barked with laughter that made him feel small, perhaps a dig at him for the line about the Awakening's sage. "And what would I tell her? That Uthron Morley transformed into mist? That I killed him—*with swordwood?*"

"No one saw us. No one would know we were there."

"Our mounts left tracks. And we *were* seen. In Southpoint. By the Little King, no less. By his city guard."

Instinctively, Zur reached for the edges of his wolfskin, to cover himself. He pictured Lorana's gift to him, tangled up with Morley's crushed corpse, and wanted to retch again. *What will Lorana think, when she learns my cloak was found with the dead lords?*

"Lord Eric." Thinking on the crimson pulp of Sundry's face knotted his insides. "Was he like you—a Barefoot Knight?"

"He was. I was a fool, to fail to see that Uthron wasn't."

"How could you have known, lord? Morley wasn't a man."

Drexan sheathed the swordwood on his staff with a clink. "Uthron *was* a man, like you or me. The pendant he wore . . . the sapphire. It was broken when we saw him revert back to man. I suspect . . . I suspect that gem had something to do with his link to the Nagarthessi. Allowed him to change his form at will."

"How did he change like that in the first place?" Uthron had frequented Hexar's court since Zur was young. A man he'd always seemed, stuffy and aloof, maybe, but not a monster.

"No one is born in service to Nagarthessi," Drexan said. "Uthron would've had to make a pact with the demon brothers. I'm certain I know when he did. Months ago, Uthron tasked a knight with making his horse a gift in Graywood."

"A gift for whom?"

"Not just any gift. Sylvanians call a blood sacrifice a Gift. And it was for whichever demon Anjan buried there millennia ago." *I regret asking,* Zur thought. "He sent him with his priest cousin, one Uther Brune, along with several pagans. They never returned to Rosbury. No one has seen them since."

Drexan looked at him. "Whatever devilry happened there, it gave Uthron power. He came for you as much as me, Zuran."

"*Me?*" The world was spinning. *No, I must be brave. Lorana would be still as stone. Jason would stand tall.* "I'm a hostage."

"There's more to you than you know, Zuran. You know it, too. I *saw* you duck that stone on the Street of Kings."

Zur could taste the blood on his lips that never was.

"Remember what I told you about the Lame King? Many believe that Eduard's Huntsman will one day appear in the sky beside his wounded king, remove the arrow, and allow Anjan's last heir to stand and ascend his throne again. And when those stars shine, we'll know the Nagarthessi have crossed over from their world into ours. They'll come to finish what they began ages ago. They'll obliterate man, once and for all." He watched Zur raptly. "Unless the Ascendant King is found. Unless Anjan's last heir can rally men, to save and rule them."

He shall shield the few, the fearful last, Zur pondered.

"The Nagarthessi know that the Ascendant King is close, and they sent Uthron to kill us for this reason." Drexan tapped on his chest with a finger. "*You* are the one who will find the Ascendant King, Zuran of Tribe Nuur. As no one else can. The Oracle and I have seen this for ourselves."

Zur regarded him warily, unsure of what was real. By law, he couldn't even squire for a knight. Yet here this chancellor was—this Barefoot Knight—telling him that he had a destiny beyond the Walls. Not just any destiny—a great one.

"But I'm one of Elzura's Children," Zur said adamantly, as if trying to convince himself. "Regardless of whether my witch ancestor descended from a Windrider, her sins poison my blood. *We* sundered Anjan's bloodline. *We* shattered Loran into thirteen realms. *We* created this chaos you say stirs demons."

Drexan studied him. "Much ill has been done to you and your people . . . and yet you're fond of it." *Fond?* That wasn't a word he'd use to describe his servanthood. "I know how you love the Walls. Lorana especially. Jason, too. Connor Tomas's melees. So many familiar faces."

Gathering himself up, Drexan brushed needles and dirt off his cloak. Firelight flickered in his helm, catching in the crow's feet that ringed its lidless eye.

"You have a choice, Zuran," said Drexan, tall and looming. "You may return to the Silver Walls if you wish. I will protect you on your journey. When we see Southpoint, I will take my leave of you. We'll never meet again."

Zur felt riddled with guilt, as if such a parting would've been his fault. "What's my other choice?"

"Come with me," the King's Crow said. "On the morrow, we'll travel underground, to the Mother of Trees, almost to her great roots. There, we'll meet the Lady Orella. She'll show you more about yourself than you ever dreamed to know. *We* will teach you. Make a Barefoot Knight of you. When you are ready, you and I will leave to find him, ascendant at birth. We'll serve him, and with him, rally the rest of man against Pathazar, Asha-Ra, and the monsters in their service."

Zur stroked his ant-bitten hand. *Make a Barefoot Knight of me. A knight.* "Must I decide now?"

"I can give you space. As much space as—"

"No. Wait." He gazed up from where he sat in the damp and his own filth. "In the forest, you told me that you have a friend who knew my mother. Is that friend the Oracle?"

Drexan smiled. "None other."

Zur thought for a moment. "Could she tell me if my mother lives?"

"Not if you return to the Walls. Once there, Lorana will coddle you, and refuse to ever let you go. You would go with her to the Golden Meadows. Her path would become yours."

Zur climbed to his feet. Embers glowed in the darkened brazier like the fireflies swirling around the ceiling. "Then we should rest tonight. Take me to the Great Tree tomorrow. I'll meet your Oracle." His stomach growled cavernously. "Some supper would be nice, first."

CHAPTER 6

Dracar

 cold wind whipped the nobleman's cloak like a banner as he climbed Mount Dracar.

Hand over hand, foot over foot, Evan scaled a rugged cliffside in the dark, blind save for starlight and the ruddy wash of campfire light from far below. He sampled crevices with his fingers and boot toes, testing the sureness of his grip before continuing up. Every few minutes, he slowed his breathing to listen for an owl that wouldn't naturally perch this far up.

I'm too old to climb a mountain, he thought, runnels of sweat trickling sideways across his neck and forehead, *let alone a mountain at night.*

Moonlight guided him onto firmer footing, a ledge as wonderfully, mercifully level as a fine wooden floor. Hauling himself up, Evan collapsed to lay sprawled on his back. Heaving air, he pawed at a dank moleskin glove until it came off, wiped his sweat bullets as the wind chilled his forehead. He stared up at the glitter of night, finding comfort in several constellations he knew well—the Merman's Trident, the Good Steward, and the Lame King, among others.

Turning on his side, he peered down a wall of chiseled cliff, to the rutted path and the campsites beyond. Several thousand cookfires glittered like candles in a chandelier, lighting the sides of tents. Pavilions resembled hubs in the wheels of massive camps that grew larger every day. In the mountain's shadow lurked the oval of Rorin's amphitheater, looking ancient and forgotten.

Beautiful sights, all, but some I would enjoy rather more on solid ground. There was little he could do. When Pigeons came calling, one had to meet them where they deemed a place safe to meet. He'd followed the false owl's hoots from camp to the base of Mount Dracar, up winding pebbled trails, and, finally, up this miserable, seemingly endless cliff.

The Pigeon had a report to make. A report that Evan needed to hear urgently, not least because of the events this week.

The Worthy Assembly was set to hold the Meet of First Declaration. Evan needed his Companymen there in force for Jason's claim—especially with Thorngale dead, and especially with Lorana late. From discreet exchanges with those already present, Evan knew this, at least: Rathos had succeeded in his mission. Thanks to Silvertongue's persuasion, the Loyal Company would throw its voting weight behind Jason Warchild if he failed to win all three Trials.

You were successful, Rathos, as I knew you would be, Evan thought. Rising unsteadily, he slipped his glove back on and summoned the resolve to follow the owl. *You made me proud—your father and mother, too.* He eased his way past a boulder to the base of the ledge looming over it. *And you were as successful as one can be in this damnable Company of mine.*

What he didn't know was *how many* voting Companymen would make the Meet's quorum.

Rathos had delivered the Company . . . mostly. Yesterday Evan had learned that the Company's other, powerful sire had withheld a count of members—Rathos included—as insurance in case the nobleman again failed his mission. On the face of it, Rezlan planned to use those numbers against Evan, to vote on whether the Company should go to war.

But Evan knew Rezlan Ambrose, knew him like his own sword hand.

Scaling rock, Evan misplaced a foot and raked his chest painfully on the slide down. He was grateful to land on his feet, at least, and not his head. Cursing himself and Pigeons alike, he continued his ascent. Even for secrecy's sake, this messenger had chosen an impractically remote rendezvous point.

I've been betrayed already, Rezlan Ambrose, he thought. *For the sake of the Fourth Wing that we both serve, I hope you haven't double-crossed me, too . . .*

Secrecy was essential. With hundreds of Assemblymen, knights, and peasants pouring into the Golden Meadows every day, eyes and ears were everywhere. Sothos's lackey lords knew what he'd eaten for breakfast, lunch, and dinner, and when he'd taken a shit, for that matter.

So someone could've imitated a Pigeon, luring him up the mountain to cut his throat and push him off the cliff. He glanced his leathery sword hilt with his wrist to remind himself it was still there. *I'll hear your report, Pigeon . . . and if you're not a Pigeon, you'll certainly hear mine.*

Evan pulled himself onto the ledge, where he heard the owl's hoot again, closer this time. Listing against a cliff wall, he navigated a ledge three feet across that led him up, his back to the mountain while he eyed the pitch-black chasm below. The narrow footpath led him round the mountain, to a pillar beneath yet another ledge.

The nobleman listened for the owl's hooting through the wind. *If it's a twice-turned Pigeon, perhaps he means to kill me by exhausting me,* thought Evan. Using starlight, he searched the ledge wall for crevices and toeholds, made a quick calculus, and began climbing.

Evan heaved himself up onto the ledge. He rested in the dirt afterward, trying to catch his breath. He ached badly, his pits stank, and sweat drenched his hair.

Hoooot, hoooot. The Pigeon's call came from around the bend of a path as flat and pebbled as fine Romarian road. Evan pushed himself to his feet. He walked uphill, past bulging rock, his breath a cone of mist in the cold. He passed a crevice, heard flapping, and ducked as a colony of bats spewed out, funneling into the night sky.

The business end of a blade stuck the small of his back. "You're awfully loud," came a whisper in his ear, "and quite stupid."

Not a Pigeon after all. He lifted his hands. "To whom are you leal?" Evan asked calmly. "Jon Redoak? Sam Gramlore?"

His assailant wasn't alone. Mocking laughter issued from the shadows, three to five distinct voices. "To the gods of field and forest, milord," said the one behind him.

The man was a Commoner. Brigands, most likely. They'd masqueraded as Pigeons and lured him up here, away from the Cloudlanders who'd defend him.

Quickly now, old man. Evan jammed his elbow into the belly behind him. The fool missed the chance to cut his throat, and Evan made sure it cost him, grabbing him by the shoulder and forcing him to stumble out. He brandished his sword and had its point pressed to the brigand's spine in half a second's time.

"I'll take that." He plucked the dagger from the brigand's hand and urged the man forward with his sword, to the edge of the cliff. Shadows took shape across the area, too many for him to fend off. "I'm worth more alive than dead," he announced. "But try to kill me, and know I'll take as many of you to hell as I can."

"But you don't believe in hell."

Evan recognized the voice immediately. As any parent would.

Into moonlight stepped what could've been his late wife's ghost, her hair a rich indigo. She wore unfamiliar breeches, gray furs, and tattered linen. And were those *pauldrons* on her shoulders?

Evan released his attacker, who repaid him with a hard shove into the cliff wall. "Don't hurt him, Dustin," Leah Sinclair pitched her voice, "or I'll do you like I did Venn."

"You seem fonder of your old family than your new one." Dustin spat to his side. "Next time, have Creature spring the trap. Bastard's tougher than he looks." He rubbed the small of his back as he strode past Leah.

A crooked smile worked its way into Leah's face. "I'd expect nothing less of the man who taught me how to handle steel," she said archly.

Evan gazed at his secondborn, incredulous, and then at her materializing Heretics, motley in their stolen armor, mail, and boiled leather. He identified a portly man, a lankier one, and one fellow built like an aurochs.

Unbelievable. "What're you doing here?" Evan demanded.

The heavyset man sucked his teeth. "Ungrateful bastard," he swore. "Night and day we traveled t'get here, all to save his miserable skin. And *this* is how he treats our Mad Lady."

In his life, Evan had known suffering. He'd lost his sister and best friend to a blackpowder explosion. He'd lost his titles and the source of his wealth to Hexar's grief and fury. His wife, Faye, he'd lost to fever. He'd kept painful secrets from those he loved most.

He'd no idea his heart could hurt more until he heard another man call his daughter the Mad Lady. *So it's true.*

"Hello to you, too, Father," said Leah Sinclair. The little girl he used to bounce in his lap rounded on her outlaws with a commander's authority. "Leave us." The skinny fellow hoofed at the dirt agitatedly, bleating like a sheep. "Go, Creature. Leave us, all of you."

"I'd like my dagger back," Dustin reminded Leah.

The outlaws traipsed off, up the winding mountain trail, with Creature mimicking an owl's hoot. When they were alone, the Mad Lady swung her arms around her father. He embraced her warmly, as if she'd never left, sopping up the comfort of his child's presence. She felt like home. So much like home.

How long had he dreamed of this? Years of anger and regret faded . . .

. . . until he smelled a perfume of horse and sweat thick about her person, until he glimpsed the pommel pitched up from her left hip, until he remembered that before him stood an outlaw accused of theft, murder, and worse.

Seeming to sense apprehension, she withdrew from him, with a pointed look at the sword still in his hand. "You can put that away now, Father."

Evan sheathed his blade, staring at her. She didn't wait to pry Dustin's dagger free of his other hand. "Why are you here?" he asked his daughter.

Leah gave him a cold, appraising look. "This is happening exactly as I imagined it," she said with a withering laugh. "You never fail to meet *my* expectations, Father."

All it took was that unruly tone. The defensiveness set in, familiar as his dank moleskin glove. *You abandoned your family and decency for a life in the wild with murderers and thieves, and you expect warmth?*

"I expected a messenger, Leah, not the outlaw child who shames her father." She betrayed no hurt. "Now tell me, why are you here? Here in Northland, in the dead of night? Did you come to filch from the nobles? To steal, kill, run?"

Leah sighed through her nostrils. "Very well, milord." *I raised her to act the lady, but she milords me like a lowborn to spite me.* "I'll be quick." She unslung the travelsack from her shoulder, reached in, and pulled out a soggy cabbage.

Not a cabbage. The wet-haired head landed on the ground with a sickening squelch, rolling until its nose brushed against the toe of Evan's boot.

Evan closed his eyes, reopened them. *How I wish Faye had never left us. Maybe then we could've saved her.* He regarded his great failure. "Child . . . what have you *done?*"

Recovering the head smattered her breeches with blood, and she wiped it off casually, as if it were mere mud. "As Pretty Phillip said, I saved you from danger." She pointed a finger at the decapitated head. "This bird you call a Pigeon meant to take your head tonight. Luckily, we tracked him and the others from the Midlands."

"The others?" Evan echoed her.

"I was sent by *Rathos,* Father," Leah said. "We saved him and his companion from Pigeons that meant to kill them."

The night air felt colder. *This betrayal goes deeper than I believed,* he thought. "Tell me everything, Leah."

Over half an hour, Leah divulged what she knew, about the Soothsayer Pigeons, the baiting of Rathos and Karl into Graywood, the Heretics' ambush of a Pigeon regiment with plans to catch Evan alone on this mountain tonight.

"You have a twice-turned traitor in your Company," she finished. "Maybe more than one; I can't say for sure. The men we killed"— she averted her eyes ever so slightly—"we tried all we knew, but they wouldn't give up a name. Whoever it is, he and your Pigeons have been bought off. And we know whom they answer to."

Evan grimaced. *The pink-handed cunt.* All the pieces of Thorngale's murder fell into place like parts of a puzzleboard.

He'd expected betrayal, of course. Just not this way. *Some Loyal Company,* he thought grimly.

"How was it you came to know of this conspiracy?" he asked her, eyeing the head. "Not just about the conspiracy in Graywood. The one against me tonight."

Leah stroked her knuckles uneasily. "I have my ways," she said. "Ways that might not honor our house, but ways that *help you* all the same."

Evan didn't want to hear more. He was ashamed of her, and angry with himself for not foreseeing this, and that arrow of shame and anger found a useful target in her. "Help me? I'd rather have died a thousand times than see you"—he gestured at her, at all of her, everything about her—"like this. Your poor mother. She'd spit on me if she saw you."

That was all it took, and suddenly they were at it again, as if Faye had died only yesterday.

"As she'd spit on me when my men and I escort peasant families to safety, so they can keep their children away from cassocked pederasts?" Leah demanded in a rising voice. "When I protect Free Believers and their flock traveling on the road?"

Yes, he knew about her friendship with Jacob Sulley, about how she helped peasants flee with their children. It didn't wash the blood off her hands. "I never asked that of you."

"No, you only reared Rathos and me on the Awakening, on Gram Reuben, on your misbegotten sense of *noblesse oblige*—what got your wife killed because she was laying rags on poxed foreheads and—"

Instinct took over, and he only realized he'd slapped her when he heard the clap of his palm on her cheek. She touched the spot.

"Faye chose her fate," he said. "But I didn't want that for you. *She* didn't want that for you—or this. This isn't your place. It's not *safe,* Leah."

Leah dropped her hand to her side, smiling sadly. "When did you ever know me to do what was safe? While Mina and Dana stitched or played with dolls, I'd take a horse and ride to Peacefield for a game of Shoot the Fruit."

He rubbed tension out of his jaw, suppressing a surprising urge to smile.

"I've always done as I will. Because I'm not your lady, or Mother's. I'm my own woman." She scooped up the head by its bloody hair and shoved it into her bag, as if it were a melon she'd felled in a game of archery. "You're playing a dangerous game, Father. It'd go better for you and this hell we call a kingdom if you let me help you."

Evan regarded her in silence. He lingered on her sword. *And now I must ask you to forgive me, too, Faye.* "My daughter is dead. I realize that now. So I'll talk to the Mad Lady."

CHAPTER 7

The Wedding Guests

n the day of the wedding, at sunrise, Sara received her second summons to pray with Cathreen Morley in the castle gardens. She'd feigned a stomachache the day before to avoid time alone with her lord's mother.

She dared not refuse her again.

Sara idled beneath the latticework of the oval boxwood hedge entrance to the gardens, fidgeting with the long, dagged sleeves of her sky-blue gown, a loan from Lady Barbara. Had she been any other peasant girl at a lord's castle, she would've adored this silken gown, relished the scents of lavender on her neck and wrists, reveled in the smoothness of her lye-lathered skin. How often had she bathed in Rosbury?

But Sara Sothron was her father's daughter. Nothing could change that. Nothing ever would.

"I see you, child," the lady's voice floated to her. "Come."

Peering within, past the hoops of low-hanging rose vines, Sara saw the noblewoman's snowy hair off in the distance. Lady Cathreen sat on her bower bench, half-obscured by the trunk of an oak tree. She had her brittle back turned. *How did she see me?* She remembered how a birdsong had alerted the Grand Inquisitor and his black-robed companion in the hedge maze at the Silver Walls. But she heard no birds.

Sara treaded a stone walkway, passing by cheerful yellow daffodils and sprigs of long-stemmed flowers. Cathreen sat beside a ring of twelve statues, tossing breadcrumbs into a pond rippling with trout.

Like Sara, the lady wore a gown of matrimonial blue. She turned to face her with the most insincere smile. "That gown suits you. Sir

Damien would be so proud to see you." *Not here, he wouldn't, you wrinkly prune,* Sara thought. "How's your belly today?"

"Better. Thank you, milady."

At her urging, Sara sat beside her. The lady placed a small, cold thing in her hands. A silver wedding band. In its exquisite silver leaves nestled a pearl nearly as big as her eye.

Cathreen regarded her with the dignity of someone who expects gratitude. "After speaking with your mother, I thought it fitting that you should bear the ring that brings her under Sir Willard's rod," she said. "A child from an old marriage should help usher in the new."

Sara flashed her a defiant eye.

Cathreen Morley chuckled. "Think you every wedding is a happy occasion? Women know better." She groped inside a bag to her left and flung breadcrumbs at the pond. "I was your age, a girl of the Kingdom of Magnes, a rose blossomed early, when I was wedded to a lord. He went to war and died, so at twelve I was promised again to the lord of an outcrop of squalid little hamlets in a distant kingdom. I protested leaving my family—aye, even when Lord Stoddard showed up at my father's gates with his horse-drawn carriages and knights with roses in their sigils. Uther Brune came with him, but his friendship was small comfort. The tears I wept at my wedding to Lord Uthron were not tears of joy. Yet I learned my place, Sara. The role I was to play in the affairs of powers I did not understand. As will you."

Her gaze had an insistence that Sara resisted. How badly she wanted to feed the ring to those trout and be done of these gardens and this old crone. She needed to find Dray.

She decided she'd hasten this along, if she could. "Thank you, milady. Do you wish to pray now, milady?"

"In short order." Cathreen reached again into her bag and scattered a wealth of crumbs across the pond, driving the fish to frenzy. "I know what you did. You helped Connor Bagman and his outlaws burn Saint Eric's."

Sara locked eyes with the noblewoman. Inside, she swam about as hungrily as the trout, trying to wrap her lips about the morsel of a lie, any lie, something. Anything.

"I saw Lord Uthron in Elf's Grove," she said. "He went into the river and came up . . . something else." A tear streaked her cheek. Her hands trembled. *Stupid girl, stupid, stupid,* she heard her mother's voice scold her, *why did you say that? What have you done?*

The barest flicker of recognition passed over Cathreen's face. She smiled without warmth. "Imagined terrors. Lies from a sad little girl. No one believes your terrible lies, sad girl. But I believe the little bird who told me about you, Bagman, Watley." She turned coolly to the pond, flinging breadcrumbs. "Willard doesn't know anything yet. But imagine his fury. You saw what he did to Farmer Grey when that peasant told him about my lord husband's murder. What worse turn would he do you once you're under his rod, and he learns that you *burned a temple?*"

"But—no—I donna—" She hadn't said *donna* in years; the lady narrowed her eyes sternly.

"Birds of a feather, Sara. And the birds you flock with?" She *tsk-tsked.* "Outlaws. *Traitors.* Had my late Lord Uthron known of your associations, why, I've no doubt he would've added your head to Traitor's Gate himself."

Her heart hammered so fiercely she thought she saw its impression in her chest, lifting, falling. Sara held her hands to prevent them from shaking, but they shook, as unrelentingly as if she were freezing.

The Red Tower. She couldn't return to the Red Tower.

Cathreen pinned her to the bench with her cold, unfeeling gaze. "I will tell no one of your treason, and you and Willard's bride-to-be will not return to the Grand Inquisitor . . . so long as you do what I tell you. Do you understand me, Sara, daughter of Damien? Do you understand what I'm saying?"

Sara wiped away her tears, nodding.

From the window of her jostling carriage, Sara watched as Saint Benjamen's pale bell towers emerged above the trees. Its bells rang, and every time they did she heard Connor Bagman and his men swearing beneath their breath inside Saint Eric's. On satin cushions to her left sat Harriett and Maeda, glum and quiet as ever, and in front the Lord Warden, playing with his toy knight beside Barbara and their lady mother. They were silent amid the sounds of creaky axles and hooves sploshing mud.

The road to temple led them through a nearly desolate Rosbury that remembered the violence inflicted on it, a main road littered with forgotten plows and wheelbarrows, cruck houses punched with holes. The thought of passing by her father's house and seeing Little Lady made her hopeful, but their coachman chose another way.

Sara would've rather avoided the depressing sights, but straying at all from her window view unfailingly invited eye contact with Cathreen. The carriage banked on a hole in the main, and the jarring movement seared her thigh with pain. In the corner of her eye, she saw Cathreen smiling faintly.

She was a noxious cauldron of fear, guilt, anxiety, sorrow, and terror, but above all, she felt bewildered.

How had the lady known about her involvement at Saint Eric's? Rittman wasn't the wiser, Cathreen had told her, nor her mother, nor any other person in the world but her. *A little bird,* she'd called the source of her information. But who—who on Odma would've told her?

Connor had made her swear to keep their involvement a secret, and she had. But had one of his men spied for Cathreen? *How else could she have possibly known about your knife, Dray?*

This was the worst day of her life, worse even than when she lost Caleb. To prevent it from worsening, Sara had to play by the terms of her agreement with Uthron's widow.

The alternative was a chamber in the Red Tower.

She remembered focusing on Cathreen's crooked yellow teeth as she drew near. "You took something from Saint Eric's," she'd said. Sara had feared the blade's immediate confiscation, but that wasn't what the lady intended. "Now it's yours. Yours always, like the shame you'll feel for your sacrilege and theft—ever sharp, never dulling, pricking you, tormenting you. You'll bear it on your person to the wedding and after that, until the end of your days. Fail me, and I'll have you and your whore of a mother trussed like sheep and sent back to Charles Burke. How would you like that?"

Such was how Sara would avoid the Tower. She brushed the object inside her gown with her thigh. *For all my life, she said. To cut and torment me.*

A mile north of the village rose Saint Benjamen's, lacking Saint Eric's grandeur and grotesques but glorious still with its throng of steeples and colonnaded front, tucked into the bosom of encroaching fir trees. Collapsible wooden seats gridded the grounds in long neat rows. Before Saint Benjamen's steps and ornamented portal gathered the guests, some forty courtiers and lower gentry conversing low, the men clothed in padded doublets and long pointed shoes, the women in fluttery silks and elegant surcoats. The ceremony celebrating Sir Damien Sothron's death was to be a fine affair.

It made Sara rot inside, to be around a temple. Earlier that week, while supping with Rittman and the Morleys in their hall, Rose had questioned whether they should hold a ceremony at the temple, in the open, what, with the arson at Saint Eric's.

But Morley's widow had insisted on it. "We mustn't show fear, or the outlaws will win," she'd said in airy tone of rebuke. "And we won't be lacking in sword and spear."

Morley men patrolled Saint Benjamen's grounds, silvered in plate and mail, some hefting spears. Their ranks included the deputies who'd ransacked Rosbury.

Sirs Luc Tolos and Bardo Lym also made rounds. Like her father, the two were from peasant households. She wondered what they had made of the deputies tearing apart their village, parting children from their parents to give to Peshar Grathos.

The carriage shuddered to a halt in the shade of a tall oak. The Lord Warden climbed out first. Overwhelmed by a swarm of wedding guests, he misplaced his foot and tumbled off into mud, drawing gasps.

Sara would've laughed had Cathreen not been there. The lady quickly descended and helped Sam to his feet, picking off mud flecks from his garments. It gave Sara comfort to imagine kicking her into the mud with him.

For a time, all anyone seemed to care about was meeting Sam Morley, expressing condolences and condemning Drexan Lorrain an evil sorcerer, up until the temple doors swung open and out came the bride.

She looked a maiden worthy of songs in her supple, frost-blue sideless surcoat lined in ermine, her face a pale oval in the mound of her silky wimple. Kind-eyed and smiling, her mother received every well-wisher with an ease that comes from joy. There was no sign of the woman who'd slept through the Red Tower.

And it must stay that way, Sara resolved to herself. *We won't go back because of me.*

She and the Morleys met her mother in the middle of the crowd. Sara hadn't spoken privately with her mother since the fight. Guilt overwhelmed her—guilt for denouncing her mother a whore and shoving her.

Yet she was stiff as ice-covered leaves when Rose knelt to embrace her. Lavender hung thickly about her mother's bosom and neck.

"How do I look, my sweet?" the bride asked her daughter, with everyone watching and listening. Her earnest expression solicited a socially appropriate response.

Sara caught a look from Cathreen. "Mother," was all she could muster, biting her lip. *I sound like Praise, asking for his mother all the time. Would you think me an idiot like him if you saw me bearing Mother's new wedding ring, Father?*

"My love," came his voice.

Willard Rittman stood at the temple's threshold alongside Geffrey and Brother Elfred. For once, the justice wore raiment that, rather than add to his repulsiveness, distracted from it: a cap of feathers to hide his bald spots and a cuirass with room for his bulging gut, over a doublet striped gold and green. The whip that'd nearly killed Farmer Grey coiled off his belt.

"Sir Willard," answered the bride, holding the folds of her gown as she ascended the steps.

Sara observed her mother's formalness. Rose had likened the world to a fire-breathing serpent. *You think you protect us, Mother,* she thought, *but Willard and Cathreen are the dragons.*

The important people ordered themselves on the temple steps, first Lord Sam, seating himself on the cushions of an oak chair nearest the doors, followed one step lower by the priest, and the bride and groom on the third. As ring-bearer, Sara was made to sit at the front, flanked by Cathreen and her miserable daughters. Guests rustled into their seats.

The wedding began under a noon sun that made sweat run down her face like tears, as well they should've been tears.

As was customary for an Elvarenist wedding, courtiers presented the couple with twelve gifts. The Morleys honored the groom in Justar's name with a quarrelsome destrier that thrashed his head wildly as a squire led him to the steps. In Sacreis's name the priest himself presented Rittman with a leather-bound copy of the Twelve Testaments. A third man announced his gift in Prospo's name, and out from the woods stumbled two lads lugging a chest between them. Rose leaned giggling into the justice when one boy lost his grip and spilled glinting lorens. Sara risked a chuckle, in turn, as Rittman made himself look like a tiny-headed turtle as he squeezed his thick neck through a gorget gifted to him in Amath's name.

Gifts in the goddesses' names were predictably boring. In Gourda's name, Cathreen presented Rose with a shiny new iron cauldron. Others gifted her mother a necklace of prayer beads in Divna's, a calendared green gown in Venas's, and freshly picked daffodils in Selyssa's, a staple of any wedding. *Daffodils for a womb that always fills,* Sara recalled the Common rhyme, grimly. In Helsar's, someone stupidly gifted her mother with a steel-tipped scabbard, which Rose, turning around, promptly gave the groom. Maetha's gift was one for Sara, a new wimple.

Only one Gift will satisfy me, Sara thought.

When it came time for Lord Sam's wedding present, the betrothed knelt together on the stairs, heads bowed. Everyone leaned close, unable to hear the soft-spoken lord.

Brother Elfred took it upon himself to convey his lord's gift. "What a proud gift, indeed," he announced loudly. "In his generosity, Lord Sam forgives the groom his bride's debts in return for her slain husband's land, house, and horse."

Guests nodded approvingly and spoke in praise of Sam Morley. Sara overheard one gentryman suggest he was already filling his father's chair. It took everything she had not to hurl the ring at Elfred. *Nothing will be like it was when you return, Father. How can you possibly forgive Mother? How can I?*

Rising, Rittman turned to face them. "And I have a gift of mine own," he declared in a tone for all to hear. He extended a hand to Cathreen. "To my fallen lord's wife, and to her family, I say this—as the Kingkiller's Curse found King Hexar's killers, I will find Lord Uthron's. I swear that I will find the King's Crow and drag him to the Silver Walls to answer for his crimes."

People began to clap. *I hope the King's Crow turns you into the toad that you truly are, Willard Rittman.*

With a blessing from Lord Sam, Brother Elfred opened his sprawling copy of the holy books in one arm and began to utter incantations in First Tongue. A few minutes in, commotion arose on the crowd's fringes, near the woods. Two men were arguing, gently but insistently. Twisting about, Sara tried to catch a look at what was happening through the guests' close-pressed bodies.

"*Brother Elfred!*" Rosbury's reader, Gary Henley, elbowed through the crowd, a grave raven amid colorful birds.

Elfred knitted his brow in consternation. He turned to the Lord Warden for guidance, but Sam Morley had the same look as the reader pressed on, demanding their attention. Cathreen snapped her fingers at the justice's deputies, urging them to intervene.

"Reader Gary, what, uh, a surprise," Elfred stammered.

The reader stood on a thick tree root, making himself seem taller. "A surprise, yes, Elfred." His eyes wandered until they found Sara. "A surprise to find Sir Damien's lawful wife marrying."

Earlier, Sara had been angry at the reader for giving his little cousin free rein in the bullying of Praise. She'd hug him now if she could.

All eyes turned to Uthron's heir, but it was his justice who commanded attention. "I have a writ from the steward herself," Rittman said defensively. He pointed at a crinkled parchment nailed to the temple door. "Princess Lorana *herself* declared Rose widowed."

The reader bowed reverently, long gray sleeves curling with his spread arms. "Which no one would dispute, Sir Will."

I dispute it, Sara thought. *With all my heart I dispute it.*

Rittman set his jaw rigidly. Sara thought she saw a little nerve fork up the center of his forehead. "Then what *business* do you have here?" he seethed.

The reader waxed with a cheerful smile. "No business, sir. Only a wish to witness these green and fair proceedings."

The groom made a face. "You'd . . . bear witness. To an Elvarenist wedding? You—*a reader.*"

"Aye, if we could." *We.* Several other peasants streamed forth from the forest, among them Clyde Hobbs, Cam Suffrey, and Stram Doling. "We were friends to the Sothrons. It donna feel right, not to witness."

Friends? None of them had associated with her father or given her mother and her charity when he went missing.

Sam Morley stood abruptly. "We welcome you," said the noble lord, in a voice he needed no one to convey for him. Sara saw Cathreen's mouth slackening. "Please friends, join us. We don't have enough seats for you, I'm afraid, but you can stand."

At that Gary Henley beamed, as if his lord had just offered him his chair cushions. "Our thanks, Lord Sam. My friends and I havnah had seats to call ours in a good long time. Standing'll do just fine." Six peasants filed in beside him.

Smiling sunnily, the Lord Warden plopped back into his chair. Courtiers muttered behind Sara, sowing panic. "Why'd he *do that?*" a woman asked. "They're here to do harm," a man said. "Let's go," Sara heard still another man urge his lady, but she said they couldn't, not without Lord Sam's dismissal.

More peasants trickled in from the forest by the second as the ceremony proceeded. Willard and Rose held each other's hands, but neither held the other's gaze consistently. Cathreen waved Tolos and another deputy to her daughters' sides. Sara counted as many peasants as Morley men. The air was boiling.

Her innards coiled up as she heard Elfred speak the gods' names in order of consort. This was the last invocation a priest made before declaring man and woman husband and wife.

Amath to Maetha, Sara understood as she heard Brother Elfred recite the pantheon's consorts, *Justar to Helsar, Sacreis to Divna, Prospo to Venas, Felos to Gourda.*

"Speak in a tongue we know!" Stram Doling cried through cupped hands. At a raw look from Rittman, Lym waddled after the offender. Doling led him into an unavailing chase around a tree, elk-spry, easily evading every grasp of his hand. Peasants heaped scornful laughter on the paunchy knight.

Sara registered in Cathreen a look that she'd never seen, not in all the years of her father's service. How often did one see fear in a noblewoman's eyes?

"Willard to Rose," Rittman said. "Forever."

"Rose to Willard," her mother finished. "Forever."

The sharp jab to her side came from Barbara. "Are all peasants as daft as you?" she griped. "What are you waiting for, you idiot? They said the words. *Present the ring!*"

Smoldering, Sara rose from her chair. She walked toward the temple steps, toward her mother and the man she could, by every law, call husband. She clutched the ring in her hands so tightly the wedding band's edges bit her flesh.

"*Turan e'sparta!*"

Something dark blurred past her cheek, fragmenting into fledgling pieces midair. Sam Morley, Lord Warden of Rosbury, wiped at his splattered cheek and lips. He examined the silken strand of brown webbing his fingers, his horror growing as it dawned on him and everyone else what'd happened.

Sara spun about. Alford Hemlock was readying the second throw, breeches at his knees, his arm working behind his rear.

Rittman flared red in his cheeks. "*ARREST THAT MAN!*" he bellowed at his deputies. "*DAMN IT, BRING ME THAT MAN!*"

Screams drowned out his orders. Peasants surged forth from the woods, overwhelming the crowd like an ocean tide. Stones showered House Morley's men from every direction. Many used chairs as weapons, whacking men-at-arms over their heads. Out came House Morley's swords. A peasant lost his arm in a spurt of blood. The guests trampled their own like deer fleeing predators.

Cathreen Morley flew to her son's side. "*Protect your Lord Warden!*" she shrieked through the chaos. Several Morley men did as bidden and made a ring around him, shields up, swords drawn. "I wasn't shown this," the noblewoman kept repeating as she pulled her boy close. "*He didn't show me this!*"

A stone whirred past Sara. Nearby, Alford wrested steel away from a knight. Gary Henley had somehow acquired the justice's destrier and mounted it clumsily, wheeling about for a wild charge, kicking at the knights who scrambled to bring him down. "*GIVE US BACK ROSBURY'S CHILDREN!*" he roared. "*GIVE THEM BACK!*"

Willard Rittman marched on the mob with his knights. Someone stole his whip and lost an arm to his sword. Whirling about, the justice plunged through a wall of men and struck the rump of Reader Gary's stolen steed with the flat of his blade, holding fast to his ankle so the rider tumbled off the galloping beast.

Sara acted before she could think.

Her mother's wedding ring left a pink welt in Rittman's temple. He gasped inaudibly as he staggered off, a tremulous hand over the sore. Up from behind him flew Praise himself, pinning Rittman beneath him, laughing hysterically all the while, as if he were playing a game. She'd never been so glad to see the pock-faced simpleton.

Alford sighted her. He had a cheerful grin stained with blood. "Once more a fine throw, our Damien's daughter!" he cried at Sara, laughing like a madman. "*A fine fuckin' throw!*"

"*Sara.*"

The girl spun and found her mother. Disheveled flowers and brown hair hung in her face. Mud spattered her wedding gown.

Rose jerked on her wrist as she headed for the temple doors. "Come with me, come quickly," she said, breathless.

"Mother, your arm." Sara winced at the blood on her mother's pale arm. "You're hurt."

"It doesn't matter. Come with me, Sara. We'll be safe—"

Her mother fell sidelong with an *oof* from Geffrey's shove. The deputy dug his fingers into Sara's arm, reeling her in close. Rage poured from his eyes, making him seem ten feet tall. "You little fucking shit," he sneered in her face. "I saw what you *DID*. You struck Willard. Your own father-to-be! Are you with them? Answer me, are you—"

Sara pulled on Dray's knife, and it ripped through her gown as easily as it pierced the metal and leather protecting Geffrey's thigh. The deputy fell at once, screaming murder. He bled his hands trying to pull the gnarled steel from his leg.

She hovered over him, feeling as tall as the Silver Walls. "*DON'T . . . YOU . . . TOUCH . . . MY MOTHER!*" she screamed.

"Sara." Her mother looked from her to Geffrey, and from him back to her. "My sweet, what have you done?" Tears clustered in her eyelashes. "*What . . . what have you done?*"

A horn blew. Around her, Sara saw deputies overcoming the gallant resistance. Praise wobbled about like a drunken giant with four men clinging to his arms and shoulders. Men wrestled the reader, Alford, Stram Doling, and Bram's father to the soil. "I want them all alive," shouted Rittman, looking crazed with his cap gone, hair matted to one side of his face.

Stealing past her mother, Sara grabbed Dray's knife and yanked as hard as she could. Geffrey's wails were in her ears, blotting out her own little whimper from the agonizing pain in her hands. She opened palms made a ruin and flush with blood that spotted her dress like crimson tears.

She ran.

CHAPTER 8

A Season of Death

eneath a sky raked with clouds, Assemblymen lined up at the Colossus—lords first, clergy second, merchants last.

They gathered for the Meet of First Declaration. The Meet decided how the Kingstrials would be judged. And here, Jason's claim would live or die.

In the thick of the lords stood Evan with the Bull and his Cloudlands vassals, clad in a cobalt doublet, gray breeches, and polished black boots. He could've risen at dawn and been first at the portcullis, like overeager Sam Wuthers and his vassals. Yet that would've only drawn more attention to himself and made *him* seem like the claimant, not Jason.

Besides, Evan thought, *I'd rather the Assembly reserve its scorn for Lorana's man in black.*

The Worthy didn't disappoint. Close to noon, a knight in filigreed black armor loped past on an onyx garron, drawing jeers. A plume of white goose feathers fluttered atop his helm. With one gauntleted hand he clutched the reins, and with his other he held an ebony rod fogged at the top by unmistakable pearl light.

As Lorana's knight rode past, Evan booed lustily with his fellow lords. Happily, even. *I missed this,* he thought.

Wexrenn seized the lord by his elbow, glaring, as if he'd just committed a grave offense. "Is that not Princess Lorana's man?" he demanded. "And is she not *still* our king's sister?"

Evan pried free of his grip. "I forget you're taking up your father's seat for the first time, Russell," he said as he rubbed his elbow.

Wexley admonished Wexrenn in Cloudspeech. "Blackstaff represents more than one king, steward, or royal house," he said in Common. "He's the crown-in-the-Assembly. We must all jeer him, or our king's claim will suffer because of our silence."

Evan didn't begrudge Wexrenn his ignorance. Even most Assemblymen misunderstood Blackstaff's role and symbolism. Well before the Long Summer Rebellion, and the Interregnum before it, Hexar's ancestor did as no king had done since and butchered his Worthy men, all of them, while they sat in this building. To prevent such a thing from ever happening again, subsequent Assemblies forced subsequent kings to agree to two rules: a monarch would never march north to the Golden Meadows with an army, and he'd send a representative in his stead, always.

Thus was Blackstaff born. Anytime the Assembly met, the king— or steward—designated a loyal man for the black armor and silverstone rod, and sent him north.

Yet a crown-in-the-Assembly was more than symbolic. Blackstaff's famous rod was the key to the Colossus. Centuries of tradition had hallowed his role, and no one entered without him first waving it about. A skeleton crew guarded the ancient amphitheater and opened it to no one, not even Assemblymen, unless the black knight rapped his rod on the portcullis and affirmed his loyalties.

It was a strange ritual, but Loran was nothing if not its traditions.

Blackstaff dismounted at the portcullis, ignoring customary taunts. Lifting his rod, the knight pounded the fist-sized chunk of its silverstone on rusted grille for three deep clangs, *THUN, THUN, THUN.*

No one answered. Such was the ritual.

High above, archers emerged from the Colossus' arcades, sunlight glancing off their crossbow bolts. Evan sensed unease among the other Assemblymen despite the knowledge that this was harmless ceremony. *Were that those bows were loyal to me,* he thought. *A few well-placed bolts, and I'd shift the Assembly in Jason's favor permanently, without need of my Company . . .*

"We see you, black knight," an archer shouted down. "Are you the king's man?"

"I AM FOR THE KING," cried Blackstaff, his voice muffled by his helm but audible.

"Show us the stone that shines."

The knight twisted about, sweeping the area with a blaze of his rod's silverstone light. The crossbows withdrew. Seconds later, the portcullis shuddered open, its winch chains clanking.

Blackstaff led the procession through the gatehouse.

Evan entered with the Assemblymen. He wasn't two steps inside before Sam Gramlore stepped athwart his path.

"You should find a seat, Sam." Evan sidestepped the Lord of Eddenwood. "They go quickly."

The lackey matched his movement, blocking him. "And you might find a lordship," Gramlore said with sneering eyes. "Attainted men can't sit with the Worthy."

"The king pardoned me on Remembrance Day. You were there, I recall, if a bit drunk. And at the kingkiller's table."

He grinned. "You were attainted."

A shadow engulfed them both. "Move, Sam," rumbled Trevor Wexley, "before I beat that grin off you and send you back to your father like the whelp you are."

Gramlore weathered the tall lord better than others. He smiled. "Were that my father still lived! He'd choke to hear that the Lord of the Cloudlands championed a seat in this Assembly for *scrorn-ner-gaith.* Do you enjoy spitting on your fathers?"

The Bull had his sword jerked halfway out of its scabbard before Evan forced him to sheathe it.

Nothing could've pleased Gramlore more. "Back so soon, only to leave again," he said, chuckling. "Lord Jon shall rejoice to hear the bastard prince has no champion."

"Why would your master rejoice, Sam?" Evan rejoined quickly, loudly, so the lords behind him heard clearly.

"Heh. Jon Redoak isn't my master." *Indeed not,* thought Evan.

Gram Sothos is. "And it's treason to bear steel against Assemblymen in the Colossus. Treason gets you expelled."

"But only when quorum is called. Has quorum been called yet? Have the Worthy changed the laws in my absence?"

Gramlore tightened his lips, unable to prove him false. Lords were agitating for him to move; someone said, "Gods' sake, Sam, we were there when Hexar pardoned him. *Move.*"

Caving to pressure, the lord gave the path. "Your sister's bastard will die, Sinclair," he said as Evan strode past. "Would she have wanted that?"

It took all Evan had not to break his jaw. Passing him, he overheard a Gelder lord calling Gramlore daft for sparring over rules with a *Sinclair,* of all people. *Yes,* Evan thought, satisfied, *my family always had a seat here . . . and today, we do again.*

Deceivingly compact on the outside, Rorin's amphitheater opened up on a grand sand arena half a mile in length. On all sides stone benches rose in tiered circles, sectioned by steps and illuminated by jewels of torchlight. The heads of fearsome beasts snarled along the walls, dragons and griffons, lions and bears, embellished iron pipes that could flood the arena with water in minutes. In the middle benches to the east nested the King's Box, a pillared platform shaded with purple canvas.

Evan marveled at the ellipse of sand, the circular benches, the oval sky, the ridged snouts of iron pipes. *Hello again, my old friend. Did you miss me, as I've missed you these many years?*

The Colossus had intrigued Evan since boyhood, and not only because nobles spilled blood here during Kingstrials. The heart of Loran pumped within these walls, not behind the walls of silverstone. Rorin Romaris had ordered his builders to craft enough benches for a realm, and here the realm had sat. For millennia the kingdom's people—its lords, clergy, merchants, knights and peasants, once, too—had met here to decide their wars, treaties, taxes, their gods and kings, their fate.

They had done it together, once.

Evan lingered on the uppermost benches, picturing a time when the Wing of the Commons sat there. Bending, he scooped up a handful of sand, watched it filter through his fingers. *I will give my life for him,* he promised his sister, *if it comes to that.*

A youthful speed overtook Evan. He led Jason's lords up the steps to the most coveted seats, those facing the King's Box, where the lord speakers presided over the Worthy Assembly. Evan wanted to be where everyone would see him opposing Sothos's minions.

The Cloudlanders didn't delay in claiming their seats. Sitting, Evan leaned toward Wexley. "I even reminded you about the laws against bearing steel, my lord," he scolded the Bull under his breath.

"Quorum hadn't been called," Wexley said with irritating smugness. He stroked his auburn beard. "You said so yourself."

"If you or any of your men are expelled, our king loses his champion. No champion, no victory today, no throne. Did you come all the way to cost Jason his chance? What of your pledge to my nephew at the *rythnoraim?*"

Wexley stared straight ahead, indignant. "A Cloudlander's word is stronger than swordwood."

"Then be still as swordwood, and let me wield you against our enemies as if you were a steel branch."

So long as you keep the Fourth Wing to Loran proper, Evan imagined the noble lord thinking. Gramlore had tried to exploit a division and prod the proud Bull into making a critical error. Redoak had probably planned that provocation, the bastard.

The Bull and his nobles warranted looks of wonder from the rest of the noblemen. Some labored to shuffle through the benches to welcome Wexley and his Cloudlands lords back to the Assembly. Evan, gone for about as long, didn't merit the same courtesy.

When lords and priests asked what brought the old lord out of exile, and whether he would end Hexar's Folly, Wexley would only promise to be there for Jason Warchild. Evan took satisfaction in their disappointment. *We are all here to make Jason your king without war. If you'd end our Silent Friendship with the Cloudlands, back my nephew.*

After the Wing of Lords came the Wing of Clergy, day and night in their stark choice of raiment, the Elvarenists in flowing cream cassocks, the Free Believers in their drab gray linen. The bishops and priests clustered about the King's Box; the readers filled out the northern benches like crows perched on boughs.

Clabbard studied faces in the crowd. "Tom Gelder has twenty lords to his claim," he noted.

Ulbridge said, "And Wuthers half as many."

"Look at the Thorngales."

Evan followed Wexrenn's finger to the southern side of the benches, near the gaping hole of a collapsed section. Gavin, Darren, and Luc, all seated in the Wing of Lords, stared back at him. The Thorngales had with them no small number of lords, maybe thirty in all. Evan counted Wess Dyvar, Kevin Stonehold, and Pesh Pettard, lords with wealth, men, and good names. He turned from their scowls.

I played no part in the Old Oak's death, but they've bent their ears to Sothos's lackeys, who've twisted them against me, he thought. *No matter. They'll see reason.*

"None of them matter," Ulbridge weighed in. "It's Shaddon we should worry about. Look at his numbers."

Grathos's flock clustered by sixty Sothos loyalists. They included Dumas Sunox, who occupied two seats by himself. Gramlore, Jacob Hexbrook, Domin Greathall, Petor Ellsby, and Aron Tuller, men sworn to Sothos, piled beside each other.

Sothos is in the Red Tower, and yet it's as if he's here today, moving the game pieces into place for Shaddon. "The odds are presently in their favor, that's true," Evan said. "The rest of the kingdom isn't."

"And our king is a young man in his prime," Wexley said. "Shaddon couldn't lift a proper sword, let alone a fucking lance. I doubt he'll even survive the First Trial."

"Three Trials, three Wings: only the Worthy crown kings."

Clabbard searched the crowd of readers. "I can't see that strutting peacock Fawkes," he said. "He's usually easy to spot in that obnoxious feathered cap."

"Assembly matters bore Lord Tomas, and he likes to make an

entrance besides." Evan nodded at the Master Reader of the Free Beliefs. "Fawkes's lords expect Jacob Sulley to defend his claim and herd readers for him in his absence."

He caught a look from Sulley. Bookended by Fawkes's lords, the Master Reader looked more a captive than the head of his religion. House Fawkes sought to pave the road to King Tomas the Second with the Wing of Clergy's one hundred fifty-seven Free Believers, who outnumbered the same chamber's one hundred ten priests.

Fawkes won't hurt our cause, Evan thought, *not if my Loyal Companymen hold to their oaths.* No matter their consciences—or whether some *were* twice-turned traitors—the readers in his Company had decided. They'd stand with Jason, no matter how Jacob Sulley went. To defy the Company publicly was to invite death in the shadows. *But will any oaths matter if we've lost the Pigeons?* he wondered darkly.

Yet appearances could deceive. The understated Jacob Sulley was easily one of Loran's most powerful officials. In a land where most peasants worshipped in parishes, the Master Reader commanded the respect of millions. It was why the High Bishop liked to slight Sulley, envious as he was that a beggarly reader shared spiritual footing with his priestking.

Sulley's power concerned Evan. Sulley himself was not a Companyman. If anyone could make the readers essential to his Company break their oaths and risk death, it was him. His hope was that Sulley would see Evan as Evan had always seen him: as a natural ally.

Near Fawkes's vassals and the Free Believers sat a trio of lords sworn to the Company, yes, but without love whatsoever for the royal family; Hexar had bedded all their wives. Samuel Ironkeep, Jeff Mohr, and Jacob Farryll looked disgruntled, and rather ready for the Kingstrials with two Eddenhold claimants to be finished. *Silvertongue cast a spell indeed if they agreed to back Jason,* he thought admiringly.

An alliance with Trevor Wexley had opened the door for King Jason, but Rathos Robswell would ensure that he'd walk through it. *You fill me with pride, Rathos, and remorse.*

Rathos had delivered the Company at a cost that twisted his warder's stomach. Leah had said that Rathos would bear his scars from Graywood for the rest of his life. "At least they're handsome scars," she'd said, as if that meant anything.

Evan remembered knuckles cracking. "Everything's a game piece to you, isn't it, Evan?" Matthus had said. "Do you even know what love is?"

Nothing has been for nothing, Matt, a small voice inside Evan reassured him. *I promise you.*

In streamed the Wing of Knights, the least powerful of the three chambers, merchants and freeholders arrayed in silk and linen. Among them were Tom Webb, Lorn Granger, and Drexyn Lauphrey, Companymen and Petitioners. Tristan Lox entered to stares and quiet asides over the sumptuary laws he plainly violated by draping himself in fox pelts. Geoff Donovan, known as the Whore Lord, trailed in bantering affably with clients.

Those and all other merchants ascended to the topmost benches that once seated the Fourth Wing. Viewing them as up-jumped peasants, lords and priests consigned them there.

But how lords and priests love their purses, Evan thought. Without the merchant class, the kingdom's outstanding debts would've drowned Loran. The Wing of Knights had no anointed men, but many among its members griped that they deserved knighthoods, so often were they called upon to rescue Loran from bankruptcy.

He lingered on the merchants' benches. *What would the Assembly look like if it had its Fourth Wing?*

The answer depended on the rank of the answerer.

Ask a lord about what he knew of the time when Worthy Assemblies seated peasants, and he was like to scorn the era's brawling, brazen thievery, and infectious lack of decorum. Ask a priest, and he could make a day of counting the vices and heresies, which ran from unspeakable carnal acts to burnings of the Twelve Testaments. Ario Pattas, one of Gram Reuben's contemporaries, had famously dismissed the Fourth Wing as "a flea-bitten rabble ignorant of sums, customs, history, and why they're even in the Assembly of Loran to begin with."

He could have easily said that about this present Assembly, Evan thought contemptuously as he scanned the amphitheater.

Yet it hadn't always been so. Over millennia, the Wing of the Commons had elevated as many saints as sinners. Willard the Wise was one of many lawmen, thinkers, warriors, artists, builders, and poets who started with nothing, rose through the Fourth Wing, and left Loran more powerful. Indeed, that flea-bitten rabble had at times overshot the loftiest aspirations of the Awakening's sages, occasionally admitting *peasant women.* A younger Leah had cherished tales about women with seats; with hindsight, Evan wondered if he'd planted the seeds of her madness by indulging her.

Evan needed only one reason to justify his life's pursuit. When the Assembly had four wings, and peasants a seat at the realm's table, everyone knew more dignity and less squalor, and the kingdom a longer peace. *To each a chair,* Evan thought, *to all a piece.*

All conversation in the Colossus ebbed as the black knight treaded to the center of the arena. Blackstaff removed his helm, revealing a man with a balding head and hard, seamed face. Evan knew this Sir Astiban Hoard. *I would've chosen a different man for Blackstaff, princess,* he thought grimly.

Hoard was not a kind man. He terrorized peasants. If the rumors about him were true, he was guilty of ripping his own bastard from the womb of a Casaanite whore and chucking it down Traitor's Pit. But he was loyal to the royal family, fiercely loyal. He supposed that Lorana valued loyalty over anything else right now, which was what Jason needed.

Astiban Hoard thrust his rod into the air, to plant it into the sand and declare the Meet open. *"One realm—one king—but three wings!"* thundered his baritone voice. *"This was King Rorin Romaris's law, and—"*

"YOU LIE, BLACKSTAFF!"

Assemblymen twisted in the direction of the voice. Men gasped or swore, or signed diamonds. Evan wanted to smile.

No one had noticed the peasant who'd tottered into the gatehouse.

There wasn't much to him. Balding and spindly, the old man looked as withered as Midland wheat. His sunburnt skin and holey tunic set him worlds apart from Assemblymen in silk and pelts. He couldn't possibly lift a sword, and yet the lords and priests reacted as if a host mustered behind him.

The old fellow was one step from setting foot in an arena forbidden to peasants for two centuries.

"There are *four* wings!" the man cried over mounting protests, his voice amplified by the Colossus's high curving walls. "You lot stole our seats! *GIVE THEM BACK!*"

Evan blinked out the tears that clustered in his eyelashes. *You see, Matthus? Nothing has been for nothing. I'll see to it that minstrels hear of this one's courage.*

"*TUREL E'SARTHA, TURAN E'SPARTA!*" the man shouted as heckling lords and priests flung stones and pebbles.

Above, a lord cried for his knights to intervene.

Grimacing, Evan craned up at the King's Box, where Greg Thorngale should've stood. Jon Redoak listed on a balustrade beneath rippling purple canvas. Beside him lurked the other two speakers, Grathos in his cassock, cloak, and ornamented miter, and Frederick Midliche, Speaker of the Wing of Knights, a plump trader attired in embroidered samite.

Sentry knights steamed forth from the northern entrance, lions on their surcoats and spears in their hands. The peasant's heels dragged ruts through the sand as Blackstaff and others hauled him out.

Evan closed his eyes and listened to what was the elderly man's last moment. "The Commons need a wing!" he wailed. "The Midlands starve! Temples burn! *Return what was taken! RETUUUURNNN . . .*"

To each a chair, Evan thought, knowing the old man's head had already been taken.

More than half the men seated shot to their feet, clapping and chanting, *"Red-OAK, Red-OAK!"*

Evan Sinclair rose and joined the applause, to looks from startled Cloudlanders and the unease of every Companyman he counted present. Free Believers crossed their arms or looked away, disgusted.

I've been away for many years, Evan thought, *but I haven't forgotten to play the game.* Yes, he led the Loyal Company. He'd spent his life trying to seat peasants again in this Assembly, for a better realm, a more peaceful realm. That was his passion.

But he couldn't be seen sitting, lest these Assemblymen think he sided with the disruption. Enough men believed the Fourth Wing promised chaos; he and Jason needed to show that wouldn't happen. Such was politics.

Striding back in with the swagger of a man who's just taken a life, Blackstaff plunged his glowing rod into the sand. The gates shut with a decisive, sonorous clang. Assemblymen stood, applauding Hoard.

When Blackstaff was gone, Jon Redoak held up his palm. "Set a watch outside for any more peasants with bright ideas," he commanded archers. "The Meet of First Declaration begins."

With the blood of peasants, aptly, Evan thought darkly.

Because peasants hadn't served in the Worthy Assembly for centuries, rumors about just what their rulers did and said spread through the realm like fire through dry bush. Pull up a seat at any tavern, and you'd hear outrageous tales men swore on their mothers' lives were true.

The worst had staying power. Assemblymen worshipped effigies of the Nagarthessi and dined on the flesh of Common infants while shackled parents watched and screamed until their voices gave out. Hidden in the shadows, Barefoot Knights convened at the Colossus to tear down thrones and unite the world under a tyrant.

Sordid tales involved Evan, annoyingly. Rathos had once overheard a Peacefield minstrel singing about how Sarah still lived and, along with Evan, performed fellatio on Companymen in the Assembly. (Evan had a reputation for dealing gently with Commoners, but hot pincers took that one's tongue.)

When Jason seats the peasants again, they'll see how things really work in the Assembly, Evan thought. Men spoke. Men argued. Passionate men. Self-serving men. Those who might've gone north to change the Assembly realized they were only as effective as the number of allies they could wheedle, inveigle, intimidate, or bribe to their side.

Making the Assembly more mysterious, the people didn't know how anyone voted. Romarians had bequeathed to them a secret ballot. It was maybe the only thing all Assemblymen still regarded as sacred. Every man was given scraps of parchment and sticks of charcoal to record their votes.

Those scraps of paper were masks Evan's Companymen wore to hide themselves in plain sight. The ancient tradition of secret voting had infuriated Hexar and made the Company the thorn that it was in Gram Sothos's side.

Ironically, what gave them the power to protect peasants also helped nurture conspiracy theories about the Assembly.

Yet the rumors weren't all wrong. Commoners said the Wing of Lords stopped at nothing to crush them with taxes, and that priests in the Wing of Clergy conspired to steal and indoctrinate their children in temples. This was quite true.

Evan found this out when he urged the Worthy to finally end family separations. He was roundly applauded by readers and many merchants, and dismissed or threatened by Sothos's allies. "You play with fire," Evan said over the noise, "you burn your hands. Be cruel to peasants, and they'll be cruel to you."

Jon Redoak ordered Evan to stay his tongue or visit a cell.

Seated beside him, Grathos agreed with a nod that made his miter slump forward. "The Hands serve, Lord Evan," said the Speaker of the Wing of Clergy. "Perhaps you forget why we gather here today. We must serve the realm by settling the Kingstrials' rules of engagement."

"And thus, settle who wears the crown," Redoak added.

Evan didn't miss the chance for a jab. "You mention the crown," he said for all to hear, "but where is its representative, and why do we meet without her?"

"Blackstaff is here. Do you not see his rod in the sand?"

"Princess Lorana isn't a king. She's steward. And she's supposed to sit beside you in the King's Box, Lord Jon."

Alyse's daughter was overdue in the Golden Meadows. In vain, Evan had tried to delay the Meet until she arrived. As one of the Kingstrials' arbiters, Lorana could thwart the gimmicks and rule-bending for which Sothos and his puppets were so well-known. *I rather wish the Old Oak hadn't been killed,* Evan thought grimly. Speaker Thorngale would've been useful here.

Laughter belted around the Colossus. Redoak had the most blood-boiling grin. "As you say, Lord Evan, the princess isn't the king. But the realm needs its king. To crown one, we must have rules, or else we'll have chaos. You're welcome to leave in protest, of course."

"You first," Evan said.

Only Jacob Sulley seconded Evan's motion for a delay—not for Lorana's sake, but Tomas Fawkes's. He wanted to fetch the Lord of Westerliche. A smatter of laughter carried through benches when Grathos asked if anyone had checked the Whore Lord's tents. Redoak invoked a rule as speaker of Fawkes's chamber to deny Sulley time to find him, a snub that surprised no one.

The laughter faded as Trevor Wexley rose to speak.

Redoak squinted down. "Lord Trevor, this Assembly is gladdened to see the Cloudlands rejoin us after years away."

The speaker's graciousness didn't soften the great lord's stony demeanor. "You'll be less glad after I speak my piece," said the Bull. "Aye, we've been away. Charles Burke betrayed my brother—"

"And yet," Redoak interjected with a voice amplified by his high perch, "you ally with the house that retains the Grand Inquisitor. Why, Lord Trevor?"

Wexley looked like he'd descend from his bench, climb to the King's Box, and crush Redoak's skull in his hands. *He means to rile you, Trevor,* Evan thought. *Speak to persuade, not to hurt.*

The Bull smiled. Not a heartwarming sight, his smile, but men listened. "I proudly support Jason Warchild's claim to his father's throne," he said. No one dared jeer, for who would, at a lord with a fourth of the country in his grip? "He is no bastard but a man of honor. He bested my nephew in a trial by sword. By rights, he should've ended his life, but Hexar's son spared him." He clenched a massive fist. "*The son of Hexar did that.* He earned my friendship and brought my men and me back to this land. A king like that is the rightful king of the Cloudlands—and Loran."

Wexley sat down amid the applause. *Lorana may not be here, but the great winnings from her gamble are,* Evan thought.

Redoak asked the High Bishop to lead the Assembly in a prayer, slighting Sulley and his Free Believers. Grathos began praying by calling this age in Loran "a season of death," with kings and lords dying like flies. He implored Justar for justice in the desecration of the South Farcombe temple. He asked Athos to lift his lamp for the lords Greg Thorngale, Eric Sundry, and Uthron Morley, and guide them to the Evergreen Isles.

Prayer offered no better time for a headcount. Evan made a count of allies and came up shy of a slim majority across the three wings. *Your doing, Rezlan,* Evan understood. *Always counting your odds, old friend, all while kneecapping progress. Are* you *our twice-turned traitor?*

Grathos dared not pray openly for his ally Sothos, but he made a swipe at Lorana with a call to "restore the friendship between the crown and the Worthy." The High Bishop stared icily at Evan as he eulogized Greg Thorngale, condemning to hell whomever slew the speaker.

Yes, yes, Evan thought as he endured stares, *blame me for these deaths, not the Hammer of the Commons—or the laws you pass in his name that pound peasants like nails.*

After prayers, a war of attrition unfolded in the Colossus. Fought bench to bench, nobles, priests, readers, and merchants all took turns slinging volleys of arrows with their voices and scraps of parchment.

This was where the Loyal Company mattered.

The Worthy Assembly had three chambers—a Wing of Lords dominated by devout nobles, a Wing of Clergy bitterly divided between priests and readers, and a Wing of Knights controlled by merchants sympathetic to the Common cause—but, truly, it had two. One side worked to remake Loran in the priestking's image; the other side vigorously opposed it. Over the last fifty years, ancient customs, new wealth, and waves of proselytizing readers had made the body into a seesaw, tipping Loran this way and that on the fulcrum of votes.

In the absence of a Wing of the Commons, Companymen in the Assembly often made the difference in tipping the realm against those with power. The Company filled a void the lords and priests did not want filled by peasants, and it frustrated their designs, all in plain sight.

Standing for recognition, Hexbrook made the first attack on Jason's claim. To a swell of laughter, he asked the Assembly to dismiss the Kingstrials and crown Shaddon. "The succession makes the need for Trials irrelevant," said the Sothos vassal. He weathered jeers and curses. "Shaddon is King Hexar's brother. With the crown prince gone, King Hexar left us no heirs. But Shaddon is here. He is the rightful king!"

Evan waited to speak until all the Assemblymen finished their insults. "Shaddon had a hand in Hexar's death," Evan said, the acoustics amplifying his voice, "and only the Worthy crown their king."

The time came to vote. Men marked scraps of parchment and passed them to tallymen on the stairs. The tallymen added up scraps, the three speakers conveyed the tally, and Hexbrook sat down, defeated.

That was an easy vote.

With the aid of his Companymen, Evan won a rhetorical clash over the Three Laws, which held that a claimant became king by showing that he could do three things in three Trials: redden his sword, lead men into battle, and prove the power of his blood.

The ancient laws were not by themselves controversial . . . until Aron Tuller petitioned for a tweak to the third one. Tuller wanted claimants to prove an "unadulterated blood lineage" to Anjan Half-Elf. A clever little maneuver that was, clever enough to fly over the heads of even seasoned Assemblymen.

Tuller's language would've been a portcullis to shut out contenders with disputed lineages like Jason. Evan rallied for the motion's defeat on grounds that it'd violate tradition. The Assemblymen scratched at papers with charcoal, passed them along to tallymen, and listened as the speakers read the tally.

Evan won the next matter less handily. Rising again, to the visible frustration of Shaddon's allies, he called for a ban on the use of steel in the First Trial. "Then you destroy spectacle," Wess Dyvar grumbled. "Better that than the loss *of every viable claimant*," Evan rejoined. "What use are the Trials if half the kings die before even the Second?"

Men scratched at paper. Tallymen counted. Speakers gave the count. The Assembly passed the rule by a difference of two votes.

Other times, he lost. Sothos's bannermen rallied for *mas in adversas*, a dusty rule permitting champions to compete in an injured claimant's stead. That could only serve older men like Shaddon. Many derided the switch rule as cowardly, and raised their voices and stomped their feet until the Assembly moved that a champion couldn't actually *win* a Trial for his absent claimant, merely keep his name in contention.

The tallymen collected scraps. Redoak seemed to bask in the applause from allies when he announced the outcome.

A few rules of engagement passed muster with everyone. Every Assemblyman voted to bar claimants from entering their rivals' camps on pain of expulsion or death. Every lord with a force also consented to respecting the outcome of the Trials under pain of expulsion and death. *At least we can all agree on that much,* Evan thought.

To anyone but Assemblymen like Evan, the proceedings had to seem painfully glacial, the rules arcane. By the fourth hour, all the Cloudlands lords but Wexley had lost interest. Thrice Wexrenn nodded off, snoring cavernously; Evan jolted him awake with a sharp elbow to the ribs.

"These are a sorcerer's trickeries," Wexrenn despaired, rubbing his flank with a miserable look. "Fucking hell, I can't even understand what I'm for or what I'm against."

"Then we should be glad that Lord Evan is a sorcerer," the Bull said in a tone of reprimand. "Do what he does, shout when he shouts, vote as he votes . . . *and stay the fuck awake.*"

The defense of Jason's claim isn't all my work, thought the warder to a ward. Rathos Silvertongue proved his value twenty times over as the

Loyal Company, so often immobilized by its infighting, fused together like the grip, pommel, and blade of a fierce sword—a weapon to hack and slash through Priestking Parlisis's machinations, one manipulatable rule after another.

Time and again, Companymen blocked rules dressed by Jason's enemies in the silk of fair play. Hexbrook advanced a game of archery in case no one won the First Trial definitively. Mohr, perhaps remembering how Fawkes had bested Jason at arrows on Remembrance Day, rallied other lords against it.

The worst rules were the ones with Elvish names only priests understood. A popular linen merchant peddled a rule he billed would allow claimants to field more warriors for the Second Trial. In fact, the *tandesh invariis* rule was an obscure Romarian custom that forgave foreigners for invading Loran to save a king unable to defend himself—something that Hexar had weighed using during the rebellion. Redoak and Grathos hoped to stretch the rule's language into a tunnel mouth that Shaddon could fit a hundred Intercessors through and use in the Trials. Companymen like Lox, Granger, and Donovan buried the rule with fiery speeches about Loran's independence that nearly moved Evan to tears.

For the Lord of Caerdon, long looking in from outside, it was a rush to watch his Companymen one by one refuse their own selfish interests and parry every maneuver from a Sothos proxy. Some, like Greathall, grew so unhinged by their defeats in the fog of war that they openly accused Evan of corrupting the proceedings.

"A Company of devils," Greathall called the men hidden by charcoal and parchment. Flustered, the red-faced Sothos vassal rallied other lords to do away with the secret ballot completely.

Joining with Assemblymen from all three wings, the Loyal Company defeated the maneuver soundly.

This is reason in numbers, he thought proudly. *Peasants may lack a Fourth Wing, but until Jason restores it, the Loyal Company will protect the interests of the voiceless.*

Tensions came to a boil over the Thorngales. With a stone in his throat, Wuthers asked to know *which* brother planned to vie for the crown on House Thorngale's behalf.

The brother he eyed worriedly had a foot propped up on the bench below him. "Why do you ask, Lord of Minor Sunder?" the Stormsword asked with a bored lilt.

Evan saw his chance. He took it, and stood. "Because you and your brothers seem confused," he said firmly. "One house, one claimant. House Thorngale makes camp at these Meadows without declaring which of its lords will represent them in the Trials. It's been against our laws since Raelin the Red."

Gavin looked elsewhere, as if addressing a Sinclair were beneath his dignity. Luc laughed at Evan from the side of his mouth.

Not Darren. He narrowed his eyes at Evan. *The truth is, you're in my sights, Darren Stormsword,* he thought.

"Against our laws?" Darren stirred from his bench, removing his boot from the seat below him. "You don't get to speak about what's against our laws, you murdering fuck."

"Yet here I stand."

"Not for long."

A glance communicated to Ulbridge that he was needed. Unlike Wexrenn, the Lord of Hapry Springs knew how to be useful in the Wing of Lords. Bundled in plaid scarves and kilt, Ulbridge rose solemnly.

"Lord Speakers," Ulbridge said in his rolling accent, "long have my kinsmen and me been away from this Assembly. But I hope its honor is intact." He pointed at Darren Thorngale. "No Assemblyman may impugn another's name in the Assembly. I move to censure Lord Darren."

Darren threw his head back, laughing. "Honor," he spat.

"Yes," Evan muttered in a voice he knew the Colossus's rounded architecture would carry to the Thorngales but keep from others in earshot, "something your father clearly never taught you."

Darren Thorngale bolted up, sword in hand. Seconds had passed before an avalanche of gasps and condemnation hurtled down on top of them. Gavin and Luc surrounded their brother, pressuring him to sheathe his weapon.

But it was too late.

Over the storm of voices, Wexley's thundered loudest. "*There is quorum still,*" the Bull protested.

Thorngale was still standing, sword unwavering and pointed at Evan, when the Speaker of the Wing of Knights gaveled the bedlam away. Assemblymen called Frederick Midliche the Fox. With his circlet of coppery hair and neat, white goatee, the silk trader rather resembled a fox, but his sense of self-preservation had earned him the moniker. As someone whom Sothos had searched for excuses to hang, Midliche preferred to avoid controversy, letting the other speakers corner the limelight.

The Fox did not stay quiet this time. He glared from the King's Box. "Not since King Hexron has someone drawn steel against an Assemblyman here," Midliche said gravely.

Any other Assemblyman would've apologized profusely for fear of losing his seat, if not his head. Not the Stormsword. Darren drew more gasps and denunciations as he pivoted his steel to the King's Box. *This is going better than I'd hoped,* Evan thought.

Above the cries rose Darren's voice, unintimidated. "I'm not 'someone,' old goat," he told the Fox. "I'm the Stormsword of Loran. Thirty-nine Uzmen tried to kill me, and thirty-nine Uzmen died on this blade. I defended my country."

"A country you blaspheme with your madness," Midliche countered, his fat cheeks growing redder by the second. "Your seat is forfeit. Sheathe your sword—*NOW*—or it'll remove your head!"

Hesitant at first, the other two speakers began to crack; Redoak and Grathos stumbled over each other to denounce Darren. *So they killed the Old Oak,* Evan realized. *To vacate a speakership for a lackey and turn the Stormsword against us.*

Their ploy had worked beautifully. After a long moment, Darren pivoted again toward Evan, glaring. "Fuck seats, and to hell with Trials," he snarled. "Evan Sinclair dies by mine hand. And Lord Warchild. I'll pledge my sword to the king who gives them to me. Alive."

With the Assembly's fury raining down on him, and the Fox threatening a beheading, Darren Thorngale relented and sheathed his blade. He said a few words to his brothers, then breezed down the stairs, his mane of rich brown hair flowing. At Redoak's command, the Colossus's defenders rolled open its gates, and Blackstaff escorted the defiant young lord out.

Inwardly, Evan breathed a sigh of relief. Of all people at the Golden Meadows, including Shaddon, the Stormsword had posed the greatest threat to Jason. Now that threat was gone . . . at least from the tournament. *The Bull will need to triple Jason's guard, but this was worth it.*

A lone figure dashed through the gates, crying something. Men bristled, likely fearing another peasant intruder.

It wasn't a peasant. The herald wore House Fawkes's colors on his vest, a griffon soaring against triangles of dusk orange. He shouted something that stunned everyone.

Tomas Fawkes was dead.

It's as Grathos said, Evan thought. *This is a season of death.*

CHAPTER 9

The Most-Sought Hand

tacks on stacks of headmasts and headsails billowed on the horizon like low-hanging clouds. *Storm clouds,* thought the steward, folding her arms uneasily. A procession of strangers in black garb marched up from the anchored ships, dipping in and out of sight amid the sandhills. *A Lonely Isle's storm, here to deluge us, if the Kingstrials deliver a king whom Parlisis doesn't fancy.*

Lorana was nervous. The unease in her belly threatened to overwhelm her, but it wasn't entirely the foreign warships. She exchanged looks with the stalwarts flanking her—Andrew Windkin, her strong and loyal knight, and her lover, confident in an emerald, open-sided surcoat, her black hair bushy.

Minutes passed long as hours as Lorana and all the men ahorse behind her waited on the prieslenne. The ocean air tasted salty. Seagulls wheeled overhead, crooning. When Anyasha reached for her hands, the princess realized she'd been practically kneading them to dough.

I told you that you shouldn't come, Yasha, Lorana thought. But Anyasha had insisted. "You loved her once, but I wouldn't accompany you out of jealousy," she'd said on their way to the Golden Meadows. "She's engaged to Shaddon. Been with her father on the Lonely Isle for two years. Who knows if she's the woman we knew?"

Thirty feet away, the procession emerged from the dunes, led by the woman whom Elvarenists said spoke for the twelve gods.

Edenia Highdaughter, the high priestess of her religion, looked as she had when she'd left Lorana at the Shimmering Bay two years before. Across the thirteen kingdoms, minstrels praised the prieslenne for her beauty, the slope of her perfect bosom, her golden tresses (and her piety, occasionally). Still, it was the glow of her smile that captured hearts. That smile was there now, turning the stone maiden malleable as moist clay.

But she was called the Most-Sought Hand in the Thirteen Kingdoms for a reason. Lithe, winsome, and fair of skin, Edenia was the picture of everything that men desired in maidens. She had a heart-shaped face and welcoming blue eyes that turned rooms around her. She buried her comely figure in a long gray overcoat and wore elbow-length gloves, protection against the blustery Northland winds.

A silken headdress made an oval of her perfect face. *You never covered yourself at the Walls, Eden,* Lorana thought, *not even when Parlisis's bishops and priests came to check on you.*

Halting yards away, the prieslenne smiled a melancholy smile. This wasn't the reunion either of them would've wanted. Lorana had a host at her back, and Edenia a regiment of silver-masked brutes whom Hexar had banished from his kingdom.

A guardsman appeared by Edenia's side, a halberd in his hand. He wasn't an Intercessor, but he looked as foreign as one in his striped cream-and-indigo uniform, crested morion, and the choke of his ruff. A gold ring pierced his left nostril. "Thank the twelve gods and be blessed," he announced in an elegant Medecian accent. "You stand before Her Blessedness, Pries—"

"Oh, Sir Vayne, there's no need for it," Edenia broke in with an air of annoyance. She crossed the sandy cobblestone walkway and folded Lorana in her arms. "My flower. Oh, my flower, I *missed* you!"

Lorana tensed. She'd played king for two years, and in that time, she'd daydreamed about this moment, about the sweet smell of the prieslenne's perfume, the chance that their breasts might brush together, or their lips . . .

But she was guarded. Anyasha was right. After two years away, Edenia had shown up with warships, her father's ghouls . . . and an unfamiliar ring on her finger. An ostentatious ring it was, a stylized band accented by tiny diamonds, including the centerpiece, half the size of an eyeball. Befitting for a dignitary engaged to a would-be king. *So it's true.*

Lorana had a thousand questions. She wanted to shake Edenia by her arms until she answered every one of them.

How, Eden? she thought. *How could you accept a marriage proposal from the man who kidnapped Erick, who procured the poison that killed my father—a king who didn't blame you for Parlisis, but doted on you as if you were another daughter? Was this a forced arrangement? Did you have any say?*

. . . and why were you silent when Jason and I wrote?

Lorana attempted a smile. "I missed you, too, Eden."

Edenia held her headdress to keep it from flying off in the wind. Seeing Andrew, she lit up, mouth agape. "*NO!*" She flitted from the princess to the knight and back again, eyes wide with disbelief. "*Windkin?* Last we saw each other, you were a squire! Barely able to lift a sword." She squeezed his bicep. "Do I sense . . . *muscles?!*"

"Sir Andrew proved himself a most puissant warrior in the king's wars in Uzland," Lorana said with an easy smile.

The young knight smirked. He'd always been smitten with the prieslenne, just like Jason and every other man with at least one good eye. "Hello, Eden."

Edenia's guardsman tightened the line of his lips. "You will address the prieslenne as 'Your Blessedness,'" he said imperiously.

Her Blessedness rolled her eyes. "Forgive this one," she said. "Sir Vayne Adrias captains my guardsmen. He swore a vow to protect me, and it's made him intolerable." *Protect you so that we can't take you hostage again*, the princess intuited. "Medecians are utterly serious bores."

"So serious their stool grinds to diamonds in their bellies, we Loranians say," Lorana quipped.

The woman who embodied the will of twelve gods broke into undignified laughter, snorting like a pig. A look at the stoic Vayne Adrias only intensified her snorts. She wiped tears from her eyes, sniffling.

"You've more the king in you than your Medecian mother, in that case," Edenia said. She sobered quickly. "Oh, Ana. I'm so sorry." She roped the steward in for a hug, then released her, straightening her posture for an alien formalness. "On behalf of my blessed father, Priestking Parlisis, I come bearing gifts that he hopes will ease the pain of the great king's passing."

Without needing to be asked, Intercessors peeled off from the procession and returned lugging wooden chests aflow with gold and jewels. They plonked the treasure down in front of Andrew, paying Anyasha disapproving looks through the eye holes of their masks.

Anyasha endured them with a coolness Elzura's Children honed over their lives. "You mean the great king's murder," she chimed. At a blistering look from Adrias, she added belatedly, "Your Blessedness."

Edenia turned to her, as if she were just seeing her for the first time. She smiled sunnily. "I can see And—*Sir* Andrew," she corrected herself with a wink at the knight, "isn't the only one to have grown like a Great Tree! What a beauty you've become, Yasha. Your suitors must be countless." She held Lorana's gaze for a split second. "And yes . . . My flower, I wept when I heard of your father's murder by those foul peasants."

"By Elvarenists," Anyasha piped. "Your Blessedness."

Smoldering, Adrias stepped forward; Andrew snaked a hand about his hilt. "I can tell this kingdom needs a righteous king," Adrias said. He glared at Anyasha. "In the Kingdom of Medecia, we remember Elzura's Curse. There, Elzura's Children would sooner fling themselves into the sea than contradict Her Blessedness in a devout man's presence."

Edenia began to speak, but the steward rode roughshod over her. "But you're not in Medecia," she said icily. "You're in Loran—*my* kingdom. You're unloved here. And no matter how many ships you sail with, or how many ghouls slither here with you, you're just visiting. Pray you don't visit the Red Tower."

"The Head speaks," Andrew said with a lopsided grin.

The knights knifed each other with their stares. Making peace fell upon Her Blessedness, a thing she'd always done well. Edenia apologized for her man's conduct; the Medecian bore the indignity in silence, looking like he'd pass a diamond.

"If recollection serves, a temple stands not far from these shores," the prieslenne said. "King Hexar once brought us north to visit it. I'd look upon Saint Alban's Temple and light a candle inside in his memory. If Loran's steward agrees, of course."

Lorana agreed.

One of her men gave up his palfrey to the prieslenne. The pair rode ahead of their forces at a steady trot, speaking in low tones as they navigated hills abloom with purple heather. Not wishing to give Edenia's handlers any cause for quarrel, Lorana stuck to superficial topics—the prieslenne's voyage, Northland weather, and the like.

It was an odd and uncomfortable feeling, to have shared her bed and endless nights spilling all to this woman, only to pretend that none of it had happened.

Some miles inland, a seagull tried frantically to outmaneuver a griff, giving them reprieve from the awkwardness with a riveting chase. The distressed gull wheeled through the sky, wailing, until the king's bird shot at its prey like an arrow and ended the game.

Gull feathers wilted around them like wintered leaves, delighting the prieslenne. "I've missed the wonders of Loran," she said, beaming as she held out her palm to catch a feather. "Griffs. Silverstone. Swordwood. Everything."

And your family here? Lorana thought. *Did you miss them?*

After an hour's riding, they came upon the splashing River Colossus, crossing a bridge so rickety it had to have been built in King Lathros's time. Saint Alban's wasn't long after that. The temple's pale steeples and columns rose before them, blurring together like a desert mirage.

Lorana swung off her horse; Edenia waited for Adrias to help her dismount. The five of them, Lorana, Edenia, Anyasha, Andrew, and the Medecian, walked to the temple's ashy doors. Remarkably, the door handles and hinges seemed in working order, if rusted orange.

"Sir Vayne, you'll stay here while we light the candle, and I'll hear no argument," Edenia said with a highborn's practiced command. "I can feel Sacreis and Divna's presence in this dead place." She tugged off her silken glove and laid her hand on a door, as if she sensed something alive in the rot. "They're still here."

Vayne Adrias and Andrew Windkin seemed to be on the same side as they took issue with the notion of either woman being alone without them. The prieslenne silenced her hound with a stern look; Lorana brought hers to heel by reassuring him that he'd remain within earshot, after all.

Anyasha wasn't reassured. Her look was a knife to the gut. *I love you, Yasha,* Lorana wanted to tell her, *but this is necessary. Not least because Eden lied. We've never been to this temple.*

The doors gave a rattling scream upon opening, and again when they shut. Inside, Saint Alban's looked like the world had ended under its holey, vaulted ceiling. Shafts of sunlight fell on overturned pews, crumbled statues, the chancel's dusty altar, a busted floor strangled by weeds.

Lorana kept silent as they walked past pews, their steps clacking. A dangling-legged insect flew too close, flushing her right ear.

Away from her guard, Edenia seemed less smiley, and less formal, smaller, even. "Saint Alban's used to be the only gutted temple that still stood in Loran," she said. "Now there are two, from what I hear."

"In South Farcombe, yes," Lorana admitted. "Peasants are desperate, and your father's grip on the Assembly prevents me and any king after me from stopping the priests who split up families and take their children to your temples."

That wrinkled the prieslenne's perfect brow. She slid her arm around Lorana's, drawing her close. "I don't agree with it," she said softly. "Is that why Jason fights in the Trials?"

Lorana shed her mask, rounding. "He risks his life to keep Loran from sliding back into war," she said. "And you've come back with foreign warships to pressure the Worthy Assembly into crowning Shaddon over him—your *true* husband."

Her tone cracked Edenia's visage. She'd rarely—if ever—been terse with her friend, her lover, the prieslenne. "You don't understand, Ana. You shouldn't have gaoled Lord Gram, taken his son's hands."

I've taken more than Justen's hands, she wanted to boast, but that had to stay a state secret.

"Your father plots my family's destruction. His conspiracy killed my father and Erick, and drove Garrett to madness." She seized Edenia's left hand in a way that would sorely test Vayne Adrias. "You lied to get me alone. Tell me, Eden—is Shaddon's ring proof that you're part of this?"

The famous warmth in her eyes faded. Edenia ripped her hand

away, chin trembling. "Of all people, you know I *hate* my father," she said in a shaky, hurt voice full of anger.

It was true, she did. But it hadn't always been so.

Edenia had been a child at the Silver Walls when the Long Summer Rebellion broke out, taken hostage temporarily, then permanently, after Shaddon stole Erick in the night. At first, she'd isolated herself in her West Tower, opening her chapel door only to take food and water or scurry to the garderobe like a frightened mouse. Passing under her high window every day, Lorana would listen to her wet-voiced prayers to Maetha, Helsar, and Divna.

This had lasted for more than a year. The weepy-faced little girl had been a ghost, and Hexar, furious with everyone and the world for Sarah's death and his son's kidnapping, had boasted at court about how content he was to let his enemy's daughter suffer in silence . . .

That was, until Lorana one day plucked a daisy from the maze, snuck up the West Tower, and slid the flower under the chapel door.

After that day, the little girl became someone else, bubbly, sweet-natured, and fond of playing games with the Eddenhold children. She became a presence around the castle, winning the king's affections. Not long after that, she requested a change of rooms to the East Tower, where Hexar's daughter by Alyse and his son by Sarah resided together. From that point forward, it was as if she'd always been with the Eddenholds—indeed, as if she'd been one of them, another child from another dead wife. No one could imagine the royal family without her.

Yet as the years went by, as Winter and Summer Solstices passed them, something else emerged. Edenia stopped praying in her chapel. She didn't talk about her father or mother unless asked. Once, Romara, heavy with Heather, had requested over dinner that Edenia pray in her father's ways; the usually serene prieslenne had stood abruptly and left without an excuse.

How she'd wept two years ago. "I don't even know him, I don't want to go back," Lorana remembered Eden blubbering on her chest weeks before her departure. She'd tried to console her, tried to tell her this was important—that Hexar wanted a thaw in his frosty relations with the priestking—but nothing she said had given either of them much solace. "He abandoned me. He's a monster. I hate him, I'll *always* hate him, flower."

The prieslenne tore off her headdress. Her lustrous flaxen hair spilled down her shoulders. "You have no idea just how claustrophobic this stupid fabric is," she said. "I've been made to wear it the day I arrived on that miserable fucking island."

Lorana had her answer. She'd built walls around herself in preparation for this reunion, and they came tumbling down as Edenia, the *true* Eden, flung her arms around her, burying her face in the nape of her neck. "I missed you, flower."

The steward held her snugly, smiling. "And I, you." Eden lingered for a moment, eyeing her lips with long-lashed eyes. Lorana thought of Jason when she pulled away. "Who forced this on you?" she asked with a glance at the ring.

Eden worked Shaddon's ring off her finger hurriedly, her lips pressed together tightly, as if every second it remained on her flesh caused excruciating pain. She glared at the ring in her palm, looking as if she meant to hurl it into the temple's dark recesses and never retrieve it.

"Who else?" she said. "The one who sent me to work and threaten you into his bidding. I refused him, Ana . . . at least at first." She held Lorana with a vulnerable look that felt like a gut punch, tears globing in her eyelashes. "The last two years have been hell for me. I *told* you I didn't want to go back, *I told you!*"

In the ruins of Saint Alban's, she confirmed what Lorana had suspected. Eden had at least tried to form a bond with her father, but he'd treated her cruelly, locking her away in *another* tower, where the Daughters of Divna worked to reeducate her. Parlisis saw in his estranged daughter a means to an end in his calculus to retake Loran and invade the Free Kingdoms. All to wipe out the Free Beliefs that threatened his iron grip.

Eden hadn't met Shaddon before her engagement to him; she'd

merely been informed of it. She'd play the part assigned to her, as wife, diplomat, and—once Shaddon bribed or killed the other claimants to sit the Silver Walls—broodmare. And if she refused, she'd be sold to the prince that Parlisis sought for Lorana to wed.

Lorana barked with harsh laughter; she cared not if Sir Vayne Adrias heard. "Your father and his delusions," she said. "He really thinks I'd agree to marry Kar Kravack, my father's nemesis?" *So that's your proposal, dear uncle. You'll regret it.*

"Kar Kravack seeks to legitimize Uzland," Eden explained. "The way to do that is through a pact with the Lonely Isle. A noble lady's hand in marriage would be the ink on that treaty. With one of us as his bride, the Lonely Isle would gain a million new souls, and Uzland a place among civilized realms."

The steward clenched her teeth. *The lengths to which our enemies have gone to destroy us, Father.* "How did you lose your wedding band?" she asked.

She flickered at Shaddon's ring, then Lorana, bewildered. "How did you . . .?"

Wordlessly, Lorana reached into her cleavage and yanked out a ring that made Shaddon's look like the work of a Common smithy. Edenia stared at the silverstone haze encircling Jason's ring.

"Charles Burke found this on the assassin who tried to kill Jason." She gave it to Edenia, who rolled it between her fingers. "An assassin sent by the *Rose Guild*, Eden."

"I lost this ring a year ago. My father would've known it was from Jason . . . but he or Shaddon would've paid the Rose Guild to orchestrate the attempt on his life."

"Or Gram Sothos. They worked together to kill Father."

Edenia shook her head, frustrated. "Jason should be at the Silver Walls. Not here. Why would he put himself in harm's way by entering the Trials?" She scowled. "*Why'd you let him?*"

Lorana let out a *hmmf*. "You wedded the honorable idiot. I wrote a forgery in Father's hand putting him in the succession, but he knew it'd likely cause a war. He didn't want to see our kingdom suffer another

Long Summer, or worse." *We have you to blame for this, too, Drexan. May Charles find you so I can be there to interrogate you myself.*

"Worse has come, Ana." Tears rolled down Eden's cheeks, smudging her rouge. "I love Jason. I love him still. Have you . . . have you told him?" Her voice squeaked when she said *him.*

"Not yet." Lorana took her into her embrace again. She bit her lip as she consoled her, stroking her back. Her blood boiled for Eden, for her father, for everyone caught up in Parlisis's far-reaching webs. These were evil times.

"Sir Vayne—he's my turnkey, not my protector," Edenia sobbed into Lorana's shoulder, tears wetting her gown. "I've always been a hostage; I am one again. It's never stopped. I'll be someone's prisoner until the day I die, Ana."

Lorana lifted her chin with her finger, looking into her glassy blue eyes. "No, you won't. I'm going to kill Shaddon. And when Jason sits the Silver Walls, he'll unite Loran under four wings. You'll never need to leave us or fear your father again. And you won't be a hostage here."

Edenia smiled through her tears. "I missed you, flower."

CHAPTER 10

The Laurels

thousand lords, lower gentry, clergy, merchants, and families shuffled through the Colossus's benches. Some men bantered affably. Some cast wagers on who'd survive the First Trial. None wasted time in claiming seats.

Evan took it all in grimly. The sight of a tiltyard in the arena lent the amphitheater a charged air, like the excitement of a hunting party hot on something's trail. These sightseers had traveled long distances to witness bloodshed. *My nephew risks his very life to keep this kingdom out of war,* he thought, *and the kingdom salivates to see whether he'll lose his head.*

He scanned the faces ringing the Colossus from his seat beside the Cloudlands lords. High in the King's Box stood the princess, dressed in fine chamblet silks, listing on a balustrade. She looked mildly distracted as she conversed with Frederick Midliche. Jon Redoak and Peshar Grathos sat well away from her, fanning themselves in the heat.

Evan was glad of Lorana's presence. Claimants always broke rules, which the judges had to settle. In that event, the steward and Midliche would cancel out Redoak and Grathos. She was Jason's first line of defense.

He spotted Jacob Sulley. The Master Reader had shaved his head to stubble in mourning for the Lord of Westerliche. Tomas Fawkes's men had discovered their lord with his throat opened in his own pavilion, naked and sprawled out on his blood-saturated bed. It'd happened during the Meet of First Declaration.

No one knew who'd slain Fawkes, or how anyone could've slipped past his guards, but everyone had a list of suspects.

Not shockingly, Evan himself topped most lists. Fawkes had been the only Free Believer in contention for the Walls and, thus, the greatest threat to Jason's support base in the Assembly.

After the Meet, Evan had launched a charm offensive, dispatching amiable lords like Ulbridge and even Lorana to mollify Free Believers.

Jason's claim required them. They'd pointed to the real culprits—the men who'd assassinated the king and Greg Thorngale.

Grimly, Evan saw that more than a few Petitioners in his Loyal Company had stubbly scalps, just like the Master Reader. *Remember your oaths, you loyal men,* he thought. *Rathos swore you one and all to Jason, should no one win all three Trials. Defy your orders, and I'll see that you join Lord Fawkes . . .*

The speeches and prayers were short. Rising to applause from the lords and priests and scowls from just about everyone else, Redoak called on claimants to show bravery. Adjusting his miter as it slumped forward, Grathos recognized the guest of honor.

The priestking's daughter lived up to the songs about her, this much was true. Lustered with golden tresses that cascaded down her front, she had a kind face, a comely figure that turned heads, and an easy touch that won admirers or at least didn't deepen the revulsion among enemies of her religion and father. *I see why you so love her, nephew. But better Shaddon slip a ring on the Most-Sought Hand in the Thirteen Kingdoms than you.*

Lorana had shared news about the betrothal with them, and against Evan's wishes, with Jason himself. Oh, his nephew had gone to rage. Grabbed his sword. Made stupid threats.

Evan had been glad of these tidings. On the one hand, the betrothal made it less likely that Assemblymen would take any rumors of Jason's moonlight marriage to Edenia seriously.

It also whittled away support for Shaddon. Nothing put fear into the Fourth Wing's supporters more than the prospect of Parlisis's own flesh and blood becoming queen consort. *It's for the best, nephew,* Evan thought. *Very, very much for the best.*

The arbiters of these Kingstrials rose to speak.

The Speaker of the Wing of Knights spoke to the need for fair contests, and then it was the steward's turn. In the shade of canopy, Lorana eulogized those whom their enemies had slain, threatening Loran with a new war—her brother Erick, her king father, and the late Greg Thorngale, of course.

Shouts echoed from the arena's northern portcullis. Evan thought it was another herald, come to share tidings of another claimant's murder. He'd welcome that.

Something absurd emerged from under the portcullis. A mummer wobbled out on wooden stilts at least twelve feet tall, draped with a loom's worth of pearl brocade. Rocks spilled out of his padded bosom as he maneuvered uneasily on the stilts, teetering, arms outstretched for balance. Nestled in his brown hair lay the mockery of a pointed crown.

The mummer was supposed to be Lorana.

It was a message from their enemies in the Assembly. *You may rule as if you were king,* it went unspoken, *but to us, you're a joke.*

Laughter issued around the Colossus. Many Assemblymen glanced at Lorana like children in on a joke about their teacher. Redoak and Grathos basked in her humiliation, red-faced and chuckling.

And to her credit, the stone maiden joined the laughter.

Swift as the wind, a rider sped out from the shade of the southern portcullis on a stallion dressed in his house's colors. The jeers faded. Outpacing guards, the rider leaned out from his saddle. He whacked the stilts with the edge of his sword, throwing the mummer into the tent of his sprawling brocade gown.

Cheers and laughter flew up from the benches, from Evan and the Bull and his noblemen loudest of all. Jason rode around the Colossus, hand clenched in the air, clouds of sand frothing in his wake. Watching him from the box, Lorana beamed at her half-brother.

Trumpets drowned out the applause and laughter as men carried the mummer out of the sprawl of his dress.

Nice try, discrediting Lorana to discredit Jason, he thought with a look at Redoak. *But all you've done is make my nephew seem more the hero.*

Astride their mounts, the four other claimants bounded into the arena from the northern entrance, some encased in impressive armor. Tom Gelder wore a helm adorned with his sigil's two-headed dragon, their snouts and tails curling about his visor. Gavin Thorngale outdid Gelder with a helm wreathed in elaborate steel antlers.

The arrogance of these Thorngales, Evan thought. *I hope Jason's lance snags those antlers and breaks Gavin's neck.*

Of course, no one was more arrogant than the late king's brother. Shaddon rode up on a white stallion with a whipping mane. He looked ill-suited in armor fit for someone ten years his junior. Free Believers pitched insults at Parlisis's champion as he struggled to steer his mount into line with the others.

Evan thought Sam Wuthers the best-suited for this match, despite the dearth of applause. The pauper lord wore nothing flamboyant, merely a visored helm and armor over chain mail.

His nephew had donned armor hammered in Gildebirg, the toughest on the continent, his gift from Trevor Wexley.

Jason had balked when Evan insisted that he wear the heavy black plates, fearful of compromising speed and agility.

"That's the best armor this side of Ansara," Evan had told him. "It's capable of even resisting swordwood."

"But the Worthy Assembly *banned* steel in this contest."

"Wear it, and trust me," Evan had told him. *As I trust the source who told me to make you wear it,* he'd refrained from adding.

Beckoned by the steward, the five claimants formed up in a line, alongside their mounts. Their squires came running up with their long lances. Evan made a quick search of the instruments for telltale signs of tampering, but if someone had painted his lance, he couldn't tell from this distance.

My source told me the truth, Evan reassured himself.

Descending from the King's Box, Grathos strode to the arena's center to pray. He asked each claimant in turn if they had any cause in their hearts the gods might grant in victory.

Shaddon urged his black stallion out of line. "The favor of Sacreis, that I might rule with his divine guidance over the First King's first kingdom, long bereft of its priestking," he said, to denunciations from Free Believers. He stretched his arm at the prieslenne. "And Divna's blessing—that I may love my wife, Her Blessedness, as I will love this kingdom."

"God save us," a merchant nearby muttered.

Jason twisted in his stirrups. He narrowed his eyes at the king's brother. "Justice," Evan's nephew said, loud and true, "not only for my father, but for every man, woman, and child in this kingdom."

Evan and the Cloudlands lords sounded their approval.

Ahorse, Sam Wuthers trotted out of line. "Justice for my house and me," he said, looking as small as his cause. He shot his rival, Gelder, a smoldering look.

Chuckling, Tom Gelder said, "I will sit the Walls in glory."

Gavin Thorngale lifted his lance, and all eyes followed its accusing tip to Evan. "Lord Jason wants justice for his father. I want justice for *mine*. The Loyal Company killed the Old Oak of Thessela. Justar grant my brothers and me vengeance against Evan the Traitor."

Evan weathered the stares, asides, and jeers in silence.

A lottery of straws determined the first match. Thorngale and Shaddon would joust. Everyone for Jason's claim but Evan seemed to breathe more easily. *Thorngale and Shaddon could be a way of making sure that neither dies,* he thought. He wouldn't put anything past these wolves. Even so, he nurtured the hope that both men would die in the sand today.

The Kingstrials began with the call of a single trumpet.

Thorngale kicked his horse in its flanks, spewing sand in his wake. Barreling down the lists, he couched his lance in the crook of his arm, his shield raised protectively over his chest and neck.

At the other end of the lists, Shaddon couldn't seem to maneuver his stallion forward. He looked an amateur as he tapped the horse's flanks with his heels, to nickering protest and head-thrashing. Parlisis's allies fixed their attention on their man as he struggled. Other Assemblymen jeered lustily at the humiliation.

Her Blessedness watched all this attentively, Evan saw.

With Thorngale closing in fast, Shaddon finally blundered into a clumsy charge. The antlered rider leaned in so far to his left he looked like to fall off, doubling the reach of his lance. His weapon struck Shaddon in his chest, exploding into a thousand chips. Off ran the stallion, nearly trampling the king's brother.

Squires rushed out to help Shaddon up. Thorngale rode triumphantly around the arena, pumping his fist as his house and allies chanted, "*KING GAVIN, KING GAVIN!*" Cantering by, the antlered lord smoldered at Evan.

Wexrenn pointed out what everyone else had observed, breathless, as if he were the first to see it: Hexar's brother had a pronounced limp. Shaddon looked his age as he hobbled off in the arms of squires, to the apothecary on duty inside his pavilion. Evan spied blood on the man's greaves.

Wexley seemed to see it, too. "A shard from Thorngale's lance must've struck him in his thigh," the Bull relayed.

Evan traded a heartened look with Jason. This was victory already. *An injury will force Shaddon to name a champion, and champions cannot win Trials for their claimants,* Evan thought. *Perhaps there's hope to be had in these crown games after all . . .*

The chants settled. Thorngale pinched another lance from a squire, trotted back to his end of the lists.

Sam Wuthers won the lottery to face Thorngale next. He equipped his lance, snapped shut his visor, and waved to his lady wife and son as he galloped off to the western side of the lists.

No cringeworthy mistakes, this time. The lords charged each other at nearly the same second, hardened on approach, aiming for the other's unprotected part. Shields scraped as the two men swept past each other, lances swaying like branches in a storm.

"I'll wager Thorngale takes him this time," Clabbard told Ulbridge.

"Is that an open wager?" Wexrenn asked him, grinning. He rolled a golden coin across his knuckles. "Two lorens on Darren Stormsword's brother?"

Evan frowned. Seeing that, Wexley rumbled to his vassals, "If you bet, you should profit from King Jason's success."

And not from the victory of the man who's vowed to take my head, thank you very much, Evan thought darkly.

Other Assemblymen showed less fealty to their kings. They gleefully palmed coins that winked in the sun. *How fat these suckling pigs will grow when more claimants die.*

For the good of the realm, Willard the Wise had confined bloodshed over crowns to the Colossus, to these Kingstrials, but men did as men had always done and wrung out profit from the contests. Critics of the Wing of the Commons tended to overlook that peasants had once banned gambling in the Kingstrials, quite virtuously.

Back in position, Thorngale and Wuthers dug their heels in their mounts' flanks and bolted. The Old Oak's son lurched forward in his stirrups for another long reach with lance. The pauper lord emulated Thorngale's winning strategy, slackening to his left to extend his reach. His lance tasted breastplate in an explosion of wood chips. Thorngale tumbled off his horse, into the sand.

A stunned silence fell over the Colossus.

Looking as shocked as anyone else, the members of House Wuthers thundered up, stomping and chanting for their king. Gamblers like Clabbard promptly paid up and refused to play anymore. Despite Wuthers being a rival, Evan found himself stirring with admiration for the nobleman. Not unlike House Sinclair, Wuthers's family had long been looked down on, an oft-repeated joke among more prominent lords.

Gavin Thorngale ripped off his helm, hurled it to the sand. Drunk on anger, he called for his sword. His squire ran out and handed him his blade. Observers leaned forward, eager to see how Wuthers would respond to this challenge.

Respond Wuthers did, with a jaunty poke of his lance that hit Thorngale just below his neck, threw him back to the sand, and won a chorus of laughter across the arena.

Thorngale's squires helped the red-faced lord off the field, and that was that.

Now there were three.

Jason and Gelder plucked at their straws. Winning, Gelder leapt onto his mount, a mare black as oil. A squire brought him a lance but he declined with a headshake and motioned for another, a gnarled, ruddy pole that caught Evan's eye.

Equipping the lance, the lord trotted by his rival Wuthers and muttered some slander that no one else heard. Wuthers lifted his visor for a red-hot stare, clanged it shut, and snatched up another lance.

"*Unhorse him, Father!*" squealed the young Sam Wuthers.

Everyone, even the steward and lord speakers, watched a contest centuries in the making as closely as they would one between Jason and Shaddon. Gelder and Wuthers were age-old enemies, as their grand-sires had been enemies. The killing of King Lathros had forced their ancestors to choose sides against each other and led to House Gelder taking control of Sunder Way, Loran's most profitable trade route, over which House Wuthers had held sway.

Evan shook off his own memories of that damnable road.

The two men couched their lances and bolted off, awash in dust fuming up from their mounts' hooves. Sailing down the lists, neither rival wavered. Wuthers huddled in his stirrups, his shield low, perhaps seeking a test skirmish. Gelder aimed his lance straight at his ene-my's heart.

A squeal of shattered steel echoed around the arena. Wuthers crashed headfirst in the sand, impaled on Gelder's misshapen lance.

Spectators inhaled sharply. Above the pandemonium came Lady Wuthers's gut-wrenching wails.

My source told me the truth, Evan thought grimly.

Gelder rode by exultantly. Wrenching his bloodstained lance from Wuthers's corpse, he made a congratulatory lap around the arena, to rowdy chants from supporters and full-throated denunciations from just about everyone else.

"That lance should've shattered," Ulbridge said, stunned.

"We *banned* steel in this contest," Wexrenn complained, as if he'd been active in that vote, and hadn't slept through it.

"That's not steel," Evan said. *One thing can pierce armor as if it were silk. And there's no way a pauper lord like Gelder could afford it . . .*

Gelder had used the one metal sharper than steel—a limb hewn from swordwood tree. The limb had been painted to look like a lance.

He'd broken a rule agreed upon at the Declaration.

Summoned to the King's Box, Gelder trotted up with his illegal lance, Wuthers's blood still dripping off it. Lorana and the speakers interrogated the claimant, a tempest of angry cries and demands swelling up all around them.

A handful of apothecaries, all sworn to other claimants, descended on Wuthers. He was determined to be dead and carried out of the arena by his sworn nobles, a few of them openly weeping. Defeated, much of House Wuthers and his men-at-arms departed with the pauper lord's widow and son. Some gathered below the King's Box, demanding Gelder's head.

Everyone was watching Gelder or the speakers, but Evan watched Jason.

His nephew was in mortal danger. Everything depended on Lorana and Midliche canceling out a verdict by Redoak and Grathos. If the speakers couldn't agree, the Assemblymen here could vote to expel Gelder. Evan—no, Jason himself—needed the Companymen to rally.

And if none of that worked in Jason's favor, the Bull's gift to his nephew had to hold up against swordwood . . .

Half an hour went by, all eyes pinned to the King's Box, where Lorana argued heatedly with the other judges. Finally, Peshar Grathos shuffled downstairs to the arena. The steward looked overcome with fury.

"We, the lord speakers," he said, "have heard you, *ahem,* and we have determined no unworth." The protests issued deafeningly, but the High Bishop's voice pierced through them, amplified by the amphitheater's acoustics. "Lord Tom used no, ahem, *actual* steel in his contest. Therefore, we hold that he shall remain, and joust with the last contender."

Now, all eyes turned to Jason.

The Bull cursed and raged and swore. Overwhelmed by protests, the High Bishop receded to the King's Box. Lorana stalked off, shoving past Redoak, hands clenched at her sides. *Midliche voted with Redoak and Grathos,* Evan realized. *Is the Fox just another wolf, easily bought?*

Ulbridge blanched. "We need to lead Jason off the sand."

Evan shook his head. "Trust in Gildebirg, Zarold." *It's the best I could do for him, Sarah.* If Jason were to leave the arena, he'd forfeit the Trials. *Even if they cheat him out of his crown in these games, we need him to play to the bitter end, and live . . .*

Gelder spurred his mount on and took up position. Jason ran to his side of the lists, couching his paltry wooden lance in his shoulder.

They charged. Gelder flew down the lists, his swordwood lance pointed at Jason's cuirass. Evan found himself praying to a god he hadn't called upon since his sister's death.

Halfway there, Jason lurched forward in his stirrups and angled his lance at the throat of Gelder's horse. Blood and sand filled the air.

Mists of sand settled. Swept up by relief, Evan forgot all gods and prayers. Gelder crawled out of harm's way, belly-down, worm that he was. His dying horse flailed about, blood gushing from the hole in his neck that Jason's lance had made.

Jason galloped over to their benches, letting admirers touch his outstretched hand and share in the glory. Chants swept the Colossus.

"*WARCHILD!*" spectators cried. "*WARCHILD!*"

Evan ignored the applause, his eyes trained on the wily Gelder, who could still challenge Jason to a trial by sword. The cunt didn't disappoint. Staggering up, he threw off his helm and shouted for a squire, who sprinted into the arena carrying his scabbard. Gelder grabbed his hilt, planted his foot on the boy's chest, and pushed off to free his sword. He made a beeline for Jason, his eyes low and dark.

Evan's heart was in his throat; he knew Jason too well by this point. *That sword could be swordwood, Jason,* he thought. *Stay ahorse, as Wuthers did. Keep the high ground.*

Jason dismounted, but of course. Drawing denunciations from every direction, Gelder didn't allow Jason to arm himself but swung viciously with his blade. He made an upswing, then a side slash, then an upswing again, and at every maneuver the bastard prince fell back on his heel. Wexley's gift slowed Jason down, but it proved its worth a thousand times over as sparks flew off his pauldrons and breastplate.

Jason's squire, a Cloudlands boy, ran up behind Gelder, nearly there with sheathed sword . . . and the cheat swiveled and whacked the scabbard out of his hands so that it whirled into the sand, too far for Jason to retrieve it.

There was no rule against this, no rule to bend or fight for. In a match like this, men depended on honor. And Gelder had none.

Jason had but one play left, and he unsheathed it from his sword-belt. The rondel dagger he wielded was feet shy of the length of Gelder's sword. Yet even with that dagger he began to block Gelder's downward arcs. He stepped and slid to evade the next slash, and in the same fluid motion brought the rondel dagger down hard on his rival's sword hand.

Jason landed with Gelder in the sand. He suddenly had the man disarmed and the point of his rondel dagger at his neck.

The Colossus's acoustics allowed everyone to hear Jason clearly through the jubilation: "We weren't to fight to the death with steel in this contest," he said thickly, "but yield, and I'll spare you."

Gelder held his hands steady in the air.

The four presiding judges left the high box, filing down steps to the crimson-splotched sands.

All smiles, Midliche handed off the crown of laurels to the steward. "*THE FIRST VICTOR!*" she cried when she had silence. Lorana extended the laurels to her brother.

Several lords bade their daughters stand and called their names as if they were merchants peddling fish. "Here, my lord, her name's Rose, she's your Virgin," cried one. Another said, "Mine is Gaela, more beautiful than any woman in the thirteen kingdoms."

Riding past, Jason didn't lay the laurels on Rose, or Gaela, or any other woman. He defied everyone, Evan especially.

CHAPTER 11

Golden Hair

 won the First Trial today," Jason said, "and yet it feels as if I died on Gelder's illegal lance instead of Wuthers."

His allies stood or sat in silence, their expressions dark and telling. Wexley and his lords crowded by the end of the table, the clinks of Russell Wexrenn's spoon the pavilion's only sounds as he diligently fished out stringy meat from his broth. Lorana sat hunched over, her chin in her palm. Her downcast eyes captured the pavilion's mood.

Surely you understand, Ana, he thought. But she didn't seem to.

His uncle festered by the pavilion's entrance, breathing steadily through his nose, arms folded. His face was nearly as flush as the red of his doublet. He looked up from his feet, eyes seething. This was the first time Jason had ever seen the man so angry. He didn't like it.

"You did well, my king," Ulbridge chimed helpfully. "With Wuthers dead, you've three more claimants to defeat in the arena. The next contest is a deadly one, and you will kill them."

"I'd say you should've killed Gelder," Clabbard added, "but your mercy bought you goodwill."

"*Goodwill.*" Evan sounded like he might laugh.

"Even so," Clabbard said, "Shaddon will invoke the *mas in adversas* rule to stay in the game." He warmed his hands over a brazier popping with embers. "Your zealot uncle will name for himself a champion, and we'll fight *him* in the—"

"Remind me, Lord Jason," Evan cut in, waxing a thumb meditatively over the blond hair on his chin, "how does one win the

Kingstrials? In Loran, how does a man become king?"

Wexrenn wiped broth off his chin with a forearm. "*King* Jason," he corrected him irritably.

The lord hadn't finished saying *Jason* when Evan shouted, "*HE'S NOT KING YET!*"

His rebuke shook Wexrenn into dropping his broth spoon. Seeming to disapprove of Sinclair's tone, Wexley narrowed his eyes.

Rogir Levan must've heard from outside, because he poked his head in, concerned, and withdrew when Lorana gestured him out angrily.

Jason saw the trap as easily as he'd seen Gelder's attempt to maneuver his swordwood lance at his heart. He decided he'd play, anyway, and crown Edenia. He'd won the first test in this tournament.

He'd reminded his prisoner wife of his love for her—that he'd defend her against his family's enemies. The Colossus had fallen deathly quiet after he crowned her. Shaddon was said to have been livid. It made Jason feel strong tonight.

Strong, that was, until cold reality seeped in.

"By winning all three—" Jason began.

"*WRONG.*" Evan gritted his teeth. "'Three Trials, three Wings—'"

"'Only the Worthy crown their kings,' aye," Jason said angrily. "Yet Hexar won all three of his Trials. The Worthy honored the rules and anointed his head with oil."

Wexley nursed a cup of mead. "I was there," he intoned.

"But rules can be bent," Evan said stridently. "Or broken outright, with everyone watching and unable to do anything but curse their gods, just as Gelder proved today. Broken rules kill men as well as their claims."

Clabbard scowled at no one and everything as he stroked his beard. "Peshar Grathos and Jon Redoak are cheating cunts," he swore. "The laws forbid speakers from taking sides."

"But they're half of the judges," Lorana said. She ran a hand through her brown curls, irritated. "That's Sinclair's point. Rules bend or break in these contests, but it won't matter if enough Assemblymen support my brother."

Evan looked triumphant, his point made by the princess herself. "After today's budding romance, we don't have enough kingmakers," he said icily. "Jacob Sulley is leaving. He's taking nearly every reader in the Wing of Clergy. We *needed* them."

He could've as well said that Parlisis himself had entered the Kingstrials. Everyone in the pavilion looked stunned.

"Leaving," Wexrenn repeated dully. "As in . . ."

"As in, they're leaving the Assembly, the Golden Meadows, and these Kingstrials. In protest." Evan chuckled in disbelief.

As if that were that, and Jason's claim were dead.

Lorana gazed at Evan, half in consternation, half in anger. "You speak as if those readers *were* your Company, Sinclair."

Evan flickered at her, then Jason. "It wouldn't matter if they are. They're disillusioned. They decamp and leave at first light, all one hundred fifty-seven. They wouldn't have backed Elvarenists like Shaddon, Gelder, or Thorngale. With Fawkes dead, Jason was their hope—*their last hope*—until he crowned Priestking Parlisis's daughter with laurels and told the world they're more than childhood friends."

Wexrenn flickered from Evan to Jason. "Are they?"

Unbelievable . . . Jason stepped toward his uncle. "Is Ana right? Is *this* why I risked my name allying with you and your band of traitors?"

The nobleman snatched Jason's ear as if he were a child. "An attentive ear. That's what I asked of you. Did you not hear me—?"

The move felt as galling as it did degrading, and after a day of unhorsing men and watching blood spill, it made Jason want to break his uncle's jaw.

He slapped Evan's hand out of his face. "Yes, I love her," he growled. "My uncle worked with Sothos to kill my father. Years before, he seized my brother Erick, and then conspired to have him slain. *Now he weds Edenia?*" He clenched his teeth. "I know that I behaved a fool. But I can't . . . *Shaddon can't take everything from me.*"

There was contempt in Evan's laugh. "But now, he will. You're so much like—" He stopped just short, but Jason knew what he meant.

You're so much like Hexar, Jason understood, *a fool king who left*

Loran weaker and made these Trials necessary in the first place.

Jason grimaced. "I love her, Evan. Do you even know what love is?"

His uncle suddenly looked shaken, as if he'd seen Hexar's ghost.

Jason sought out a sign of support from Lorana, but she refused eye contact. *Even you, sister?* he thought. *You, who told me about Edenia's forced marriage to begin with?*

Edenia had been forced into this twisted relationship by her calculating father, curse him. It'd kept Jason awake and restless all night. He'd paced for hours. He'd dreamed up mad dreams of grabbing his sword, sneaking into his enemy's camp, killing everyone in his path to free her, his wife, his innocent wife.

Jason had almost ventured out . . . but he'd known that to trespass into Shaddon's camp would be to invite the removal of his claim, perhaps his head. Redoak and Grathos wouldn't miss an easy opportunity to keep him off the throne.

He'd known better than to pull a stunt like that, to crown his clandestine wife the Virgin of Venas. But with adrenaline pumping through him after the joust, seeing his wife up there in the benches, alone, he'd wanted them all to know.

He'd wanted Shaddon to know.

Above all, he'd wanted *Edenia* to know. He'd sooner forsake all the world's crowns and thrones than risk her thinking that he'd abandoned her.

"There's more to this than a crown," Evan said soberly. "If we can't make you king, the dream of the Fourth Wing dies."

"Perhaps it's better that it does," Wexrenn muttered, to an unhinged look from Evan.

Jason massaged the bridge of his nose. "What now, then?"

Evan grunted. "I have no clue. I do know that the solution to this problem won't involve *you*." He made a headshake and waved off Jason. "Years in the making, seconds to destruct. Damn stupid . . ." Trailing off, he turned and departed through the pavilion's flaps.

Jason listened to his uncle's fading footsteps. He regarded Wexley. "And what of you?" he asked testily. "Would you curse me a fool to my face, or threaten to leave, like Free Believers?"

The Bull gripped his shoulder, squeezing. "People forget that we Cloudlanders had gods before the Elvarenists," he said. "We accepted their religion, but these skirmishes between this religion and that one"—he shrugged indifferently—"it matters less to us than honor. I pledged to make you king. And I will."

The Bull said something with his look—*So long as your honor holds, and our arrangement regarding the Wing of the Commons stands.* He patted his shoulder father-like, poured himself mead, and stepped out, swishing his cup.

On the way out with Wexley, Wexrenn slapped Jason on his back. "I'm not sure what I was thinking by likening some *scrorn-ner-gaith* whore to a beauty like that," he said, his smirk doing little to help. "Personally, I'd be more concerned if you *hadn't* fucked her." He seemed to ignore Jason's furious look as he left the pavilion with Ulbridge and Clabbard.

That left Lorana, who stood clutching the back of a chair, all slouched shoulders and dark eyes. With everyone gone but them, sounds of drunken laughter from Cloudlanders filtered in, feeling completely out of place.

Jason regarded his half-sister. "Edenia always felt alone, an outsider among us," he said. "She's mere feet from us after two years, and she's more alone than ever—"

That drew Lorana's hard gaze from the floor. She went to him, cupped his hands, and slipped something familiar into his palms. "You told me to look at this if I suspected your reasons for gambling us on this dangerous game." Silverstone radiance glowed through the spaces between her fingers. "Now look for yourself. Was this worth it today, brother?"

Jason clenched his palm tight around his wedding band, tight enough to feel the silverstone's sharp edges. "Shaddon's taken everything from us. Father. Erick. I can't—"

Lorana clasped his head between her hands, drawing him so close that their noses nearly touched. "I told you about this wicked betrothal because I thought you deserved to know. I didn't expect you to act like a witless, heartsick idiot, brother."

"I deserve that."

"*You deserve the crown.*" Lorana released him from her shaking hands, returning to the chair. "If Jacob Sulley leaves tomorrow, if it shortchanges Sinclair's Company, you may not wear one. Now, we may have to suffer King Shaddon, or King Tom, or King Gavin. Eden will pay the price, and we'll have the war you said you'd pay any price to avoid."

"My passions clouded my star of reason." Jason went to her. "The Loyal Company was always a backstop. We've still got two more Trials. The *naumachia* and the griffon."

Lorana watched him in disbelief. "Wait until you see the griffon. You might wish that you'd fought that dragon after all."

Turning from him, Lorana swept her mantle off another chair's backside, slipped it over her shoulders, and cinched it at her neck. There was something else in the lines of her face. She had to be desperately worried about Edenia, too. She'd always been a sister to Lorana, her truest friend, besides Anyasha.

"Where are you going?" Jason asked her.

"Where else?" She lifted one of the pavilion's flaps. "To see if the Master Reader will see the star of reason."

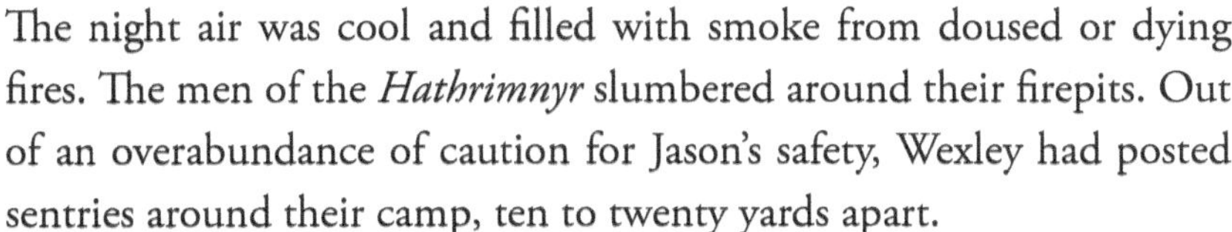

The night air was cool and filled with smoke from doused or dying fires. The men of the *Hathrimnyr* slumbered around their firepits. Out of an overabundance of caution for Jason's safety, Wexley had posted sentries around their camp, ten to twenty yards apart.

These were the men Jason needed to slip past unnoticed; they'd stop him and raise questions, or report his leaving to the Bull.

I'm supposed to be king, but I feel like a prisoner, Jason thought. Dressed as one of the *scrorn-ner-gaith,* he timed his departure through their movements carefully. Leaving camp behind, he waded into a sea of reeds that swirled against his skin.

Heading east, toward his enemy's camp, he stayed close to the roads rutted by wagons. A great bonfire towered over Sam Wuthers's camp as his men mourned their fallen lord. Decisions were being made there this night. Hard decisions. Wuthers's titles had passed to his namesake, and that boy of eight would decide whether to decamp and return to bury his father at Sunder Castle, or forfeit his claim and stack his loyal nobles behind another claimant.

I'm so sorry, child, Jason thought, as if Sam the Younger could hear him. *I've also seen my father slain before my eyes.* After these Kingstrials were over—after he'd killed Shaddon and freed Edenia—he'd grant Lord Sam the Younger whatever he asked of him. If he couldn't kill Tom Gelder in the Colossus, he'd behead the cheating bastard.

Farther on, he walked past another dead lord's camp. On Tomas Fawkes's grounds, he heard no jubilance, or chatter, or sounds of mourning. The camp's bonfire had guttered already some days past. Fawkes's vassals and sworn knights could've left, but Evan had said they wanted to wait, to decide whom they should throw their weight behind.

It won't be me, now, Jason thought grimly. He recalled the last time he'd seen Fawkes alive. It'd been his first day in the Meadows, and the Lord of Westerliche had insulted his sister, mocked his claim, and been anything but someone who should be dead in a few days' time, his throat slit by nameless killers.

I agreed to the Kingstrials to keep a succession war from breaking out, Jason thought, *but that doesn't make any of this more civilized.*

Up the way, men in unfamiliar raiment stumbled on the road; Jason receded into the reeds. He waited for them to pass. A quarter mile on, he spotted camps on the Colossus's other side, a maze of pavilions, wagons, makeshift stables, gutted fires, and blanket heaps shaped like sleeping men. He stood to risk a glance at the shadowy hills of enclosures.

This was where Jacob Sulley and his one hundred fifty-seven slept. He wondered if Evan and Lorana were there; he hadn't seen either of them return. *Surely Sulley has to know that staying to support my claim is the best and only path for Free Believers. Elsewise, Parlisis recaptures this realm.*

"Jason?"

His heart skipped a beat. The reeds parted for a shadow, but he knew her voice. Edenia stepped into the sparse starlight, wrapped snugly in a gray cloak that made her seem a specter. Flaxen hair curtained her elegant shoulders.

They embraced at once. He tasted the beeswax of her lips, inhaled the lavender on her neck, caressed her hair and hips.

"How did you find me here?" she said between his kisses. "How did you know?"

"I was coming to find you."

He couldn't see her smile, but he felt it as he pressed his lips against hers. "And I, you," she said breathlessly. "My love, my sweet love, my true husband . . ."

He had her in the dirt, her stay over her hips, his breeches down to his knees. She shivered as he slid inside her sweet soft wetness. Her breasts shuddered with every thrust. She coiled her legs around his waist and sucked on his bottom lip, begging for his seed between breaths that fogged in the cold night air. It was as if they'd never left Sarah's Fountain. And the terror of being caught, by anyone, mingled with the joy of having her again. It made the sex electrifying.

He exploded inside her.

They lay together in the earth afterward, veiled by reeds, arms and legs crisscrossed. They kissed each other relentlessly, gently, trying to make every second compensate for two years apart.

Jason gazed into her eyes, wishing there were daylight so he could see her sky-blue irises. "Each day in the Brace, before a battle, or in my cups, I thought of you," he whispered as he touched her cheek. "You kept me alive. Kept me fighting. I still love you, Eden."

"And I, you." She ran a hand through his damp raven hair. "But . . . my love . . . you shouldn't have given me those laurels today."

He gave a small, embarrassed smirk before kissing her again.

CHAPTER 12

Mercy and Justice

unlight gleamed through pockets in the forest canopy, stinging her waking eyes.

Sara heard the songs of life, cicadas droning on, crickets performing lustily, the rushing of a river. Grass roughed her skin as she stirred to consciousness, and it was then that she remembered the terrible pain that had wracked her palms.

A pain she no longer felt.

Hesitantly, Sara flexed her hand, half-expecting a rush of familiar burning, the burning that had made her flail and sob, that had nearly led her back to Rosbury. It'd been an unending nightmare.

But now . . . nothing.

Am I dreaming again? She feared so. She feared she was still in the Red Tower, beside her fitfully slumbering mother. *If I am, is Caleb beside me? Or has the Inquisitor's Shadow already taken him through the door to hell?*

About her loomed oak trees dressed in moss. Sitting up, she inspected her gown, a wrinkled ruin of faded umber stains covered in blades of grass and pine needles. *Lady Barbara will be furious with me,* she thought, *when she sees me . . .*

All at once, it came rushing back. The wedding, Lord Sam picking Alford's refuse off his face, Rosbury's peasants clashing with House Morley's men, Reader Gary ahorse and demanding the return of the stolen children in a high, clarion voice. Geffrey Chaffer's thigh, lanced with Dray's knife like a speared fish. Her palms, overflowing like engorged rivers after a red rain.

Sara held her open hands side by side, comparing them. The worms of ugly scars ruined and rutted her palms, but she saw no blood, not even bloodstains. She couldn't remember how the blood had stopped, only the running and stumbling, the sounds of steel meeting steel and her name in her ears. She remembered coming here, to Elf's Grove, slumping against a tree trunk, slapping off ants, crying and bleeding before finally, *finally* giving into sleep.

I'm healed. But . . . how?

But she already knew.

Rich, gentle music wafted into her ears, rising above the mutterings of River Harriet. Dray stepped out from behind a tree, strumming his lyre, a smile on his face. He looked not like a pauper now but a golden knight, a seamless cuirass plate and faulds fitted over his golden doublet and hose of gold. A crown of posies nestled in his perfect silver hair. *He is truly a prince of the lost elves,* she thought.

"*Joy, joy, Damien's daughter thought,*" the elf-prince sang in his musical voice, "*for her barter every tear had bought. That Gift could be made, the price paid, to deliver a soul ere sunlight's fade.*"

Sara leapt to her feet and threw her arms around the elf-prince. She'd never been so happy to see anyone. "Oh Dray," she said, "I'm so so *so* sorry I wasn't here! It wasn't my fault. Sir Willard took Mother and me back to Thorn's Keep. He *married* her!"

Dray caressed her hair. "Words were said, words not meant by the mother. They joined hands only in the eyes of men, not the old gods'."

His words gave her small comfort. "And my hands . . ." She flipped her palms over, studying the grisly, swollen scars.

"Were healed by Dray," the elf-prince finished for her. "Though these scars will remain until flesh cannot, child."

For her barter every tear had bought, Sara thought. "What have I done, Dray?" she asked herself more than him. "I threw Mother's ring at Sir Willard. I . . . I hurt Geffrey . . ." She'd never liked the rouge-toothed deputy, but she knew with a sinking heart that she might've hobbled him—maybe even *lamed* him. What did that make her? *I've done things I never thought I could or would do.* "And Lady

Cathreen, she knows I had a hand at Saint Eric's."

"And it will all be worth it," Dray told her. As he caressed her hair, she remembered Caleb, and it gave her comfort.

She checked over her shoulder. Sunlight glinted off the misshapen steel of Dray's knife where it lay in the grass. "We can still make your Gift?"

"Yes," Dray said. "And the Gift will do as the Gift should. It will please the old gods and return your father." He stood back from her, eyeing her seriously. "But afterward, when the knight is back, you must both take his horse and go. Immediately."

"Go where?" she asked softly. "To escape Lady Cathreen?" Uthron's horrid widow had threatened Sara and her mother with a Red Tower cell. The last she saw her, she'd looked not like a figure of authority but a frightened mother.

"Not only her. A darkness festers upon the land like blight. You saw that darkness yourself once." Dray turned to stare at the river, where Lord Uthron had descended beneath its frothy currents. "This is the ancient power that stole your father from you. When Sir Damien returns to Rosbury, you and he will take your horse and go at once."

"But go *where*?" Sara asked again, confused.

Her tiny reflection watched her from his perfect blue eyes. "You and Sir Damien will go west, past the forest of steel, to the Great Tree, where griffons nest." Fear ripped into her like talons. "A friend of yours will be there, and you—*we*—will see him."

"We?"

Dray made a slow nod. "You've a role to play, Sara, you, your father, and the boy called Zuran. As do I."

Zuran? She hesitated. *The boy in the Silver Walls's kitchens.* She went rigid with remembered resentment for the Casaanite, but it felt small, even silly, after Red Tower cells and weddings-turned-battles. "What of Mother?"

"Her fate is now her own. Dray can heal flower and flesh, summon the dead from far away, but a stubborn heart is not mine to change. Men were given freedom, and over that I am powerless."

Sara said nothing for a long moment. "Will I . . . will I see her again?"

"One day, child."

Tears blurred the corners of her vision. *Mother, I'm so sorry. For calling you a whore, for ruining everything, now for leaving you. But this must be done. For Father . . . for us . . .*

The sun was setting. Dray led her to the knife. With the utmost care, Sara recovered the warped blade, enfolding it in the sheath of her gown's folds.

Sara worried that she'd need to search for a hare, which seemed nigh impossible on an empty belly, with a raw, thirsty throat besides. But she didn't need to look far. As if prompted, a white hare hopped out of the weeds nearby, nose wiggling. He came to them willingly, pliant as a kitten.

Dray picked him up as gently as he would a beloved pet. He knelt by the river, at the same place where Caleb had made his Gift. The knife felt strange in her scarred hands as she knelt beside him.

She stroked the hare's ears with a free hand, holding back the knife in her other. She glanced at Dray. "Will he feel pain?" she asked shakily. She'd catch a million hares if that was what it'd take to bring her father back, but she hated the idea of causing this sweet animal the same pain she'd felt.

"Very briefly," Dray told her, "and then it'll be over."

She looked into the hare's guileless black eyes. "Will he see *his* father again?" she asked. "*His* mother?"

The elf smiled gently. "Yes, child. For you mortals, death can be cold, frightening. So the old gods clothe what frightens in the warmth and joy of the familiar. As this creature passes, he will again see the love that was there at his beginning."

Oddly, his answer both comforted her and didn't. She prepared to do the awful thing, raising the knife over her head. Dray clutched the hare's ears together like a gift of flowers. He circled his finger about a spot on the animal's exposed neck.

Closing her eyes, Sara brought the blade down like a bolt of lightning. Warm blood slathered her hands, seeping through her fingers, reminding her only too well of her own. He pulled the blade from her grasp, gently.

She opened her eyes.

The elf-prince stood over her, holding the limp hare to his chest as a mother would her child. Golden sunlight framed his body and yellowed the pale posies in his hair. "It is done, Sara," he said. "Your father waits for you at his house."

Sara leapt up, dizzy-headed and flush with emotions she couldn't number. She jumped up and down, smiling despite the tears. "Thank you Dray, thank you thank you thank you *THANK YOU!*"

Dray caressed the Gift they'd made, smiling. "Go at once, child. Your father will not know you at first. Lead him to the stables, mount your horse, and go west to the Great Tree. We will meet Zuran there."

Sara didn't need telling again. She ran in the direction of her village, of her house, of home, hands warm with the hare's blood. She threw a look at Dray as she bolted off and saw him clutching the hare in the crook of an arm, his other palm raised in farewell.

At the Great Tree, then, my prince, she thought. *My friend.*

Sunlight winked on the thatched roofs of Rosbury's huts. Sara crouched behind bushes on the outskirts, eyeing the few who peopled the main.

Villagers strode by briskly with baskets and buckets. No one walked alone. Rittman's deputies escorted people to and fro, hands resting on the pommels of sheathed swords. Two women bickered with a deputy who just stood there, laughing at them. Overhearing them, a third deputy came by, listened patiently to their complaints, and backhanded one across her face. Sara felt the sound of the slap in her own cheek.

Father, you won't recognize our village. She mourned for Rosbury. Things were worse than ever here, and now she was leaving. Doubtless the deputies were all searching for her.

She'd be safe once she was with her father, a knight anointed and trained with the sword.

But would Sir Damien know *her?* Dray said he wouldn't, not at first. She couldn't puzzle out what that meant. *You'll remember, Father,* she thought. *You'll remember me when you see me, I know it.*

While waiting for the deputies to leave, Sara lifted her hemlines above her knees and tied a makeshift knot at the hip, to keep the fabric from snaking about her ankles. She hastened behind the waterwheel, then behind the cone of the dovecote. Doves flapped about anxiously, cooing.

Sara abandoned the dovecote for a maze of several other buildings. She padded around Twelve Mercies, rounded past the pillories, and crawled on her hands and knees through the muck behind a weed-choked sheepfold.

Deputies walked past on the other side, speaking in low tones about the wedding revolt. "Poor Sir Will," one man kept saying. He laid the blame for the violence on Jon Watley and Evan Sinclair's Loyal Company.

It wasn't Firemouth or the Company, Sara thought. *It was you lot and Sir Willard! You took the children. You're no better than thieves, and Rosbury raised a proper hue and cry.*

When the deputies were gone, she crossed a well-worn dirt road to shelter behind a house. She peered around the corner, and her heart swelled. She could see their house, *right there,* the edge of the rickety fence, and through stable beams, Little Lady's strong hindlegs.

The sight of her horse comforted her like warm honey tea.

It also made her think. If her father wouldn't know her at first, would he remember how to ride? Rose had always cursed the courser half-mad, but an unconfident rider could pitch her into frenzy. The question added to her anxiety.

I have to trust in Dray, she reproached herself. What she trusted less was herself at a Great Tree with griffons, the great winged terrors that flew off with bears like hawks clutching cats. *I hope I'm worthy of mercy and justice . . . and that you'll be kinder to me when we meet again, Zur.*

Finding courage, Sara darted up the path as quickly as she could without drawing attention. She hid behind Farmer Grey's house, yards from her front door. Little Lady stamped her hoof excitedly.

"*GIRL!*"

She froze at the familiar, husky voice. Bardo Lym waddled over from a space between houses, clenching the front of his breeches together after what looked like a piss. *I can outrun Sir Bardo,* she thought headily. *I can make it to Father.* Bardo was fat and easily winded.

She couldn't outrun the other one. The young Luc Tolos emerged beside Bardo Lym, lean and handsome in his armor. He blocked off one end of the road as Lym straddled the other, hands outstretched to net her if she fled.

"No use running, Sara," Tolos warned her in a hard voice.

No. NO. They surrounded her. *Not like this. They'll take me to Thorn's Keep. Father and I have to leave!*

Neighbors of theirs poured out from their doors. Among them was Farmer Grey's wife, looking concerned. "What're you doin' with Sir Damien's daughter?" she demanded.

"Back inside," Lym snapped. "Not your business, woman."

Tolos looked at Sara in a way that made her feel ashamed. "I can't believe what you did, Sara," he said in a more familiar, incredulous tone. "*God,* look at your hands." He gripped her by her shoulder as if she were a criminal and led her to the door of her house. "Your father's waiting for you."

They could've forced her on with a spear to her backside, and still she would've smiled. "You've seen Father?" she asked, squirming with glee.

"He's been waiting for you," Lym said gruffly, striding by them. "Figured you'd return for that malcontented beast. Little Lady? Little Bitch, more like. She bites."

"Don't call my horse that," Sara protested.

The door swung open . . .

. . . and Sir Willard Rittman emerged. Inside, a pot boiled over the firepit. *No. Why's he here?*

The justice flitted from her to the knights. "Where did you find her?" Rittman asked.

Lym pulled off his kettle helm, slicking back the thorns of oily hair. "Right over there, Sir Will," he said. "Found her first I did."

Rittman thanked the knights and sent them back to their posts. Wormy lips quivering, he snatched Sara by her shoulder and hauled her inside. A bee whirred by her ear as he slammed the door behind them.

Heedless, Sara bounded left and right, searching corners, the shed, the loft above, everywhere. "Father?" she yelled out, growing more hysterical with every passing second. "Father? *FATHER! Where are you? FATHER! FAAAATHER!*"

"I'm here." Waning sunlight silhouetted Rittman at the window. He seemed to soften with worry. "Maetha have mercy, Sara. Your hands! They still have Geffrey's blood on them."

"It's not his." Sara surged forward. "*What did you do with my father?*" she demanded. "*Where is Sir Damien?*"

The justice looked at her as if she were mad. He hooked a stool with his ankle, dragging it close. "Sit, daughter."

Her revulsion, her fury, her disappointment, everything swirled inside her like a storm. "I am *not* your daughter, *Will.*"

Rittman laid a hand on the back of the chair, sighing. "For the love I bear Rose, I'll withhold my hand. Gods be with me, I wish to show you mercy, if I can."

Sara spat on him.

The justice was there in two quick strides. "*EVIL CHILD!*" He dug his sausage fingers into her arms, shaking her so hard she grew headsick. "Do you know what you've done? Geffrey will have a limp! Would you take another friend of mine? You disarmed Tom with that apple you threw at his head. And now Geff. Do you know the misery you've caused your mother and me? *Do you?*"

"Father," she kept saying as the sobs poured out, "Father, where Father, where are—"

"*I'm your father now,*" Rittman seethed. "I'm responsible for you, twelve help me, I am. Lady Cathreen told me after she saw you stab

Geffrey. Told me about Saint Eric's. I couldn't—I couldn't believe her! You did it under my nose." Fear mingled with the anger in his eyes. "I don't—*I don't know you right now, child.*"

"Dray, please, Dray," she wept, "help me, HELP ME!"

"Who's Dray? Is he with Connor Bagman? Were you in on Sweet Tom, too?" Rittman unhanded her. He stalked off to the window. She clung to the ridgepole, sobbing softly.

"Sara," he said with his back turned. "I care for you. You lost your father—yes, you did. I lost mine, too, when I was your age. I worry over you as I wish my father had looked after me." He circled about. "But Sara, you must tell me everything. I can protect you if you come out with it. I know Connor Bagman and Jon Watley burned the temple. Did they have a hand in Sweet Tom's murder? Who was with them that night in Southfar?"

She glared through her tears. "Uthron Morley."

"I warn you."

"It was Sam Morley. He burned your stupid temple."

The justice seized Sara by her wrists. She kicked at his shins. On the backswing her left heel slammed the ridgepole, detaching it from the ceiling beam so that it wobbled over them like a spear pinned in the dirt.

Rittman gasped sharply. He swatted at the air, then at his arms, at his cheeks. The beehive lay about them like chunks of soggy clay. Sara saw a bee wriggling its stinger into her arm.

She flew past the justice, bees giving chase. She hurled open the door and made for the stable. Startled, the knights Lym and Tolos barreled after her. Rittman's cries quickened her feet. People watched from their windows, as cowardly as the peasants at the Red Tower. Others opened their doors.

Dray, I have to get to Dray. Inside the stable, Little Lady pawed irritably at the soil. *Come, Lady.* Sara was scrambling through two stable beams when something latched her ankle.

Rittman hauled her halfway out. With a face pimpled with bee stings, he looked as hideous as Praise. "*SARA!*" he cried.

"No, leave me be!" she kept repeating. She kicked Rittman in his nose. "YOU WON'T TOUCH ME LIKE THAT AGAIN! Leave me alone!"

Little Lady tensed protectively, snorting, squealing her whinnies as Rittman crawled through the beams. Outside, the two knights headed off Farmer Grey's wife as she marched up, demanding to know what was happening. Four other villagers flanked her. *I wish they'd been with Caleb and me in the Tower,* she thought.

Once inside the stable with her, Rittman chased her round and round and round. Sara bolted toward the courser's rear, keeping the animal a barrier between them. He ran to head her off; she pitched the other way. On and on this went.

The game ended when the justice caught her by her ankle again. He dragged her under the horse, halfway out to the other side. He was shouting at her.

Willard Rittman looked afraid, she realized. Below Little Lady, she couldn't make out anything he said.

The world was quaking all around Sara, hooves falling like meteors in plumes of smoke. In the fraction of a second, amid the blur of hooves, Sara noticed the tuft of hair tracing her courser's belly like a white road. How had she never seen that?

Then, fire. Everything was fire.

Her chest burst as her poor palms had when she'd gripped Dray's swordwood knife. The pain was her mother's dragon, unclenching its snout for a blast of white-hot flame that incinerated her. She was the tinder of a sacred temple, all its hardwood pews and rafters, eaten from the inside out by an uncontrollable inferno.

She couldn't move or breathe. Fire turned her to ash, and then as swiftly as it came it was out, snuffed like a candlewick. Voices towered over her like a storm-whipped wave, but she couldn't answer them.

She was underwater, listening from a remote place.

Numb, faintly aware.

Between, it seemed. Between everything and nothing. Between a grove of miracles and the darkest corner of the reddest tower. Between the first kiss a mother offers to her newborn and the wistfulness of the elderly.

There. Not there. Everywhere.

Slipping . . . a tiny grain of sand tumbling out to sea . . .

Then she heard her name. He slipped unnoticed through the crowd with a smile warm as sunlight after a passing storm. He hoisted Sara up and twirled her through the air, laughing.

Safe Passage

hifting torchlight revealed disheveled pebbles at his feet and chalk drawings on cavern wall.

"We're coming to a grotto," the King's Crow announced, to echoes amid the incessant patter of water. "Tonight we'll sleep there. We're close to Westland."

Close. Zur trudged behind him, nearly losing his footing on a pile of pebbles. As promised, Drexan had guided them deeper into the earth, with a lay of the land that only Barefoot Knights would have, through vast, stalactited caves rife with bats and claustrophobic passages that forced them to duck their heads. They subsisted on salted hare, icy water from the runnels that guided them, and the heat of torchlight that Drexan kindled by drawing blood with swordwood.

Zur had no sense of time, no sense of how long to sleep or when to rise, save when Drexan snuffed out his torchlight or stirred him awake. He'd been sorry to see off their mounts at the first cavern, but traversing dark, tunneled earth wouldn't have been kind to hooved animals.

"The way to the Great Tree will be longer by foot, but it's less likely that griffons will see us when we surface," Drexan had reassured him.

The boy who'd spent his life a hostage had discerned the unspoken truth. *Better that no one see a Casaanite boy astride a donkey in the open,* he thought, *especially if the Grand Inquisitor is searching for one.*

He expected Lorana to search for him, her little brother. Drexan had shared as much that first night in hiding. But the King's Crow— the man who'd set a brazier ablaze with a drop of blood—had told him that her path would become his if he returned to the Silver Walls.

He rose every morning and slept on the ground every night wrestling with his decision, missing home.

Missing the only family he'd ever known.

But he had questions. Questions that only the Lady at the Tree could answer.

In his mind, he fiddled with truth until it sounded less like truth. *I need to know, Ana. You and Jason need to know, for times will come when we need to face shadowkings, all of us, together.* It did nothing to allay his guilt over leaving, with Jason in the Kingstrials, with two lords savaged in a forest. *What must you think of me, princess?*

The stream they were following thinned and whispered into a hole. Torchlight flickering, Drexan led them through a tunnel that branched into other creviced passages. A turn here, a turn there, and they entered a high-ceilinged grotto littered with the signs of domestic life.

It was an eerie scene. Below a smoky ceiling was a firepit ringed with the tangles of wool blankets. About the living area lay wooden spoons, bowls, shirts, wimples, even dolls. Older-looking braziers dotted the grotto. Here, as elsewhere in these caverns, white chalk graffitied the rocky walls. Tunnel mouths promised only more labyrinth.

Zur wished away the prickle of gooseflesh on his arms. "Are we expecting . . . more friends?" He eyed the dark tunnel mouths.

"Not until we reach the Great Tree. This place is long abandoned." Drexan went about lighting braziers, until the grotto was ruddied brightly.

Zur knelt by the firepit. He picked up a wooden toy knight, stroking the yellowed goose feather that curled off its helmet. "Abandoned by Barefoot Knights."

Drexan nodded. "The Solemn Order called this place Rorn Abeth. In Medecian, it means 'Safe Passage.'"

"Was it a shadowking who drove them out?" Zur asked hesitantly. It'd taken him time to be able to say the name. To acknowledge that real evil existed and had a name.

"Until Morley, I don't think there's been a shadowking on this earth since the First Days," Drexan said as he looked about. "More likely, some lost the faith, abandoned their oaths to the Ascendant King, and moved into villages, to live out their lives, safely anonymous."

"But not your ancestors."

Drexan smiled from one corner of his mouth. "No."

Zur treaded left to the nearest wall, to a score of graffiti patterns that seemed to repeat, almost like music notes rising and falling with staves. A circle vortexed endlessly inside itself. Helixes spiraled across wall, sloppily at spots, as if the artist had been fevered.

Some of the drawings were of men. A tall knight hovered above the vortex, clad in the thousand tiny ovals of chainmail. A crowned king arose on the wall to his left; to his right knelt a bowman, doing homage.

"The Lame King." Zur traced the foot of the knight with a finger, accidentally smudging chalk that he wiped on his tunic.

Drexan joined him. "And his Repentant Huntsman."

But who's the knight? The grotto whispered with the slips of their footsteps as they headed left. Forks of lightning lanced across the wall like cracks in a pane of glass, gathering beneath a scribbled cloud. Under the storm sat the God Who Rebelled and Died, unmistakable with his sinister bat wings and goat horns. Two companions flanked Dracar, one a warrior clad in skulls, the other a figure hooded and cloaked.

"The two brothers," Zur said. "*Nagarthessi.*" Uttering that name here raised the hairs on his neck; he shook off the feeling that something watched him, and disapproved.

The Crow touched the grainy, hooded figure. "Asha-Ra wears the cloak." He dragged his finger to the skull-armored warrior. "Pathazar wears death." He looked at him. "But what distinguished one brother from another?"

Zur thought on what he knew. "Asha-Ra was the trickster, a changeling," he said, staring at the cloaked figure. "A herald to Pathazar, the real threat to elves and men."

Drexan nodded. "Like Uthron Morley, Asha-Ra came to the unsuspecting as a trusted friend, changing form as a man changes clothes. In the First Days, this made him the perfect spy—a terror to those secretly loyal to Anjan Half-Elf."

Fixating on another drawing, Zur walked right. A woman lay sprawled on her back, belly erupting with the volcanic ash of squiggled insects. "Selyssa," he named the ill-fated goddess.

"'The Nagarthessi burst from their mother's womb like spiders,'" Drexan recited from the First Testament, "'after the fallen one, Dracar, raped the goddess to deliver elves and men to destruction.'"

"I thought Barefoot Knights despised Elvarenism," Zur said, a glint of mischief in his eye.

"I told you, religion is a house of lies built on truth. This isn't just a depiction of Selyssa." Drexan pointed at the spiders. "As Asha-Ra and Pathazar were born, so they'll be reborn. The brothers will be freed from their prison to enter the world of men once more."

"As spiders from a woman's womb?" Zur shuddered to imagine such a thing. Shadowkings were traumatizing enough.

"It's a metaphor for force. For creation without consent. Anjan and his mages dispatched the Nagarthessi back to hell, and with deception, they'll crawl back. A human host is the key they need to unlock Anjan's door, as it were, and step into our world again. As Dracar disguised himself to rape Selyssa, Asha-Ra and Pathazar won't come into willing hosts. So the father—"

"—so the sons." Water pattered steadily in the tunnel mouths. He lingered on one. "How long will we stay at Rorn Abeth?"

Drexan placed a hand on his shoulder. "Listen to me well, my servant." He pointed to the passageways with his staff. "Do not go beyond the grotto. The Barefoot Knights who came here were desperate to flee hounds and stake burnings. Lady Orella told me that some survivors delved into . . . the darker mysteries of their Windrider blood."

For supper, Drexan produced berries from his travelsack. Every berry was delicious, a warm explosion of flavor sweet as wine. Zur had a handful, savoring the juice as it coursed down his throat.

They made a fire in the firepit, as Barefoot Knights before them had done.

Zur bolted up from his place by the fire, panting. Cold sweat drenched him. The braziers were still crackling, but their fire had dwindled. He tugged on a moth-eaten blanket and shut his eyes, eager to forget whatever it was, find sleep again.

That was when he heard wings. A blur of feathers and fur shot by his face. Furos glided to perch on a boulder, scratching the surface with his talons. He turned his feathered head this way and that, regarding the boy curiously.

"Furos?" he asked, as if the bird would respond. "Lord—"

He flipped on his side and found himself alone. Zur rose and shuffled around the chamber, checking every crevice and tunnel hole for his protector. Drexan's swordwood staff leaned on the wall by the grotto entrance.

"Must you always leave me alone in the dark, Drexan?" he called out. His echo called back, *Drexan, Drexan.* He asked for him a few more times, to no avail.

Zur approached the king's bird, showing him his palms for goodwill. "How'd you find us here, Furos?" he asked. The griff opened his beak, panting. *A stress response.* "Where's your master?"

The griff shifted posture, eyeing the tunnel mouth. Zur ventured close, listening for any sound beside the patter of water. *Perhaps Drexan didn't heed his own advice. Perhaps he went deeper in search of something, fell, twisted his ankle.* He imagined the chancellor asprawl on a bed of rocks, unable to call out to him. *Why else is Furos here, if he didn't summon him?*

"Drexan?" he called out to the darkness. "Are you hurt? Drex—*Anyasha?*"

The shape of her face, her nose and chin, took form in the darkness of the tunnel. Anyasha smiled. He saw the pale sole of her foot as she fled into the dark. Before he could say anything, Furos flew after her, vanishing.

"Okay, then." Zur ran a hand through his sweaty curls. He found a short, damp plank of wood and held it over a brazier, expecting it to catch flame. When it didn't, he tore off a piece of blanket, wrapped it around the wood, and blew on the fire to encourage it.

I won't go far, he assured himself. He passed into tunnel, shining his torch on creviced wall and the pebbled path at his feet. He stumbled over uneven ground as he pawed about the wall, glancing over his shoulder to make sure he hadn't lost sight of the hoary orange oval of the tunnel entrance.

Echoes of footsteps and Anyasha's laughter urged him on. She was fast. The faster he walked through the dark unfamiliar, the farther she seemed.

The cave narrowed and stopped abruptly at a crossroads, where Furos waited on a ledge, tail writhing. In sparse light, Zur spotted chalk graffiti at either side of the tunnel entrances.

It's a sign, he knew. *The Barefoot Knights must've left these signs to guide them through Rorn Abeth.* One symbol looked like a seated king; the other, the kneeling bowman. *The Lame King is for kings. I'll take that path.* Just as he began to enter tunnel, the griff broke into wild flapping, shrieking.

"Don't go, little brother," he heard Lorana beg him.

Zur held aloft his torch, ignoring Furos. "I must." He took one step into the tunnel mouth . . . and gave a short, panicked cry as he plummeted into darkness.

Seconds later, icy water overtook him, filling his throat. He sank until his feet touched slick rock. He sprang up, kicking furiously until he burst through the surface, scrambling for dry ground. Desperation landed a score of painful scrapes on his hands and wrists as he clambered out of a rippling cavern pool.

Shivering, sputtering, he took in his new surroundings. The torch lay somewhere, oranging the cave slightly, enough for him to see. He crawled to the pool . . . and discovered the gleaming star of the torch at the bottom, beneath all the water, *still burning.*

"Some survivors delved into . . . the darker mysteries of their Windrider blood," he remembered Drexan saying.

I can't say whether this is magic, Zur thought, bewildered, *but I'll be lost without light.* He took a deep breath and plunged back into freezing water. Once, Jason had shown him how to tread water; he paddled his hands and feet just so, swimming vigorously until he reached the well-lit bottom. Grabbing the torch, he kicked his feet and rose, careful to hold the wafting, waterproof flame away from his person. *What a shame it'd be, if the first person burned underwater were a Casaanite.*

He hauled himself up and raised his magic torch. Grotto light gleamed in the daggers of stalactites, catching in ripples on the pool's surface. Staring up, he saw that he'd tumbled off a ledge some twenty feet high. He scoured the area for ways out but found no easy footholds, no hewn steps, no ancient ladders. A short distance from the pool lurked another tunnel mouth.

Furos whooshed down, darting into the tunnel ahead. Zur peered as far inside the cavern mouth as his torchlight let him. "Furos!" he cried, too late. "Shit."

Entering the tunnel mouth, he pawed his way past sharp rocks, after the sound of feathers fluttering. He ran as fast as his feet could carry him. He swelled with hope when he saw the orange oval of a fire-lit tunnel mouth fifty yards out. *Drexan's there,* he thought. Walking up to it, he lifted his torch to sear through the veils of spiderwebs. *Maybe he entered this cave another way, made a fire . . .*

Vanishing silk gave way to a chamber of treasures. Zur's torch lit hundreds of reflective surfaces: silver dishes, ornate chests overflowing with bounty, fixtures of iron draped with bejeweled gowns and shirts of mail, pearl necklaces, swords with golden hilts, and tables piled high with coin.

Thirteen mirrors ringed the room, long, shiny ovals with exquisitely foliated golden borders. He neared one, passing a rack of lances. In the first mirror was his reflection, armored neck to toe. *I'm a knight!* he thought, gratified at the luster in everything from his gorget to the greaves and sabatons.

He tensed at the sight of someone emerging from behind his reflection. It was a woman—a *Casaanite* woman! She was old, perhaps the oldest kinswoman he'd ever seen. She had a stern countenance, seamed cheeks full of ginger freckles, and a mop of thick gray braids upon her shoulders.

Yet her eyes were warm and brown as the earth after a spring rain, and when they met his, he stopped shivering.

A word nearly escaped his lips: *Mother?*

The old woman touched his reflection's pauldron, and he felt her fingertips graze his own flesh. "I'm not your mother," she answered him. "You're dreaming, Zuran of the Tribe Nuur." Smiling, she gave him a gentle push. "Fly like a griffon."

The foliated mirror frame burst into flame, as if slathered in oil. Backtracking, he bumped into the rack, dislodging lances that clattered on the floor. All at once, fire exploded in the frames of the other mirrors, flooding the room with light.

Looking at the first mirror, Zur no longer saw himself or the woman but a chamber at the Silver Walls.

Where am I, he thought, *if not in a dream?*

He walked past each mirror, seeing familiar faces in their glass. In the first, Lorana accompanied King Hexar in the Hall of Memory, passing silverstone-smelted statues. In another was Jason, comforting Garrett in a ship cabin. Heather giggled with Lorna Durros in another mirror, as Evan Sinclair's ward loved a purple-haired woman in another. In the fifth portal, Drexan navigated the castle hedge maze with Charles Burke, the trains of their garments snaking after their sandaled feet.

Darker visions awaited. He saw Lorana's chosen speaker, Greg Thorngale, porcupined with arrows, expiring in a pool of blood as his sons wept and swore vengeance. *Is this portent, or past?* In another, a knight groped weakly for a wooden idol just beyond his reach, impaled on the misshapen lances of glinting branches. On Zur walked. In a drab hovel, a young man knelt before the charred husk of a dying woman, delivering twins.

The ninth oval showed a Red Tower engulfed by chaos. Scores of peasants gathered outside its walls, beating someone frantically trying to escape their clutches. A hue and cry, raised to apprehend a thief, he judged. But through the ruck he saw justice yield to horror. Men held down the offender while others knifed his chest open. One knifer pulled out the heart and ripped into it with his teeth, as if it were prized venison. Zur breezed past.

He stopped at the tenth, arrested. *You.* The girl from the kitchens stared at him from a glade noisy with a river's rush. She steepled her grimy hands together, as if in prayer.

Mock me, Sara, Zur thought in challenge. *Mock me, you . . .*

From behind Sara emerged a tall, pale man, naked save for the faulds of leaves twined around his waist. He held the girl's shoulders so protectively that Zur mistook him for the farmer Caleb. Lanky ears slanted out from his silver hair.

It's an elf! Zur realized.

As Sara closed her eyes, the elf opened his, returning Zur's stare with an expression that felt . . . unkind. His eyes were a deep ocean blue that bordered on black.

Eager to move on, Zur headed right. In the eleventh mirror he found the grove again, devoid of elf and girl. His curiosity was guiding him away when . . .

The elf stepped into the mirror. He'd passed into the grove reflected in the eleventh frame as if the mirrors were all connected, as if Zur were watching him from inside a house, the mirrors merely windows looking out on the same forest.

Zur felt cold all over and stiff in his joints, as if he were still sodden wet from the icy pool. The elf had no eyes or ears. Skin covered the shallows of his eye sockets, as if he'd never had eyes, as if some cruel god had deprived him of them.

Breathe, he reminded himself. *Breathe . . .*

The boy stepped right. The elf seamlessly stepped right with him, matching his every movement, as if he were his reflection. Zur opened and closed his right hand, and the elf opened and closed his left one. Another step coincided with another step. Zur backed up two paces, and the elf mirrored him precisely, retreating beneath the shade of a mossy tree branch.

Zur hastened past the twelfth mirror, averting his gaze from the movement that followed him in the glass.

Against better judgment, he looked. In the mirror was the same grove—and there again, the creature. This thing was following him.

Only now . . . the creature lacked a nose and mouth. He was an eyeless, earless, noseless, mouthless horror, a mockery of a man. Yet the muscles in the creature's face tensed as if the thing were grinning.

This is no elf, Zur thought, his heart in his throat.

"Zur." He spun around.

Anyasha stood behind one of the tables. She'd traded her bleak wool for a sumptuous cloth-of-silver gown that flowed so naturally with her curves that she seemed hewn from marble.

"Yasha, thank god," Zur panted.

She curled a ringlet of her charcoal-black hair around her finger, smiling.

"Yasha . . . how—" he began, running a hand through his hair. "I think I'm dreaming."

"We are all of us in a dream, Zuran of Tribe Nuur." She circled the table, dragging her finger across its dusty surface as she approached. "The only question is who does the dreaming."

She came within a foot of him. He saw his tiny reflection in her brown eyes. "Did Lorana send, um, uh . . . Yasha . . ."

As casually as she would if she were behind closed doors, alone, Anyasha began to wriggle free of her gown. He reddened fiercely at the sight of a dark brown nipple. She slipped a strap off her arm, and the gown rolled gently off her hips and down her shapely legs, piling up around her feet.

She grinned at his discomfort. "I've seen how you look at me, Zuran." She guided his hand to her left breast and teased the bud of her nipple with his fingertips. "Have you seen how I look at you, sometimes, my kinsman?"

The taste of her lips had the strength of mead, lulling him into acquiescence. Giving himself to her, giving himself totally, Zur planted sweet tender kisses on the nape of her neck. She took his hand, lured it to the patch of moist hair in her nethers.

"Love me," she moaned between kisses. She sank to her knees, ignoring his halfhearted resistance as she unfurled his breeches. She giggled. "*It's a dragon!*" He shut his eyes, trying not to tremble. The flames in the mirrors brightened intensely, ruddying the chamber.

"Give it to me, give me your sweet seed," she begged as she licked his shaft. "*Giiive it to me, to meee, to meeeeeeee!*"

Zur opened his eyes . . . and recoiled from the corpse girl who held his member between shriveled rotted lips. Her skin flaked with green decay. She cackled madly, beating him with hands rent to bone. Zur got up, ran, tripped on a cobwebbed stool. He landed on the floor, entangled with the corpse.

"*Don't you want to fuck me?*" Skeletal hands throttled his neck. Centipedes spilled coiling from the flaps of her decaying mouth, pelting his face.

He couldn't breathe. He was in Sarah's Forest again, the shadowking crushing his windpipe.

Out of nowhere flew Furos, descending with talons drawn to tear at the creature's face. Zur bolted up, reached for a lance to defend himself, and heard a heartbreaking sound.

Anyasha was gone. Where she'd stood swirled a plume of smoke, and the smoke took form. Uthron Shadowking snapped Furos's neck in his pebbled hands. With starlight for eyes, the mist swirled soundlessly after him.

"*Drexan, Drexan!*" he called out as he ran tripping into the tunnel mouth. Behind him, mirrors fell and smashed into each other, one after another, throwing glass everywhere.

The old Casaanite woman waited for him by the entrance. She pointed to a recognizable glimmer at the tunnel's end. *The pool.* Zur raced past her. Glancing over his shoulder, he saw the mist blossoming like gray flower petals, opening to pull him in.

The glimmer began to fade, as if a door were closing. *No, NO,* Zur thought. He came to a dead end, beating his hands on rock. His torch fell, sputtering out in a shallow puddle. All was darkness . . .

Until there was light, as much light as the flaming mirrors had cast. Torches crackled to life in the iron braziers that lined a wall, the sight of which filled his heart. *The South Tower,* Zur knew. He marveled as a claustrophobic cavern morphed into a corkscrew stairwell, rocks calcifying to brick. *The South Tower!*

The shadowking was feet from him. Death's cold touch rasped at his backside as he ran up the stairs. *I'll jump out of the window in*

Drexan's study, if I must. As he ran, he wrestled with doorknob after doorknob, fleeing, frustrated. He was still running when he heard a deep rumbling at his heels.

The South Tower's walls trembled.

As one foot left a step in the stair, he saw, the step preceding it quaked loose, tumbling into darkness. *This is a nightmare, it's just a dream,* he thought, but he remembered that he'd imagined the attack in Sarah's Forest a dream, too, and as he fled up the stairs, more steps fell away, the stones in the walls with them, whirling into oblivion.

A husky laugh reached Zur as he fell screaming. "Round, round it spins," came a voice, "until off it rolls again."

In a whir of wind, something caught him, stopping flailing descent. A musk of death cloyed in his nostrils. Massive black paws clutched his arms and thighs. Struggling to look up, wind blinding his eyes, he beheld a belly rippled with black fur.

The griffon from the Kingstrials. The griffon has me. He wasn't sure which had the worse death in store for him—the shadowking or a griffon. Craning his neck, he met the beast's sharp dilated gaze. "Until off it rolls again," the stranger said again.

The griffon released him, and he fell out of wispy clouds, everything churning wildly, head over feet, the crowded city rushing up from thousands of feet below. Zur alighted abruptly on the battlements of Southpoint's walls, graceful as the king's bird and completely unhurt.

Zur bent over, hands on his knees, panting. *Land like a griffon,* he thought incredulously. He began laughing despite the horrors. *I'm a Windrider's descendant, after all.*

His joy was fleeting.

Loran's capital city burned. Pillars of smoke towered into the sky. Fire gusted through cobblestone streets like hurricane wind, nearly wresting Zur from his perch and sucking him into the inferno. Daggers of flame punctured daub-and-wattle walls, thatched roofs, discarded wains, piers, anything that fire liked. Everything crackled in the city of light and shadow, the manors of the rich and the hovels of the peasants, the Great Temple and the Free Parish of God, Westcheap and

Eastcheap alike. Through the firestorm he saw the ashy remains of people, piled on street corners like heaps of autumn leaves.

Beyond the burning city was the Shimmering Bay, red as blood. Corpses floated like drowned ants. Above the red water, in smoky heavens, there twinkled a lone star, cold and remote. Sounds of a pitched battle, of wailing men and snarling things, reached him on the city walls.

Zur swiveled. The city was alight, but the First King's castle stood still, as it had for ages, its pearl aura ruffling in the giant smokestacks.

This isn't a dream, Zur understood, at last.

Absorbing the devastation, he turned and beheld Traitor's Gate. Even at the end of the world, someone had still managed to mount several tousled-haired heads on its spikes. A wind picked up, wafting smoke and flame . . . and whispering something.

Broken lines and thirteen crowns, he heard the wind say.

A figure approached from the western battlements, its cloak rustling in searing wind. A hood shadowed its face. Again, his voice carried on a wind, repeating like an echo: *That's what Elzura the Witch begot.*

The spectral figure was at least a hundred feet away, but with each step it covered thirty paces, lightning-fast. Searching for a weapon, Zur spotted a loose brick. He gripped it tightly as the figure moved within throwing distance. It held something under its arm.

The apparition floated nearer, its cloak rippling, as if it were underwater. "No closer," Zur warned. "Name yourself."

With a pale hand the figure drew back its hood.

"You've been following me," Zur said. Courage rattled in his chest. "What are you, if not an elf? *NAME YOURSELF!*"

And the wind hissed in response, *She cast a spell . . .* . Zur heaved the stone, and it passed through the faceless creature as if it weren't there. Eyelashes uncurled from the sockets like the legs of insects emerging from two burrows, their blue eyes flaring as elfin ears elongated . . .

Before withering to drooping earlobes, as gossamer silver hair wound tightly into cotton patches on the head of a collared priest . . .

And dirty-blonde hair flowered richly, tumbling down her shoulders, amber spilling into those hazel eyes like molten gold filling an iron mold. The girl faded to facelessness again.

"I know who you are," Zur told the shapeshifter, defiant.

And we love her children not, said the wind. Drawing the object from under its arm, the shapeshifter impaled it on the one spike remaining.

Zur finally saw them, the other heads, the only family he knew. Jason had met death with honor, his mouth a tight line, but Anyasha, with her hanging jaw, had screamed. He wept when he saw Heather's head, ashamed of his ill feelings toward her.

Lorana's head was the last one added to Traitor's Gate.

My family. As Zur sank, throat raw from crying, the wind roared. His faceless tormentor vanished and reappeared over the Silver Walls, a gigantic specter clenching its fist, a single eye socket flaring with pointed starlight.

"Stop this," he pled, to the shapeshifter, to bloody sea, to god and gods, to himself. "*STOP THIS NOW!*"

A brilliant light erupted on the horizon, bright as morning sun. Wails pitched from tens of thousands of demons unseen, a single shriek loudest of all.

Rubbing the glare from his eyes, Zur saw the sea's color wash into a vibrant, natural blue. Gone was the giant specter, gone the lone star, gone the firestorm, heaped bodies, Traitor's Gate, the heads of his family. Trees of every kind burst through the cobblestones, leaves asprout, spring-green. Their flowers spiced the air.

Zur saw that a knight walked upon the sea as if it were solid ground. Whorls of emerald green and earthy brown flourished in his armor like leaves and roots quarreling on forest floor. On his brow rested the source of light, a crown inlaid with sun, moon, and stars, the brightness of their light obscuring his face.

Are you a god? Zur marveled.

God said nothing. Instead, he *grew.* He grew to twice his original height, then four times, and then tenfold, up, up, up. As clouds burst on the points of his crown, his emerald pauldrons sprouted leaves, his metal arms furrowed with tree bark, and the tentacles of pale coral polyps writhed about his ankles. Still, he grew. Waves that would've capsized galleys crashed futilely against the cliffs of his greaves. And the knight grew, his body filling the sky like a living mountain.

A shimmer of light pranced up his breastplate and faulds, and steel plates as vast as kingdoms shattered like glass. The fissures widened into canyons, revealing in their chasms a rich mosaic.

Peering up at the patterns, Zur gasped. In every tile was a face, every man living on Odma, everyone dead and yet to be. Zur spotted faces young and old, gaunt and well fed, dark-skinned and light with eyes of sea blue and emerald green and royal purple and earth brown.

He saw *everyone*.

Piece by piece, the nameless god's cracked armor toppled into the ocean with avalanche force, spitting jets of foamy turquoise water hundreds of feet into the air. What remained was a giant radiantly covered in the stained glass of the smiles, frowns, scowls, and tears of millions of faces. Seagulls flocked to his crown, circling.

Not seagulls, Zur realized. *Griffons!*

Above the giant shone the jewels of the Lame King, and beside it a Repentant Huntsman, kneeling to pluck the arrow from Eduard's wounded ankle so that he could stand and rule.

A voice reached Zur, gentle as leaves rustling in a breeze:

> *Go and tell the realms of men:*
> *The lame shall rise, the blind see,*
> *And the deaf hear the herald's din*
> *When a king wades through sea*
> *And comes to reign again.*

It was the king. He ruled alone, without Assemblies, and the world was better for it.

Zur knelt before Anjan's last heir.

With his crown scraping clouds, the Ascendant King acknowledged the ant-sized boy with the slightest, most generous nod. *Find me,* the breeze commanded him.

"Lord, where will I find you?" Zur asked.

Zur never heard an answer. As suddenly as he'd come to vanquish the darkness, the apparition disappeared. With him went the sunlight and seas, fading all at once to a damp, firelit grotto.

"Easy, Zuran," Drexan said. "Easy now."

When he opened his eyes, he saw about him the familiar grotto, awash in the orange flicker of the fire. He lay cradled in Drexan's arms, drenched in sweat he mistook initially for cave water. The King's Crow watched him as Zur thought a parent would, and tears stung his eyes as he realized he quite wished he'd known his tribesman father.

"It was—was a dream," Zur stammered. He glanced at the tunnel mouth to hell, stunned to think that he'd never even left.

"Forgive me, Zur, I deceived you," Drexan said softly.

"Deceived?" *Again?* he nearly added.

He nodded. "I needed you to see it for yourself." He gazed at graffiti on the cave walls. "Rorn Abeth does not mean what I told you. 'Sight Perilous,' that is its true name. Barefoot Knights wanted answers. Here, they received them."

Deceived again. "What did you need me to see?"

Drexan creased his brow, his green eyes full of pity. Zur knew without needing to be told.

He'd seen the Great Burning.

No, he thought bitterly, crawling to the crackling fire on hands and knees, as if it were salvation. *Let this not be a vision.*

His lord got up, unthreaded his brooch, and draped his servant's trembling shoulders with his cloak. He sat with him by the fire.

"How did the world end?" asked Drexan, his eyes flat, as if he knew every word Zur was about to speak. He spoke as if this were all for Zur to come to his own terms.

Images flashed through his mind in the color of crimson. His heart hammered in his throat. "One of *them.* The foes of Anjan. The foes of man. Southpoint, burning . . . blood water." He shook to remember the mounted heads. "The dead. And . . . and . . ." He raised a shaking finger to graffitied cavern wall.

Drexan sighed through his nostrils. "We can stop him from crossing over."

"No, we can't." Zur stared at the drawing of the cloaked figure. "He's already here."

The Suitor

orana slipped the sterling silver ring over her finger. The circlet fit her stubby finger as snugly as if it'd been cast for her. She admired its jade centerpiece as she heard out Sinclair.

"... as foolhardy as your half-brother's crowning of the prieslenne," he was saying, restless. "I understand your desire for closure. More than most, I do. But Your Highness, there's no reason for you to attend a meeting like this if"—he lowered his voice—"*if you feel you can trust her to do this for you.*"

The steward caught her reflection in her pavilion's mirror glass. She wore the silver chamblet dress she'd had on that day she took Justen Sothos's hands. An ermine-lined mantle draped her shoulders. In the mirror she saw Sinclair, hands on his hips. He looked as poorly as one of his peasants, shaggy in his beard, a cape curtaining one shoulder.

Their eyes met in the mirror. "Foolhardy," the pardoned lord repeated himself softly, "and imbecilic."

The look she paid him channeled her father.

Sinclair averted his eyes apologetically. "All I mean is—"

"If tonight goes well"—*if Shaddon dies, and with him my warlord suitor,* she pondered but wouldn't dare speak aloud, not even in the sanctum of her pavilion—"Jacob Sulley will have cause to return. Wouldn't you agree?"

They'd been over this. Word had reached her that Charles couldn't sneak a hired knife past Shaddon's Sons of Sacreis and Intercessors. He'd been trying for years, but this piled tinder on the fire of her frustration with him. Part of her was beginning to question the man's loyalties.

But she'd planned for failure. Before leaving the Walls, she'd procured a common, very traceable poison from Jon Applewood, as insurance. *Why would I rely on a man to do a woman's job?* she thought. *Indeed, a job for* two *women?*

A few nights before, Edenia had snuck out of Shaddon's encampment, risking her turnkey's ire. Meeting at Lorana's pavilion, they'd hatched a plan to visit poetic justice on the man behind her father's poisoning.

Shaddon had invited her to his pavilion for supper. It'd be his last mistake. It'd never occur to the sanctimonious fool that the Most-Sought Hand in the Thirteen Kingdoms, his betrothed, the high priestess of his faith—and a woman, no less—had the gall to poison him. *For she doesn't love you, my dear, idiot uncle.*

But she wouldn't just sup with her uncle. On the surface, the dinner was a démarche with House Eddenhold, to declare Shaddon and Parlisis guiltless in Hexar's death, push for Gram Sothos's release and Jason's exit from the Kingstrials.

It was also a meeting to introduce Lorana to her savage suitor—the one whom Parlisis wanted her to wed so he could tighten his grip on the continent. It was as laughable as it was insulting, and confirmed much about her enemies. Parlisis and Shaddon believed women were blameless doves who lived to lay eggs.

But they've got the wrong bird, and the only eggs I lay are ones with plans to save this realm. She and Edenia would poison them both. Edenia would pretend hysteria. Lorana would limp out a victim, blaming her uncle's death on Kar Kravack, whom he'd treasonously, foolishly invited into his brother's kingdom.

Parlisis's handpicked king, found dead with Hexar's great foe. The realm would be outraged. Shaddon's guilt would be undeniable. The Master Reader would learn of Shaddon's death and be like to return with his voting readers, shoring up Jason's claim . . .

Better still, Edenia would've made it all possible.

Sinclair, like Anyasha, didn't see it all falling as neatly into place. "Why go in person, if someone else can do the deed?" he asked.

Lorana rouged her lips with beeswax and pressed them together. "One wonders if you've grown fond of Lady Alyse's daughter, Sinclair."

Evan studied her a long moment. "In truth, I have, Your Highness. You show a cunning that I wish your half-brother had. I admire you because of it."

She returned his look through the mirror. She might've taken offense at the comment about Jason, but she couldn't deny he was right. "If only my beheaded mother were alive to hear you say it," she deadpanned.

Evan allowed a quick smile from one corner of his mouth.

"But with Sulley and his flock gone, no thanks to your fickle Company, I'm also obviously needed as a judge."

"Of course. You're more important to your brother and the Fourth Wing than ever. *Why risk yourself?*"

She reached for her headdress.

"I fear you've lost the star of reason, Your Highness, like your brother," Evan added with license she wasn't sure he had.

Lorana showed Evan her ring hand. "Remember this?"

He stared at it dully. "The ring my sister gave your father."

She studied the crowfeet etched into the band. "He never wore the one my mother gave him, but Sarah's stayed on until the day he died. I pulled this ring from his corpse."

Lorana fitted the headdress over her scalp, tucking rogue brown ringlets underneath. She lingered on her reflection, her thick brow and knob of a nose, signature Eddenhold features.

"I had two mothers—your sister and the Lady Romara—but just one father," she said. "I want to see his killer's eyes as he lay dying. As they cloud over. I want to know that it was him who ordered my father and brother slain." She gazed at him in the mirror. "And tonight, I will."

Sinclair wisely held his tongue.

She dabbed her finger in a pot of lavender on her stand and

applied it frugally around her neck. "Not a word to him," she said softly, catching his eyes in the mirror.

The nobleman's eyes were still when he smirked. "You needn't even tell me."

Where it stood on a hill, Shaddon's tent looked like a crown, its cream-and-indigo canvas supported by gilded wooden beams. Listless banners lined a mud path leading uphill, and in the light of Andrew Windkin's torch she could make out griffons prancing in their folds.

At Shaddon's campsite, there was no shortage of Sons of Sacreis, or Intercessors. They were as many as his men-at-arms, all about some business or another, always in groups. Lorana ignored the unnerving stares of silver-masked men as she and her knight beelined it to the pavilion entrance.

A Medecian met her at the entrance flaps. Adorned with that starched ruff and crested morion, Vayne Adrias looked cut from Shaddon's tent in his striped regalia. His nose ring glinted gold in torchlight. *How fitting that Eden's turnkey should guard her betrothed's entrance,* Lorana thought.

"You're expected, Your Highness," Adrias said with cold courtesy. He sharpened at Andrew. "He's not."

"It's a curious thing," Andrew said, "how the man who'd rule Loran prefers the company of Uzmen and Medecians to *actual* Loranians."

Adrias flitted to her, outraged. This one had a talent for appearing outraged. "Fool of a woman, you'd break faith with your uncle?"

Lorana chuckled. *As he broke faith by kidnapping Erick and arranging for my father's murder.* "Sir Andrew is my most trusted knight. What I know, he knows." She turned to Andrew. "But Sir Vayne is correct. Return to my brother's encampment. Tell him that I was still in good health when you saw me last." Andrew knew to share this with Sinclair, not her half-brother.

Andrew bowed stiffly, parting with a poisonous look for Adrias.

When her knight was well away, the Medecian turned rigidly on his heel and guided her through pavilion flaps, into firelight's cozy orange glow.

The canvas entryway opened up on a spacious interior columned with wooden beams. An ornate table sliced through the middle, surrounded by crackling braziers with elaborate soaring griffons in the latticework. Without so much as an introduction, Adrias left.

At the end of the table, nearest the entrance, sat two men not of the civilized world. Uzmen. You could tell not just by their mottled furs, but also by the fairness of their skin, so pale they seemed ghostlike from a distance. One looked like a god hewn from marble, his furs shaped by his musculature. A mane of wild, creamy hair flowed around his hard young face. His frost-blue eyes followed her with hints of malice, distrust, and lascivious curiosity.

So this is the elusive Kar Kravack. He was tall, strong, and handsome, with even a cleft chin. If she enjoyed men, and if she were as traitorous as Shaddon, her legs would quiver like jelly to ride this pale stallion. He dwarfed his companion, a frail, hooded Uzman, probably a servant or slave. Uzmen enslaved even their own.

Her traitor uncle sat at the table's other end, a sulking foil to the barbarian—Hexar, but fatter, jowlier. Shaddon wore a thinly trimmed auburn beard to suggest a jawline. His miniver-lined mantle failed to hide the hill of his plump belly.

Shaddon was so grim that men said he shat bricks, but he brightened when he saw her, smiling. "My sweet niece," he said as he limped up. "Gods be good, *you're grown!*" His belly jiggled as he boomed with his late brother's laughter.

That startled Lorana—she wasn't expecting her father's laughter. Yet Shaddon donned his mask, and the stone maiden donned hers—an understated smile to suggest courtesy while honoring the estrangement and distrust in their relationship. She performed a curtsy, and made sure to tense with surprise when he embraced her warmly.

He held her close for a long, stifling moment. He wore a heavy cologne of frankincense, like an altar boy.

She noticed that he was shuddering. *Did you poison him already,*

Eden? she wondered.

No. Not dying. He was *weeping*. Sniffling. *What a show.*

Shaddon peeled away with glassy eyes. "My poor child. I've prayed for you—for our family. Twelve times a day I pray, to Helsar for your father and brother, to Maetha and Divna for you. It began when I first heard of my brother's passing."

His murder. By you, through hired hands. "Thank you," she said. "And when Erick died?" Anger tinged her voice.

His chin wrinkled as he fought back tears. "Oh, oh. Child, I . . ." He wiped his nose with his wrist, snot sticking to it. *Your calling is in mummery, not kingship, kingkiller,* she thought. She refused the urge to pick up a table knife and stab his neck.

A guttural voice awoke. Kravack was saying something in his tongue. It was only when his companion nodded that she understood Kravack spoke to him. The other Uzman listened as if his life depended on it. *Definitely a slave,* she thought.

"Princess Lorana," said the short, thin Uzman, in an accent that shortened the *o* and stretched *i* to *ee*. "The gracious Kar bids me to tell y—" Kravack silenced him with a backhand so hard and vicious the thunderclap was likely heard outside.

Even Shaddon flinched. Kravack watched his countryman as if he meant to kill him before dinner.

The Uzman rose, hand shaking over his face. Firelit blood glistened on his lip. Before he could utter anything else, Lorana asked Shaddon, heatedly, "What is this? I thought you wished to introduce me to a suitor, make a peace. If I wanted violence, I'd wait for the Second Trial."

Shaddon stumbled over himself to handle the situation, hardly kingly. "I—yes, forgive me, niece. I, uh . . . This is *Vossar* Kar Kravack. *Vossar* means—"

"Chieftain, yes, easy enough," Lorana cut him off. "Though it might just as easily mean 'mindless savage.'"

Without missing a beat, the slighted Uzman translated for his chieftain. Grinning, Kravack responded through his slave, emphasizing whatever it was he said by thumping the table with two meaty fingers.

He spoke loudly, not seeming to fear discovery, despite being in an enemy kingdom.

Just like Gram, the brute's under a priestking's protection, she gathered, *and he flaunts it in a vulnerable, kingless land.*

The interpreter sought permission from his *vossar* with a glance, and then said, "The great Kar bids me tell you that he fist me because I did not stand when I spoke for him. It is an"—he stopped, seeming to struggle for the right word—"an insult if a dragoman does not stand for his *vossar.*"

"And what were you trying to say, before he 'fist' you?" asked Lorana, her contempt plain.

A nervous glance at Kravack, and the translator replied, "He heard you mention the prince and wanted you to know that your brother was a godly man. He died as a man should. It is by Prince Erick's example that our people have been led to the light of the twelve true gods."

"When would you have met my stolen brother?"

"When he went to proselytize in Uzland on behalf of His Holiness," Shaddon interjected. He sounded proud.

Lorana tugged on her father's ring, to remind herself of why she was here, to play the game. Erick was her trueborn brother, and a hole inside her she'd never been able to fill. If Parlisis had sent Erick to Uzland, it would've been before his service in the Brace . . . before Shaddon arranged a Muhregite arrow for him half a world away.

"Translate this for me, dog," Lorana responded after a lull. "You've described your master as 'gracious' and 'great,' but I've seen that he is neither. My king father was great. Your *vossar* shows that he's craven. Tell him what I said, dog."

"Not dog, Your Highness." The interpreter smiled as if *she'd* made the *faux pas.* "Dung."

She glanced fleetingly at Shaddon. "In unforgiving Uzland, I've learned, men who are not warriors are given . . . unsavory names," her uncle said. "Yes, the *vossar's* dragoman is called"—he flushed with embarrassment, unable to finish. "As I wrote you, His Holiness believes it in the interest of Loran and all the realms to seal a peace with Uzland.

But sometimes godly work requires a woman's earnest love, as Divna loves Sacreis."

Lorana looked over the dragoman skeptically. Pale and feeble-looking, he was a far cry from his master. Mismatched eyes of jade and amber flickered at her from under his hood. "Dung, is it?"

"At your service, Princess Lorana." And Dung turned to the great Kar, translating breathlessly, fearfully. The *vossar* erupted with husky laughter, which Lorana matched with hers, until he stopped. Kar stared at her, offended.

"Tell me," she said, her voice rising to a level acceptable for the affront, "why should I consider your intentions a second longer? You enslave your own and beat them like dogs. You're my enemy." She could've threatened to walk out and share with all the camps that Uzland's enemy was among them, but that'd ruin her ploy.

Her uncle looped his arm around hers and drew her close. "He's not as brutal as this," he said softly. "On the love I had for your mother, I promise you I haven't led you into danger. Kar is a proud leader of his people. He's sworn by the gods he'd treat you with as much respect as Uzmen do their own womenfolk."

She almost burst with laughter again. Uzmen were known for nothing if not for beating their women like sealskin. *You're a damn traitor,* she thought as she looked into his brown eyes. *And more dim-witted than I imagined . . .*

Shaddon stiffened indignantly. "This is my niece by Lady Alyse," he told Dung. "And this is my pavilion. I am to be king of this land! Tell *Vossar* Kravack he'll treat her with courtesy, or His Holiness will condemn your souls to hell with my brother's murderers."

Lorana regretted that she hadn't retched during all that.

The Uzmen conversed in their tongue, with Kar Kravack look-ing appropriately chastened to save face. Dung composed himself, hands at his sides, as if he were Kravack, apologizing. "The tender Kar would ask forgiveness of Her Highness, if such a word ex—ex—" He shook like a leaf, obviously screening for the likelihood of imminent pain.

I don't think I've ever met a more pitiful creature. No wonder these vermin ran and hid from my king father.

"Existed," Lorana filled in the blank for him.

"*Existed*," the dragoman exhaled with relief, smiling, "yes, as it does not in Uz." He swept his hand at her. "He's heard tale of your beauty, Princess Lorana. Though our realms might be foes, he would make you his, give you child, and seal a peace."

Lorana squelched a good smirk. *I'm ugly and all the world knows it,* she thought. *It's legitimacy you want for your savages. A seat at the table. For every man who pursues me, the door to a great chair lay between my legs.*

Kravack rested his chin in his hand, elbow on the table, watching her for her reaction.

She looked forward to watching those frosty eyes shut forever. As there was no word for forgiveness in their tongue, she nodded by way of reassuring him in hers.

Shaddon seemed satisfied. "I'll summon my betrothed," he told Dung, "and we can pray, and eat. And the *vossar* can attempt to prove himself worthy of my niece's affections."

Nodding obsequiously, the dragoman conferred with his chieftain in their harsh dialect. The chastened Kar agreed.

Shaddon dispatched Adrias to find Edenia. In that time, Sons of Sacreis dutifully padded through the pavilion, coming and going as they set the table with salted trout from the River Colossus, pantlers with buttered bread, bowls of spiced beans and peas, and almond cakes. It was a sumptuous spread that seemed to impress Uzland's chieftain and hog his attention, to the point that she wound up making more small chat with his sickly-looking interpreter.

"I grieve for my late brother," Shaddon told Lorana as shirtless zealots set water basins and flagons of wine on their table. "Had I been there"—*and why weren't you, precisely, you fiend?*—"I wouldn't have *ever* allowed peasants to handle food." He stressed "ever" with the kind of fierceness and resolve that he should've summoned before he fell on his ass during the First Trial.

He interlocked his thick fingers like someone convinced he was conveying a truth never spoken. "I would've reminded him of divine laws. The twelve gods wisely consigned lowborn men to rule by divinely appointed rulers. It is with good reason they have a place at our feet." He watched Lorana. "Not seats at our tables."

The dragoman translated for them, and then Kravack. "The wise Kar bids me to tell you that the next king of these lands speaks true," he said. "We have rats in the same barrels."

She segued to another subject with the ease of a courtier seasoned with controlling the flow of conversation in unsavory company. Her gaze meandered to the topped-off flagons, dully bronzed by firelight. *Did you bless the wine, Eden?*

Two nights past, Edenia had crossed the Golden Meadows in hood and cloak, risking snakes and Adrias's anger to reach her tent. There, they'd hatched a plan. At first, the idea was to kill the kingkiller, as Tomas Fawkes had been slain in his bed anonymously. People would suspect or even accuse Lorana, Jason, and Sinclair. No one would have proof.

No one would accuse Edenia of assassinating her would-be husband. She was the high priestess, above reproach among priests and Sothos's vassals.

But there was that other gem. Edenia confirmed that Kar Kravack *was* passing through mountains, into Loran. To meet Hexar's daughter and woo her. At that point, she'd decided to play. In one stroke, she'd avenge her father, eliminate their two foreign enemies, and clear a path for Jason in the Kingstrials.

Heaven and earth, Jason, she thought presently.

"Leave it to me, flower," Eden had told her. "I'll have the Sons of Sacreis let me bless the wine. At dinner, we'll abstain from it—you, out of understandable suspicion, and I, because I'll still be drunk from the night before." She'd snickered. "I've been drunk since my father commanded me to marry that oaf. Your Uncle Sacreis shamed me for drinking like a whore during the voyage. He'll be glad I'm sobering. He won't ask questions."

She dwelled overlong on the flagons. Kravack flickered at her.

The trout was beginning to cool, and the famished Kar beginning to lose patience, by the time Adrias emerged from the flaps to announce his captive's arrival.

Yet Edenia entered the pavilion looking less a prisoner, more a queen. Rows of gemstones sparkled along her perfect bosom. Her golden hair bounced freely along her shoulders. All eyes lit up at the sight of her in that supple, form-fitting white gown.

All eyes, except for those belonging to Edenia's betrothed. Shaddon glowered. "Even a priestess should cover her hair," he scolded her softly when she came near, more parent than king.

The chieftain seemed to find the Most-Sought Hand as appetizing as the trout. Lorana stirred protectively as his eyes followed her. *So much for my renowned beauty . . . but I can't say I blame him.* Lorana relished the wetness between her legs. *I'll fuck you well after this, Eden.*

"A special occasion, my love." Edenia bestowed a chaste kiss on Shaddon's frumpy cheek, then seated herself left of him, near Dung. She crossed looks with Lorana so fleetingly that the princess herself nearly missed it.

"Now we can pray," Shaddon said. Her uncle had the high priestess lead the table in prayer.

Edenia bowed her head, steepled her hands, and closed her eyes. So did Shaddon and Dung. The princess didn't shut hers. Neither did Kravack. He smiled crookedly at her as the prieslenne issued soft-spoken prayers to Amath and Sacreis.

After prayer, the Sons of Sacreis filtered in, pouring them copious amounts of wine that spilled over their cups. Lorana held a hand over her cup, shaking her head at the cupbearer.

That seemed to bother Kravack. He made a quick aside in Uz with his dragoman. Once his chieftain finished, Dung rose.

"Is there a problem, err—what was that name again?" Edenia smiled apologetically.

"Dung, Your Blessedness." He gave a slight bow. "The all-seeing Kar bids me tell you it is considered an insult in our culture for a guest to refuse drink. He would ask Princess Lorana, why do you refuse wine?"

His master raised his cup to impress his meaning upon them, as if Dung's fear of imminent violence wasn't enough to compel honest translation. Shaddon narrowed his eyes at the princess, showing that he wasn't entirely a fool.

She'd prepared for this. Lorana held her hands in her lap. "Tell your 'all-seeing' Kar that if he truly sees all, he'd realize that I lost my king father to a poisoned chalice," she said.

Shaddon stroked his beard. "I understand, my niece, but worry not. It's not peasants who served us wine, but devout Sons of Sac—"

"It wasn't peasants who killed my father," Lorana said sharply.

It was you, she thought angrily. *I know it was.*

Kravack set down his cup, eyeing the wine inside warily.

Edenia smiled. "There's no reason to fear," she said. "I took the liberty to bless our wine before the meal." Without hesitation, she lifted her cup and drank thirstily.

Lorana suppressed the cry in her throat. She edged off her seat, wanting to smack the cup out of Edenia's hand, but it was too late. Edenia set down her cup, smiling.

Nodding gratefully, Shaddon quenched his thirst with a cupful of wine, and beckoned a cupbearer for a generous refill. Kravack didn't avail himself until after Dung had his refill, and only then sipped tepidly.

Lorana stared at the prieslenne, speechless. *Edenia, what have you done?* Another Erick-shaped hole was driven through her as she waited for her friend, her lover, to collapse and die. Jon had assured her that the poison pumped through the heart more efficiently than the Sphinx's Kiss. In minutes, Eden would be dead. *And I only just got you back . . .*

Seconds passed long as hours. Nothing happened. No one slumped on the table or off their chair. Eden enmeshed herself in the role of hostess happily, smiling as she picked at her trout and beans. Dung spooned supper greedily into his mouth as her father's enemy did his best to show her a different side of himself.

A breeze sighed through her pavilion, rustling her hair. Lorana sat before her mirror glass, her headdress dashed to the ground. The rowdy laughter of Wexley's *scrorn-ner-gaith* drifted in from outside.

She gazed at her reflection, thinking on the times she'd pled with Eden to break the curse of her ugliness with a kiss. Behind her, the flap curled open, and Anyasha stepped through tipsily. She was achingly pretty tonight, garbed in a plaid shawl that did nothing to obscure her cleavage.

Lorana turned about, smiling wanly. "Where did you get something like that, dearest?"

The girl smiled faintly. "I'm afraid, I'm afraid I'm drunk," she said with a chuckle. "I've been worried about you, Ana—"

"You've been drinking with Cloudlanders," the steward said. In another mood, on another night, she'd feign her mock displeasure a little more earnestly.

Anyasha sighed. "Their liquor tastes *awful.* Like a horse pissed into a pig's mouth and the pig pissed it into mine."

"Do they have more? I'll have some."

"I drank it all." Yet Anyasha was sober enough to navigate the short distance to Lorana. "Your uncle and his guest live, I take it."

Her big brown eyes offered the comfort of liquor, at least. Lorana wanted nothing more than to rip the shawl off and lose herself in her lover, lose herself and consign tonight's failures . . . and terrifying questions . . . to hell.

"They do."

Anyasha eased herself into her lap, curling one arm behind her neck. Lorana smelled foul liquor on her breath. "Eden didn't do it?"

Lorana shook her head tiredly, staring off. "She'd blessed the wine. The savages drank, and they spent hours treating me like a simpleton. Trying to get me to see the magnificent Kar's humanity—to forget that my father spent the last years of his life throwing his verminous people back to the mountains." She scoffed softly. "I tolerated insults to my half-brother, thinking perhaps I was wrong, that the poison would take effect."

The princess fiddled with her father's ring. "I told Sinclair I wanted to look into his eyes, to know it was him." She gazed up at her. "But I don't think Shaddon killed my father."

There was commotion outside her tent. Anyasha slid off her lap with practiced ease as footsteps approached hurriedly.

Rogir Levan barged into the pavilion. An unfamiliar man flanked him, no Cloudlander, his dark hair disheveled. He had on a partly unbuttoned tunic and muddied breeches and boots. Anyasha pretended to straighten garments where they lay on her bed, glancing distractedly at the stranger.

"What's the matter, Sir Rogir?" Lorana asked. "Who is this?" *Was I wrong after all?* she wondered. *Is Shaddon dead?*

"It's a rider from Southland." The knight glanced at the panting, disheveled horseman. "It's Rosbury, Your Highness. Villagers killed a justice of the peace. They're . . . rebelling."

CHAPTER 15

Kinsman

he King's Crow stood on a hilltop, the sun's glare in his helm, eyes closed. He held outstretched a gloved hand, palm open, as if he were a farmer hoping for a drop of rain in these parched parts. His cloak stirred faintly in the breeze.

Zur watched Drexan from the shade of a tree. Minutes passed. Finally, something shattered the silence of a forest in hiding, *urrrEEP, UReeep*. A brownish-gold blur, Furos sailed to them from the woods. He alighted on Drexan's cowhide-gloved arm like a pouncing monkey, a vine of berries in his forepaws, hind legs tensing as his tail straightened for balance.

"And like so," Drexan said as he descended to the clearing, stroking the griff's feathery head. "A griff is a Barefoot Knight's best friend. If you can summon one, you'll see the world as they do. Even save yourself a foraging trip." He plucked a berry from its stem and ate it.

Zur felt less rooted as he took note of black sickle talons that could rend flesh, the hook of a beak that could gouge out eyes. "My lord, I think I need more time."

"Did Uthron give you the benefit of time?" Letting fly the griff with a leisurely wave of his arm, Drexan unsheathed his staff's swordwood top. "Did any of the horrors you saw?"

The horrors. Five days after leaving the Barefoot Knights' caverns, Zur still fought off day's nightmares, the memories of what Drexan had told him was a vision. Not a day had passed that he wasn't glad they'd transitioned from damp earth to the dry heat of the tri-regional area, which Southland shared with Westland and the Midlands.

It'd taken a day for his eyes to adjust to sunlight again. He took in his surroundings with a new appreciation for fresh air, warm sunlight, and green above all. Dust from the Midlands filmed the horizon with an ochre haze, but here in Southland's hills, willowy grass tickled their skin, birds sang in the crowns of hazel trees, and wind blew softly.

Drexan reached for Zur's arm and sliced it with an easy sleight-of-hand maneuver. He winced. This was the price he'd pay. It was a painful learning curve, to be sure.

"Do you not feel pain when you do this?" he asked him.

"Of course I do," replied his lord, dabbing at Zur's blood with a cloth that was plenty pink by now. "Just be thankful we need sword-wood to do this. It cuts easily, but it also—"

"Channels the power in our blood," Zur finished for him.

"As nothing else can."

Drexan began folding the cloth around his arm. His flesh was fast becoming a scratching post, scored several times over. Lorana, Anyasha, Jason—anyone who knew and loved him would all be furious if they saw his scars.

In a life before shadowkings and apocalyptic visions, Zur would've wept at the sight. But this was life after revelation. He was in a war, Drexan liked to remind him. A holy war, battling the ancient enemies of all living things. Drexan and his Oracle would knight him to fight them, to find the only king worthy of ruling over everything.

I suppose my scars are badges of honor, in that light, Zur thought, trying to harden himself.

His mentor ambled uphill, listing on his staff. "If I learn to master Furos, will you show me how to master a griffon?" Zur called after him. "Perhaps . . . to ride one?"

Drexan laughed as he climbed. "I told you, lad—no one's mastered a griffon or ridden one since the First Days. If I could do it, do you think we'd be walking on foot?"

"But you pacified the griffon at the Walls."

"I did no such thing. The griffon reacted to *you.*" Drexan crested the hilltop. "But don't think you can harness a creature like that to your will. It'd be like trying to leash a lion. It'd kill you just for trying."

"King Anjan and our ancestors bound them to their wills. They rode griffons through the sky like mounted knights."

"And no one has since. Griffons may tolerate men, as they do the Oracle—but *riders?*" He shook his head, chuckling. "Until we find Anjan's heir, I'm afraid gloving a griff is the closest you or I will *ever* come to the glory of flight."

I suppose that's the challenge of the Third Trial, Jason.

"Close your eyes," Drexan instructed him coolly.

Zur shut the world from his mind. He inhaled crisp forest air, let his mind roam as freely as he could, to the place where earth and soul met. He felt the throb in his new scar, listened to the wind and birds.

"His heartbeat—do you hear it?"

Zur listened. He heard only rustling leaves, the distant scream of a hawk. He was restless until he heard what sounded like a drum, low at first, then louder, louder . . . *dum, dum, dum.* Straining, he nodded.

"Let yourself be one with the land, the flesh and bones of our king. Be one with the land, and the griff will let you in."

The flesh and bones of our king. Zur was with his kinsmen again on the Street of Kings as stones flew like hail. He stood on city walls as Southpoint burned to cinders, pillaring skies with smoke. He shook off memory and vision alike, isolated the sound, *dum, dum,* flexed and coiled the fingers of his will . . .

"You have him," Drexan said, a smile in his voice. "Tug the reins gently."

But I don't even know how to ride a donkey. In his mind's eye, Zur felt the griff bristle in challenge. He grasped with his will, clumsily. Grappling with the griff was like trying to bag a cat. *Gently,* Zur thought . . .

He envisioned the hooded one, the muscles in his faceless face shifting for a grin.

He was in danger as soon as he opened his eyes, and he knew it. The griff leapt out of a tree, talons protracted. Wings spread, Furos descended on Drexan, who slapped at the beast, losing his travelsack. The creature shot at Zur like a bolt.

Zur closed his eyes initially, seeing if he could slip into the griff like a hand its glove, but something inward batted him off angrily. Furos harried him, wings slapping him, talons raking his forehead. He sprang downhill, ducking, hands over his head as the griff gave chase. *But you protected us!* he thought wildly.

He tripped on the spring of a tree's root and somersaulted onto his back. Furos spiraled down on top of him. He didn't feel the wind as it thrashed the tree, but he felt the griff recoil from the whip of the limb, heard him fly off.

The boy clutched his forehead, moaning slightly.

Sunlight flickered as Drexan came into view. "Griffs are sometimes as wily as griffons." He sounded condescending as he lectured Zur. "They bristle at the touch of a clumsy, forceful will."

His lord offered him a hand. "An untrained will," Zur said as he took it, lurching up. He resented the insinuation that he, still a squire, of sorts, was clumsy or forceful. "Perhaps I need more training before I attempt to control a griff like this."

Drexan made a thin line with his lips. "And you will," he said. "It's something you will master, with time. Like swinging the branch of a tree to ward off a pursuer."

Zur realized what he was saying. He flitted from Drexan to the tree limb that had whacked Furos. "I had nothing to do with the limb hitting Furos."

"Didn't you?" Drexan nodded at the palm Zur had used to massage his scratched forehead.

Unclenching his hand, he saw that it was smeared with blood. He dabbed his forehead dizzily and rubbed his fingers together, seeing how sunlight lightened the crimson.

"I told you, there's power in blood," Drexan said. "Only blood summons that power."

Zur stared at the tree. "I did nothing intentionally."

"The instinct to protect yourself worked its way into the tree, which listened."

"I spoke to a tree and it hit Furos?"

"You make it sound ridiculous." Drexan seemed proud suddenly. "We are the heirs of power over the elements that King Anjan conferred upon our ancestors."

Rubbing blades of grass off his tunic, Zur sighted a shred of cloth from Drexan's travelsack dangling on a limb. His gaze meandered to a scatter of contents that Furos had let out, bits of food here, a wooden spoon there.

Drexan sighed as he scanned the mess. "If only Furos were as loyal to me as a fucking tree is to you. Help me pick this up."

Zur understood what he meant. For one thing, these were Drexan's possessions, necessaries for their travel on foot, but they couldn't well leave something for someone to find. They'd left the cold damp of the Barefoot Knights' caverns for dry heat and open air, and with that came danger, requiring vigilance. They'd been burying the dross of their cookfires and dashing any tracks visible in the soil.

"Furos attacked me because I tried to control him . . . less delicately than you would, I suppose." Bending, Zur recovered the spoon, handed it to Drexan. "But why did he attack *you*?"

The chancellor made a hammock of his ruined travelsack for flotsam, diligently unthreading food from blades of grass. As he walked uphill, Zur followed him, eyes on spilled contents.

"Griffs and griffons are bound to our blood, we to theirs, but they're animals," Drexan said. "Even hounds can bite hands that feed them."

Zur spied a glint in the grass. He picked up a still-intact glass vial that bore a griffon sigil. *This is from the Silver Walls.* Every vial in Jon Applewood's stores had the same imprint. He turned the vial over in his hand, watching as the salt-like white powder inside shifted around. *The sleep agent.*

He spotted yet another vial, this one broken by its fall. A faint bluish liquid stained its shards of glass. *What was in this?*

Drexan was attentive. "Let me handle that, Zur," he said. He tore cloth from his cloak and went about collecting shards, pawing at each piece with a safely wrapped hand.

"Why the vials?" Zur asked.

"Oh, that was a valuable gift that Lord Jon made to me," Drexan chuckled with some disappointment. "An expensive potion for a stomachache from Penatho."

"I'd have thought it'd come from Tesos. They're better known for their potions."

"We learn something every day, don't we?" He had Zur help him cover the stained-blue grass with soil until it looked like a small anthill. "Worry not about foreign potions, but the griff you need to master. It's the first lesson Barefoot Knights have their squires learn. You can kindle fire and call tree limbs to your aid, but why do battle, if a spy in the sky can warn you about your enemies' movements?"

"'There were no lies when King Anjan saw through ten thousand eyes,'" Zur recalled a verse as he watched Drexan.

Drexan smiled amiably as he scooped up fleshy berries. Something was off, and he wasn't telling him. "A king isn't a king unless he can protect his subjects," he said. "And Anjan needed his spying griffs. Especially since the two Nagarthessi counted among themselves a powerful shapeshifter."

He stopped to look at Zur. "The faceless shapeshifter you met at Rorn Abeth was Asha-Ra."

They hadn't said that name since leaving the cavern. The grotto was behind them, but Zur couldn't sleep at night. Drexan had mercifully spoken of the demon indirectly, beating around the conversational bush until now.

"I still don't understand why," Zur said.

"Rorn Abeth means 'Sight Perilous.' But that sight doesn't come to just anyone. It came to you, as it once came to me."

"No, not that," Zur said. "The girl he"—*Asha-Ra,* his mind prodded him unhelpfully, but he refused to name him—"that the shapeshifter appeared with in the mirror."

"Yes, you met her on Remembrance Day, you told me."

"I can't stop wondering . . . *why?* Why her, with him? Why would an ancient demon take an interest in some lice-infested Commoner?" *A brat, at that,* he thought, but he regretted his disdain for her. She'd seemed so adrift in the glass. Hopeless, even. At night, her amber gaze haunted him.

Drexan scratched his coppery beard, longer, unruly, and a darker shade of brown after days underground. "The demons aren't like you, me, men, or anything alive today," he said. "Like elves, they were created by the gods themselves. And like elves, they can live for eternity."

"Perhaps that's why the demon appeared as an elf."

"It wasn't out of a fondness for elves that Asha-Ra the Deceiver would've appeared as one of them," Drexan said. "The Nagarthessi despised the elves. But like elves, the Nagarthessi were prescient. Farsighted. In the First Days, Asha-Ra and his brother exploited this gift to make sport of men. Play them off each other for their diabolical ends. Of the two brothers, Asha-Ra was the best at it. He played men as if they were chords on a lyre, their discord his music."

"And if he appeared to the peasant, he would've chosen a form she'd trust," Zur intuited. He felt terrible for this girl, and more terrible still for having treated her so meanly.

Drexan nodded grimly. "Prince Garrett left on a strange ship, bound for who knows where, over a vision he'd received telling him to find the elves." *I understand the power of visions, now, crown prince,* Zur thought. "He did it because in all lands, through almost all religions, it's taught that elves were friends to men."

"What will become of Sara?" Zur asked.

"If what you saw has already come to pass, she no longer exists," Drexan said simply. "There lives a type of hornet that preys on spiders. It'll kill the spider, carry it to its nest so it can lay eggs inside. Its young then feast on the arachnid when they hatch. So it is with the Nagarthessi when they target a host."

"Only the Nagarthessi are both hornet and egg," Zur said. "They deposit *themselves* in their future hosts." Drexan gave an admiring nod.

"But why choose a Common child? How would it benefit Asha-Ra to possess a little girl's body?"

Enlisting a noble lord like Uthron Morley made sense. A Lord Warden had castles, wealth, men, connections at court. After all, Drexan's trust in him had made the shadowking an ideal assassin.

Peasants like that girl had no power, not without the Wing of the Commons. No easily understandable value.

"It's frustrating," Drexan agreed bitterly. He gazed west. "Damn it, Charles. We had their vessel. *She was in your hands.*" He leaned heavily on his staff, as if the burden of knowledge were too much. "And you let her go."

He suddenly remembered Drexan accompanying Charles Burke in the mirror. "He was focused on the people who killed our king," Zur said. "The girl was innocent. She should've been protected in the first place, not gaoled."

Drexan had a grave look. "We're at war, Zuran. In war, you don't invite your enemies to compete against you in the Kingstrials. You *kill* your enemy. Your vision showed you why."

"I was shown other things." Zur paced off, putting space between them. "A woman appeared. A woman I've never met. A Casaanite."

"Your mother."

"She wasn't, and told me so." He described her to Drexan, her freckles and thick cheeks, the hunch of her shoulders.

A look of recognition passed over Drexan. He smiled. "So you met her. At least I won't have to make introductions."

"Who?" Zur asked. Seemingly satisfied that they'd cleared the area of scattered contents, Drexan poked forward with his staff, gaining up the hill in swift strides. Zur hastened after him. "But that's impossible. The Lady at the Tree couldn't be—"

"Have you ever seen her at court?" Drexan asked airily, almost aloof. He forged ahead through tall grass. "Has anyone ever told you she was, like you, a Child of Elzura?"

"No! But—"

"But surely someone *should've* told you. That princess you call your older sister, the Warchild—"

"Don't call him that." Zur halted to make his disapproval plain. "Lord Jason may yet be your king, *King's* Crow."

"May." Drexan swiveled about, his brow knitted. "Such insolence. I've never been addressed by a Casaanite this way. I suppose that's why the king and his court kept the truth about the Lady Orella's heritage from you. From all Loran's hostages."

Zur stared at him in disbelief. It was impossible. Across the continent, his people served. They served in penance for Elzura's sin against humanity. In every one of the kingdoms, Casaanites were barred from holding or learning how to equip weapons, from holding lands and estates, from earning income. He and his kin were taught this from birth, as if it were math.

"She's a Casaanite," he said with mounting frustration. "*In an Ansaran kingdom.*"

"And who'd trifle with her? Hexar was a blustery fool, but even he had to recognize her power." Drexan measured him with a note of mockery that infuriated. "No army of his or his lords' could assail a person constantly surrounded by griffons."

Yes, but that's not the question. That there was a *Lady* at the Tree, and not a lord, had spurred enough controversy at Hexar's court. She'd never paid homage to the king directly, or been received at Eduard's Keep. Yet hers was a long shadow. Lorana had admired Orella from afar. "My father has a love of spymasters," she'd told him, once, "and how *delicious* is it that it's a woman who keeps an eye on his griffons and Sylvanians?"

Ana, have you lied to me all my life?

"You've seen the end of the world, and yet this isn't plain to you," Drexan said. "Thirteen kingdoms conspire to capture your people and keep you in arrears over an ancestor's debts. But their motive isn't religious. Not entirely. They take people like you for self-serving reasons. To rob Casaan of manpower and keep it a backwater in perpetuity, not a power Ansarans and their kings must reckon with."

He was furious. Furious with himself for never seeing it. Furious over the lies. Furious with Drexan's patronizing tone, and *his* lies. "Stop, lord."

"To preserve a pool of unpaid labor for lords and save them the hassle of paying peasants higher wages," Drexan continued witheringly, as if he *meant* to antagonize him.

"*I said stop it.*"

"To keep the rabble chained with gratitude that at least, *at least* they're not an accursed people reviled by all Odma."

"And by withholding Lady Orella's identity," Zur said with a step forward, the knuckles of his fists flaring dangerously, "to keep my kinsmen and me ignorant of a Casaanite with *actual* power in this kingdom."

"*That's it!*" Drexan spoke with relish. "It's the truth."

"The truth! God and gods, you play games as much as Asha-Ra—"

Drexan raised his hand suddenly, as if to strike him, and held it suspended. "I'll. Allow. That. Once." He punctuated each word through gritted teeth.

Once, a feud with the King's Crow would've turned Zur's legs to jelly. But he'd survived living shadow, seen his blood ignite kindling, witnessed the world's end. And time and again, he'd been deceived by his protector. Right now, his legs felt like pillars of stone. "You participated in this conspiracy," Zur said. "All while making out to be my friend."

Drexan bent forward. "I am your friend, Zur. And I'd keep that from you again, as would any courtier who valued his neck in Hexar the Mad's court."

The sorcerer whipped his head about suddenly, closing his eyes. The griff's cry cut through the air, *URReeEEP, urrEEP*. Furos glided over their heads, into the treetops.

"Be silent," Drexan said direly. "Follow me."

They darted up a hillside fortified with trees and hazed with midges, finding shelter behind boulders that overlooked the clearing.

Zur peered out from behind. It was minutes before he saw the forest shift down below. His chest felt crushingly tight. He realized that he was expecting a dark, living mist to swirl into the clearing. It terrified him to the point of nausea.

Instead, a man ventured out of the wild, camouflaged in an earthy cloak. Sunlight veined the scars that crisscrossed his left cheek and left arm.

It was another Casaanite. The most formidable one Zuran knew. He was a walking armory, a sword hilt protruding from the recesses of his woodland cloak, daggers at his waist, bow slung across his chest, fletched arrows bushing up his back.

Jhazar of Groth waded through high grass, cautious-eyed. The baldheaded strongman scoured the area as if he smelled them, sifting through grass, peering in the direction of trees. He kicked at the dirt hill that covered their leavings.

Rolling up his sleeve, Drexan added to the scores on his arm with a clean cut from his staff, all without taking his eyes off Jhazar. *They have similar scars,* Zur thought. *And he fears this man . . . as well he should.*

Jhazar pulled something out of his cloak and thrust it into the air. Zur's wolfskin robe draped his scarred arm like a slack banner, still ruddied with blood, from the looks of it.

"*ZURAN!*" Jhazar thundered. Hearing someone other than Drexan not even say but shout his name made it sound spoken from another world. "Kinsman, I speak to you now! I bring you the gift of a sister's concern. You are loved. You are missed. You haven't been blamed for those your lord slew. Say something, if you hear me. Leave a sign; I'll make you safe. I swear it on the blood we share with Elzura of Casaan."

The Inquisitor's Shadow scowled at the wilderness. "Now I speak to the man who kidnapped you," he boomed. "Give up the boy, you coward! *Give up yourself!* Those who sent me seek answers. They'll show mercy if you give it to them. But run and you'll have no mercy. I swear by the power of the Red Tower."

From the corner of his eyes, Zur watched Drexan for his reaction. *I wasn't the only Casaanite to speak to you insolently,* he mused somewhat darkly.

The hulking Casaanite remained there, glancing about, as if he expected Zur to take his offer and emerge at any moment. He swiveled at the sound of a shriek. Furos bolted into the blue sky, crying as he zigzagged from tree to tree.

Jhazar tracked the animal's flight pattern with a rapt gaze. He nocked an arrow, stretched his bowstring, and ran after the king's bird, his speed unflagging as he moved through the high grass.

Drexan snatched Zur by his arm. "I used Furos to buy us time, but we need to leave," he whispered. "Remember what you saw in the grotto. Remember the truth."

Yes, truth. Zur lingered on the clearing. *I'll never forget it.*

CHAPTER 16

The Stars

"I haven't seen those stars before." Mina peered through the eyepiece of her father's enormous, coal-black skyglass.

Rathos swished the wine in his cup, eyeballing the spatter of stars she studied. He couldn't hope to focus on what his wife was seeing. From the Moon Tower's topmost floor, its paneled roof drawn like shutters, he viewed a night sky that dwarfed all below it. The air was crisp and cool. Somber notes from Dana's restrung harp drifted up from the courtyard.

"You're sure you haven't mistaken the Lame King?" he asked her.

From atop her ladder, Mina reared up from the eyepiece, looking annoyed. She wobbled precariously. Rathos pitched forward to catch her, but she steadied herself against the skyglass, an iron-cast device so towering that the unlearned man would mistake it for an upright cannon. He set down his wine cup to hold the ladder.

Mina waved him up with irrepressible, almost childlike glee. "I think I may have made a new discovery," she said.

Rathos helped his wife down and climbed. Through the eyepiece, he beheld a vast, purplish canvass painted with gobs of white stars. Twisting a knob crystallized pale spherical blurs into gemstones. Tugging another knob enlarged the view.

"I can't believe it." A necklace of eight stars hung together a small distance from the Lame King. "The closest stars of that luster were always several degrees southeast—the Cupbearer."

Mina was beaming, dressed in a silvery samite gown that complemented her violet hair and accentuated the curve in her belly.

She looked radiant. "A new discovery, then."

Rathos descended. "By the Lady Mina Robswell. While with child, no less!"

"I'll record it in Father's constellation book." She crossed the chamber, retrieved Evan's tome, and splayed it open on the table. She picked up the quill, resting its feather on her bottom lip. "What shall we christen this constellation?"

He strained for another naked-eyed look. "The Repentant Huntsman," he volunteered.

Mina inked the nib of her quill. "You think it's him? After all this time, King Eduard's crippler finally returns to draw the arrow from his ankle? One might say he's on time."

"I don't hear any temples or parishes ringing their bells," Rathos remarked dryly. "What about 'The Just Steward'?"

"Be serious."

He curved his arm around her and drew her close. "I am." He traced a shape in the heavens. "It even looks like you. Two stars for your hands, two for your eyes, one for your heart, and three for the babe in your belly . . ."

"With that belly that large, I'd be a hog."

"Aye, my delicious hambone." He teased her with a lecherous-sounding growl.

He planted kisses on her neck. She smelled of lavender. "*Hmmm.* There's a lot to draw from twelve stars. What about 'The Star-Crossed Lovers'? Perhaps after my cousin and his priestess." That stung, and she seemed to sense it. "Sorry, my song. Too soon for jests?"

Rathos chuckled with disgust. "We're far from alone in laughing. Can't you hear the rest of Loran?"

And what a joke you've made, Jason Warchild. Of me and Evan both. A week ago, word had come to Caerdon Castle of Jason's First Trial triumph—and how the bastard had promptly and damnably squandered it by crowning Parlisis's accursed daughter the Virgin of Venas. Commoners were irate.

Rathos didn't need to guess where the Loyal Company fell on the matter. Win or fail, Rezlan had sworn, Warchild's fate in the Kingstrials would be his and Karl's also.

Any day now, he expected to receive summons to the Last Elflord Inn. But he was at a loss for what to say, for how to even begin to sell Jason's betrayal. Companymen still in Wessex-by-the-Sea would've backed their darling Tomas Fawkes, but he was dead. Not even Rezlan's popularity could keep Reubenites from revolting against Jason, or from beating Rathos himself to a pulp if they saw him. It'd occurred to him that he could send Karl in his place; sadly, Dana seemed truly smitten with him.

Lord Evan, we gambled the Company on your nephew, he pondered. *They call me Silvertongue, but the fire of their fury will be hot enough to melt silver.*

The stargazing tonight had been his wife's suggestion, to allay his troubles. *At least I can retire. Be done of treason.* He'd promised Mina that he'd leave the Company after the meeting in Wessex-by-the-Sea, but Rezlan's report about the kingdom's deadliest swordsman coming for her father and cousin had put an end to that, at least temporarily. She still wanted him to exit the Company after the Kingstrials, no matter the outcome. *And after this embarrassment, I will,* he swore inwardly.

His wife drew his hand over her belly. "Do you feel that?"

He smiled. "A kick." He felt another movement.

"I have a name for these stars. 'The Awaited Child.' I see a babe there"—she traced lines between the stars—"the mother and father holding it."

"I like that."

They kissed. He held her tightly, as if by releasing her he risked losing her to the wind. He listened intently. "Do you hear Dana playing?" he asked.

Mina was already inking *The Awaited Child* on the book's calfskin, with a flourish of penmanship. "Neither her harp nor the sweet lovelies she's whispering into Karl's ear." She smiled crookedly.

A horn blared. A man's cry interrupted the second blast. Rathos peered outside the window, seeing tongues of torches below and countless stars above. Something whistled up, *pfft.*

He'd already whirled about when a second arrow struck a wall inside the Moon Tower, clattering to the floor. "We're under attack," he said. He shielded Mina with his body as they flew to the door.

Feet thundered up the tower steps, echoing. Two people. Whoever had loosed the arrows was in the Moon Tower with them, *now.* Inwardly, Rathos cursed himself for neglecting his sword-belt. Making do, he scooped up the arrow. He had Mina shelter behind the skyglass. He flattened beside the door, heart in his throat.

The door flew open. Rathos stopped shy of lancing Karl's jugular with the arrow. Drenched in sweat, the Reubenite held a bloodstained sword. With his other hand he held a panting Dana by hers.

"*DANA!*" Mina said. His sister stumbled past Karl and embraced his wife, trembling.

Rathos jerked the Reubenite close by his shirt. "Who?" he demanded.

"Pigeons," Karl gasped. "They're . . . *they're climbing your god-damned walls!*"

Mina stared at him. "That's impossible," she said. "Our outer walls are seventy feet high. There's a moat."

"They got over with grappling hooks, I saw them glinting, told the herald before one gutted him," Karl said breathlessly. "I killed the one who did the herald."

Rathos bared his teeth. "*Then they're inside.*"

As if on cue, a storm of voices and boots swelled up the stairwell. Mina backed off, clutching at Dana. Her watery gaze ripped him up as if he were weed. *This is my fault. You told me to leave the Company, and I didn't. Rezlan's making good on his promise.*

Karl readied his blade as if he meant to fend off all their attackers by himself. "Stay back, all of you," he said. "I felled a Pigeon below. I'll take the rest before I let—"

Rathos forced his arm low. "*Shut up,*" he hissed at Karl, "*and help me move the skyglass.*" He pushed past him.

The Reubenite had a crazed look, as if he'd told him they'd fly to safety through the window. Moments later, he joined him by pressing his shoulder into the skyglass that weighed at least two-hundred stone.

THWOOOM, the skyglass tumbled down, shattering lenses inside and shaking what felt like the entire tower. Clutching the device by its thick rims, all four, even Dana, strained to lift and push it, grunting. They propelled the barrel forward, glass crunching beneath their feet, until the topmost shaft teetered on the first step of the stairs.

Half a stubbly face emerged from behind a wall, a lookout. Too late he cried out. The cannon of the skyglass silenced him as it hurtled down the stairwell, *DHUN, dhun, DHUN, DHUN.* The screaming, the sounds of it shuddering leadenly off each step, smashing into walls, went on and on, endlessly, *DHUN, DHUN, dhun, dhun, dhun . . .*

Cries echoed in the courtyard. Rathos swiped Karl's blade. "I'll go first," he told them. "We make for the crypts."

Mina bit her lip. She was thinking of the castle servants, he knew, as much as the castle itself. *The steward hesitates to abandon her people, her family's ancestral seat, but Evan would understand. House Sinclair is more than mortar and stone. We'll reclaim it . . . and avenge anyone whom the Pigeons slew.*

"How?" Karl balked. "Pigeons are out there. Waiting. We'll make it no farther than a few yards outside the Moon Tower."

"There's a secret way," Mina said.

Rathos nodded. "Follow me."

They descended in haste, stepping past bodies crushed by the skyglass's tumble down the stairs. They all wore the forest-green cloaks of Pigeons.

The first man's head was smashed like a melon; Rathos stole his blade, Karl his longbow and quiver. The fourth Pigeon they found crawled in agony from broken legs; Rathos ended his suffering with a stab of his sword through his neck. The skyglass had scuffed the walls and crimsoned the stairs.

Rathos peered out from behind a wall. The skyglass had lodged in the Moon Tower's entrance, plugging it mostly shut. Outside, Pigeons gathered noisily, trying to worm through.

Karl leaned past him for a look. "How do we get to this 'passage-way' now?"

"Trust my brother," Dana said chidingly.

Rathos turned his gaze to the floor, hunting. "There," Mina told him, pointing at one ill-fitting stone. He wiggled his fingers through the crevices, prying the stone free and lifting.

Twenty years before, a mute and broken Evan Sinclair had returned to Caerdon Castle determined never to become a prisoner again. He'd dug new passageways to the crypts, from Oliver's Hall, the two towers, even the stables and his forge.

Rathos and Karl heaved the cumbersome stone aside. A hole big enough to squeeze through emptied into dark earth pungent from residual blackpowder. He had Karl go first, to test ladder steps and check for Pigeons. After him went Dana, followed by Mina. Rathos descended last. He tried wedging the stone snugly into place, but it was too heavy, his reach from the ladder too tenuous. Last he saw, a Pigeon was scrambling over the wall of the skyglass.

The ladder deposited them toward the end of the crypts. Sparse light from the Moon Tower's hole sketched contours of empty black-powder barrels. They waded through.

Rathos discerned a faint blur of light through the entrance far ahead. "The undercroft with the crawlspace," he whispered. "It leads to Sylvanwood."

Rathos and Mina advanced briskly, behind Karl and Dana. They checked fleetingly inside every door they passed on their left and right, trying to single out the dark shape of a bench.

His mind was racing, working out all the details of a plan. *We'll exit the tunnel that leads to Sylvanwood,* he thought, *then head for Nocastle.* The Sinclairs were on good terms with Lord Bard.

Dana halted abruptly. "I hear fire," she rasped.

A sword cleaved the air, nearly catching Mina in her arm. Rathos parried the Pigeon's thrust, steel ringing. Another man in hood and cloak emerged right of them, ruddying the tunnel with his torch. He barreled toward Dana and fell headless from a stroke of Karl's sword.

Rathos cornered the first Pigeon with a flurry of strokes. By the time he stuck him in the belly, spilling his insides, more Pigeons flooded the tunnel, with more swords and torches. He counted seven. Karl was the wind with his steel, disarming one and holding off another from Dana skillfully. More green cloaks swarmed them, separating the couples.

 Suddenly there were five swords to his one. "You three, on the Reubenite," one swordsman barked to his companions. "The Mad Lady and the deputy's the ones we need."

Mad Lady? Rathos grabbed Mina by her hand. They ran. Pigeons gave chase, sounding like horses stampeding behind them, cloaks aflutter. If they could reach the ladder, snatch a torch, set aflame the barrels dusted with blackpowder . . .

Mina gave a shriek that made his blood run cold. In one chop, Rathos cleaved hand from wrist the Pigeon clutching at Mina's hair. Fists and flats of swords clobbered him in ruddied hell, completely overwhelming him. He puddled to the soil, his mouth flooded with the taste of his blood, only dimly aware of the shuffling feet and his wife's screams.

They beat her. They beat his wife. As blows rained down, he could do nothing but call for her, to let her know he was still here.

Seconds passed like hours. Pigeons hauled him up and led them stumbling out of the crypts, up the cracked stairs, into the night, into the hands of shadows assembled against the inferno of stables. They'd been waiting, setting House Sinclair's castle ablaze.

Their captain solved the mystery about the identities of the sackers, and which master they served. It wasn't Rezlan.

The Soothsayer mocked him with the laughter in his eyes. "We meet again, Silvertongue," Varn said. "You seem so fond of killing my friends. A clever use of the—what was it? A fucking *skyglass?*" He broke into astonished laughter.

Rathos spat on him. "Bastard."

Varn's men thrashed him. Mina wept, begging mercy for him. Forced shaking to his feet, Rathos glanced skyward. The stars in Mina's constellation twinkled remotely. Indifferently.

Varn frowned at the blood on his cloak. "I'm not a bastard, but I think *you* know one," he said. "I'll take you to him, Deputy Speaker. You can say hello to Lord Jason when we mount your heads beside each other." A grin spread over his face.

Loyalty

 majestic world rushed below him, and he watched it all through a magnifying glass.

Nothing was hidden from the griff's keen eyesight, or his hearing. Bands of sunlight flickered in his eyes, colorful as the rainbow. Wind rustling his feathers, he basked in the glory of an endless blue sky. He focused on how the earth curved like a marble around its faint edges, on the Rotwood's jade sprawl.

Incredible, Zur marveled. He relished Furos's senses. *The earth is round, just like the Awakening's scholars held centuries ago.*

He heard the flutter of wings not his own. Focusing on the forest far below, he pinpointed a robin leaving her tree to hunt for her chicks. A snake slithered up the branch with her nest, flicking its long red tongue.

Peripheral movement lured his attention to the dot of a white rabbit. Even from miles up, gliding through cloud vapors, he heard its heartbeat. Sickled talons protruded from his paws. He hungered.

"I hear it," he heard himself murmur from another world, and even as his human self said it, his griff self heard him say it from high above. The effect was jarring. Misplacing the rabbit's heartbeat, he narrowed again on the grove with the Casaanite boy and his lord near the S of a weed-choked cobblestone road. The griff was hard to steer, hard to control.

"Very good," Drexan's voice reached him. "Now, find the robin's nest again. Flex the griff like you would your fingers in a new glove."

Zur flexed the fingers of his will. "Silence helps," he said. Furos was learning to heed him, but controlling a griff through Windrider magic felt less like slipping his hand inside a glove, more like trying to collar an eagle.

Something on the horizon shimmered as brightly as gems in the sun, riveting Furos. Under blankets of consciousness, Zur felt the griff stir uncomfortably.

Don't fly south, he intuited from the griff. *No green in that sharp place. No prey. Sharp leaves, sharp bark. Pain and death.*

"I can see Graywood," the boy told his lord.

"Yes, it's near," Drexan said. "But I asked you to find the robin's nest and the snake. Must I ask a second time?"

Zur bristled at the rebuke, nearly slipped out of the griff he gloved. *Easy, my feathery friend,* Zur soothed Furos. He shut out a world of noise to concentrate on the snake in the tree.

He listened and heard . . . men. Yes, men. And the slapping sounds of fists colliding with flesh. A woman, crying, her grief as loud to the griff as if she were feet away. The disturbance came from the road. Zur narrowed his griff eyes and saw them . . . saw *him*, of all people . . .

Zur fell as he'd fallen in the dream at Rorn Abeth, through cloud, sky, and forest, into himself again. He was rubbing his head when Drexan tried to help him up by his arm and pressed his fingers around a fresh swordwood cut.

The boy jerked his arm away.

"I was trying to help you stand," Drexan said, apologetic.

"I can stand, thank you, lord." Gloving a griff had a way of making his senses seem lackluster by comparison. The forest was all muted greens and browns, with a dearth of detail that felt wretchedly mundane. He yearned for his wings. "There are men on the road not far from us."

Drexan looked alarmed. "Who?"

Zur pinched the bridge of his nose, trying to ward off a mild headache, his price for possessing a griff. "Not Jhazar. A small company of men. They have prisoners—a woman."

At once, Drexan retrieved a branch from the ground and brushed their tracks with it like a broom. "Help me clean up," he said as he worked diligently. "We need to leave."

Leave. Zur knew what he meant. They'd discussed it a day before, venturing into a new cavern, scuttling underground like beetles in the dark, all to elude Jhazar of Groth. They'd lost him the day they'd sighted him, but Drexan said the Inquisitor's Shadow tracked like a bloodhound. The way to the Great Tree from here was through cavern only, and no way elsewise.

Zur wasn't looking forward to the sleepless dark again. But that wasn't what made him plant his feet. "We can't leave yet," he said.

Drexan continued to dust away tracks.

"Those men have Evan Sinclair's ward as their prisoner," Zur said. "I saw him through Furos."

Kneeling, Drexan stuffed belongings into his stitched-up travelsack. "Charles's Shadow is the best huntsman this side of the Free Kingdoms," he said. "If there are men near, he'll have heard them. We need to leave."

Or is it you *who need to leave, Lord Drexan?* Jhazar had promised Zur safety, and not Drexan, who stood accused of kidnapping him. The tracker's words had hung over them for the last week like a dark cloud.

Yet he was mastering griffs. Learning about the Solemn Order. Learning that Lorana and her father's court had misled him and his people about the Oracle. *But I'm still loyal to them,* he thought. *I'm to be a knight, after all. And they are my family, whatever that means now. I've never known any other family—even if Drexan's Oracle might have once known my mother.*

"Rathos Robswell is Jason's ally," he told Drexan. "I'm investigating." He headed north. "Alone, if I must."

Zur ignored his lord's insistent, strained calls for him as he pressed on through the Rotwood. He didn't need the griff. The old road wasn't far.

He stopped at the clutch of oak trees spilling over Midway Road.

Over the ages, feet, hooves, wheels, and rain had rubbled this proud highway into weed-ensnared gravel. More feet and hooves were coming round the bend. Zur crouched behind an oak, peering out.

Up the road plodded the men he'd seen through the griff. There were dozens, a motley bunch appareled in patchy tunics, breeches, and cloaks the color of the forest. They looked rough. He'd figure them for the Loyal Company's Pigeons, but those in charge rode horses barded with cloth of cream and violet.

The Lonely Isle's colors, Zur registered. *Quite the display in Westland.* If the Silver Walls didn't catch wind of this sight first, courtesy of Jhazar or someone else, peasants passing by would be like to teach these men a hard lesson. Westland was a province sparse with temples; the Elvarenists should've known better than to broadcast their religion. *And yet here they trod, proudly the priestking's men . . .*

Leaves rustled. Zur rounded on the King's Crow. Wroth, Drexan looked like he'd turn him into a toad this instant, if he could, but the men distracted him.

A shrill scream cut through the air like a knife. A footman shoved a woman to the debris road. *A merwoman?* he thought, astonished by the sight of her violet hair. "Walk faster, whore," the footman growled at her.

Not a second later, Rathos Robswell hurled himself into her attacker. He throttled the footman's neck, apoplectic. The man tried for the dagger at his waist, unable to evade the blows raining down on him.

Zur remembered Sinclair's ward from Remembrance Day. Lorana had told him about Jason's alliance with Lord Evan, the role Robswell would play in delivering the Loyal Company and swinging the Worthy Assembly's votes, if that was what it took to crown Jason. On the night of Hexar's death, Rathos had been regal in cape and doublet, a vision of a young man in his prime.

The man pummeling that assailant looked nothing like Rathos. His face was lumpy from beatings, filthy from travel, his hair tousled so that the ward looked crazed. Rathos bared his teeth like an animal as he savaged his victim. Four men flew to their companion's aid, but it took five to drag Rathos off.

"I told you," Zur said for Drexan's ears. The King's Crow pressed a finger to his lips for silence.

One of the riders dismounted with a flourish of cape. He had boyish good looks, a shock of chestnut-brown hair and the smiling eyes of a bully. He approached the men beating Rathos into next week with an easy gait. The man Rathos had accosted was avenging himself on the woman; the rider kicked him off.

"Easy, Gareth," the rider said with a bored lilt.

Gareth staggered up with a face that Rathos had bruised purple. "THE FUCK, Savan?" He clutched at his belly, where the rider, Savan, had struck him. "That purple-haired bitch is *mine*. 'Specially after this indignity." He pointed to his bloodied face. "She's—"

Savan half-drew his sword, sunlight glancing off its blade. Zur noticed his elaborate pommel, a lion on its hind legs. "That purple-haired bitch," Savan said, as if Gareth were simple, "is more valuable than you or any other idiot in this company." He walked toward Gareth, who looked intimidated. "If you *ever* use my name again . . ." Zur heard Savan trail off.

One of the men who'd subdued Rathos stepped forward. He was lacking several teeth. "You let us have the Sinclair bitch days ago, Varn," he told Savan. "Called it an advance, you did."

"Aye," chimed another man, a bearded butterball. "Called it an advance on the wages we're owed. Gareth's had her more than anyone else. My turn was next, Varn. I was promised."

Zur looked at the poor woman. Sinclair's daughter wore the tatters of a gown, one strap dangling off her porcelain-pale shoulder. Dried blood caked her front. *Monsters.* Zur twisted at Drexan. *We have to do something. We will . . .*

Savan—or Varn, rather—seemed to lose his swagger as a third companion joined the fat one. The three of them closed in. Others watched from a distance, as if gauging to see if they should join. Riders tapped their horses' sides, flanking Varn protectively.

The three brutes were advancing, muttering complaint, speaking over each other. "You told us Caerdon Castle would be the end of it," the toothy one said. "Told us we'd get what's ours," the fat one added. "A whole year of this, Varn, and it's *still* not bloody over," growled the third one.

"Ants," Drexan said just below a whisper. Zur grimaced.

Varn studied the three men. He cut the tension with an airy, effeminate laugh. "Very well, rape her," he said with a shrug. Rathos wrestled with his captors, incoherent with rage. "But you won't hurt her face or ruin that hair. Those parts of her remain unspoiled."

The toothy one produced a dagger. "Or how 'bout we take the loot from Caerdon right now. How can you stop all o' us?"

Zur preferred a conflict. *It'll make it easier to help them if their captors kill each other.* Would it be easy as all that?

Varn uncinched his scabbard. He tossed his sword at the men's feet. "Go on, kill me," he dared them. "Kill the rest of us, too. Take Mina Sinclair and her husband, palm whatever riches you can. I'm unarmed. You little birds certainly outnumber us."

The first two men cast each other sidelong looks. The third one took a shaky step forward, dagger glinting in his hand. They were afraid of this Savan, or Varn, whatever his name.

Varn regarded the man and his dagger disinterestedly. "Of course, you'll get *much* less today than what you're owed—and it won't go far. What you pocket you'll spend quickly. And what remains of your very sad, very short lives you'll spend running. Looking over your shoulder. It'll be as if you suffered from the Kingkiller's Curse." He menaced them with a step closer, over the line of his sword.

The third man laughed nervously, a row of black teeth on his bottom gumline. "He's powerful, I'll give you that. But he's *not* the fuckin' king—"

"Actually, he is. Call him a king without a crown—"

"Aye, king of the Red Tower—"

"And yet," Varn said with a light smile, "he sacked a castle from his cell. Infiltrated your paltry band of traitors. Turned birdies like you with the lure of a little gold." *Birds.* Finally, Zur understood. *These* are *Pigeons.* "Point is, lads—you can kill my friends or me, but can you kill all of Lord Gram's other friends? They'll flip this kingdom over like a rug to find you."

A long moment passed. The toothy one finally lowered his dagger. Those who'd stood by, watching interestedly, tried now for disinterestedness.

Wet, labored laughter drifted into earshot. Legs quivering, Rathos Robswell struggled up in the arms of his captors.

Shut up, you fool, Zur thought. *Don't make this worse for you and your wife . . . especially when help is near.*

Varn turned his flat, emotionless eyes on the ward. "What's so funny, Robswell?"

"Your name," Rathos said with a crimson grin. "I like it—*Savan.* Easy to remember. It's not often that I hear of someone in Loran named after another kingdom's capital. Are you from the Kingdom of Penatho, Savan? You don't hide your accent well."

Sighing, Varn beckoned to his men. One of them flung Sinclair's daughter into Varn's arms. Rathos wriggled in his captors' arms, no longer laughing.

Varn regarded Mina skeptically, as if he were checking an apple at market for blemishes. He lifted her violet hair, sniffing, and exhaled rapturously.

"That *hair.* I bet people ask you lots of questions. Like, do you have any webs?" He checked her gaze for permission she didn't give, then inspected her right hand, splaying her fingers apart. "Hmm. No webbed fingers. Toes?" He glanced down at her bare, bloody feet. "No webs there, either. What about fins? You've got a merwoman's hair. You *have* to have fins."

Varn seized fistfuls of her gown and sheared it down the front. She maintained a steely dignity as he probed the sides of her breasts. "Where the hell are your fins?"

Chains clinked like bells as Rathos lunged. "KILL YOU," he vowed, "I'll fucking *KILL YOU*—"

Whirling, Varn landed a vicious blow on Rathos's face that puddled him in the other men's arms. He popped his knuckles and turned to the fat Pigeon as Mina cried out for her Rathos.

"You'd said you were promised her next," he said. "Off the road. Make it quick." He grabbed his shirt and drew him close, a finger in his face. "Remember, leave the face and hair unhurt. A kingdom needs to recognize her."

Zur winced as he felt Drexan dig his fingers painfully into the place between his neck and shoulder. "Come. *Now.* I'm not asking."

There was no debate. The King's Crow hauled him up and forced him uphill to safety as if he were a parent, and Zur the child. Drexan pushed him on for fifty yards. When they were a quarter-mile out, Zur pried free of his lord's grip.

Drexan had a disgusted look. "You put us in danger. If you wish to be a knight, think like one." He continued his relentless march uphill, cloak rustling.

"Stop." Zur chased after him. "I said *stop.*" He reached for Drexan's elbow; the Barefoot Knight jerked away. "Goddamn it, in the name of the king—*STOP!*"

The chancellor turned about. "There's but one king who concerns me, Zuran. But one whom I serve."

Zur realized he was panting. Sweat beaded his forehead. "I thought his name was Jason, son of Hexar."

"The Warchild isn't king."

That damn vile name. "But he could be. Before we left the Walls, Lorana told me of her plan to make Jason king through the Kingstrials. Rathos Robswell was one of the centerpieces. He was to deliver the Assemblymen in Sinclair's Company for Jason, in case he didn't win all three Trials."

"And you propose . . . what, exactly?" Drexan pointed at the road, the sleeve of his cloak gaping under his wrist. "Those are armed men. Servants of Gram Sothos. We're outnumbered."

Zur rolled his sleeve to his elbow to show his scarred arm. "God and gods, we descend from Windriders! You've shown me that blood has power. Cut me with swordwood, and we'll—"

"We'll *what?*" Drexan snapped. "Send Furos to harry them, so they can kill him and deprive us of his sight?"

"They're *defiling* Evan's daughter as we argue," Zur said. "It's happening off the road, out of sight. We can circle round on her attackers, destroy them with fire. Wait for the next men, destroy them, too." He'd never spoken of murder so glibly. "Let us do this thing. For Jason. For Lorana. Let us do this thing, this one kindness for our family. Then we'll leave."

The most indelicate, patronizing smile worked its way into Drexan's face. He laughed grimly.

"I didn't know loyalty was a laughing matter, Chancellor."

"It isn't." Drexan hardened. "I just wish I understood how a lifetime of lies and forced servitude endears one to captivity." He snorted. "'Our family.' Really, boy."

"You've lied to me, too, if recollection serves. About the Oracle's identity, for starters."

"Because I valued my neck, like anyone else. If I'd told you the truth about Orella, Hexar would've had me led to Traitor's Pit and beheaded. Who would've taught you about your proud lineage, then?"

"You once told me you like honesty in your servants. That if you're wrong, I should correct you."

Drexan rolled his eyes, sighing. "Spare me."

"Tell me the truth," Zur insisted. "You're the one who told Jason that he could enter the Kingstrials. You set Lorana and all of them on this path! *Why,* lord, if you had no interest in seeing Jason crowned king in the first place?"

Drexan tugged on his cloak. "We've lingered in the open for too long. Jhazar and the Pigeons aren't the only ones we need to watch for. You have a choice, Zuran. The same you had before. Do you wish to be a knight, to serve the *real* king? You need to decide."

Zur was grasping for anything now, any piece of Drexan that would convince him to stay and fight for the royal family. "You saved Evan Sinclair's life, once. Would you not save his daughter and ward?"

Drexan veered away, his lips pressed firmly together.

"What of Sinclair's cause? The Common cause. You saved it when you saved his neck."

A fury was in his lord's face when he whirled about, as if Zur had insulted him, the Solemn Order, the Ascendant King himself. As Drexan descended toward him in long, unbroken strides, Zur remembered that he was dealing with a sorcerer. He towered over his servant, green eyes flaring wide.

"His *cause?*" He spat. "I despise nothing nearly as much—except maybe the man himself! Evan Sinclair brought the curse of war upon us for that ill cause—he *and* his whore sister's."

People still spoke of how the King's Crow had gambled his post—even his life—to rescue Sarah Sinclair's brother from an ignominious end. Even when critics carped about his strange appearance at court, or cited rumors of sorcery, they'd admit, begrudgingly, this one thing: Drexan Lorrain had been a true friend to Evan Sinclair in the nobleman's darkest hour.

Yet here he was, listening in disbelief as Sinclair's savior renounced one of the few stories that spoke to his goodness.

Drexan had a raking smile. "You think me hateful. Disloyal."

I'm not sure what to think anymore, Zur thought.

"You don't know Sinclair. He preaches justice for the poor, but he's a liar. A fiend. A spider spinning webs to catch kings, Assemblies, and those he claims to love so he can suck out their blood when it suits him. Worse still, the spider thinks himself a savior. He's so convinced that seating peasants in the Assembly will deliver the kingdom from destruction—make his suffering and the suffering he's caused worth it—that he ensnared Jason, even Lorana in his plot. 'To each a chair.' A seat for the rabble." He spat to his side, as if he were expelling bitter ale. "In the act, Sinclair would unleash something crueler and deadlier than a million shadowkings."

A million shadowkings? Zur shuddered involuntarily. He was at Rorn Abeth again, watching as Southpoint burned, as a sea of blood crimsoned the bay. *Was that what I saw?* "You're not serious."

Drexan didn't seem to hear him. He stared downhill, as if he could see Rathos and Mina. "Sinclair compared himself to a cork in the poison vial." He chuckled mirthlessly. "He and his precious Commoners are the poison, more like, ready to spill out on our heads." He eyed Zur strangely. "Only the Ascendant King can seal the vial. Keep us safe from its poison."

An awareness stole over Zur, an awareness that stunned and dismayed him, that enraged him. He saw as Furos did—saw everything, as if he were flying over a forest.

Only, he didn't need a griff's eyes to see the truth.

Zur lunged. He grabbed hold of the strap of Drexan's travelsack and unslung it, spilling its contents. He snatched glass from the grass.

"No closer." Backing up, Zur stumbled on a tree root and nearly lost his footing. He held up a blue-stained shard of glass as if it were a sacred relic, and he were warding off evil. "Tell me what this is."

There was no fury in Drexan now. Only fear. He beckoned to Zur with an open palm. "Please give that to me—"

"TELL ME WHAT THIS IS."

"Keep your voice low. If we're discovered, I may not be able to—"

"What, protect me? Is that what you'd have me believe?" Zur held the broken vial away, out of Drexan's reach. "Tell me. What. This. Is."

"Something that could hurt one of us." He gestured again.

It was Zur's turn to laugh out his contempt. "I thought it was a spice. This is the Sphinx's Kiss. It's the same blue I saw in King Hexar's veins the night he died. Is this not it?"

"Zuran—"

"You killed Hexar." As soon as the words left his mouth, he knew it was true. Damnably true. *You poisoned the king.*

Drexan was the kingkiller.

"It's been staring me in the face this entire time," Zur said, horrified. "A Barefoot Knight of the Solemn Order. Like your forebears, you killed a king to seat someone else. A puppet."

"Puppet." Drexan sneered. "You saw the Ascendant King in your vision, did you not? A giant clothed in faces. Did *he* look like a puppet to you?"

"But you had to have help to cover your tracks," Zur went on, refusing the debate. "Who else worked with you? Was it Jon Applewood?"

They descended into argument, neither one allowing the other a word in edgewise.

But Zur would never reason with a kingkiller.

He was loyal.

"The old gods showed you the same future they showed me." Drexan sounded almost desperate. "The same vision—"

"The same vision! You gave me berries to eat before I had that vision. Was there something in the fruit, the way there was in the sleep agent you doused me with—"

"You'd rather me have left you there, in Sarah's Forest? You ungrateful—"

"*UNGRATEFUL?*" Zur blazed. "Jhazar had the right of it. You kidnapped me, Barefoot Knight. But I don't have to stay." Snake-quick, he retrieved the travelsack, slipping the shard of glass inside. "You were kind to me, Drexan. You saved my life. Showed me that magic exists." A tear irritated his right eye. "If you follow me—if I see Furos following me—I won't remember all your kindnesses. I'll tell Lorana everything. *Everything.*"

Zur tried not to shake where he stood. He'd threatened a sorcerer. Not a rumored sorcerer. A real sorcerer. He held his breath, tensing as he expected Drexan to shower him with fire, or gut him with his swordwood-tipped staff.

Drexan merely seemed resigned. "Go, then," he said. "Fight for your family. I won't follow you."

They remained watching each other for a long moment. The King's Crow turned and marched uphill, poking forward with his gnarled staff. With his back bent, he looked like a frail, old man. Not a Barefoot Knight. Not a kingkiller.

Zur watched him until he disappeared over the hill. He felt conflicted. Remorseful. He'd never see Drexan again, this man of miracles.

Perhaps never fly as a griff flew again. Never meet the Oracle.

Never become a Barefoot Knight of the Solemn Order . . .

Never learn about his mother, or whether she lived.

Nor should I want to, he chastised himself. *Sorcery or no sorcery, I'm no kingkiller. I'm loyal.* Tears slipped off his face.

He trudged downhill, toward danger. Drexan's mockery replayed in his mind like echoes at Rorn Abeth. What did he—an unarmed hostage, without even the swordwood necessary to summon power from his blood—hope to accomplish? How could he hope to rescue Rathos and his wife from Sothos men and treacherous Pigeons?

Yet with every step he took, passing columns of trees, Zur felt a weight lift off his shoulders. He was doing what was right. *I'm no traitor.*

As pale cobblestones came into view through the trees, he conceived of a plan. Jhazar was his salvation. He needed to find the tracker, tell him of Caerdon Castle's sacking, of Rathos and his part in securing a victory for Jason in the Kingstrials. As his kinsman, he'd help him, surely. The Grand Inquisitor would've told him of Jason's alliance with his uncle, surely . . .

He remembered seeing Drexan with Charles in the mirror at Rorn Abeth. *What if Charles helped Drexan kill Hexar?*

On the wind came voices, men's voices, disgruntled and wary. Zur followed the rhythm of boots and hooves, staying in the shade of trees along the road.

He half-ran, half-walked a quarter-mile before he caught up with Varn and his turncloak men. They were laughing and fielding insults for the shackled prisoners. Rathos staggered at the column's head like a blind man. Zur couldn't see Mina.

UrrrrrrEEEP. Zur looked up and glimpsed the pennions of wing feathers as Furos glided overhead. A Pigeon glanced his way; he ducked behind a tree. *I've made a mistake,* he realized. *How could I possibly hope to help Jason? I'm just a servant of the Walls, not even trained. And I've seen a shadowking. Drexan was right.*

As he turned to leave, he smacked into Drexan's chest.

Not Drexan. A hideously disfigured Commoner stared at him.

Beads of saliva oozed from the crusty scabs on his lips and cheeks. *Shrrip,* he slurped. He plunged his fist into Zur's belly.

Zur fell to his knees. An arm looped around his neck, another around his chest, holding him in place as the fists came, smashing his soft belly like hammers.

A one-eyed man snaked out from behind a tree. "Weeslaw donna like Elzura's Children," he said, tickled. "D'ya, Jacob?"

The one called Weeslaw savaged Zur, all while sucking up spittle that drizzled from his ruined lips, *shrrip, shrrip.* Soon he had fists and feet flying at him from all sides.

"Silence, all of you," came a stern, hushed voice. "They'll hear him squealing if you're not careful."

The fists relented. Zur was wracked with pain he'd never known. He coiled up on the soil, clutching his stomach, gasping inaudibly.

A Mumbler stepped out from behind a tree, his sandaled feet crushing grass. He wore gray robes soiled from woodland travel, stringy along the sleeves. The most exquisite emerald ring adorned his knobby finger. He looked familiar . . . yet Zur had never met him.

Other men stepped out of the forest, young and old, a boy with coal-black hair, two taller men with coarse stubbly faces, the last a pig of a man with yellow teeth in his grin. The fat one cinched Zur's wrists behind his back with hempen rope, tying it tightly. A cloth was tied over his mouth, gagging him.

A hostage taken prisoner while trying to free prisoners, Zur thought. His vision blurred with tears. *Drexan, you were right about me.*

Water

 tinny, clinking rattle deepened into a series of haunting groans, migrating through the amphitheater walls and shaking stone benches. It was as if the frightening heads of beasts along the walls were snarling their displeasure. Jets of water chugged out of their ridged iron snouts, gallons each second, inundating the Colossus arena with impressive speed.

Assemblymen applauded as ancient pipes gave proof they still worked after hundreds of years. After several hours, after the sun's climb to noon, the churn of river water turned the arena into a bronze-brown lake patched with lilypads of sand. Longships bobbed in the arena's corners. Trumpets blew. As the water jets thinned to trickles, a fine mist of rain began to sprinkle the lake.

Rain running down his face, Jason faced the lake with his twelve rowers from the western stairs, clad in a shirt of mail, a helm over his raven-haired head. The other claimants massed near their ships, Gavin Thorngale with his twelve, Tom Gelder with his. As was his right under the *mas in adversas* rule, his craven uncle substituted his role in this Trial with a champion, a Medecian Intercessor named Teryll Quathor. In the shadows of their black cloaks, twelve silver-faced men huddled behind the maskless, square-jawed Quathor, oars ready.

The Second Trial. Lorana and Charles Burke had secretly seen to it that Sir Gordon Whitecastle didn't return to Loran with a dragon. The Assemblymen had decided on a new contest for the next king, to prove that he could lead men in battle.

A *naumachia* was no dragon-slaying, but neither was it a cakewalk. To win the Second Trial, one of the claimants would need to fight their way to a manmade island at the center and be the first to seize laurels slung on the stake of Blackstaff's ebony rod.

Every man had a sword, but only one claimant could take the laurels and call himself victor.

This is a mad game, Jason thought as he looked out across the lake, at the men he and his oarsmen were about to kill. *But I much prefer it to war engulfing us all.*

Yet war *was* engulfing the kingdom. One week past, word had reached them of a violent peasant revolt in Rosbury. A justice of the peace had slain a child in broad daylight, and now uprisings were spreading through Loran like wildfire. Keen to encourage their lords to stop the upheaval, the Worthy saw in this Second Trial an opportunity to remind the realm about the perils of giving peasants power. This deadly laurels game was a way to weed out kings as much as a timely little history lesson.

To see how, one needed only look out at the island's six defenders, peasants all, pathetic and small with their wooden swords and shields. None of them had volunteered to be here.

High in the King's Box, Jon Redoak pointed at the island. "Two centuries ago, Sir Bradley Durhurst and his Treasonous Twelve killed their king and sacked the Silver Walls," he said, his voice echoing. "Not idle were Ansara's other kings. They built an armada to blockade the Shimmering Bay and starve that kingkilling mob out of Anjan First King's castle."

Yes, it's almost a history lesson, Jason thought grimly. The blockaders hadn't fought each other, or rammed galley against galley, as the claimants were about to do.

Redoak stared down at Jason, a sadistic smile curling in his face. "Stop me if any of this sounds familiar."

Jason bore the derisive laughter in stony-eyed silence. *They make light of my father's murder, despite the fact that it was Elvarenists who did Sothos's bidding . . . and, by extension, Shaddon's and Parlisis's. Will they still laugh when I win?*

Standing beside him, Trevor Wexley muttered something in Cloudspeech that drew scowls from Derek Clabbard and the six Cloudlanders. Clothed in ringed mail, all of the Wall knights but Rogir Levan stood to his side. The old lord had insisted on joining Jason despite the fact that he couldn't swim well.

They could each of them fight if the situation demanded it—and give their lives for his. He did not wish that. He'd try at all costs to avoid loss of life. He'd steered Loran into Kingstrials to avoid war, but he wouldn't have his men die for spectacle.

Evan rose from his bench, to boos and hurled pebbles. The kingdom's rulers were blaming him for peasant violence, conveniently forgetting that the lord had spent his life warning them about the math of oppression.

"It does sound familiar, sadly," Evan answered Redoak, his voice carried by the amphitheater's acoustics. "As I have warned repeatedly, you risk our necks by denying the peasants a voice in this Assembly." The boos turned to venomous curses. "You've stuffed your ears with wax and will not hear me." He swept a hand at the pathetically armed island defenders. "Now, you stoke the flames of war by making sport of these people."

Peshar Grathos quivered up in the King's Box, listing on a balustrade. "Peasants bite the hands of the lords and priests who feed and protect them, and even now, this traitor stands with them," he said.

Jason sized up a much sparser amphitheater. He saw an overrepresentation of lords, garbed in doublets and silks, and priests, ghosts in their pale cassocks. Jacob Sulley had made good on his threat to leave, taking most of the Free Believers with him and cleaving the Wing of Clergy in half.

He *had* to win the second and third contests, indisputably. *I wish you'd shared how easily your Companymen discard their oaths, uncle,* he thought with a look at Evan.

But he'd been a fool. He should've squashed the impulse to defend his wife's honor. The laurels he'd crowned her with had meant something to his dear wife, but it'd cost him dearly in Assemblymen.

He searched the sea of faces ringing the arena and found Edenia in the southern benches, dressed in a sumptuous red gown, her golden hair pooled about her shoulders, nuggets of emeralds around her neck. Inwardly, he smiled. *She wears my house's true colors, not Shaddon's false cream and violet.* Edenia was signaling Jason as much as the rest of Loran.

He remembered their lovemaking in windblown reeds, and her vow to him by Sarah's Fountain two years before: *I take you as husband, and love you forever.*

Lorana sat in the King's Box with the other judges, her brown hair flowing down her shoulders, framing her round face. He followed her line of sight to Edenia. *We both love her, sister. We'll free her from Shaddon, as we should've freed Erick.*

The steward leaned past Redoak and Grathos before they could cast any more aspersions, wrapped in an air of contempt. "Are we here to talk or watch a king prove himself in this great sea battle?" her voice rang out. "*SHIPS AND OARS!*"

The Assembly's approval thundered in his ears as Jason and his men rushed into his longship. Their ship wasn't wide, only four feet across; caskets had more space. The Bull and his Wall knights seated themselves portside, to face danger, while Clabbard sat close to the bow with Jason, his starboard rowers behind him. One of his men flailed as he skidded on rain-slick wood.

As Erick Seam severed the rope tethering them to a wall, Jason shared one last fleeting look with his mother's brother.

They'd agreed last night that two of the claimants would try to bleed Jason first. "Teryll Quathor will try for the island while Gelder and Thorngale ram your vessel," Evan had told him. "Gelder because he's a bought whore, and Thorngale for his misplaced vengeance. You'll need to ram Quathor's ship first, kill him, then deal with the others."

With rain pattering his helm, Jason raised his fist, and his portside oars clapped the water, rowing the vessel toward his uncle's champion. Shaddon's longship set out smoothly from the northern side, straight as an arrow flying at the island. The maskless Intercessor stood at his bow, eyeing Jason fleetingly.

The other ship captains were doing just as Evan had predicted they would, sailing straight for Jason, to intercept him before he could ram Quathor. Mired in a patch of sludgy sand, the rowers on Thorngale's ship struggled frantically to free their oars. Gelder's oarsmen pulled ahead in fine, muscular strokes that set the vessel on a collision course with Jason's.

Clabbard barked orders in Cloudspeech to the oarsmen that surely meant *brace for impact!* "ROW!" Jason shouted in Common.

The bow of Gelder's ship bore the iron snout of a dragon's head that could smash the hull of Jason's ship like a battering ram. Sunlight glanced off the blade Gelder drew as his rowers slapped their oars through muck water twenty feet away, now fifteen, now ten . . .

Jason turned to see his portside rowers distracted by the imminent collision, hands on their sword hilts, not their oars. "WE HAVE TO INTERCEPT SHADDON'S MAN," he snarled out. *"ROW! ROW!"*

Clabbard snatched him by his elbow. "Lord, beware the water," he said with a nod at the distinctively rust-red murk. "Its color . . ."

"The cunt may use swordwood again—leave him to me," Wexley said as the oars splashed water, and it was what Jason heard last before a whip-sharp *CRAAAACK* erupted in his ears and he went flying into Clabbard. He was still righting himself as his longship took on water, rust water torrenting through a hole stuffed with a dragon's head inspired by nightmares. The entire world tilted right.

Gelder's oarsmen herded into his sinking vessel, slashing their swords. The applause roaring from all sides of the arena sounded insane and surreal.

No, Quathor. Listing on his ship's lurching lip, Jason saw Shaddon's *mas in adversas* champion sail cleanly for the island. He plucked a spear from the orange water and hurled it for a clear throw across the lake. It impaled one of Quathor's rowers, barely slowing the ship's momentum. In a matter of seconds, Shaddon's men would beach the island and kill the peasants.

It was over. The Second Trial had been lost, and with it, any hope of winning the Kingstrials.

His life and the lives of his rowers were in even more danger than before.

Damn it, damn it all, Jason thought as he unsheathed his sword and cut through a Gelder rower's arm, spraying blood. He was back in the Brace again, sword hewing through some Muhregite's silk and leather. His men clanged swords against those of Gelder's oarsmen, their backs to the ship's edge, some toppling overboard as their vessel tipped dangerously to one side.

I've lost hope of becoming king, but my Assemblymen can throw any outcome favorable to Shaddon into doubt. Maybe Gavin Thorngale will be forgiving if we throw our weight behind him, make him king . . .

Jason gasped at the blast of white-hot fire in his shoulder. He whirled on Gelder, who wobbled unsteadily with the ship's sinking churn, a sword in his gauntleted hands. It was a blade notched like tree bark. *More fucking swordwood.* He recoiled as the blur of Gelder's blade shortened his sword into a dagger.

"Send your slut mother my best, Warchild." Gelder raised his sword. Two huge arms the size of branches wrapped snugly about him, their biceps plated in black Gildebirgean armor.

Gelder screamed haltingly as Trevor Wexley crushed him in his embrace. The little lord couldn't unhand the swordwood; its merciless edges snapped the rings of mail over his chest like icy twigs. Wexley meant to use the swordwood to saw through Gelder, through armor, flesh, bone—centimeter by centimeter.

"Swordwood cuts both ways, you fucking cheat," Wexley rasped in the much-smaller lord's ear. "My armor can take it. Can yours?"

Amid Gelder's ragged pleas, amid the sound that Jason's sword made through an oarsman's heart, the Colossus turned deathly quiet, and he heard only the songs of swords, sloshing water, and the clacking of planks. There was a scream, followed by a towering uproar.

A glance at the island turned defeat on its head. Quathor lay unmoving on the packed sand, run through by a peasant who'd somehow equipped one of his rowers' swords. Around the arena, Parlisis's puppet lords and priests bellowed curses at the peasants, who'd been enslaved to serve as killable props. Shaddon paled as he saw hope slip through his fingers. Seated beside him, Edenia flashed Jason a smile.

Defenders, indeed, he thought, renewed. *This Trial is over for you, Shaddon . . . but not for me.*

The impact from Thorngale's ship plunged Jason headfirst into ruddy water. He was in another world, a red one. The cut to his flank sizzled as if it'd been dunked in oil and set afire. He inhaled metallic water that turned his throat raw and sickly.

He could just drown, he thought. Let the wars for peace be over. Let someone else fight these contests. Let the metallic water burn through him and drown him . . .

Jason surged to the surface, past the half-submerged wreck of his longship. Rain pounded down in thick bullets, roiling the surface and curtaining the air in silver so that he couldn't see two feet ahead of him. Someone screamed over him and crashed into the water.

A vague shape floated ghostlike in the mist of rain. It was Gelder's longship, still intact. He swam toward it, through hell, navigating a flotsam of oars and corpses, throat stinging, flank pounding, trying to keep water out of his mouth and nostrils.

Rain thinned to needlepoints. A parting curtain revealed Thorngale's ship cutting through red water, straight for Jason. Gavin Thorngale pointed through the rain and urged his men to row. He had no intention of reaching the island. He just wanted to kill the man who'd refused him the head of old Greg's falsely accused murderer. *All the damn world's bent on vengeance for dead fathers,* Jason thought.

With their ship reducing speed, Thorngale and his men leaned off the edges, as if they meant to pull him up. They had their swords pointed down at the water. They'd spear Jason as if he were a whale.

Jason swung back his arms, kicking his feet, fighting to put distance between himself and Thorngale quickly. It was no use, against a ship. Their swords fell like the rain, piercing the lake surface. Jason cried out raggedly as a sword raked his shoulder. He submerged himself, swimming as low as he could, burning as rancid water relished the taste of his wounds.

He swam out as far as he could, trying to outpace the ship. He bolted to the surface, gulping down air, throat burning as if he'd swallowed a torch.

Still the teeth of swords came. The seam of Thorngale's ram sliced through rust water like a demon blade. Jason spun to swim away. He heard waves splitting behind him, the clap of oars.

A great cry made him swivel.

Trevor Wexley lunged out of the lake in a burst of water, latching onto the longship's edge with both hands. These were light ships built for speed, not weight, easy to ram, easy to sink, and Wexley was an anchor. He dragged the longship down like a hungry kraken, catapulting Thorngale and his men like pitch. The ship flipped over on Jason's great champion with a hollow thud, belly up.

Trevor! He swam toward the sinking vessel, but then . . .

The rain lightened a little, and Jason saw more clearly, saw that the island was a dozen yards off, easily within reach. The shadows of Quathor's Intercessors stood tall on the island, surrounding the laurels, the peasant defenders motionless at their feet. He counted four of them, down from twelve. Four. They couldn't claim the laurels for Shaddon, only obstruct and kill anyone else who tried.

Six peasants slew nine Intercessors? he wondered, incredulous. *I would've seated them in the Wing of the Commons, had they lived . . .*

Six feet away, a man swam into view, sloshing through the water. It was David Bridge, his knight. A sword wound colored the entirety of his left arm crimson.

"Are the others alive?" Jason asked him amid the thick of rain bullets. "Trevor, he's not coming up."

David shook his head, rain trickling in rivulets through his moustache and the dark hair clinging to his face. "I don't know, lord. This water . . ."

"We have to end this," Jason said. "The island." He nodded at the Intercessors watching them. "Can you do it?"

David nodded slowly, as if pulling himself together. "Four foreign-born bastards on two Loranians, I'll take those odds. Let's win this shitshow Trial."

They plunged ahead for the island. In a few breaststrokes, they waded out, stumbling up packed sand, soaked to the skin. Before their feet left the water, David handed off his sword to Jason. They scooped up two of the peasants' shredded shields.

The Intercessors charged them. A heavy sword stroke nearly tore apart Jason's shield. He let the brute land another blow before he drove his sword through shroud and abdomen, giving the Intercessor a terrible death. David had a new sword, and that blade opened the next Intercessor's throat.

Two on two. *I like these odds even better,* Jason thought. Rain sheeting down, Jason and David danced with their last foes. The bastard prince vaulted at one, sinking his steel into his heart for a jet of blood that half-blinded him.

David screamed wretchedly. Swiveling, Jason saw Gavin Thorngale wrench his sword out of the Wall knight's flank for a gush of crimson that gave Jason to bloodlust. Cheering voices echoed around the amphitheater as Jason clashed wildly with Thorngale and the last Intercessor.

Jason spotted a vulnerable sliver of gambeson between Thorngale's pauldron and chain mail. *There we are.* He stuck him with his sword, forcing a retreat. But that maneuver left him exposed. He gasped as pain erupted through his backside. Turning on the Intercessor, he cleaved him shoulder to heart.

"It's just us, Warchild," Thorngale said through the rain.

The bastard prince circled on Thorngale, who clutched his chest. Dark, shoulder-length hair matted half his face. He gazed at the sea of faces around them, listening to Assemblymen who called on him to spare the kingdom this Jason Warchild.

But Thorngale's vengeance had blinded him.

This was still a game.

As casually as if he were reaching for a cup of wine, Jason unslung the laurels from Blackstaff's rod. Cheers for Thorngale turned into bitter curses. "This contest is over, Lord Gavin," he said. "Yield, if you value your life."

"If you valued your life, you'd have given us Sinclair."

"Yield."

Gavin Thorngale did not. They traded blows, their steel ringing. Jason parried a swing at his leg, then another that would've taken his hand. It was a wonder that his wounds had blood to give at all. He was tired. Sluggish. His exhaustion gave Thorngale the opening he needed to bleed Jason's left flank.

Jason staggered forward, touching his flank, withdrawing his bloody hand shakily. Thorngale lunged. But he failed to see the peasant's corpse, snagged his foot, and landed on a knee.

That's that. Jason drove his sword through Thorngale's young, handsome face.

All the world jeering, Jason stumbled to recover his prize from the sand. *Such a small thing, bought at such a steep price.* He waved the laurels about clumsily, then fell to sprawl on his back. He breathed shallowly as the gray skies wept and wept.

"And you," Garrett's voice echoed in his ears, "*you* are the cause of all of it."

CHAPTER 19

Lovers' Quarrel

hen the princess was young, a great storm rolled into Southland. The storm of a hundred years, Drexan Lorrain had called it. Days before, Jason, then a boy of eight, had ventured out with Garrett and Connor Tomas on a boar hunt. They didn't return before the gale struck. They wouldn't return for weeks.

Most believed the king's sons dead. How bitterly Lorana had wept. Her father had only recently beheaded Romara, and it seemed the fickle gods would take her beloved half-brother from her as well.

Inconsolable as the storm, Hexar had a hundred men ahorse and his huntsmen's hounds ready before the lashing rain had abated. That was the first time the king handed the thirteen-year-old girl his realm. It was a lonely posting, with Anyasha only a year older than Zur, both too young for her to befriend, and Heather still a squalling babe.

With Erick gone, that left only her ladies-in-waiting, all insufferable, and the Silver Walls's most valuable hostage.

Hexar eventually came bounding across the drawbridge with his sons in tow, alive and laughing about how they'd had to nest in a tree above a flooded forest floor. How everything had changed during their absence.

For a young Lorana had learned to lead . . . and love.

Edenia had begun to sneak into her bed, listening as she wept, brushing her hair to soothe her.

"I have you, my flower," she remembered Edenia telling her every night, her breath steady on her neck. "I'll always have you."

Her face was warm in the firelight as she watched a Bull's apothecary work to rescue Jason from another storm. His bony hands flew from task to task as he cauterized his wounds with a knife bright red from flame, and then stitched them shut with thread, needle, and a healer's touch. Her half-brother lay on a bed of pillows in his pavilion, skin balmy to the touch.

"That water was foul," the apothecary, a snowy-haired man, Eorl, explained in his rhotic accent. He stirred a lumpy gray tea with his pestle. "I fear he fights the same infection as Lord Trevor. He'll need to drink this to fight it off."

Lorana held the mortar perfectly still in her hands while Evan Sinclair tilted open their king's jaw, and she poured in the brew. The three of them quickly dipped fingers in the salve and smeared it over the jagged sutures in his wounds.

"Redoak and Grathos bent the rules for Gelder," Lorana told Evan as they worked. "Now they use poison."

"You could be right," Evan said. "Yet it could've been rust, or something else. Those pipes are ancient and untended."

"And Redoak and Grathos knew it."

Evan agreed with his silence.

Eorl dampened Jason's beaded forehead with a wet rag. He lingered on him with Lorana and Evan, and then excused himself to tend to the other wounded. "He's an Eddenhold," the apothecary said. "If he's like his father, he'll win this trial, too."

This trial, Lorana mulled as she watched Eorl exit through the pavilion flaps. *Spectacle, more like. And what a show it was.*

The Assembly's applause had echoed off the Colossus's walls while bodies drifted on the lake surface, listless as dead leaves. The corpses included Gavin Thorngale and dozens of oarsmen, his and Gelder's, along with half of the men who'd rowed for Jason. Tomorrow morning, Lorana would lead her sibling's camp, lighting candles to pay tribute to David Bridge, Derek Clabbard, and the other fallen. After that, she'd draft a letter to Sir David's widow, explaining how he'd died, and what his loss meant for the kingdom.

Let this all mean something, Jason. Acid stung the back of her throat as she hoped that candles wouldn't also burn for her half-brother.

Wexley had suffered sword-piercings, and yet he'd swum to the small island and clutched a shallowly breathing Jason to his chest until help arrived. Only then had the Bull succumbed to unconsciousness.

You weren't wrong to hold out hope for Wexley, Father, Lorana thought. *But you were right to withhold all knowledge of bastard rights from your son. Now look at us. All this pain and suffering. To stop a war that men seem intent on starting. A war we should've started after you were killed. Whose fault is it?*

In the dimly lit pavilion, she imagined their faces. Faces she cursed twelve times over. Parlisis. Sothos. Shaddon, no matter the facts of his culpability. The King's Crow, for planting the seeds of the Kingstrials in Jason's head to begin with, then absconding with Zur, as Shaddon had once kidnapped Erick.

Jason, for trying to save a kingdom hanging together by a thread, even the half that reviled him.

Herself. She blamed herself. *I should've locked you in the Red Tower,* she thought with a smoldering look for her brother she meant twice over for herself. *Crown you king and let you rule there, until all the realm was on fire and we'd crucified our enemies' corpses.*

"It's better not to blame yourself. Trust one who knows the futility."

Sinclair slouched in his chair by Jason's bedside. He rose, turning on her with puffy eyes. The lord had helped rush Jason out of the Colossus; his nephew's blood cracked down the front of his tunic like dried mud.

"Agreed," Lorana said crisply. "I blame you."

If the nobleman took offense, he didn't show it. "For the revolts."

"No, you saw the revolts coming. You spoke truth to power. I respect that."

And why couldn't I have foreseen it? she thought grimly. Night after night, she'd tossed and turned in her bedsheets, a sheen of sweat on her as she gratingly remembered the Little King's words about her reviled justices.

Because I was proud . . . no, she corrected herself. *Because I tried to beat lords like Gram Sothos at their own game. To do the job Hexar couldn't, and rule this realm and her subjects like a hen who'd protect her chicks from the fox.*

She'd lain a sword on the shoulders of men like Willard Rittman and called them justices of the peace. To keep coffers full during the Kingstrials, she'd signed an order that had these justices flip villages over for extra income. It was a symbolic gesture to appease greedy lords, who'd suspected her of foul play with the dragon and refused to draw on their own coffers. She wished she'd used more of her political capital in that, and sacked Rittman for the good of all.

Now that prodigious tax collector was food for the crows, dead at the hands of furious villagers after killing one of theirs, a child. Rosbury's fire was roasting the kingdom. *I did what I had to,* she pondered stubbornly, *and Commoners repay me by taking up arms against us.*

The Commoners couldn't have chosen a worse time to revolt. Lorana and Sinclair had billed Jason as the king who'd return peasants to their Colossus, and peasants were giving ample evidence as to why they *couldn't* be trusted with power. *Perhaps my father and Shaddon had the right idea about these vermin, after all. Perhaps* you *were right, too, Charles.*

"I don't blame you for the revolts." She side-eyed Sinclair. "Drexan planted seeds in Jason's head to fight for crowns. But you nurtured that seed. Convinced him."

Sinclair was unmoved. It made her more wroth with him. "Your brother saw what half this kingdom meant to do to the other half," he said in a low voice. "Hundreds of Loranians call themselves 'noble' because they were born at a castle. But what Jason has done—that's *truly* noble. The very height of nobility in men."

"The height of stupidity," Lorana snapped back. "As was his decision to ally with you." *Our decision.* She hastened in his direction as if she meant to slap him. "An alliance with you has bought us nothing but a rug ripped out from under our feet."

"Jason ripped it out from under us," Evan said matter-of-factly, his eyes not shying away from hers. "As the prieslenne pulled it out from under you. Why else is Shaddon celebrating his nephew's victory mere yards away?" He strode past her, to the chair draped with his hooded cloak, which he slung across his shoulders. The sigil of Zarold Ulbridge's scaly mermaid tail swam down one side of the cloak.

"Where are you going?" Lorana demanded. Sinclair made a useful whipping post, but she found his company reassuring in this hour. Her misery needed some company, her thoughts a way to keep from devouring her.

Sinclair threaded the brooch of his cloak and covered his head with its hood. "To see to it that an alliance with me hasn't been for nothing." He ran a hand through his nephew's matted black hair, watching him as a father would. As Hexar should've more often. "My nephew has Sarah's strength, but we must be careful. Double the guards outside his pavilion, Highness. Our enemies smell blood in the water."

Sparing not another look, Sinclair bolted past, through the pavilion's flaps, a man on urgent business. *He goes to meet with his Companymen,* she thought. *What good will it do to keep them won for a king, if that king has fallen?*

When she could no longer hear his footsteps, the stone maiden removed her mask. She sunk into Sinclair's chair, stroking her half-brother's limp hand. Tears coursed through her eyelashes and ran down her face like rain.

"You stupid, *stupid* fool," she whispered thickly. "You *have* to be Hexar's son. Why else would you be so stubborn? You and Heather and I, we could've avoided this hornet's nest."

Why hadn't he accepted her forged succession letter? She'd warned of the terrible Trials. Jason could've been safe behind the Silver Walls. *Height of nobility,* she thought. *Was it worth it, to be noble for this hateful, broken kingdom, Jason?*

She traced one of his long fingers. "But I've also been the fool," she admitted. "A fool in love. I betrayed you, brother—and worse, it was with someone we both love. She was there for me when few others were. Now I wish she'd never come back, for all the trouble it's given us."

A wind whipped strands of her hair. "Is that true?"

Lorana whirled. Anyasha stood in the entrance, one hand keeping the flaps above her, silhouetted by the fires aglow in camp. She wore a mustard kirtle over her white blouse—gifts from *scrorn-ner-gaith* who'd come to admire her beauty. "Do you wish Edenia had stayed on the Lonely Isle?"

"Yes."

"Why?" Her brown eyes pierced Lorana like steel. *She knows. Of course she's known . . .*

She remained in her chair, words heavy on her tongue. "Because I betrayed you, Yasha."

Her servant stepped inside without permission. Light from the fire bathed her beautiful skin in hues of indigo and mahogany. Lorana resisted the urge to run to her, to beg for forgiveness.

"When?" Anyasha asked coldly.

At court, Lorana Eddenhold had been feared. Before this girl, with her brother fighting death one foot from her, she was a speck of sand from the amphitheater floor. She was nothing.

Lorana told her all. Edenia had kissed her at Saint Alban's, it was true. That betrayal would've been forgivable, had a kiss not turned into nocturnal visits. For the past few weeks, with Jason mere yards away and the Worthy and their soldiers all around them, they'd made love, at first in the field, like beasts, and then later in her bed, after Lorana had shared the hours for guard rotations around her pavilion—when Anyasha was least likely to pay her a visit herself . . .

After every parting, Lorana reviled herself. Cursed herself a traitor and a fool. And then, come the next night, she'd forget all revulsion and curses, all for Edenia's tender kiss, for their lovemaking.

Anyasha responded as only one without recourse would: "You're a princess," she said, emotionless. "I am merely your servant—"

"No, Yasha." Lorana ran forward, hands out as she tried to explain, to reassure.

"I am a hostage," continued Anyasha, averting her eyes as she came within inches of her, "cursed by Elzura to serve."

"You're the love of my life—"

"Am I?" Anyasha looked at her without hate or anger. "'A fool in love.' It's what you said when you thought no one was listening. So love the one you want." She exited swiftly, through the haze of cookfire smoke outside.

Lorana fluctuated between grief and, shockingly for her, a royal's anger. No one had ever walked out on her. No one.

I deserved that . . . worse. Lorana collapsed into her chair, running her hands over her tear-wetted face. *I'm a scoundrel . . . as terrible to my loves as Father was to his.* She glimpsed Jason on his bed, his chest only slightly rising. *How right you were, Father,* she thought as tears freshened in her eyelashes. *We're all traitors to our own hearts.*

The prieslenne was an intoxicating ale, and neither she nor Jason had ever kicked their addiction to her.

An hour or more had passed when she woke to the wind ruffling her hair. Lorana glanced over her shoulder tiredly. Sinclair stood in the entrance, a mermaid's tail curling in his cloak's folds.

She twisted back to Jason. "Did you meet with as little success as I thought you would?" She sighed. "Sincl—Lord Evan—I'm sorry for what I said earlier. You've done more to protect Jason and see him enthroned. More than our father, in fact, ever did. I've been glad to have you around him."

A hand clasped her shoulder. A younger man's hand. By the time Lorana stood, both hands laced her throat, hard as iron. She opened her mouth to scream, but nothing made it out. He squeezed and squeezed. She chewed into a wayward pinkie finger, tasting the iron of blood.

Grunting, he hurled her to the soil. On hands and knees, she staggered up, stumbling to the flaps, calling for Windkin. For Sinclair. For Yasha. She heard only a pitiful, painful rasping.

Her attacker had her again, pinned her to the soil by her wrists. She was kitten-weak against him. Through the brazier light, she saw inside his hood perfectly, the trim of his all-too-familiar goatee, the stone in his throat, the golden ring glinting in his left nostril.

"I'm not here for you," Vayne Adrias said in his elegant accent. "Be still, by Selyssa, and drink this"—he latched her throat in the vise-grip of one hand, and drew from his cloak a colorless vial in the other—"or I'll shut you up permanently. Your uncle needn't know." He chuckled faintly. "Idiot prefers the dark."

A chair slammed into Adrias, throwing him off her. Lorana heaved for air.

"HELP, THE PRINCESS NEEDS HELP," Anyasha cried over her. Footsteps thundered toward the tent.

By then, Adrias scrambled to his feet at Jason's bedside. Firelight winked along the curve of his dagger as he fixed it over Jason's chest, ready to plunge it into his heart.

Windkin and Levan flew inside, with men to spare. "Kill him," Lorana tried to tell Adrias, "and your master will never leave these shores." But her voice rasped pathetically.

Adrias gasped as another blade punctured his abdomen, below the ribs. Clutching the dagger hilt weakly, Jason twisted the apothecary's small knife.

Still abed, Jason had stabbed him. He was awake, barely, seeing Adrias through one fluttering eye. He wouldn't defend against a second attack.

A dagger twirled into Adrias's neck. Blood sheeted down his cloak. He grasped for the hilt as he stumbled forward, onto the points of the swords of Loranian knights, who finished him off in a few strokes. Adrias's blood soaked the soil, spreading.

The arm of the dagger-thrower stretched past her face. Blaring-eyed and panting, Anyasha of Tribe Nuur looked as bewildered by her precision as the knights flanking her. Her practice with a blade had paid off beautifully.

Lorana threw her arms around Anyasha, thanking her in painful croaks. She flew past men-at-arms trying to check her for wounds, over Adrias's oozing blood puddle, straight to her brother.

Jason lay motionless, on his back. It was as if he'd never woken. She checked his sweat-drenched body; lifted bloody, clammy hands.

"AN ASSASSIN TRIED TO KILL KING JASON!" Levan blared as he stormed past other men, back out through the flaps. "*AN ASSASSIN!* SEARCH THE PERIMETER! LIGHT TORCHES . . ."

Windkin knelt beside her, greaves clinking. He swung from her bloodstained palms to Jason. "Is he—?" he began.

Lorana shook her head, filled with relief at the sight of the ruptured suture in her brother's abdomen; it was his one and only wound, it seemed. She massaged her throat as Windkin brought her a waterskin, realizing belatedly that she'd marked her own dress with crimson handprints.

Lorana spun on Adrias. She felt the fabric of his cloak. It was Evan Sinclair's raiment . . . on Edenia's sworn guardsman.

"Something's happened," Lorana grunted out, her voice gravelly. She pointed at Ulbridge's borrowed cloak.

CHAPTER 20

Of Foxes, Thorns, and Wolves

he night journey northward wasn't as treacherous as his mountain climb weeks before, and for that, Evan Sinclair was grateful. The nobleman kept his mare's trot slow, tapping his flanks with his heels. Starlight guided him through reeds, past the wiry branches of trees that looked like ghoulish arms.

His heartache ran deep. He'd preferred to remain with his nephew. *The wounds weren't fatal,* he reassured himself. *He'll recover with time.* He trusted in the apothecary Eorl's skills. He had to.

After a half hour of riding, Saint Alban's columns took form in the dark. He circled the ruins, whistling low and soft. Nothing. He whistled again, then heard a fluctuating chirp.

"Hail, Pilgrim," came a voice from the temple's door. He recognized Tom Webb's effeminate voice.

Evan slid off his horse. He searched the doorway vainly. "Hail, Eyes of the World," he answered softly.

"Where does the sun rise and set?"

"It rises in the west and sets in the east," Evan replied. He approached a side entrance thronged with high weeds.

"Which star shines the brightest in darkest night?"

The man Evan didn't see behind him bagged his head with burlap, blackening his world and muffling everything. He was summarily relieved of his sword and Ulbridge's cloak.

"Don't struggle, Lord Evan," Webb whispered through the burlap. "Don't make this any harder than it needs to be."

So you are the twice-turned traitor, Tom, Evan thought to himself. But Webb wasn't alone. He heard other traitors, voices belonging to Lorn Granger, Drexyn Lauphrey, Geoff Donovan, and Tristan Lox. His own damn Petitioners. Every one of them.

Evan straightened his shoulders for dignity. "Would you kill me here?" he asked flatly, unemotional. He didn't want to give them the pleasure of knowing he was frightened. "At least remove this hood so I can see your traitor faces."

No one responded.

"Take his horse," Lox instructed someone coldly. "Get the cloak back to camp." *They mean to impersonate me for some ill deed,* Evan gathered. *I hope Jason's guards are alert tonight.*

Callused hands, a merchant's hands, fastened his wrists behind his back with rope. He was led off several paces, then forced astride a horse clumsily. Webb mounted up behind him, kicking their horse into a hard gallop. Hooves rumbled at their sides, keeping pace.

Swaying, Evan remembered what Gram Reuben had once written: *Fate is a name we give the unknown, and the unknown is fear.*

An hour passed in the swaying dark before the rich smell of cedar filled Evan's nostrils. *Wesswood,* he knew. Wesswood was a cedar forest some miles east. Owls hooted from up high. They scaled a hill, passed under branches that scratched at his hood. Flames crackled into earshot.

He heard men's voices. He knew them all . . . one better than the others.

The traitors helped him dismount. Off came his hood. His eyes adjusted slowly to a forest grove populated by shapes of men. Ruffled cedar trees loomed over a fire licking at a spitted hare.

Around the fire stood nobles, including Jon Redoak, Petor Ellsby, Jacob Hexbrook, Domin Greathall, and Aron Tuller. Sam Gramlore leaned against a tree, chomping into an apple. Seated on a log by the fire, Dumas Sunox worked his teeth on a haunch of hare. The plump lord glanced up at Evan, belching.

Gram Sothos sat on a stool, his pink hands splayed neatly upon his knees. He looked gaunter than Evan had remembered him, his eyes sunken and grave. *That's what captivity in the Red Tower will do to a man,* he thought. Yet here the kingkiller sat, free of constraints, garbed in a handsome green doublet and ermine-trimmed mantle. Firelight flickered in his storm-gray eyes and across the dome of his balding head.

Evan looked at his betrayers. Tom Webb, Geoff Donovan, Drexyn Lauphrey, and Lorn Granger refused to meet his eyes for too long. Draped in his exotic pelts, Tristan Lox looked on smugly. The shadows of archers lurked among the trees, their longbows nocked.

At least the Stormsword isn't here, Evan thought as he was forced down on a tree stump on the fire's other side, opposite Sothos.

Sothos returned his stare, unflinching. "Dumas," he said in that sonorous voice, the voice of a man who's won, "be a good man and fetch Lord Darren. He isn't far. He's grieving Gavin's death with his brother Luc." He breathed through his nose with deep satisfaction. "Tell him we have his father's killer."

Evan gave him a poisonous smile. *I know who killed Greg Thorngale, and it wasn't me . . .*

A moment's silence turned awkward. Sunox seemed embarrassed. "Uh, my lord," he said, "my knees, they're, uh . . ." He tapped a thick knee. "I fear climbing the amphitheater's stairs did me in. I will go, but it may take me longer to fetch Lord Darren."

Sothos exhaled his annoyance. "You should climb stairs more often," he chided him. He flitted to Gramlore, who was already unhobbling his horse from a tree. "I should keep men like you around me more often, Sam."

"Good to see you've been pardoned, Pinkhands," Evan interjected. He creased his brow, pretending confusion. "But doesn't that take a king? I don't believe we have one—"

Someone struck his jaw, ringing his ears. Lox popped his knuckles. "You'll talk to your better with respect," he growled.

Evan worked his jaw, glancing at the Petitioners. "What was the price of your betrayal? Lordships? Coin? Women?" He singled out the fanciful Lox. "Boys?"

Lox arched his fist, but Sothos signaled him down like a kennel master his dog. "Can't you see, Sinclair?" Sothos asked. "They weary of your treason. They long for a strong king. A righteous king."

"Shaddon would be a righteous king, but strong?" Evan shook his head, *tsk-tsk*ing. "He will kneel to the east. Which I don't think you'll all like."

"Lord Gram has delivered what you never could," Granger stammered out like a defensive child. "When Shaddon comes to power, we'll never again fear taxes on our trades."

"Lords regard merchants as Commoners with riches," Evan replied, unimpressed. "A King Shaddon would change that?"

Webb stepped forward. "We never fought for a Wing of the Commons," he said. "That dream was yours and Rezlan's."

"Nor would they see a bastard king," Sothos intoned.

"And *you*"—Evan gazed at Sothos through the flickering fire—"how long have you had Charles Burke in your pocket?"

Sothos betrayed nothing. "If what you're implying were true, it'd be the other way around, old friend."

The realization that Burke had betrayed the royal family sank in with a weight and bitterness only someone who'd been tortured by his king could know. *Hexar, you blind, blundering idiot,* thought the nobleman. *You tortured and attainted me, and all along, the real traitors were in your inner circle. Men your children called family. You should've listened to Trevor Wexley.*

Evan chuckled scornfully, overwhelmed by implications. "We're old, but we're not friends, you vile cunt," he retorted.

Lox raised his fist threateningly, and Evan shot him the darkest look he could muster, as if to say, *I may be tied up, but I know enough about you to still be dangerous.* And he did. Evan had compromising information on everyone here—enough to sow discord in this circle of friends, even now.

"Aren't we?" Sothos tilted his head just slightly. "You were the one who approached me in the Red Tower like a friend. Has our friendship not profited our claimants, Evan Sinclair?"

Evan stretched his wrists behind his back, testing the slack of his bindings. "There was no friendship. No profit."

But there *had* been an arrangement between him and the man who murdered his sister, a highly profitable one, if all had gone according to plan. A devil's bargain.

It'd happened at the Red Tower, an hour before Evan had charged Rathos with delivering the Loyal Company. He'd gone to the Tower's high cells to visit with Gram Sothos, alone.

Rathos had called the imprisoned Sothos a lion pacing in his cage. Evan had need of long claws he knew not even a Red Tower could contain.

Charles Burke had strangely given him space alone with Sarah Sinclair's killer, and with hindsight, Evan understood why. Caerdon and Saxhold had traded bitter insults, at least until Sothos understood that he wasn't reciprocating.

"We both have horses in these Kingstrials," Evan had told his sulking enemy through his cell bars. "And horseflies."

Sothos would languish in a cell for killing Hexar, at least for as long as it'd take for Evan, Jason, and Lorana to seat the Fourth Wing and unite their weakened kingdom against the Lonely Isle and its allied realms. Gram Sothos was under the priestking's protection. Nothing could befall him. Prison walls might as well not even exist. Evan knew that all too well about the man called Lordsbane.

An understanding here, an understanding there, and the lifelong enemies shortly arrived at a mutual agreement. "I will block the fox from your henhouse," Sothos had said at last, as grave-eyed as a haggler, "if you remove the thorn from my toe."

Fox had been a winking play on Tomas Fawkes's name, and *thorn*, an abbreviation of Thorngale.

The calculus had seemed as straightforward as the gains. With all his youth, charm, and smirking disdain for Elvarenism, Fawkes was a darling of the Free Believers, a fact helped by his friendship with a Master Reader. This was as true in the Loyal Company as it was in parishes across Loran. It made Fawkes as insufferable a threat to Jason's prospects as Shaddon's, the man whose brother Sothos had slain to make him king.

Evan needed Sothos to dispatch Fawkes. Westerliche was famously well-guarded, and so admired that no one in his inner circle would turn against him. No one but his favorite whore, a Tessian spy in Sothos's employ. Just so, Evan couldn't be caught sneaking a hired knife into Fawkes's pavilion. All his work—all of it—would be undone if that happened.

Greg Thorngale was another matter. Evan liked the Old Oak. He admired him. The aging lord had done nothing less than pull Loran back from the brink of destruction . . . and for Jason to don his father's crown, he had to die.

Sothos had an obvious reason for wanting him dead. The steward had named Thorngale his replacement as Speaker of the Wing of Lords, and that maneuver bore an intolerable risk to Sothos. It was also an intolerable injury to the pride of the man who'd held the office like an iron-fisted tyrant for decades.

Less obvious was why Evan would give the order for his Pigeons to kill Thorngale. Sothos had worked hard to convince him of the need. "The princess seeks to replace me with a lion, but she'll get a lamb," he'd said with a penetrating look. "Greg's an old man unsuited to Loran's divisive politics. A hero he may be in the minds of many, but he wants the realm to remember him for his olive branches, and he'll extend one to the lords. My lords. Your lords. He'll make concessions that'll hurt Warchild as much as Shaddon Eddenhold."

As much as Evan reviled Sothos . . . he knew he was right. That sense was borne out when Thorngale slavishly agreed to the lords' outrageous demands to trap a dragon for the Second Trial, with the already-indebted Silver Walls on the hook for it. His olive branch had prickly thorns, and it'd fallen on Lorana to toss it out—all after she'd harnessed peasant fury to make him her man in the Assembly in the first place.

"I mean to kill you one day," Evan had said. "How can I trust you to uphold your end of the agreement? Or you, me?"

"Self-interest," his enemy had replied smoothly. "Isn't that the god you men of the Awakening worship?"

"I *do* trust your self-interest. Your self-interest will lead you to betray me, as mine will lead me to betray you. We need some other assurance we can give each other."

Sothos had watched him through his cell bars without hate or anger. "You love my wife Tess as much as I do. You always have. And you know I love her more than life. Let us swear on our love for Tess. We'll honor this grand bargain."

"Then we'll kill each other?"

Sothos had nodded without breaking eye contact.

So Evan had sworn on his first love, as had her husband. He'd agreed without shaking a pink, gnarled hand. That, he'd never do.

He left Sothos in his cell with the impression that ridding the Kingstrials of the aging, outwitted speaker would benefit them and their preferred kings alike.

That was half-true.

Greg Thorngale was indeed a lamb, and Sothos had access to Fawkes, but neither of those reasons would've been enough for Evan to slay the peacemaker. Lorana had made a shrewd calculation in naming the Old Oak to a post that at once steered the Wing of Lords and held sway over the rest of the Assembly. Greg Thorngale would've ensured fairness in the Kingstrials' outcome, not least because of his popularity with peasants.

And that was why the lamb had to be slaughtered.

For Evan was done with olive branches. Done. He was done playing the lamb in a kingdom of wolves. He and Sarah had tried to seal the Fourth Wing's reinstatement by wooing Hexar, and they'd failed. Guilt-ridden for decades, Evan had exhausted petitions . . . and for what?

Hexar's refusal to even consider seating peasants again had hammered one of the final nails into the coffin of Evan's peace. But the king's assassination that same day had showed him the star of reason, illuminating Rezlan Ambrose's truth vividly. It was a truth he'd refused to see for twenty years.

There was no doing business with these wolves. Sothos, Grathos, and all of Parlisis's Assemblymen would torch Loran in another Long Summer before they allowed peasants to sit with them and make laws. They'd corrupt any proceedings like the Kingstrials in the name of an Elvarenist Loran they wanted to last a thousand years. Compromising with their enemies wouldn't aid their cause. Neither Thorngale nor the steward nor anyone else could make these Trials winnable for Jason.

For Jason to become king, he'd need people without seats in the Assembly. And peasants long bereft of those seats would help him by reclaiming them . . . by force.

Nearly every uprising in the history of uprisings had an inciting event, something that lit the fuse of mass unrest and inspired the aggrieved to rally. Most believed the Interregnum began the day King Lathros insulted Free Believers by telling them to make their altar in his garderobe, but violence had fanned across Loran well before then—the result of a beloved clergyman losing his head at Traitor's Pit.

As soon as he'd learned that Lorana had rallied peasants for the beloved Old Oak's speakership, Evan knew he had his fuse. His sacrificial lamb. Whether Sothos kept his promise and slew Fawkes wouldn't matter, for Pigeons would kill Thorngale and his sons disguised as Daughters of Divna, leaving scraps of their veils on the lords. The scraps could've well been tinder.

It'd played out in Evan's head like a choreographed dance. Furious Commoners would blame their Elvarenist oppressors for the peacemaker's death. From Eastland to Westland, from Southland to Northland, peasants would rise up as one. They'd take back their seats. Loran would be made whole against the powers trying to slice her up like pie. *Nothing will have been for nothing,* he'd reassured himself in times of doubt.

There were a hundred ways this could go ill, so Evan had tried lighting other fuses. The great temple in South Farcombe had been one. Jon Watley was a reliable dog, keen on barking everyone into war by himself, and if caught, Rezlan would face consequences in the Loyal Company, not Evan.

Thus would Evan, with one hand, stoke flames of revolt, and with the other play the Kingstrials. He was no warmonger at heart. He still had hopes. Perhaps Rathos could deliver the Loyal Company, and perhaps Jason could win his Trials like Hexar, or if not, with help from the Company's Assemblymen. He'd hold nothing back in that pursuit. Nothing.

All the same, Evan had something else in mind for Jason in the event the Kingstrials didn't yield him a crown . . .

Every uprising sprang from the sparks of a fuse, a martyr or rallying cry, but *victorious* revolts depended on something else. Evan could orchestrate the Old Oak's killing, and leaders would percolate to the surface like froth in a boiling kettle. But to win, they'd need something more than ordinary mortals. He didn't have faith in the Loyal Company to lead them, and he felt vindicated by the betrayal of these twice-turned traitors.

A child of destiny would need to lead them. A man chosen seemingly by fortune, endowed with a compelling story, denied the Silver Throne from birth by the craven elite that had cursed their serfs with a hardscrabble existence and stolen their children. A man who shielded Common girls with his own flesh, who—rather than plunge his kingdom into war for his glory—abided by ancient laws and constrained that hell to an arena. A man cheated out of his own seat in rigged contests.

A Warchild.

For men followed leaders, not titles, not congresses. Thus would peasants enthrone Jason, and Jason seat peasants again. A turn for a turn, a seat for a seat.

Matthus's last words echoed in his ears. *My nephew wasn't a game piece,* Evan thought in rejoinder, as if the knight faced him from Sothos's stool, chiding him still. He'd gambled with his blood. He hated himself for that. But after the foiled attempt on Jason's life, and then Hexar's assassination, he'd believed the lad safer by his side, even in a viper's nest like the Kingstrials.

And if Jason fell . . . there was always his sibling. That one wouldn't be king. Yet the Commoners would have their seats. Rathos had the location of the fire that had killed Sarah and Matthus. A flask of black-powder could incinerate a carriage, and there were five hundred barrels' worth at Barley Tower.

But god had mocked his designs. *Not god. Not gods.*

Of all people, a peasant girl had played the fuse. She'd been slain by one of Lorana's ham-fisted justices of the peace. Revolts had exploded across Southland, and the realm knew Jason as her half-brother. Coupled with his crowning of Edenia, his besotted nephew likely had no chance now to rise on the wave of peasant anger.

Worse had happened.

Indeed, Thorngale had been a fuse—the *wrong* fuse. Evan had ordered Old Oak and his sons hacked to pieces on a dusty road. His Pigeons had dressed not as Daughters of Divna but in the camouflage of their woodland cloaks, slinging arrows from trees. Unbeknownst to Evan, they'd slain the old man and given his sons scratches, leaving them very, *very* much alive . . .

Alive to swear bloody vengeance against Evan and Jason, by extension. Now Gavin was with his father, and the deadliest of the brothers was on his way to this forest grove right now.

Evan regarded his enemy through the snapping flames. "I should've guessed your oath on Tess would mean nothing," he said. "As I'm sure you felt nothing when the princess beheaded your firstborn son."

Sothos looked like he'd chuck Evan into the fire. "I could kill you now, before Darren Thorngale arrives," he said through clenched teeth.

"But you won't. Nor will you allow him to kill me." *I'm too valuable. I always have been.* He ignored Lox's stare. "But what eludes me is *why*, Gram. Why even play this game with me? You had my Pigeons in your employ all along. You had Fawkes's whore. *Why bargain with me at all, if you held all the chips?"*

Sothos smiled coldly. "To prove what I've known about you all these years. You've always thought yourself better than other men. Better than me, certainly. Evan Sinclair, man of the Awakening, beholden to his star of reason, here to save us all from our selfish, cruel, unreasonable selves. To save your flea-bitten rabble." He waved dismissively. "But you've always been that snake, Evan, flicking its tongue at our fragile peace."

"My words about you, to Tess," Evan jabbed him, smiling.

"A man as ruthless as any of us," Sothos spoke over him before he could finish saying *Tess.* "Ruthless to start a war, all so you can dishonor Rorin's amphitheater by seating"—and he wrinkled his face, as if he smelled rotten egg—"Commoners."

Evan shrugged. "They sat there with us from the start, until King Lathros made the same mistake you and Parlisis's lackeys are making. I want to hear you admit it, goddamnit."

Sothos arched an eyebrow. "Admit what?"

"YOU KILLED THE KING," Evan said venomously, voice carrying through the night. "JUST LIKE YOU KILLED HIS WIFE. MY SISTER." *And you, Matthus. His hands bleed from killing you.*

The nobleman's smile widened. "I didn't kill Hexar. Even if I had, there is only One True King, and that idiot wasn't him."

"Spoken like the man who wedded Stoddard Trambar's daughter." Evan stared straight into Sothos's eyes, unblinking. "So what now, Pinkhands?" He tensed his bound wrists. "You brought me all this way . . . just to prove a point?"

"No, I want what Hexar asked of you in the throne room." Sothos steepled his pink forefingers. "I want their names, all of your Companymen. The ones in the Assembly. Tell me them, or I'll have done more than kill that whore sister whose legs you opened to Hexar for your seat for the rabble."

That's all I wanted, Evan thought. *An admission.* He tilted his head at Lox and the other Petitioners. "You want names? Ask them. You should be able to—"

"ENOUGH. GAMES!" Sothos rose to full height, towering over the fire. "I've sacked your ancestral castle. I have your daughter and ward being marched here. I want the names of your Companymen in the Assembly. Only you know them all. Give me names, or I swear by every one of the twelve gods, I will peel off your daughter's skin and make you wear it for a cloak."

Steel glinted at Gram Sothos's neck, and a few seconds passed before anyone registered that Dumas Sunox held a dagger at his liege lord's throat. "Will my name do, my lord?" the vassal hissed in his wide-eyed liege's ear.

Nothing felt so gratifying for Evan as seeing the open-mouthed dismay of his betrayers and enemies.

Of all the lords in his Company, the Lord of Ramsport was the catch Evan prized most. Years before, Rezlan Ambrose had discouraged him from seeking to turn Gram's most loyal vassal. But Evan had heard songs about discord between the houses of Sothos and Sunox, and he knew the key to a man's heart wasn't always ambition, or treasure, or even ideas. Oftentimes, it was as simple as grievance. A desire for revenge.

Long before Lorana had nicknamed Sunox Lord Gut, he'd suffered endless mockery at Saxhold Castle, where his lord had indulged even less courteous names—the Whale of Ramsport, His Portliness, Thunderarse, among others. No one could recall where the bad blood began between liege and vassal, but the humiliations went beyond name-calling. Sothos often neglected to invite Sunox on hunts, dismissed his voice in the Assembly, and overlooked his sons for coveted sheriffships. Evan relished nothing so much as discovering a man's hubris, and Sothos had *so* much to exploit in this toxic relationship.

Evan's relationship with Dumas Sunox began with desires for vengeance. Over time, it became something richer and more satisfying: a genuine friendship. Sunox's star of reason led him to support the Common cause.

The years proved Sunox a valuable asset, even when Sothos kept secrets from him. The Lord of Ramsport tipped off Evan about Gelder's swordwood in the First Trial so that Jason would wear his thick Gildebirgean armor. He'd warned Evan that tonight, the Petitioners would betray him, guttering out the Loyal Company's flame.

Redoak whipped out his sword, trembling slightly. "He's your liege lord, Dumas," he said shakily, eyes wide with fear. "You want the High God's curse on you? You'd orphan your motherless children?"

Sunox tripled his chin with a smile. "My lord, you talk of the Kingkiller's Curse. On that account, I have nothing to fear. I'm a man of the Awakening besides. I don't believe in the rubbish of religion."

A Loyal Companyman, indeed, Evan thought.

Evan winced as Lox pressed a dagger to his neck, forcing him to his feet. "Well well well!" the merchant hissed. "Who'da thought? His Portliness's a fucking Companyman."

"More loyal than you lot, you cockstain." Sunox tightened his grip on his dagger, drawing Sothos back with him.

"Look around you, fat ass," Lox snarled. "Every man here has steel on him. Look at your liege's men in the woods! You'll never leave here alive."

"Neither will you, Tristan," came a woman's voice.

Out of the forest stepped Leah Sinclair, disguised as an archer, her hair a rich purple in the firelight. She steadied the arrow in her bowstring at Lox's neck.

Soft-footed as wildcats, the other archers emerged with her. *My daughter's men,* Evan thought as a huge Uzman lurched out, and beside him the gangly Creature, more than two dozen, all dressed in surcoats emblazoned with Sothos's prancing lion. In every Heretic's hand was a longbow, in each bow a fletched arrow. They surrounded the grove.

Swords flew into the hands of Ellsby, Hexbrook, Greathall, and Tuller. "Fucking traitors everywhere," Tuller muttered.

Leah stretched her bowstring, eyes fixed on Lox. "Release Sinclair," she said in a low voice, "or every arrow finds a neck."

Lox fronted Evan toward his daughter, shielding himself. Lords curled their hands around their sword hilts a little more tightly, as if bravery could stop arrows.

Bravery wouldn't, but skill could. Darren Thorngale leapt off his horse as it thundered into the grove, accompanied by Sam Gramlore and men-at-arms. His hands flew to opposite ends of his waist and unsheathed swords. Two swords.

The bastard's ambidextrous, Evan thought, stunned.

"Gods, FINALLY!" With his rictus grin, Thorngale looked insane. He advanced on the Heretics fearlessly, a butcher with his cleavers. "I've been so fucking bored."

Arrows flew, many felling the lords' hobbled horses, one catching Lox in his throat, as the Mad Lady had promised. Her outlaws mounted their horses and rushed in, Dustin mowing down Tuller, Murg slashing his two-sided axe wildly, Creature crowing as he hacked left and right with a falchion.

No one was a match for Thorngale. The Stormsword flew like a whirlwind of steel, hacking off hands, arms, and heads in fluid strokes. The flying of his swords startled Dustin's horse into throwing the outlaw.

The Mad Lady soared through the fire on her sleek black mare, embers swirling about, Faye's purple hair sailing from her griffon's skull. She dealt death with both hands, burying a sword in Webb's chest and flinging a dagger at Thorngale that Loran's greatest swordsman blocked in a blur of steel.

Leah reared up on her horse, a vision from hell. "I'll free you," she said in a skull-muffled voice. Evan spun around; she sundered his rope with a clean arc of her sword.

She twisted about for a look at Thorngale, and couldn't see Sothos marching determinedly behind her, sword steady. Evan grabbed a discarded blade and swept low, deflecting the sword that would've lobbed off his child's head.

The clash of their steel sang through the forest. Stoddard Trambar had trained Gram Sothos like he would a son, and his methods didn't disappoint as Evan's adversary moved with a dancer's grace. He lunged, and Evan faded back. Evan hacked and he blocked. Lunge, slash, pivot. Lunge again, hack again, slope, hack and slash, slash and hack. Decades of mutual hatred turned their swords to piercing rain that fell relentlessly. *You killed my sister and friend,* he kept thinking, *you killed them.*

Evan deflected a sword stroke, a terrible mistake, an old man's mistake. A dagger flashed in Sothos's left hand, and he moved so single-mindedly that he failed to see Leah charging in until it was too late. She reared high on her horse, front hooves kicking wildly at House Sinclair's nemesis.

Sothos fell hands first into the smoking fire. He wailed as he rolled off, flailing to put out the banners of flame rippling up his chest and arms.

Like overdone pork, he thought.

"*UP, UP, COME ON!*" Leah cried at Evan.

Evan climbed behind her. Sunox mounted up with Pretty Phillip, and Murg heaved Dustin over his saddle as easily as if the man were a satchel. They plunged into forest, the thunder of their mounts' hooves mingling with Gram Sothos's terrible screams.

CHAPTER 21

To All a Piece

amn stupid boy, you spilled it on me doublet you did," the rat-faced knight said. He twisted in his chair with a livid expression. "Y'know how much this cost me? D'you?"

"Forgive me, Sir Jeremy," Tyler Rolfe said. "Didn't mean to spill wine, sir."

The apology only seemed to infuriate Sir Jeremy Hunt. He pinched the corners of his blue doublet's pomegranate-colored stain. "More than what you earn in a year, I wager. Y'know I got this in Tesos? Can't find brocade like this anywhere else. Supposin' you'll go back to Tesos for me and buy it new?"

"Forgive me, sir, I—"

A dagger appeared in Jeremy Hunt's hand, catching light from the candles in their pavilion. *In his cups again,* thought Tyler. *Will I die tonight over spilt wine?* Sir Jeremy had slain a peasant one moon ago for less.

A knight leal to House Eddenhold could do anything.

"Jeremy." The voice issued flatly from the other side of a round table crowded with dying candles, crumb-dusted dishes, and empty flagons. Sir Astiban Hoard, the Blackstaff, said the knight's name again. Jeremy lowered his dagger sulkily.

"Easy, Jeremy, easy." Seated across from Jeremy Hunt, Sir Hortus Gallivar raised his wine cup for Tyler to fill. He wore a broad, conciliatory smile. Tyler liked Hortus. "A night like this, with company like ours? I can't see why you're wroth. Besides, you can find finery like that in Westland."

"Don't wanna go to Westland," Jeremy said. "Traitors out there. I remember you tellin' me."

Tyler poured more wine. He caught a look of himself in the water of a flagon that torchlight rendered as reflective as windowpane, his bowl of black hair, the lump in his scrawny neck, the flared ears that people called elvish. He adjusted his tunic and went back to serving Princess Lorana's knights.

Jeremy pivoted abruptly to the evening's entertainment, Jaina Nadley, a skinny, cream-skinned Southland girl clad in a wool gown and girdle. He grabbed her by her bony hips, forced her into his lap, and buried his nose in her hair, inhaling lustily. She adjusted the comb in her hair, giggling.

Tyler cleared his throat and went to refill a flagon for the three knights sworn to the Silver Walls. He located the sliver of a crescent moon through the canvas flaps. Crickets screeched incessantly outside. *When will this night be over?* he wondered.

Wine had flowed in this pavilion tonight like the blood of lords in Rorin's amphitheater. A dozen cups had put the usually stern Blackstaff at ease, as Tyler knew they would. This was the seventh time he'd served the three Eddenhold knights at their get-togethers since the Meet of First Declaration. Tyler came into the role shortly after Blackstaff beheaded his predecessor, another serving peasant.

The first serving peasant had done nothing wrong, he'd learned. Sir Astiban Hoard had a temper, and he'd needed to express it the night that old peasant doddered into the arena and shamed him a liar before the realm's lords, priests, and merchants. Never mind that the old man had died for his crime.

For his part, Hoard had only shown Tyler courtesy, even paid him a loren at each get-together. By this point the knight seemed fond of him, even—not a bad thing, especially since Blackstaff played so visible a role in the Worthy Assembly, and especially because he also paid Jaina Nadley to wench on these occasions.

Still, Tyler had to be careful. Had to keep from spilling any more wine. Had to keep his hands from trembling.

Hortus licked his wine-smattered lips. "I think my mind's changed about Westland," he told Jeremy with a tipsy grin. "Don't think you'll find traitors there. Think they'll be in short supply most places, actually."

Tyler pretended he didn't hear that. Nights like this one usually ended with gossip, and Hortus was a spigot for secrets Blackstaff wouldn't leak to Jeremy. Feigning disinterest, the peasant began collecting flagons and plates from the table.

Jaina giggled as Jeremy tickled her pits, grinning. "That so, Hort?"

"So I heard." Hortus drained his cup. "Little bird told me."

"Pigeon?"

"Heh. Not a Pigeon."

"Don't be coy. Tell me, Hort."

The two knights conversed as if Blackstaff weren't there, and truthfully, he wasn't; the high-ranking officer stared off in a drunken stupor, eyes dark with whatever thoughts pleased or comforted him tonight. Tyler glimpsed the rod of his office leaning against a chair, its silverstone aura pulsing in the edges of its thick cowhide sheath.

What could that fetch at market? Tyler thought. Peasants lost their hands for stonelust. Not so, their kings and lords. He noticed the men's swords, propped up against the same chair.

"Better shown."

Hortus beckoned for Jaina. Ragging a plate, Tyler watched from the corner of his eye as she slipped off Jeremy's lap. The other knight jerked her close by her girdle.

"Such a pretty lass," Hortus said as he pulled at strands of her chestnut hair. "Wasted on our homely Jeremy."

Jeremy didn't glare at him for long in Sir Astiban Hoard's presence. "Just show me already, you sot."

"Very well. Let's say Jaina here is Loran." Hortus placed hands on her hips and slid them up her ribs, watching Jeremy for his reaction. "I reckon these are the Midlands, and these"—he cupped her small breasts—"the Iron Mountains."

Jaina smiled meekly. Jeremy stirred. "Jeremy," Blackstaff slurred reproachfully.

Hortus released her. "It matters not. For all intents, she is Loran. Now, say I'm a mighty lord from somewhere. Or rather, my cock is, and recently returned from abroad. I've come to win back Loran from the traitors who hold her captive. This"—he plucked at her girdle—"is the Loyal Company. Look at how it holds her rags, keeping Loran's spoils from my lordly eyes. If only it could be removed."

"Loyal Company?" Jeremy seemed less jealous now, more aware of the game. Tyler refilled his cup. "Go on then, Hort."

Tyler cleaned another plate. Somewhere outside, a nightbird hooted.

Smiling lopsided, Hortus unfastened Jaina's girdle, letting it slack to her feet. Jeremy bounced his leg, intrigued.

"You're saying—" Jeremy began.

"I'm saying nothing. I'm *showing*. I just removed a girdle. And now it's gone." Hortus kicked the girdle away. "*Forever.*"

Wide-eyed, Jeremy looked to Blackstaff for confirmation. Hoard gave none. Tyler stacked the crumb-free plates near the Blackstaff's rod.

"And now what's left?" Hortus hoisted Jaina's gown over her head. He admired her in her shift. "Mere ceremony."

The Loyal Company is gone, Tyler realized. *That's what Sir Hortus is saying.* Blackstaff and his men weren't fond of Sinclair or his designs to reinstate the Fourth Wing. The royal family's anointed men wouldn't make their opinions known, for fear of angering Lorana, but the rank-and-file despised her for trying to seat peasants again instead of knights. The Wing of Knights had once seated *actual* knights, after all.

Knights like Astiban, Jeremy, and Hortus considered this treachery by their betters, but all they could do was drink and quietly rejoice at the Warchild's setbacks.

But this was different. These men had news of something.

Jeremy reclaimed the wench, drawing her onto his thighs. "If that's true, then we must drink." He raised his wine cup. "To a king who will put his knights before the fucking peasants."

At this, Hoard regained his senses. The three men clinked their cups. "To the end of Evan Sinclair, saint of the flea-bitten," Hortus said with rosy-cheeked cheer.

Smirking, Jeremy slurped his wine. What a fine moment for him, Tyler understood. By slipping such information, even cryptically, Blackstaff had conferred on Jeremy Hunt an honor. Jeremy was like Hortus, now, someone with an informant in high circles—that informant being Hoard himself.

The knights drank deeply. The nightbird sounded again, louder. Still in Jeremy's lap, Jaina stretched for a yawn. As she lowered her hands, she embedded the swordwood-needled rake of her comb so deeply into Jeremy's throat it vanished in all the blood that founted out. The knight lurched off his seat, knocking aside dishes in a god-awful clatter.

Hoard slurred *traitor*, too sodden drunk to speak clearly. But he could stand. He brandished his greatsword and slid it through Jaina Nadley's belly as effortlessly as if she were made of butter.

Tyler stifled an anguished cry.

It happened in a blur, Jeremy's dagger finding its way into Tyler's hand, and then straight into Hortus's chest. The knight seized Tyler by his arm with a giant's strength. Hortus released him with an almost-quizzical look, a grief for life as it slipped fleeting through his fingers, just like the peasant's tunic.

Hoard circled the table, a bear approaching in the dim candlelight. He easily had a foot over Tyler.

Blackstaff gritted his teeth. "I, I will carry your head . . . all the way to Traitor's Gate." He tightened his sword grip. "Rolfe, you fucking bastard. You're with the rebels?"

Shaking pathetically in his grip, the dagger might've been a feather quill, for all the good it did Tyler. He'd never taken up steel against anyone until Hortus, and even then he'd taken the knight unawares. Sweat trickled down his nose, mingling with tears.

Tyler glimpsed Jaina curled up in a corner, dying. Closing his eyes, he prepared himself for excruciating pain. For death.

Seconds passed. He was still alive. He opened his eyes.

Blackstaff held his sword suspended midair, as if some invisible force ensnared it. He looked frightened. "I shall . . . have your heads," he said faintly. A last rattle of courage.

Tyler steadied himself as the other peasants formed up beside him. He glanced sidelong at all their faces. *They came, they really came,* he thought with fierce joy. He counted twenty, praise the One True God, *at least twenty* peasants with him in the pavilion. Men and women. All carried weapons—swords, dirks, axes, hammers. Their steel reflected candlelight dully.

"Might be better f'you put down yer sword and parley, Sir

Blackstaff," said the peasant Roryn Cook, tapping his palm with his hammer.

Astiban Hoard flitted from one face to another. "A lot of old rag-tags and poxed bitches. *Against a trained knight?*"

Roryn shrugged. "We killed the four guards outside easily enough. Reckon we can take one drunk."

They descended on Blackstaff like wolves, piercing flesh with the teeth of their steel. Sir Astiban fell to the sixth sword, but everyone wanted a piece. By the time Roryn forced an end to the knifing, the peasants, all of them in bloody tunics, sucked in air like they'd been drowning.

Tyler couldn't hear them. He couldn't hear the crickets outside, either. All he heard was Jaina's shaky breathing. He cradled her head in his lap, caressing her blood-matted hair.

Her blue eyes found his. "*Turel e'sartha,*" she whispered with a bloodstained smile.

They dragged the bodies of four guards into the pavilion and left with only stars for witnesses. Roryn Cook led the band of twenty with their sacred prize firmly in his possession. Had Blackstaff been anyone else sworn to the royal family, Roryn and the others would've certainly had to kill more sentries, but Sir Astiban Hoard had staked his pavilion on the edge of Jason's camp, far enough from Hexar's children so that he and friends could drink, gossip, whore, and kill without scrutiny.

Hoard's debauchery had made their plan tonight perfect.

Almost perfect, Tyler thought hollowly as he watched his friend in the moonlight. Jaina's bloodied body swung to and fro like dressed game as Tyler and three others bore her by her hands and feet. Only Jaina had perished in the standoff with Sir Astiban, and bitterly, men were hailing it a miracle. *You were the miracle, Jaina, my friend.*

They wended past camps asleep in the dead of night and trudged through barbed reeds, breath fogging, utterly silent save for reeds occasionally snapping underfoot. He glanced over his shoulder to see if they had pursuers and saw the dark arrowhead of Mount Dracar against the sky.

After an hour's brisk walking, the peasants spotted their rendezvous point, the Bony Yew, a pale, withered tree west of the Golden Meadows. Midland peasants often ventured north to pray at this tree for a good harvest.

Tonight, they'd pray for a different kind of harvest.

They weren't alone. Peasants crowded round the yew and spilled across the field. Maybe a hundred, he thought. Enough mourners for a decent peasant burial.

Tyler felt betrayed. "We need more, or Jaina gave her life for nothin'," he muttered to Roryn as they walked together.

"More'll show," the peasant leader reassured him. "Have faith, Rolfe."

"As they'll have faith when they hear about Lord Evan?"

Roryn said nothing.

Without needing to speak or be told, the gathered people cleared a path to the pale yew. They knew a sacrifice had been made tonight. Not a Gift, in the tradition of the Sylvanians, but her life *was* a gift—a gift to those here and those not, to those living and yet to be born.

Tyler and other peasants carried Jaina through the crowd, unspeaking. Under the tree's splayed limbs, they began digging a grave in the cold earth with their hands. Tears dampened his cheeks as other peasants knelt to help them, enduring ant bites together.

When Jaina Nadley lay in her grave, arms folded across her chest, a Hexwaite reader bowed his head and gave rites, and they buried her. Tyler willed himself against tears. Too many tears would fall on the Golden Meadows this night. *We cried enough while you lived, Jaina Nadley,* he thought.

They had never been lovers, though many a man who saw them together had told Tyler he should marry her. They'd been friends from earliest memory, since before a Ramsport sheriff had separated Tyler from his parents, and after he'd run from Peshar Grathos. Jaina Nadley had hailed from a shire two miles from Ramsport. They'd gone north together for the Kingstrials.

How long it was after they'd buried her that a dozen more peasants showed up, rustling through reeds, Tyler didn't know.

More arrived after those. Many more, in pairs, in bands of dozens, and then in droves.

Hundreds.

Thousands.

Their coming was like the fingers of a hand closing into a fist. They came from nearly every lord's camp, peasants from Gram Sothos's camp, from Tom Gelder's, from even vanquished houses, Thorngale field hands and Wuthers rustics, even some who'd seemingly dispersed to Westerliche. Two-hundred kilt-clad *scrorn-ner-gaith* marched in from Jason Warchild's camp, defying expectations for the folk under Trevor Wexley's cloven hoof. Astonishingly, Commoners even trickled in from outside the Golden Meadows, from as far south as Grayport.

They came armed. Tyler beheld an army of peasants fitted in jacks of plate and gambeson. Glare from the moon and stars and flickering torches shone in their helms, their swords and axes, the discs of bucklers, the points of their spears. Those who'd come straight from shires and villages hefted pitchforks, rakes, scythes. Some armed themselves with elk antlers.

Scanning the field, Tyler stirred. He saw more faces than reeds, a sea of peasants. Crickets, screeching before, fell eerily silent now. *They came,* he thought bitterly, fiercely, unable to restrain his tears. *They came, Jaina . . . and it may not be enough.*

One by one, torch-bearing peasants streamed forth from the reeds, coalescing into a group. A war council, as it were. He recognized Jonathan Smith, a thick-armed Thorngale man. Like Roryn, he was a veteran of the wars in Uzland and commanded respect among peasants.

"Stay close," Roryn instructed Tyler in a low voice. "When I say, you tell 'em what you tol' me. God be with us."

Tyler understood his nervousness. *Will they fight when they learn we won't have archers and horsemen we promised?*

Twenty-three peasants crowded around Roryn, huddling so close together their reek overwhelmed. An old woman Tyler didn't know staked a position here, listing on a double-bladed axe. Disheveled gray hair framed her weather-beaten face; a mustachio of black whiskers fuzzed her upper lip.

"D'ya have it?" a Redoak footman asked Roryn.

Roryn Cook strode to the Bony Yew and returned with the luminescent rod of Blackstaff balanced in both hands, its pearl luster lapping like waves at the edges of the cowhide sheath. Peasants congratulated one another with huzzahs and hearty backslaps. Tyler did not, could not rejoice. The price of the key to the Colossus had been steep.

"Well done Roryn," Jonathan said with an admiring smile.

"Donna thank me. Thank Rolfe." Roryn pounded Tyler on his back so lustily the peasant lost his balance. "Thank the lass we buried just before ye got here."

"We'll pray for Tyler Rolfe and the lass."

"Her name was Jaina," Tyler blurted out. "Jaina Nadley. She was my friend."

Jonathan nodded solemnly. "We'll pray for Tyler Rolfe's friend, Jaina Nadley. Roryn, did y'find the Master Reader?"

Roryn shook his head, eyes low. "Na. He flew away wit' his flock. Heard from Commoners on the road they flew to Giant's Pass, even Tesos, thuddo they was a bunch of silly pokeys and dalcops I spoke wit'. The Fawkes men wit' us canna say."

Pokeys and dalcops, Tyler thought. Peasants where Roryn was from had a strange way of speaking.

"What about Lord Evan and his Pigeons? Did any o' your men make contact? I havnah seen no men in green cloaks. Nor Lord Evan."

"Na, na. There's more. Brace yourselves." Roryn folded his arms. "Tell 'em with you tol' me, Rolfe."

All eyes focused on Tyler. He cleared his throat nervously. He wasn't like Firemouth; speaking publicly scattered his wits. Yet as he shared the terrible truth Hortus had demonstrated by disrobing Jaina, as Blackstaff himself had confirmed about Lord Evan and the Loyal

Company and the Warchild, as it all swirled out of his mouth, Tyler Rolfe found that yes, he had a voice.

Disquiet fell on the peasants in earshot. Tyler understood why. Rosbury had inspired Roryn and these leaders to rally the peasants from other camps, to unite them against the lords in a mighty show of force. Tonight was to broker an arrangement that gave the peasants back their seats . . . and, failing that, to fan the fire kindled by Rosbury to every corner of this broken, hateful kingdom.

To unleash a second Long Summer Rebellion, fought not by lords and priests over a king's marriage but by peasants for their own voices in the Worthy Assembly.

Sinclair and his Pigeons had factored into their decision-making. Conferring with Tyler and others at the Bony Yew on a moonless night weeks ago, Roryn had painted visions in their heads of a Loyal Company openly banding together with them as they overran a mutual enemy's camp, of arrows whistling at Shaddon's men and warhorses charging beside them. They'd capture Shaddon, gain entry into the Colossus, and there hold him hostage until the Worthy granted them what was theirs . . . or die in the trying.

But now Sinclair and his Company were gone—gone like Jaina's kicked-away girdle—like Jaina herself. *Forever,* Tyler recalled Hortus saying moments before he carved a hole in the knight's chest.

"By the One True God," Jonathan breathed shakily when Tyler finished. "We *needed* Lord Evan's bowmen! What can we do?" He searched other faces in their circle for answers, ghostly pale in the rod's silverstone aura.

A scrawny Wuthers peasant closed his eyes, pinching the bridge of his nose. "We can do nothin'," he sighed. "We needed Sinclair. Without him, without his archers, we'll be like trout to griffs out there."

"What of the Warchild?" the old woman piped up. "We can still parley wit' him."

An old Cloudlander with a long snowy beard spoke too hastily and thickly for anyone to understand him. A Cloudlands peasant translated: "He's seen Warchild. Says he lies abed, with fever. Says he and the Bull both. Says Warchild would hear us, but our northern lords wouldn't, even if we tried."

"'Cause we're shit beneath their boots," the footman said disgustedly, making an obscene gesture. "I told you—we can't rely on a bastard whose heart is for the priestking's daughter and whose strength comes from the Cloudlands."

Men muttered their agreement. Weeks ago, after Rosbury, Tyler and others had balked at the idea to recruit the Warchild, but Roryn quashed their refusal on grounds the bastard prince was like Sinclair—for the Wing of the Commons.

Jonathan stabbed his finger at Roryn. "You said Warchild would fight with us," he growled. "The brave men who sent me to talk with you—*those men back there*"—he cocked his thumb over his shoulder—"came here believin' he and Sarah Sinclair's brother would muster if we marched against Lord Shaddon. If Warchild's not long for this world and the Company is done . . . Roryn, we *needed* the Companymen. We donna have the men for this. We needed the fuckin' Company—"

"No," Tyler interrupted him. "We never needed the Loyal Company." His interruption startled even himself.

Jonathan turned berry-red in the silverstone light. "*Did ya hear me?* We. Donna. Have. The. Men. The Worthy have all their men here. Trained swordsmen, and they outnumber us. Maybe we could form up tight to fight their cavalry, but it's still not enough, not on flatland. What've we got without Lord Sinclair's bowmen?"

"Ourselves."

Roryn had the most incredulous expression. He broke out into hearty laughter that would've been contagious, if not for the stakes tonight. "*Look a' you!* You kill a man and suddenly you're ready to storm hell and take on Pathazar and Asha-Ra yourself—thuddo we might as well march on the White Citadel with your mighty heart." Roryn mussed his hair; Tyler stiffened indignantly. *How quickly he forgets my work in Southfar.*

"We cannot take Shaddon with this little arms," Jonathan said adamantly, directing his frustration at Tyler. "Not without mounted men and Pigeons." He faced Roryn. "We can go back. Maybe the lords will take mercy on us. Maybe—"

Roryn strode within an inch of the farmer's face, so close their noses nearly touched. "There's no goin' back," he snarled. "We left Blackstaff an' those knights butchered like swine. Took the armor *an'* this fuckin' rod. Piled sentries into their pavilion. We've got to march *now* or we've lost the surprise—an' our lives—an' killed god knows how many other Commoners just because they're peasants. The One True God brought us here for a reason. *We have to try to take Shaddon.*"

"But we donna need to take Shaddon." Tyler regarded each man coolly. "Nah when there's another Eddenhold, and her camp lies vulnerable."

For a long moment, no one said anything. The old woman grinned. "So *this* is the lad who knew Sara of Rosbury? He's got her spirit. He should lead something."

Tyler Rolfe led only by persuading the war council to take Princess Lorana hostage. That was enough. He wasn't seasoned in war. He'd never even slain a man until tonight.

It was a shock when Roryn pulled him aside and told him that he wanted him in the van. Tyler balked. "You need battle-tested men to take the Colossus," he urged the peasant leader.

Roryn smiled archly. "Aye, an' the van shall have forty such men. But you used Blackstaff's confidence to gain us his rod." He saw a glimmer in Roryn's green eyes. "Reckon it's only fitting that you should be the lad to signal us all."

A final insult to Hoard, as much as the princess who named him Blackstaff. Roryn had a sense of irony often lost on others.

Before more than four thousand peasants descended on the Golden Meadows, a small van would advance stealthily to the Colossus. In the van was a man nearly identical in height to Sir Astiban Hoard, and he'd don Blackstaff's guise and pound his rod on the portcullis. Waiting inside ground-level arcades, Tyler and forty men would charge and kill the gatekeepers, as quickly and quietly as possible. Tyler himself would ascend the ramparts, wave the glowing rod like a torch, and signal Roryn to escort the hostage Lorana into the conquered Colossus.

Thus would Commoners, after two centuries barred from even setting foot in the Colossus, sack and hold it, and therein keep Hexar's daughter, a hostage worth her weight in gold, in exchange for a prize worth their lives. Shaddon wouldn't lightly treat the life of Lady Alyse's daughter. A bargain would have to be struck for her freedom.

If all went as planned, that was. If the moving van didn't stir the camps awake. If the dozen archers on duty inside the Colossus didn't uncover the ruse and shower them with arrows on sight. If Roryn, Jonathan, and their four thousand could take and escort Lorana uninjured through the portcullis.

If a thousand-man crown formation could withstand the charge of armored knights on warhorses . . .

. . . and if a beast caged within the Colossus still protected those that god deemed worthy of mercy and justice.

Roryn gripped his shoulder tightly. "After you sack the Colossus, you signal me wit' the rod. But Rolfe." He was grave. "You clothe that rod quick, an' keep it far, *an' I mean far*, from the beast's sight. He sees it, he'll raise hell. Every man here dies if someone in the Colossus isn't alive to open that portcullis."

"Aye." Tyler wasn't sure how to reassure him. "We'll open the portcullis for you and the princess."

Roryn patted him on his shoulder. "Be worthy of Anjan's mercy an' justice, Rolfe."

"We *are* Worthy. *Turel e'sartha*, Roryn."

"*Turan e'sparta*." Roryn Cook left him on a hill, stalking off into the night to speechmake and stoke fire in the hearts of his four thousand rebels.

As Roryn's voice rose, Tyler circled about for a look at the souls gathered downhill. He went to the men he might die with tonight.

Some wouldn't march with the van, or the army. He saw dozens of them gathering about small, overturned boats. These were Grayport fishermen. Tough lads. They'd spent their night pounding wooden planks into makeshift vessels. Roryn wanted a welcoming party for the priestking's armada. While the rest of the peasants stormed the camps, these burly fellows would head to the northern coast.

Tyler stirred as he watched the fishermen heave their boats onto their shoulders with ease and start off into the night. *Give Shaddon's ships a warm welcome, lads,* he thought.

The van itself consisted of peasants seasoned in war like Roryn and Jonathan. All of them wore tunics paid for or filched from merchants over their gambeson and jacks of plate. Shreve of Hexwaite was the exception. In his looted armor, his combed helm tucked under an arm, "Blackstaff" could pass for Astiban's ghost, bald as he was like Hoard, if a little fatter in his cheeks. Shreve held the rod tightly against his cuirass, as if he feared theft.

Everyone welcomed Tyler, repeating the Romarian motto as the first and second parts of a greeting.

The old woman from the war council, Shannon Ironkeep, handed Tyler a quilt of gambeson. He listened for any sound of mockery as he struggled into it; none. Shannon handed him a sword sheathed in its scabbard. He buckled his sword belt.

I've never even worn a sword before, he thought.

Tyler sized up the Midlander and her cracked axe. With her stocky frame and muscled arms, Shannon seemed built of hard stuff, but a woman she was still, even if bewhiskered.

Shannon smiled wanly, black whiskers splaying over her lips. "I know *that* look. Seen it all me life. You wonder whether this is more than a cane. What good this axe'll do a wrinkly ol' bitch like me."

"Yes," Tyler admitted. A night for battle was not a night for lies, he reckoned.

Grunting, the grandmother swung her mammoth axe with practiced ease, forcing Tyler to duck. She rested its long handle on her shoulder. "Keep 'way from me axe, lad," she said. "It's as ill-tempered as meself."

Another hour passed in the darkness before Roryn gave word. Four thousand men and women began their march to the Colossus and their lords' slumbering camps. The crickets of the Golden Meadows sang a ballad for them as their feet, many in ratty boots, many in grass-stained cloth felt, took them closer to death. Closer. Closer. Closer, ever closer.

After an hour's march through scratchy reeds, under the eye of the moon, the Common host came to a halt impressive in its orderliness. Before them was a swath of night sky as vast as a mountain, devoid of stars.

Hand signals ordered them to shuffle apart. Shannon led Tyler and the van through the peasants to take position behind a family of boulders. Beyond them sprawled the camps and the candles of fires flickering against smoke shafts. Tufts of clouds slashed the moon, ribboning the ancient amphitheater in pale stripes. The road there was almost a quarter-mile wide. Guards watching the path would see not a van of armed peasants, only a group of greedy merchants carving up space for tomorrow's business. Roryn gambled that sentries were more concerned with incursions from rival camps.

Tyler Rolfe inhaled softly, thinking on all that had brought him to this moment. The injustice. The death.

The tyranny of a kingdom built on the bones and blood of peasants like him. A realm utterly lacking in mercy and justice for honest people.

It had to *stop.* That was what Tyler knew in his heart, and Jaina would tell him he had a good one beating in his chest, a knight's heart. He pictured her soft unspoiled face, the narrow bridge of her nose, the mole wedged into her upper lip. Tears wetted his cheeks, cracking his mask of soot and dried blood.

It had to *end.* That was what Tyler knew from grief. Days before he and his friend Dorian were to prepare Remembrance Day, they'd listened raptly to Firemouth in Westcheap. During the attempt on Jason Warchild's life, Tyler and Dorian Fielder had, without speaking, formed up with others around Watley and escorted him to an alley—to safety. A hay wagon had been waiting there to trundle the prophet out of Southpoint. "May the One True God protect you," Watley had said, locking eyes with Tyler, "and long live the Fourth Wing."

The One True God had heard Watley's prayer, protecting Tyler, but only him. On Remembrance Day, he fell ill with fever. Dorian went to help roast the boar, got accused in the king's murder, and—on Princess Lorana's orders—was drawn and quartered before an audience. Jaina had accompanied Tyler to the execution to keep him from vengeance.

Dorian would never have killed the king. Over every cup of mead with Tyler, Dorian had toasted Hexar the Bold. Always.

Now Dorian and Jaina were dead.

It had to *stop*. It had to *end*. The children stolen and given to priests. The families ruined. Tyler remembered how Peshar Grathos had followed him to chapel when he was a boy, curse the evil fucker. The lords' cruelty, their bowing and scraping to priestkings, their refusal to unfreeze wages. The high price of bread. The squalor of neglected Midlanders. Sara of Rosbury, Tomas Fawkes, and Dorian Fielder's deaths. The steward and her justices of the peace. Warchild and his prieslenne lover.

The knights, who butchered peasants with impunity. He clenched his teeth, trying to suppress tears as he looked upon Blackstaff's pavilion on the edges of Warchild's camp.

Everything about Loran *was wrong*.

Damn the lords and priests, he thought. *Damn the royal family. Damn them all . . .*

Tonight, by the hands of Commoners, the corruption and injustice would *wither* like the tapestries at Saint Eric's as fire consumed them. Tyler swore this to himself, to Jaina, to the parents he was parted from, to the One True God. The peasants would wrest back what lords had stolen.

And the cruelty would end.

"May the One True God protect you," Tyler remembered Watley telling him as their gazes met, "and long live the Fourth Wing."

The crickets suddenly resumed their ballad, deafeningly. "To each a chair," a peasant said hoarsely amid the singing. "To all a piece," Tyler and others answered him together. Others echoed them in the night, *to each a chair, to all a piece, to each a chair . . .*

Tyler remembered the night he accompanied Watley and other peasants to South Farcombe. Connor Bagman had shared the motto with Sara Sothron—so earnest, so courageous for a small girl. She'd missed her father so much she'd coped as only a child could, imagining quests from elves to resurrect him.

Sara hadn't known Tyler of Ramsport. Before that night in South Farcombe, Tyler hadn't known Sara.

Now every peasant in the realm knew Sara's name.

Will they know my name? he wondered. Tyler wept—for Jaina. For Sara. He pledged his heart, his soul, his blood to the Common cause. *We'll find justice for you. For all of us.*

"For Sara of Rosbury," he said, like the closing to a prayer.

"*For Sara,*" many around him said as one. "*For Rosbury.*"

We are Worthy. Tyler Rolfe drew his sword.

CHAPTER 22

Common

he sound rushing toward them was that of an avalanche barreling down a mountain. Inside the pavilion, Lorana stood near Anyasha, her hand laced tightly around hers.

Rogir Levan lifted one flap over his head and peered out. He bared his teeth like a dog tensing to fight.

"Sounds like men," the older knight said. "Armored men. Your uncle's assassin wasn't successful, so they sent a force to finish the job. Vile coward!"

How would they have known Adrias wasn't successful? a voice inside prodded Lorana. She would've wondered aloud, had Vayne Adrias not squeezed her windpipe moments before.

In the flickering firelight, Andrew Windkin seemed more the boy he'd been some years back. "That's madness," he said. "Shaddon would forfeit his claim. The Assembly agreed no lord can invade another's camp."

"They just sent an assassin for King Jason." Levan glanced over his shoulder, as if to make sure Adrias still lay dead, and her half-brother was abed, relatively unscathed. "I don't think Shaddon cares for Assembly rules."

Lorana clutched at her throat. "Banners," she managed to squeak with great pain.

"Sirs," Anyasha said imploringly, "we need to call the—"

Levan silenced her with a slash of the hand that made Lorana bristle. Anyasha had just saved Jason's life and hers. "We called for more guards," the knight said. "That'll do."

Lorana could've punched the prideful old man.

But then they heard it more clearly. Much more clearly. A pitch of noise on the fringe, like the growl that rattles low in a beast's throat just before it lunges. Screams. Cursing.

War cries.

The voices didn't sound regimented or proper, the voices of men raised and trained behind castle walls. Even from inside the pavilion, on what sounded like the outskirts of battle, she heard the broil of voices that were . . . Common.

Anyasha latched onto Windkin's arm. "Sir Andrew, please call the banners," she insisted.

Levan wheeled on the younger knight. "We stay put," he commanded his lesser.

Lorana clapped a hand on Windkin's pauldron. "Do it," her voice snaked out.

Trading looks with Levan, then Lorana, Windkin nodded. "Will you be safe?" He evaluated the motley group of footmen whom he and Levan had woken to confront Jason's would-be assassin; they surrounded their king's bed.

Lorana shoved him. "GO," she managed.

Without needing to be told again, the younger knight flew to the other side of the pavilion, lifting the canvas. As soon as he was gone, a man stumbled almost drunkenly into the tent's entrance. He was a farmhand, no knight, protected only by the filthy rags of a tunic and hose. Unsteadily, with shaky blue eyes, he lifted a ramshackle scythe that a strong wind could blow apart.

Trembling like he'd flee, the farmhand spun and shouted at the top of his lungs, "SHE'S HERE, I FOUND HER, I—"

Levan was the wind that blew him apart, slicing the young farmhand from shoulder to hip with his sword. The Commoner fell in pieces, splattering everyone with his life's blood.

"Fuck." Levan wiped some of the spray from his eyes.

Outside, the campsite came alive with the sounds of steel scraping steel. Just outside the pavilion, Lorana saw shadows scrambling up around their cookfires, donning armor, arming themselves.

Anyasha gripped Lorana's hand benumbingly tight. *Thank god these men remained here and didn't walk the perimeter,* the princess thought, *away from Jason, Yasha, and me.*

From inside the pavilion, they all watched as Commoners, more than they could count, surged past the campfires. *Scrorn-ner-gaith* footmen readied their swords, spears, and hammers, shouting orders to each other.

Something strange was happening. The intruder peasants lowered their steel—scythes, clubs, and rudimentary spears—as someone, a leader perhaps, emerged. He pumped his palms repeatedly at the Cloudlanders, as if calling for a truce. And the realization struck Lorana like a lightning bolt: he was telling the Cloudlanders to lower their weapons.

To *join* them.

Hope fell apart inside of her as here and there, Jason's Cloudlanders wavered.

"What is this madness?" Levan watched everything with the same confusion and fear. "Why aren't they making sliced ham of these fucking peasants?"

"Because they have more in common than not," Anyasha said with trepidation. "They're Commoners, Sir Rogir."

Levan looked as if Anyasha had told him up was down, the sky the ground, and in that ground, a crevice opening up before them, to swallow them all.

Spoken so well, my love, thought the princess, *as only you would know.* Elzura's Children had a great deal in common with Commoners. The two classes were both oppressed, distrusted, and hated. If not for the centuries of mistrust and loathing that religion had baked into peasants, Casaanites and Commoners would make natural allies.

And it's highborn like me who keep from you the truth that solidarity would free you all alike, she thought guiltily. *Why else does the Oracle's heritage remain such a closely guarded secret?*

Some of the *scrorn-ner-gaith* shot looks their way. Lorana seized Levan by his arm. "Jason," she croaked.

Her loyal lover translated: "They want Jason. We need to get him away, north, where the Bull's knights camp together."

Lorana looked down at the two pieces of farmhand. *But he told the others "she" was here.* She eyed Anyasha. *Casaanites. That's what they mean. I hate organized religion.*

As Anyasha, Levan, and the others surrounded Jason, to lift him off the bed, in their arms, the princess filched Adrias's dagger where it lay by his body.

Three harts pranced in the embossed sigil on its hilt. *It was you, Eden,* Lorana thought furiously, even as all the world seemed to teeter over an abyss larger than any of them, larger than everyone. *You sent Vayne Adrias to kill Jason. You wouldn't poison Shaddon because you betrayed us. Why, damn you?*

She slipped the blade into the loop of her girdle, lingering on Anyasha. *I betrayed you, darling. But now, I will protect you, with my life if need be. And if we live, I'll tell you everything I've kept from you . . .*

There was no time to lose. Marauding peasants—and a few of the Cloudlanders from outside—strode determinedly toward the pavilion, poorly armored but bold. There had to be fifty or more . . . and their numbers were increasing. Rapidly.

Levan lifted the canvas so the footmen could bear Jason through, some holding him aloft, their hands under his back, arms, and knees.

Without being told, two men stayed to keep the advancing mob at bay while Lorana and the others carried their king over their heads and out the pavilion. Lobstered in steel, they easily sawed through the first raggedy peasants storming inside. But within seconds the mob encircled the brave protectors, and all Lorana could see were the shapes of scythes and swords falling and rising like knives slicing meat.

As she stumbled off with Anyasha and the men bearing Jason aloft, Lorana did something she hadn't done in years.

She prayed. She called on Maetha's godface. *Mercy.*

Bellowing like beasts, Commoners barreled after them. Everything rose up to trip her feet: smoldering cookfire logs, pots and pans, tousled blankets. She fell thrice, skewering her calf on the razor's edge of a discarded vambrace.

God wasn't there, but she didn't need him, or his twelve faces. Anyasha's hand flew out of chaos and darkness, catching her arm and forcing her up. Anyasha herself stumbled, and the steward thanked Andrew for filling in for Justar's godface as he stood athwart the path of the mob, allowing Lorana to help her out of the way of running death.

They ran on breathlessly, a few knights joining Andrew to batter back peasants gaining at the rear. Lorana realized she'd lost a pointy-toed shoe. Her calves burned as fearsomely as her throat. Peasants were picking up speed, with some outpacing others, their faces twisted and livid.

Where are the men? Ahead was glittering night sky, a sea of rolling reeds, and the islands of tents. *We need an army, not sleeping men!*

If that was a prayer, god answered. A gale of voices and clattering armor rushed up to meet them. Cloudlanders, lords, knights, and footmen, ahorse and not, coalesced around Jason, Lorana, and their party. She waved her arms through the air like a fool, fearful they might be mistaken for the Commoners giving chase behind them.

At least the *Hathrimnyr* seemed to know the difference. Swords clanged against bucklers. A spear whistled over her head. Everyone about them raged and screamed and killed.

Relief quickly gave way to terror, sheer terror. Jason's army might not have mistaken Lorana and her party for the peasants, but they didn't shepherd them out of the chaos of battle, either. They were all caught in the thick of it, like birds fluttering about a chamber filled with griffs, the door shut and nowhere to go as talons came, too many to count.

Lorana clutched at Anyasha and reached in vain for Jason, his unconscious body rolling on the bed of shoulders pressed together for him. She reached for them both, as if she had the magical power to extend her arms and keep all her loves safe.

It's like it was with you, Zur, she thought as a fletched bolt whistled past her ear. *I can't save you all . . .*

Vicious swordplay between an ox of a peasant and a smaller, armored knight embroiled her. Anyasha saw the needlepoint of the latter's gothic couter headed for Lorana's eye and shoved her off. "*Yasha!*" Lorana cried out, her voice stronger and healing.

She crawled like a rat through night's battle. A sword sliced the air by her face, missing her ear by mere inches. A destrier collapsed to the earth beside her in a thunder; the animal's black eye screamed its terror.

Deep in the reeds, she shielded her face with her arms, pitching side to side as men trampled the earth, as some, even House Eddenhold's knights, trampled her. She screamed. No one seemed to hear her. Men toppled beside her, piling up like autumn leaves. Dead and dying men would bury her alive.

Fools, Jason, she thought as she prepared for death. *We were fools to think the Wing of the Commons would do us any good. Look what it's brought us. Charles was right. Fools . . .*

Fingers closed around her left hand and yanked her up from hell.

She'd kiss Andrew Windkin if she preferred men, and she thought she might just kiss him, anyway. The knight swung his sword efficiently to protect his princess. He parried a peasant's pitchfork with his blade, burying it in the boiled leather over the man's chest.

The knight's lips moved, but she couldn't hear what he said. He led her through reeds at blinding speed, maneuvering past corpses, past the blur of charging war horses.

"YASHA, YASHA," Lorana kept crying at him, searching for her lover in desperate, over-the-shoulder looks. "STOP!"

"We can't, Highness," Andrew kept repeating haggardly. "Need you safe. You're the king's daughter. The crown."

Lorana tried to force him to stop. Seconds before, she'd wanted to kiss him; now she was pulling at his windswept hair. "My brother! JASON! Stop, I said," she demanded. "GODDAMN IT, ANDREW, STOP!"

And suddenly, he did, plunging headfirst into the reeds. She thought he meant for her to duck with him, but then she saw the arrows sticking him like porcupine needles. A third bolt impaled his throat. His hand clutched hers weakly as he bled out in the middle of nowhere.

Minutes passed like hours as battle raged on behind her.

Suddenly, she became aware of the wall of unfamiliar faces surrounding her. Sooty faces. Bodies so malnourished that she saw the patterns of ribs around their bellies. They brandished axes, swords, and torches.

The ring of peasants tightened around her like a noose.

To Each a Chair

292

hen the portcullis began to shiver open, the swords and axes came out.

Shannon Ironkeep rushed in first, burying her axe into the first guard's chest. The second guard, a boy no older than Tyler, slid forward on Blackstaff's sword, mouth agape as he bled out, spilling intestines.

Blackstaff's impostor planted a foot on the boy's chest and kicked him off his sword. He seemed to lose himself in his rod's mystical aura, transfixed.

The woman boxed his helm as if it were the big man's ear. "Donna stand there like an oaf, Shreve. Work needs doin'." She swiveled on the peasants and thrust her bloody axe into the air. "*To each a chair!*" she cried.

"*TO ALL A PIECE!*" the peasants thundered together.

With the pretender beside her, the warrior-grandmother led the way into the tunnel of the gatehouse, running with the light from Blackstaff's staff fidgeting all around them. Peasants disguised in silks ran after the bobbing light, swords in the air, their war cries echoing.

Lost in a loud, sweaty, silverstone-lit stampede through the gatehouse, Tyler tried to stay alive by staying on his feet. Running behind the pack, he nicked his chin on someone's shoulder and tasted blood; he stepped wrong and winced at the pain in his ankle. Ahead, past the charging people, at the end of the gatehouse, he glimpsed a sand arena.

He felt hope. Mad hope that mingled with his grief. Roryn Cook's van had managed to slip through the Golden Meadows almost entirely unnoticed and unsuspected. Walking alone, one cassocked priest, an Assemblyman, had made eye contact with their Blackstaff, but he didn't make inquiries or raise alarm.

Undraping his staff, the man called Shreve had knocked its stone against the portcullis a little lightly at first, harder the second time, after Shannon prodded him. Everyone held their breath when the impersonator misremembered Blackstaff's traditional exchange with the guards, stammering out, upon them querying his allegiance, "AYE, uh—*I'm for the king.*"

But no one took issue. No one questioned his identity or spied Commoners lurking beneath the archways of arcades, waiting for the portcullis to slide open. The man who donned Blackstaff's armor, who wielded his rod, was someone whose significance lay in ritual. Who feared treason from a symbol?

Roryn's plan was working. If they could take his kingly namesake's amphitheater—*if they could hold it*—they could hold the steward hostage and force the lords to return to the peasants what was theirs. Everything felt possible.

As Tyler ran through the gatehouse, he remembered what his tanner papa had once told him. It was a memory that stayed with him, one he'd shared with Jaina just yesterday.

Satin, he remembered.

"Satin," the elder Rolfe had told his son in their house one night, patting his rock-hard stool seat. "*Satin!*" he'd repeated with childlike wonder. "Can you believe it? When the Wing of the Commons still had seats, Commoners sat *on satin cushions* beside their lords, clergymen, and merchants. To this day, the Worthy men sit on cushions when they meet to make law." He remembered his father's poignant smile. "As peasants will again . . . one day."

That day is here, Papa, Tyler thought as he ran toward sand and moonlight, toward salvation. *The long night of our Common folk is over.*

Arrows whistled at the entrance, studding sand and flesh. The peasants at the front of the van, who would've been the first Commoners to set foot in the Colossus in centuries, were the first to fall. A corpse heap formed at the entrance, slowing their advance. Tyler huddled with Shannon, Shreve, and other men under an archway as arrows peppered the sand feet away.

Even as arrows showered the sand before them, calamity arose in the Golden Meadows behind them, orders bellowed into the night, horses whinnying—and, distantly, the peal of steel striking steel. *Be worthy of mercy and justice, Roryn.*

Tyler urged Shannon and Blackstaff's impostor to move forward, *for god's sake, move forward.* "RORYN," he shouted as he grabbed the woman by her arm. He jabbed his finger at the camps behind them, told her the Colossus had to be taken.

Shannon cocked her thumb at the sand arena, her eyes so wild that she seemed younger suddenly. ". . . *CANNA . . . IN,*" he heard her shout over the riot of cursing and dying, and pieced together that she was saying *we cannot get in.*

Arrows rained down relentlessly, catching dead men, *pfft, pfft.* With a crazed look, Shreve said something. Only afterward did Tyler understand this man spoke for the ages.

Into the storm strode Blackstaff, convulsing as his body took on arrows, *all* the arrows. By some miracle, the hero *still stood* nearly a minute in, his black armor pierced by so many that he looked like a bush made of fletched shafts. Shannon, Tyler, and other peasants bounded past as Shreve collapsed. Doing his duty by Roryn, by all peasants, Tyler picked up the luminous rod in Shreve's stead.

Peasants fanned out across the arena to make themselves harder targets. That ploy might've served the remaining two-dozen peasants well, but a muck of wet sand slowed their pace dangerously. *The Second Trial,* he remembered. *The arena's a huge mud pit thanks to all that water.*

Worse, the luster of Blackstaff's rod made him a moving, well-lit target. He plodded through sand, ducking what felt like dozens of arrows. One plonked by his ankle; another singed his cheek. Commoners fought a skeleton crew of eight archers in mail and boiled leather, but their perches in middle and upper benches made them seem a hundred. The Colossus's sackers scattered like insects, seeking cover or dying in the mud.

Tyler sighted a crossbowman in the benches, not twenty feet off. Loading a bolt took precious time. Tyler charged with weights on his feet, his blade up.

Pain exploded in his ankle like a fireball. He collapsed in the soggy sand, limped up, and fought to hop away on one foot, screaming every time he put pressure on his skewered ankle. He looked down and saw an arrow protruding from his ankle, and all the blood that marked his trail. *That'll do it,* he thought.

A bolt from the crossbowman whistled past his shoulder as he half-stumbled, half-crawled for cover. *But where?* Tyler forced himself to think through a wall of pain. He considered sheltering beneath a bench until he saw a peasant below one, hand dangling out, an arrow through his head. *WHERE, GOD?*

The One True God didn't disappoint. The answer was in front of him, a dozen yards off. Evading arrows, he hadn't yet noticed the giant cagehouse at the center of the arena. A silver tarp blanketed the enclosure, leaving visible only sand-caked wheels.

The griffon, Tyler thought. Deep ruts in the sand led from the wheels to the gatehouse. Trappers had carted the king's bird here for the Third Trial.

He staggered in the cagehouse's direction as people fought for their lives around him. An over-the-shoulder glance showed him that the crossbowman hadn't given up on his prey. Their eyes locked as the enemy cranked his bolt.

Tyler reached the cagehouse. He struggled to ease himself flat on his belly, clenching his jaw to weather the fire founting up his leg. Clutching his sword and Blackstaff's rod, he crawled to safety beneath the cagehouse on his elbows. A crossbow bolt *thwopped* by his feet.

Perhaps the best I can do right now is keep the staff safe, Tyler thought. *We'll need it for Roryn to know we've taken the Colossus . . . if we take it.* He saw so little around him.

Tyler worked fast. He unbuttoned the gambeson, jerked out a wad of his cloth shirt, pulled it out and over his head. It was a good shirt and had served him for years; he ripped it in two pieces. He folded one piece around his inflamed ankle, the arrow too, trying to stanch blood loss.

As he finished tying the knot, thunder rumbled overhead. *A storm?* He gazed at the gatehouse, hoping that it was Roryn Cook arriving with his peasant army, Princess Lorana bound by rope. *Were the lords and their men-at-arms so easy to dispatch?*

Pain and panic had wiped Tyler's mind, and the next growl helped him remember what he sheltered beneath.

The growl wasn't a guttural expelling of air, like that of a bear. It was nothing like menacing vibrations in a wolf's snarl. Griffons shared parts with cats and eagles, but nothing of those beasts echoed in the discord that rattled two feet of solid iron floor above his head.

The griffon's growl crept out as a moist hiss, swelling into a deafening rumble that sounded to Tyler like a cyclone tearing up a village. He felt the growl in his bones, as if nothing—not even his flesh—separated him from the beast. Sand misted the air as the cagehouse shook side to side violently, as if buffeted by wind, jingling nails and iron bars. Talons raked the topside of the iron floor, and he prayed it'd hold.

Through it all, despite the battle raging around him and the blinding pain of his ankle, Tyler somehow remained still and silent. Then he saw the snake gliding over the sand. Not a snake—a griffon's tail. Thicker than his arm, the appendage plumed so thickly with fur at the end that it resembled a black flower on a black vine. The tail moved almost with a will all its own, searching for a source of disturbance. Searching for him.

He felt his heart hammering sand. *Please, god. Please . . .*

Tyler squinted at the aura pulsating from Blackstaff's rod. Roryn's warning returned to him: "You clothe that rod quick, an' keep it far, *an' I mean far,* from the beast's sight. He sees it, he'll raise hell."

Of course, he thought. *Silverstone drives griffons mad.*

As the tail wended by his cheek, he took the other half of his torn shirt and draped the rod. This accomplished nothing; the pearl aura bled radiantly through the shirt. At wit's end, he plunged the silverstone into sand, and that snuffed its light.

The shaking quelled. He realized he could hear himself breathe. Peasants were scouring the benches for archers, communicating in low voices. "Did Rolfe fall?" A man called out. "I donna see him," another answered. "But we need him, least that silverstone. He took it off Shreve."

Seconds passed before Tyler realized no one was loosing arrows. He crawled halfway out from under the cagehouse; he left Blackstaff's rod sheathed in the sand. "I'm here!" he cried.

Shannon Ironkeep descended from the benches. The old bewhiskered woman lumbered in his direction, dragging her axe listlessly through the sand. She, too, had taken an arrow; a broken shaft poked out of her arm, and she breathed heavily. She halted a distance away, eyes ablaze with fear.

"Get up an' outta there, Rolfe," she urged him in a strained voice. "I dare nah get closer."

"I canna walk!" he whispered loudly, fearful of stoking the griffon's wrath. "I took an arrow in my leg."

"Then throw the rod. Roryn needs the signal. We've taken the Colossus."

Hope unlooked-for washed over Tyler. He was about to tell her he couldn't, that the griffon nearly smashed its prison to bits over silverstone light, when cheers and cries of joy filled the night air. Of the forty people who'd breached Rorin's amphitheater, only ten still drew breath. Some of them tended to the wounded and dying. Others celebrated.

A young Midland farmhand ran around the arena for no other purpose than to rejoice. "*WE DID IT,*" he shouted as he leapt exultantly through sand. "*WE SACKED IT! WE DID IT! WE FUCKIN' TOOK THE COLOSSUS!*"

Shannon watched him wearily as he darted by. "It's not done, ya fool. Roryn'll be comin' with Her Highness. It's one thing to take a building; another to keep it, make demands."

Barely anyone listened. A man broke down and wept into his hands. Another lifted his hands skyward, giving thanks to the One True God of readers and peasants for their hallowed victory over vicious priests. The farmhand running laps started cartwheeling and fell splayed out in the moist sand. He laughed madly, triumphantly.

A middle-aged man savored the moment with dignity. He sat on a lower bench, face forward, back straight, hands round on his knees, as if he were a child in school. Blood oozed down his face from a gleaming head wound, but he didn't attend to it. It was as if he'd decided that nothing and no one would move him, even if he bled.

That was when Tyler realized it. The benches were bare! *I'm here, Papa, I'm here for you and Jaina and everyone . . . but I donna see your satin cushions.*

The blaze in his ankle outweighed disappointment. Tyler motioned for Shannon. "Help me upstairs so we can give the signal," he said. "Roryn wanted me to do it."

A fletched bolt blossomed in Shannon's heart like a red rose, and she fell clutching her axe. Another bolt flattened the farmhand where he lay in the sand.

"*THEY'RE COMIN' FROM BELOW!*" someone shouted.

No, Tyler thought. Fresh archers swept across the arena, stringing their bows. With them were knights in heavy armor. They streamed out from the northern portcullis—from *below* the Colossus. There were more men than he could count.

It took the Assembly's forces under a minute to kill the remaining peasants. Tears falling off his face, Tyler shuffled back under the cage. Fear made him desperate. Trying not to scrape the arrow in his ankle, lest he cry out, he inadvertently nudged the staff. It was as if he'd dug up a moon. The blast of silvery radiance brought on another terrible growl.

Near where Shannon lay, a company of men halted in their tracks. "There's one under the cagehouse," a dark-haired archer told the others.

"Is that . . . is that *silverstone* he has with him?" asked another, incredulous.

"Blackstaff's rod," said a crossbowman, an Eastlander by his accent. "It's how the little Common fleas got in. Good thing word reached Redoak about Lordsbane's visit here. Elsewise, he might not've had us posted here tonight."

The same fear that had stayed Shannon Ironkeep haunted the archer's eyes. "A *griffon's* in there. I'll go no closer."

"You don't have to." The crossbowman approached with his weapon pointed. His footsteps came softly, as if he thought to reassure the griffon. "Is that a star ya got with you, lad?" he called out. "Bright light, that. I can see you clear as day. From here, I could stick you between your eyes. Kill ya quick."

He remembered their faces, their voices. Dorian. Sara of Rosbury. Roryn. Shannon. Shreve. His papa. Jaina most of all. They kindled his courage, but her face and hair and voice, her laughter, helped numb the fiery throb of his leg. He heard a low rumbling—not from above him, but *out there,* like the rush of a wave gaining momentum before it crashes ashore. The battle continued, and it was because of her sacrifice, the first of many.

Tyler took heart. "We're nah alone," he piped. "Nah t'all. An army's comin'. Big brutes with swords and armor. Let me live, an' I'll reason with their leader to let you men live. You've done nothin' wrong, just your duty and your lords' orders."

Guardsmen laughed obnoxiously.

A maddening grin worked its way into the crossbowman's face. "*Nah,*" he mocked Tyler. "I'll let you live so we can ask ya questions. If you've got friends comin', well, this bolt will fly through your stomach instead of your head. Not so quick, that sorta death. And if ya stay under there, well . . ." He paused so that all anyone heard was the cagehouse shaking. "I reckon that vicious beast might just save me the trouble."

Tears coursed down Tyler's face. *Forgive me, Roryn. I see no other way.* On elbows and knees, he crawled through muck, the rod with him, spilling light, throwing shadows wildly. The cagehouse creaked as the creature inside paced anxiously. The drag of his injured leg dragged out the surrender.

The crossbowman sighed impatiently. "Gods, what is this one, a snail or a peasant? I repeat myself, I s'ppose." Laughter rang around the Colossus. "Sitting, resting, taking your sweet time—that's for lords and priests. Not for dumb serfs like you."

Tyler held aloft the rod of light; the cagehouse quaked about in response, jingling iron bars. The plumed tail curled out, silver tarp rising with it. He trembled under the glare of a massive eagle's eye, a golden disc forked with amber. He saw his reflection in its black pupil.

The crossbowman was still snickering when Tyler Rolfe tossed the spear of Blackstaff's rod into the cagehouse.

The scream was monstrous and frightening. Inside, the rod spun round like a bottle, scrambling darkness with light, offering fleeting glimpses of vast arched wings, the mustard beak and sickle talons working furiously to uproot iron bars. A few bars gave way, but a few was all it'd take. The cagehouse tilted over him precariously.

Give me mercy and justice, beast. I've never had none.

The enclosure capsized the other way, the staff twirling out and away, its static light fogging a swath of sand. Iron sheets and iron bars whirled through the air. A great shadow vaulted free of the cagehouse, wings beating air, whipping up a sandstorm that flung Tyler and the archers away like leaves in the wind.

There was no mercy in how the fall broke the boy's legs, or justice, as many of the guardsmen fled to safety. But before debris tumbled down on top of him, darkening his world, Tyler saw a shadow angel spreading its wings, blotting out stars, and he remembered why peasants worshipped griffons.

CHAPTER 24

Better by Birth

n the glow of their windswept torches, she saw them.

Their faces were gaunt, their skin leathery and taut over their bones, men and women alike. Ribs patterned their bellies. Layered in boiled leather, studded jerkins, gambesons, and a scatter of pauldrons, they looked like misfits, but underneath all that their bright-dyed tunics and hose clung fiercely to the dignity legally permissible for their station. Men donned cloth caps, women tucked their hair beneath wimples, and many of both sexes wore shabby helmets.

Some were as young as Zur and Heather, others older, but most looked to be in their twenties, thirties, and forties.

They handled castle-forged swords and axes filched from new corpses. Others gripped scythes, spears, and pitchforks as worn as their clothes. Everyone pointed steel at the princess as if she were the most dangerous person in the world.

She counted sixty. At least sixty, all around her in a ring.

Lorana was outnumbered and surrounded in a remote part of the Golden Meadows. Sounds of night's battle carried thunderously over the field, horses squealing, steel clanging, jarringly loud, as if it were all happening feet away.

Yet they felt miles away. Dead at her feet, Andrew had led her south in a vain attempt to make her safe, but he'd also put space between her and the *Hathrimnyr* and her royal force. On the horizon dwelt the Colossus, the giant jagged tooth of Mount Dracar, and beneath it all pavilions ablaze, shadows frolicking across their firelit canvas walls like demons run amok.

"They're too far to hear ya, yer high royalness," came a voice, his Southlander's accent thick. "We want a parley."

A man parted from the circle of peasants. He removed his dinged helm in a baffling sign of respect, loosing a mop of dirty-blond hair. He had a handsome cleft chin, a nose spotty with pustule scars, and pale green eyes. He took a step closer.

Lorana reached for the dagger in her girdle. As soon as her fingers glanced its hilt, scythes and spears jutted forward. She fell shaking, tears slipping down her cheeks, hated tears. She wished she'd been born a man so she could die with a sword in her hand tonight. Die with dignity.

The Southlander held his palms outward in a sweeping gesture, as if to placate everyone. He offered her his right hand. She flitted from the hand to his eyes, searching for trickery.

The peasant smiled. It wasn't a mocking smile. "We're nah like you perfumed folk, yer high royalness," he said. "If we kill ya, we wonna do it like sneak thieves."

In the corner of her eye, Lorana saw Andrew's sword half-protruding from the reeds. She accepted the peasant's callused hand; it felt rough as sun-rotted leather.

The Southlander brought her to her feet. His hand lingered near hers, thumb waxing over her palm. He smiled rapturously, as if he'd tasted a custard tart for the first time. "Royal skin is diff'rent," he said. "Is it the silverstone in the First King's castle? That why your hand is so soft?"

"Soft how, Cook?" another peasant barged in. He had a large frame, dark hair, and squinty eyes. He sounded genuinely curious.

Cook's smile widened. "Soft like silk. Like it's never known harsh lye or a scythe's splinters."

A hard old nail of a woman said something that her argot jumbled up, but Lorana saw the disdain in her weathered face easily enough.

The steward straightened her shoulders, affronted by the fascination with her. As if she were some five-legged dog. "Who are you?"

she demanded. "What do you want from me?"

Cook's smile faded. "We want what's ours." A bright flash of fire-light drew his attention north, other peasants' gazes with it. With a look, Lorana measured the distance between her and Andrew's sword.

One sword will do nothing in my untrained hands, she thought. *But if it comes to it, I'll die as my father would've . . .*

"Name it, whatever it is," she said. "I'm not sure what I can do, but it will be done."

Cook looked her in her eyes. "Aye, it will be done."

"*It will be done,*" several other peasants all around her repeated him, speaking over each other.

"Roryn, we need to move soon," the squinty-eyed peasant broke in.

"When Tyler waves his rod," said Roryn, or Cook, or whichever his true name was, his eyes still fixed on Lorana, "an' not before."

They were keeping their schemes hidden, and in her exhaustion and frustration, with Andrew dead at her feet, anger burned through her fear like dragonflame.

"You say you're not like the highborn," Lorana said in a hard tone. She flushed hot under all their gazes. She hesitated at the sight of their steel . . . Then, she remembered these were peasants.

She was a princess, the steward of Loran, King Hexar's daughter.

She was better than them. Better by birth.

"We're not, yer royalness." Roryn spoke without anger, a hint of fear in his voice as she spread her griffon's wings. That emboldened her. *I'm a parent among children. Isn't that what Drexan always said of kings, Father? That we were the god on earth they needed . . .*

"You say you'd kill in the open, not like sneak thieves," she said. "You sprang an attack on your lords' camps in the middle of the night, while everyone slept. You've slain my loyal knight. You've cornered me. You say you want to parley, but parleys involve some trust. Some honesty."

At that, Roryn's mouth turned hard, his eyes wide. "*We are honest people,*" he said fiercely, as if she'd insulted him in the worst way. He leveled a soot-stained finger at her. "Your lot took what wasna yours to take. We've suffered for years—*HUNDREDS OF YEARS*"—as his voice loudened, other peasants urged him on, in front of her, to her side, behind her—"while you lords an' ladies made whatever laws you wanted without us. Made us poorer." Ayes chorused him. "Mumbler-poor. Poor as slaves. Made us toil in your fields an' take low wages, gaolin' us if we canna pay our rents an' taxes."

She'd crossed a line. *Remember, you fool princess, they're the ones with steel.* On the other hand, she realized it was all the better if they continued speaking this loudly in the night . . . *Yes, alert Jason's men to our location.*

The squinty-eyed peasant lurched forward, clutching his axe. "Your priests steal our li'l ones like egg-suckin' snakes, 'an your justices o' the peace rip father from mother so *NONE O' US* can do NOTHIN' but see our babies leave us forever." His voice cracked raw.

Lorana understood suddenly. It was all clear as day. *The justices . . . What's theirs . . . They want the Wing of the Commons. And they seek it from me, for I am their steward—the steward who blighted them with justices like Willard Rittman.* Sinclair's truth glared at her like these peasants.

"Justices like the one in Rosbury," another muttered with anguish. "HE KILLED THAT POOR GIRL!"

"Sara of Rosbury," Roryn said gravely, staring at Lorana.

Hauntingly, everyone repeated the name, as if hers were a closing to their prayer: "Sara o' Rosbury," "Sara Sothron," "Sara, god bless her soul."

The child who was killed in Rosbury, she understood. *So she has a name.* "You've come to petition me," she said with a start. "For the Wing of the Commons."

Roryn's eyes flared with recognition. "'To each a chair,'" he said. "But petitions, they're small peas, your royalness. As worthless as a priest's soul. The kings an' lords have shown us this. We know you lot better than you know yourselves."

Lorana saw her opening. "You needn't petition me," she said. "My brother—the Warchild—fights with Evan Sinclair to restore your ancient seats in the Assembly. *We* are doing this. All you need do is stand down. Lay down your arms. Go home, and we will seat you again."

Roryn traded glances with his fellow peasants. He shook his head. "Time's past for highborn promises the highborn canna keep," he said. "The First King made a covenant. That's what readers teach us." He pointed his finger at her, as if she symbolized every wrong inflicted on peasants for the last two hundred years. "That covenant is broken. We donna trust your promises."

A chill spread up her spine as the peasant started toward her, his eyes low. "You said you want a parley." She dropped her fist in her palm like a hammer. "Then parley with me. I am steward. I can—"

"If you coulda done it, just like that"—Roryn snapped his callused fingers—"why havnah you already done it?"

"The Kingstrials," she said, trying not to show fear. "My father was killed." *By peasants,* she pondered. *I thought their religion made this Interregnum different . . .*

"Highborn games. They mean nothin'. Your king father never gave Sinclair or his Loyal Comp'ny what they sought."

"You're right, Roryn, I know," Lorana reasoned with him. "This is why my brother—"

Roryn's headshake was long and slow. "We mean you no harm, yer royalness, not you nor the Warchild," he said. "We shan't hurt you. But we need you." He beckoned with a hand, his pale green eyes iron-hard. "You'll come if you wanna make this right for the people this kingdom has robbed for years an' years. For those children your justices have hurt. Children like Sara Sothron. Do you wanna make this right?"

Staring into his eyes, she suddenly felt small . . . small as an ant. Small as a Commoner of Loran. "Where would you take me?"

Roryn opened his mouth to speak, and then shut it with a wild look. He and other peasants fixed their gazes north, then northeast, searching the night as thunder rumbled closer. They clutched their weapons close.

Lorana listened intently. Immediately, she knew what it was—a mounted army, coming for her, hooves pounding soil, plate armor and harnesses jingling together in a symphony of greatness. *My half-brother's men put down the attack.* It sounded like a monstrous force. A force mustered to put down a violent revolt and rescue a ruler. The peasants drew close together, their weapons shaking visibly in their hands.

Her trouble wasn't over. If anything, it'd worsen. She had to set the pace for what happened next, or they might kill her.

"Roryn," Lorana said. He looked at her as if he saw only her. "That's the sound of a cavalry. My brother's *Hathrimnyr.* They will ride you down where you stand." He tightened his grip on his sword, as if to prove her wrong. "Lay down your arms. I will protect you."

A peasant fell headlong, impaled through his stomach by a spear. The night sky exploded with spears and arrows, catching peasants in their heads, their legs and arms, all over. The worst pain she had ever known ripped through her left arm; she fell, screaming bloody hell.

An arrow pierced her arm. She flopped side to side, and then remembered that Connor Tomas had taught her once that one must break the shaft. She tried to break the arrow in half and stopped, thinking she might die from the effort.

Then, horses. Peasants fell beneath the hooves of muscled destriers swarming them. Hooves nearly took her in the face. She crawled away in agonizing pain, into the cover of reeds. She curled by Andrew's corpse, shuddering. *This is hell.*

She heard no begging from the peasants as knights ahorse stuck them with spears. Dismounting, others ran them through with their swords.

Not knights. The throb of her left arm was nothing next to the fear that seized her now. *Intercessors.*

The priestking's silver-masked brutes lived up to their reputation as they butchered peasants like meat. It wasn't long until they found her in the reeds, clutching at Andrew's sword.

Mounted or afoot, Intercessors parted almost uniformly for a destrier barded in cream and violet. Her uncle looked so imperious, even regal, plated head to foot in filigreed armor, the finest that a priestking's treasury could buy.

Shaddon wiped blood off his sword and sheathed it with the air of a victor. His eyes softened when he saw her, more so when he spotted the arrow in her arm. "Oh, what your mother would say." He nodded at the Intercessors. "Take my niece into custody. We'll dress her wound inside the Colossus."

"Your ghouls shot me, you idiot," she breathed raggedly.

Shaddon narrowed his eyes. "I told you where the rabble belongs. Why did you not learn when they killed my brother?"

Intercessors didn't treat her gently, because she didn't go gently. One of them simply flicked the arrow in her arm to gain her cooperation. They tied her wrists tightly behind her back. *I follow in your footsteps, Erick,* she thought. *Now he has me, too.*

Silver-masked brutes had her leg halfway onto her horse when a great clamor traveled across the Meadows. It sounded like a building crashing down, and it issued from the Colossus. She felt hope suddenly, a mad hope that rebels had destroyed the amphitheater and rendered it useless for Shaddon.

Intercessors pointed at the sky. Panicking, some among them dove into the reeds. Staring up, her uncle looked as if he might join them.

Lorana wasn't like them. Squinting up, she felt no fear. A shadow sailed overhead, beating huge wings, obscuring stars. They all watched, transfixed, until the griffon vanished behind a wall of cloud.

Mine sigil abandons me, she thought.

Elzura's Child

wo days passed in the wilderness before Zuran spotted signs of civilization. A weave of smoke twisted high in the sky above the Rotwood. *At last,* he thought gladly. He widened his arms, tautening the rope that bound his wrists. *Some hope.*

His unspeaking captors seemed less enthused about the smoke-stack. They'd been traveling off Romarian roads, up a winding, dirt-beaten path he heard someone name Flint Way.

The Mumbler, Uther, brought them to a halt in a grove of oaks. He scaled a root-entangled hill, nimble for a man so old. He stood still as a cat lying in wait for its prey, staring ahead, as if his eyesight pierced miles of tree and shrubbery.

"The village isn't far." Uther hopped down with ease, adjusting Drexan's confiscated travelsack on his shoulder. "Stay close."

The decision met with glum looks, but no one contested it, not openly. The boy understood why. *They keep me in the dark,* he knew, *blind as well as bound.*

Yet Zur kept a watch on his captors, day and night, same as they never let him out of their sights, and over two days, he learned. Despite the beatings he'd endured during attempts at escape, despite his hunger and thirst, he learned about these ragtag peasants.

Their Southland accents gave themselves away as men of Southpoint or a village nearby. Despite wearing a Mumbler's tattered gray robes, the old man carried himself like nobility. Silver-haired twins Orthos and Owen handled themselves well with steel and served as Uther's muscle. He couldn't figure how Bill, a one-eyed man, and Tom, a fat one, fit in; they liked to heckle Zur about Elzura's Curse. A boy close to his age, Devan, trudged at the line's end, never speaking unless spoken to.

Orthos, Owen, and Devan left him alone. Bill and Tom the boy could tolerate. But Zur preferred them and their heckles to the one called Spittlelip.

Raggedy, unkempt, and hideous, the man was a hateful shadow in this group. Porous scar tissue honeycombed his cheeks, making it hard to look at him for too long. He sucked at his disfigured lips incessantly for an irritated slurping sound, *shrrip-shrrip, shrrip-shrrip.* He glared at Zur when their gazes met and knocked him off-balance when he strode past.

Everyone followed the Mumbler's lead, but no one—Uther included—prayed to the twelve-faced god of the Free Believers. Every night Uther gave Zur over to two watchers while the others found a place to pray, all bowed heads and cupped hands and whispered words. *Sylvanians,* he grasped. *Sylvanians pray in the wild like that.*

But he didn't think they were really even Sylvanians.

While feigning sleep, Zur had overheard Tom pining for a pint of ale at The Golden Dragon. He knew of the inn because it was a favorite haunt of Prince Garrett's.

Southland accents. The Golden Dragon. Prayers to gods I do not know. An old man named Uther Brune. Dread closed about his heart like a fist. *These are Lord Uthron's pagans,* he realized. *The ones who sacrificed a knight to make Uthron a shadowking. I should've gone with you to the Great Tree, Drexan. To Orella. To find the Ascendant King. To learn about my mother . . .*

Now the Nagarthessi's servants had him.

Zur kept what he knew a secret. The men forged ahead in single file, the twins at the front with hands on their pommels. Bill and Tom handed Zur off to Jacob and Devan. Uther kept a watch at the end of their line. Three miles on, the smokestack billowed higher into clear blue sky, thickening until it flattened above them like a raincloud.

Briefly, wildly, he wondered whether the King's Crow was lighting the Rotwood to smoke them out. *Are you still my friend, Crow? Or would you protect me for your own ends, like you did Evan Sinclair?* Right now, it wouldn't matter to Zur if the king's chancellor protected him for his own ends or not.

He was blind. In danger. Where his captors were taking him—to whom they were taking him—he didn't know.

Once more Uther Brune scuttled up a hillside. He gestured for Orthos to clamber up. The men conferred together quietly.

After days of silence and beatings, silence and beatings, something in Zur boiled up. "You're quick for an old man," he said. "I take it you must've eaten well in a lord's service. Whom did you serve, Reader Uther? Whom—"

A fist clapped his jaw. Zur staggered off, gasping at pain. Jacob loomed over him, cracking his knuckles, *shrrip-shrrip-shrriping.*

"None too bright, are ya?" Orthos called down.

The priest hopped down, spry as a boy. Zur was surprised when he helped him up, even more so when he tried to wipe the blood off his lips with his sleeve. "I'd stay quiet, if I were you," Uther said gently. "Jacob doesn't like you or your kin."

"Well, I don't like Jacob. Where are you taking me?"

"You'll understand soon enough."

"Oh, I understand well enough," Zur shot back. "The question is, do you?"

Jacob Spittlelip hauled him back by the sleeve of his tunic.

"We understand that you're a twat," Tom snickered.

"*Heed me,*" Zur fumed. "I have powerful friends—allies who could pay you ransom—or lock you in the Red Tower. Whether you prefer coin or a slow death, that I don't know."

The threats didn't faze Uther. "I understand you're afraid, Zuran of the Silver Walls. Your trials will be over soon enough, I promise." He came so near he could smell the reek of broth on his breath. "But if you aren't silent as a mouse, Spittlelip will cut out your tongue. Then you'll be just like him, a lipsucker." He shrugged haplessly, as if he were at a loss for what to do. "Then how would you be able to make all your empty threats?"

I've met a Barefoot Knight, Zur thought. *How empty would a threat like him be when he burns you with his blood magic?* "Maybe they're not as empty as you—"

He recoiled with a gasp, clutching his cheek. Blood leaked from the cut Jacob's dagger made. The cretin opened his lips to expose the worm of his misshapen tongue, grinning. Saliva bubbled in his cheek holes.

"Don't test my patience, Zuran," Uther added as he strode past. "Nothing would give Jacob more pleasure than to deform you. 'Twas one of your own who made him this way."

Spittlelip seized him by the arm and shoved him forward. Up ahead, Tom and Bill sang the Common rhyme about his kin, *Broken lines and thirteen crowns, that's what Elzura the Witch begot . . .* right until Owen told them to shut it.

The company stopped in its tracks at the sounds of someone *else* singing. Spittlelip forced Zur behind a tree, sliding a dagger against his throat to ensure silence.

Through a fern's blades, Zur made out peasants. They defied sumptuary laws with their clothes: jerkins with shiny buttons, silken pantaloons, leather boots. A handful cinched swords and dirks at their belts. He counted twelve.

"*She was a rose I swore I'd make mine,*" sang one in a rich timbre of voice, "'*til all her petals you plucked. She was pretty and sweet and brittle, lovelier than all the others you*—folks up ahead," he warned his companions, suddenly serious.

"A Mumbler," piped another, surprised.

Uther strode athwart their path, the sleeves of his stolen wool spreading with his arms. "Good day to you, my brothers," he said with ingratiating cheer. "My friends and I would pass this way in peace."

A blond-haired peasant laughed sharply. "*Peace?* Aye, *you* may pass in peace, Mumbler. Less so, this lot."

Zur saw the peasants had captives with them. At a gesture from the blond-haired companion, the singer yanked on a rope connecting the captives so they all shambled ahead together. A cassocked priest landed on his knees in the dirt, dragging with him two knights shucked like corn in their tattered gambesons. They'd been beaten worse than Zur.

The world must be ending, Zur thought, stunned. He never imagined that he'd see peasants treating priests and anointed knights like slaves. Indeed, like Casaanites. *A revolt's happened,* he understood. *A village burns. That's why there's smoke . . .*

"Which means you're in luck," the singer clarified warmly. He stood tall and straightened his shoulders, beaming, as if he were a dutiful man-at-arms. "We have charged ourselves with keeping peace on Flint Way today. Those who would not be a slave to priest-kings or the king of his making, or Hexar's bitch daughter, we call our friends."

"May Justar's godface be with you on your quest," Uther responded agreeably. "'Bout time the priestking's devils paid for the evil they've inflicted on our country. Would you point my companions and me to safety, then?"

"Where ya headed?"

"Grayport."

The blond-haired man turned to point south. "You'll want to keep on Flint Way. Less danger for you than on a Romarian road. Our lord's north at the Trials, but many are those loyal to his rotten house. Even some peasants."

A captive knight struggled up from his knees, red-faced and defiant. "No one in this lot'll be safe, *not ever*," he swore. "*Dracar take you! When Lord Greathall returns—*"

Three peasants fell on him with fists and the flats of their filched steel, beating him until he fell over, moaning faintly. The other prisoners watched in mute horror.

One subduer, a tall, burly man, ran a hand through his hair, flinging sweat. "When ol' Domin returns, he'll know only *one* god rules over Loran," he said. "He'll see his Commons had their fill of his poll taxes and parish fines and . . ." He twisted at the blond-haired man. "You hear that?"

Shrrip, Zur heard his captor slobber. Spittlelip covered his ruined mouth with a sleeve. *Shwwip,* Zur heard nonetheless.

"Who else's out there?" hollered the singer-peasant.

"Someone's behind that tree." The blond-haired peasant stared in Zur's direction. "Better you be true with us, Mumbler. We're guardin' this town and Flint Way. I count six of you. Who else—?"

Zur bolted from Spittlelip's grip and out of the ferns, into view.

The peasants sauntered back, wide-eyed and wary. It was a familiar suspicion, and he wasn't surprised. These men likely wouldn't help him.

But he was counting on something else to sway them to his side.

"Help me, help me please," Zur pled. Orthos ran up on his heels, seizing him by the arm. "These men have taken me. *This man*"—he pointed at Uther—"he's no Free Believer. He serves the Nagarthessi!"

No one said anything. The peasants each asked for the other's thoughts with glances, and for the first time Zur noticed a woman among them armed with a spear.

The blond-haired man pivoted to Uther. "Why would a Mumbler," he began crisply, "have in his company a fucking Casaanite?"

The tall fellow stabbed a finger accusingly at Zur. "Only them that's part of a noble house walk with Elzura's brood."

I need you to look past my ancestor's sins, Zur wanted to say. "No, I'm not with them," he protested.

"Donna matter, Child of Elzura," the blond-haired man said. "You lot's coming with us. We serve Connor Bagman of Rosbury. You'll answer to him, Mumbler, or whoever you are."

In a few strides the tall peasant was upon Zur, drawing his sword. Owen inserted himself between them quickly, his sword catching sunlight as he clashed with the man. Uther's other men, including Spittlelip, charged the peasants.

Zur fell to the ground. He crawled off on hands and knees, cursing the rope binding his wrists.

Owen deftly countered a hearty swing, but the tall man had at least a foot on him. Bill leapt up snake-quick, uncoiling a dagger from behind his back that he shoved into the tall one's liver. Bill's triumph was short-lived; a dagger speared his thigh.

The peasants' numbers were helping them prevail against Morley's men. If Orthos, Owen, Bill, Tom, Devan, and Spittlelip had been sworn knights, if Uther Brune had not his crippling age, maybe they'd stand a chance.

But what happens to me? he wondered wildly.

Zur caught frantic looks from the captive priest and two knights. *They could help me,* he realized. On elbows and knees he crawled toward a discarded sword, careful of the whirl of feet and steel.

He laced fingers around the sword's pommel. *First me.* Balancing the sword between his knees, he pressed his rope into the edge, sawing it back and forth. An unseasonably cold wind whirled past him as the ropes snapped apart.

Yes, yes! Zur could've kissed the sword. He glanced up, expecting to find the priest and knights eager for rescue . . . and saw them twitching on the ground in puddles of their own life's blood. Their necks looked like they'd been chewed by wolves.

Hands had him, furious fingers that dug into his shoulders painfully. Hurled on his backside, he saw the rebel peasants all dead, all sheared through by some wild thing. Spittlelip's fists rained down on his face, again and again, *shrrip-shrrip.*

"Li'l bastard," Bill snarled. He hobbled close, clutching his bleeding thigh. Blood bathed his fingers and drenched his leg. "Gods-damned li'l prick! He gave us away. I'll gut him for that, I will, I'll—"

"You'll do no such thing." Uther loomed over Zur. The emerald ring he wore on his finger had a brilliant luster that quickly faded, as if clouds were passing overhead.

Tom clutched at Bill's wound with both hands to stem the blood loss. "*I'VE BEEN STABBED!*" Bill protested. "Were it not for him—"

All it took was a look from Uther to silence Bill into submission. "You will not hurt him, Bill," he said with soft menace. "Besides, it was Jacob's lip-sucking that drew the rebels' suspicion."

The priest gazed up at the smoke-strewn sky. "A Summer Solstice draws near." A smile passed over his lips as he turned back to Zur. "And the true gods will expect a Gift."

Spittlelip grinned.

Zur was turning onto his side when he spotted a familiar shape in the sky, feathers rustling. None of his captors seemed to notice the griff, preoccupied as they were with Bill's wound.

Drexan, he thought. *You haven't abandoned me.*

Uther rummaged in Drexan's travelsack. He opened the vial and took a whiff, smiling. "I know what this is," he said.

He flung the sleep agent at Zur's face.

The Wrathful King

ustin lay dying.

He shivered under a blanket of wool and leaves, moaning. The crone named Lisha kept him company through the night, whispering incantations by the fire, rattling a bowl of chicken bones over his perspiring face. Thorngale's sword wound in his belly bled profusely.

Evan watched from his place by a tree. Turning, he saw his daughter yards away, observing the Sylvanian death rites, arms folded under her chest, dappled furs clinging to her back and shoulders. Their gazes never met, but he could tell she was upset. With her, he could always tell.

Somehow, it felt wrong to observe his daughter without her knowing, the moment too intimate, as if she were in a state of undress. He'd only ever seen Leah Sinclair watch one other man the same way. *She knows this Dustin in a manner I would not approve of,* he realized sullenly.

A tree shifted in the corner of his eye, and the tree turned into a man, an Uzman, rather. The warpaint Murg wore peeled and cracked around his chin and cheeks. "The Heretics died for you," he rumbled.

Evan nodded his acknowledgement. He decided his watch probably seemed disrespectful, and left to find Dumas Sunox in the woodland gloom. Cedar trees bushed a landscape that rose and fell with hills. Crickets played their violins unceasingly.

They were on the far side of Wesswood, near the realm's borders with the Free Kingdoms. The canyon Barbara's Gorge wasn't far, which meant they were also near Shoaltown, where Stoddard Trambar had hanged Rezlan Ambrose's father on a tree limb.

Passing under cedar trees, stars glittering overhead, Evan wondered if any limbs he saw had been the one. *How soon until I join your father, Rezlan?* he thought. *Maybe I should choose my own limb . . .*

He'd see the sunrise soon. Evan had to wonder whether it'd be his last. On his orders, Leah and her Heretics had saved him and Dumas Sunox from torment and death. The Petitioners had betrayed him, while Dumas outed himself as one of his few truly Loyal Companymen.

For all Evan knew, Gram Sothos lay dead or dying from his burns in that forest grove. It was poetic justice, proof the gods existed, and it made Evan feel a hundred feet tall. How often had he dreamed of seeing Sarah's murderer—Matthus's murderer—writhing and wailing in flames?

It's the least you deserve, you bastard, he thought. Sothos deserved that and worse . . . but his solace was fleeting, swept away by the flood-waters of a father's agonizing, all-consuming fear for his children.

"Father."

Leah stepped out from behind a tree, her hair a shade of indigo. The tangle of her plaid skirt drooped from her sword-belt, wafting by her knee. Starlight revealed the red of a scar on her cheek. She flinched slightly when he reached out with a hand.

"Is a father's touch so terrible?" Evan asked her.

"It can be, when it's yours," she said. "Last you saw me, you slapped me."

He hung his head apologetically.

Her hazel eyes found his in night's darkness. "We lost ten men to the Stormsword back there—eleven, once Dustin dies." She glanced away when she said his name.

"It's why I'm out here, rather than there," Evan said. "You always preferred your privacy." He clasped her shoulders. "Get some sleep, child. Have the dwarf see to that cut. I have some thinking to do."

He turned on his heel, knowing that wasn't the end of the conversation. With Leah, it never was.

She followed him up the steps of smooth pale rocks that by

starlight half-looked like a mother wolf crawling with cubs. "That's it, you prick?" she snapped. "You rope my men and me into this—and then you walk away?"

Evan swiveled on her. "You were the one who chose . . . *this*," he said with a scornful sweep of hand that encompassed all of her, from her leathery boots to her pauldrons and scars.

"It's just like when Mother died. You and Rathos tell me I'm the one who left, but it was always *you* who left first—"

Evan took her calmly by her hands. They felt rough with callus. "Leah, I love you. But you're hurt. You should—"

"*You don't get to act like you care.*" Her voice dripped with grief and anger. She shook slightly as she ran her hand through her hair. "My men weren't pleased to have lost their friends for your sake and Lord Sunox's. They were even less pleased that we lost them to rescue an ally of the Hammer of the Commons."

She gave him a searching, wrenching look. "Gram Sothos and I were never allies," he assured her.

Leah clutched at her arms, as if she were suddenly cold. "Then what were you to him?" she asked hesitantly, and Evan realized that she actually feared him. "*Who are you?*"

Evan lifted a bang from her forehead, smoothing it behind an ear. "I am your father, and a desperate man in this kingdom of wolves," he told her. "I struck a bargain with Sothos I never intended to honor. He was to play into my hands, and thereby deliver a crown for Jason and seats for peasants, through either the Kingstrials . . . or war."

"But you played into his. And as a result, I've lost men." It was her turn to slap him. "Is that why you asked the Mad Lady to stay in Northland? To use her and her men as game pieces on a checkered board shaped like Loran?"

Evan placed a hand over his flushed left cheek. His little girl had learned how to land a blow. "Nothing will have been for nothing, Leah. You'll see."

She peered up through glassy eyes that shimmered with starlight. She was beautiful, his daughter. "Tell that to Dustin," she said thickly.

"Tell that to Mina and Rathos."

Evan caught her as she fell into his chest, wetting his tunic with tears. "Gram Sothos is a liar," Evan soothed her. *As am I . . .* He stroked her indigo hair. "We don't know anything yet."

Leah withdrew, wiping her eyes. "We don't, you're right. But my scouts just returned from the Meadows, and they've a story to tell." Her smile wasn't a kind one. "Rejoice, Lord Evan. The summer will be long. You've got your war."

It would've been impossible to sleep. Evan walked the perimeter of camp with the Lord of Ramsport, talking about the earth-shaking events that had unfolded during the clash with Sothos and his lords.

Incited by the death of the Rosbury child, peasants had surged north and stormed the Assembly's slumbering camps. They'd attacked their lords, priests, and merchants like mad dogs. If Leah's scouts had spoken true, peasants might've well freed the griffon . . . which meant they'd done what no peasant had in two centuries. They'd entered the Colossus.

They did it, Evan thought, as tipsy from the implications as he'd be if he were in his cups. *They fought to reclaim their seats.*

But Leah's scouts had also seen slaughtered Cloudlanders strewn across the Golden Meadows.

"They attacked indiscriminately," Evan said, troubled.

"No one attacks indiscriminately," Dumas said. The portly lord still had on his raiment from earlier, an azure doublet that stretched over his bulging belly, black boots scuffed during the skirmish, a cape ribboned by blades that had come for his back. "Those peasants organized on their own. They acquired steel on their own. They came for their enemies." He clapped Evan on the back with a thick hand. "You were the canary in the coal mine, my friend. You were a prophet."

"I prophesied to the deaf." Evan tripped on a gnarled root, and

Dumas caught him before he fell. "Years, Dumas! Years we wasted trying to petition Hexar, to warn the Assembly."

"Nothing has been for nothing," Dumas said with a glint in his eye. "You were right. War is the only way. And your nephew is poised to lead Commoners against the priestking's tyranny."

Evan raked a hand over his stubble. It'd been a long night. *If he's alive,* he thought darkly. *You'd find me and kill me in hell if he isn't, my dear friend, wouldn't you?* He kept searching the heavens for any sign of a vast winged shadow. *Or would you, Hexar?*

Sunlight soon washed over a misty cedar forest. The two lords farewelled each other at a rugged mountain path dotted with boulders. Outed as a Companyman, Dumas had to make safe his children. He wanted to reach his castle while Sothos's vassals still had revolts to contend with.

"Where will you go?" Evan asked Dumas as the lord threw a thickset leg over his horse. Pretty Phillip had traded him that horse for his wedding ring.

Sunox scanned the eastern horizon. "Tesos, maybe. I have cousins at King Grisholm's court. Redoak will give my land and castle to some undeserving shit, no doubt." He gazed sadly at Evan. "I'd invite you to leave this land with me, but I know you must see to your own children. I wish I could aid you—"

Evan shrugged off his entreating look. "You did aid me. The Kingstrials are finished, anyway. Shaddon will be king." The admission tasted bitter in his mouth. He had no doubt the priestking's allies would capitalize on the worst uprising since the Interregnum.

Dumas watched him intently. "The Company is finished now, Evan. You owe them no more allegiance than they owe you. If our secrets can help you find grace for your daughter and her husband, or for your nephew, trade them."

Tellingly, he didn't mention any grace for Evan himself. "Which star shines the brightest in darkest night?" he asked.

"The star of House Sinclair," the Lord of Ramsport replied pensively, "which never truly shines alone."

Evan smiled wanly. He shook Dumas's hand, patting the knuckles. "Safe travels, my friend."

Dumas clutched at his reins, readying his horse with a few light taps from his heels. "If you see Princess Lorana again, tell her I never resented being called Lord Gut. I've always thought of her as the *real* Most-Sought Hand in the Thirteen Kingdoms, that brilliant woman."

I'll try, Evan thought, *if she herself still draws breath.*

He watched Dumas tear off in a cloud of dust, and then headed back to the grove. The sun blinkered through forest canopy; the fire was ash; and Dustin lay belowground. Lisha chanted by his grave in a lost language while other Heretics looked on. He felt accusing stares as he passed by.

I feel alone, though, Dumas, maybe more than I ever have. Fear fell over him like a growing shadow. *Where are you, Mina? Rathos?*

An answer came soon enough. Around noon, Leah loped ahorse through the trees. Violet hair erupted about her face. "We've found them," she said, breathless.

"Show me." He scrambled up into her saddle, behind her.

Leah handpicked several outlaws to travel with her, Murg and Pretty Phillip, and two others, a Casaanite named Lethabo and another called Stonehands.

Creature meowed pitifully when she didn't choose him. "You're too loud, Creature," Leah told him. He hissed like a cat.

Off they went, fast as their mounts' hooves could carry them, over rugged terrain, in the shadows beneath mountains. The sun glared down like an angry white eye. Leah dispatched Lethabo and Stonehands to watch a ridge north of Sunder Way, where Evan had lost Sarah and Matthus two decades before.

Lethabo returned an hour later with report of a sighting. "If they're on Sunder, they'll have to pass beneath the Wrathful King," Evan predicted. "We should make for Barbara's Pass."

The four men showed him cold courtesy. *They wait for her,* he marveled. Queens had been forbidden to rule in Loran for centuries, and here his daughter had murderers and thieves to wait on her every command. Pride mingled with his unease. What made a Mad Lady? *What terrible things could my flesh and blood have done to earn their respect?* He'd seen some of these things the night before.

"The King it is," Leah said finally, and her men fell in line.

They saw the Wrathful King's sword first, an enormous blade of rusted bronze that curved over the canyon. When they rode to the cliff's edge, the rest of King Temron came into view. Millennia after the Romarian tyrant's death, the three-hundred-foot monument to his madness stood still, his legs athwart the canyon walls of Barbara's Pass, a skirt of bronze about his waist. Below knelt his victim, his bronze head bulging out of canyon wall, his expression twisted with the terror one would expect from a man about to lose his head.

When Rezlan argued forcefully about the need to remove crowns, it was this monstrosity that he cited. "No king has ever inflicted himself on the land like Temron, or set such a *perfect* example for his successors," he'd said.

Evan couldn't disagree with his reasoning. The Wrathful King was an eyesore in Loran, and the tale behind it made the monument preposterous. Someone unlearned would see the victim and think him a mighty rival, maybe a traitor, but he'd be gravely mistaken.

No, Temron's victim was a cook who'd made his king's bowels run from a spicy broth. The king sent orders to build a monument that would forever enshrine the chef's moment of reckoning. Birds circling the head honored the king's gigantic likeness with fecal stains that striped his face like white sweat beads.

"There they are." Leah pointed at the train of horse and men winding up the canyon trail, small as ants. She reached inside her furs and produced a skyglass that shuddered as it clinked open, cylinder upon cylinder. *I'd been looking for that,* thought Evan. *She must've filched it off me on Mount Dracar.*

She peered through the device, lips twisting with raw anguish. "Those fucking bastards."

"Let me see," Evan demanded, "and *get down,* damn it."

Leah handed him the skyglass limply. He adjusted the instrument until the world he saw through its lens sharpened with perfect clarity.

Down below, an army marched through the gorge, four columns abreast, knights on destriers, footmen with pikes, at least two hundred or more. Sothos's lions danced upon their surcoats. *Reinforcements,* he knew. *They march to supplement Shaddon's forces. The Worthy will see him king.*

A woman plodded on foot at the front of the procession, near the head of Temron's victim, hair bedraggling her face like purple moss. A rage, a grief, a terror, an anguish swept over the woman's father. The skyglass trembling in his hand, he beheld her husband, trussed in manacles over a horse like a prized fish to be gutted.

Evan handed the skyglass to his daughter. "Send for your archers," he muttered through clenched teeth. "From here, we can kill them all."

His secondborn touched his shoulder with a gentleness that felt strange. "Father, they're too many—too well armed—and we could hit Mina or Rathos if we loosed arrows—"

He swiveled on her, and the fright in Leah's crumpled face made him feel as tall and ugly as Temron. He suddenly had his sword in hand, and he was up and headed north, to the stairs of a sidewall trail that zigzagged down to the canyon floor.

Leah restrained her father as he frothed at the mouth like something rabid.

"*Let me go, damn you, LET ME GO, let me go, let me go,*" he pled, twisting like an eel in her arms and theirs. It took all five of them to keep Evan from flying down the sidewall stairs and killing the first man he met, from killing them all.

"Father, Father," she kept saying as he protested. "You're *a man of reason.* Think! Expose yourself, and they'll kill you, or take you prisoner. What good will you be to them then?" Her tears dampened his rage. "*What will I do then, with everyone I love taken from me?*"

He remembered Matthus standing over him on Sunder Way. "Everything's a game piece to you, isn't it, Evan?" he'd said, cracking his knuckles. "Do you even know what love is?"

CHAPTER 27

Three Trials, Three Wings

ason lay on a sweat-soaked bed, groaning as men wailed and horses whinnied all around him. Falling in and out of consciousness, the bastard prince found himself by Erick's pyre on the shore, then aboard *The Drunken Adventure*, Garrett's cold sword flat across his throat. He felt his half-brother's tears running off his cheeks, heard his mumbled apologies.

He sat up suddenly, gasping. Everything hurt like hell. The slightest move brought a stab of pain up his chest, through his thigh and flank. He felt like a child's stuffed doll, unraveling at its seams, seams he'd never known existed. Everything in him willed him back to bed, back to dreams, until he saw the grim faces around him.

The apothecary Eorl eased him onto his pillow with such familiarness that Jason mistook him for Jon Applewood. "Easy, my lord," the Cloudlander said. "Your stitches . . ."

Fire snapped in the braziers in his pavilion's corners. The pale eye of a morning sun watched from the flaps. Around him stood everyone, all his nobles, their faces grave.

Almost everyone. Trevor Wexley loomed over him, Zarold Ulbridge and Russell Wexrenn and his other noblemen, plus Sir Rogir Levan and several Wall knights, all but Derek Clabbard and David Bridge. *They died,* he realized, jarred by the burn in his flank. *They died for me. They died for spectacle . . . my crown.*

Jason licked his chapped lips. He gave suck from Rogir's waterskin until the leather pouch deflated.

"My sister," he said hoarsely. "Where's Ana?" Everyone seemed to hesitate, trading looks with Wexley.

The Bull had a dark look made darker by the pavilion's gloom. "A force of peasants attacked the lords' camps while everyone slept." The seams around his mouth tightened when he said *peasants*. "Our bravest men died protecting us. They tried to kidnap your sister, the Princess Lorana."

Jason wondered whether he was still dreaming. *A force of peasants . . .* "Tried? Where is she?" No one elaborated for him. "Damn it, am I speaking in First Tongue? Answer me!"

Wexrenn stroked the flaxen whiskers along his upper lip. "Shaddon entered our camp in the confusion," he admitted. "He kidnapped the princess, along with her Casaanite servant." He raised his gaze from his feet. "Your traitorous uncle's taken her to the Colossus, which his armies now hold."

Jason looked at them each in turn. "Where's Lord Evan?"

Ulbridge shook his head drearily. "No one knows."

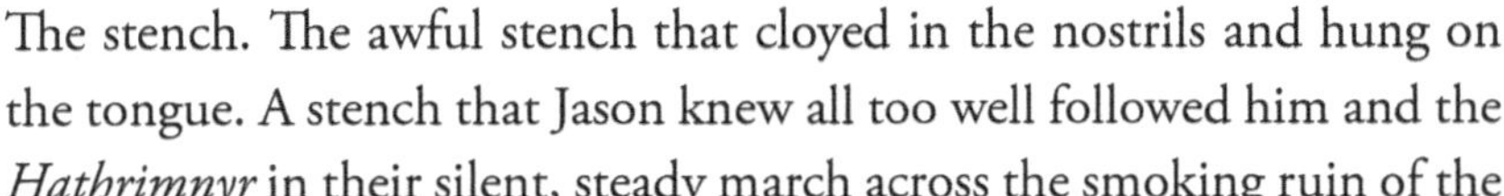

The stench. The awful stench that cloyed in the nostrils and hung on the tongue. A stench that Jason knew all too well followed him and the *Hathrimnyr* in their silent, steady march across the smoking ruin of the Golden Meadows.

The earth bled like an opened scab, splotched red with death. The dead were not in short supply. Peasants from all over Loran cluttered the way to the Colossus, preventing easy passage. Their killers had lumped the bodies into untidy hills. Crows hopped among the bodies, cawing their complaints.

Jason counted the dead. Young men. Old men. Women. Boys no older than Zur.

These are the peasants Evan warned us would rise up, he thought. They hadn't only sacked the Colossus. His noblemen said they'd also torched Shaddon's galleys off the coast in the night. *And here my enemies stand, behaving as if they've won, as if they're impervious to more violence . . .*

Such was the field of silver that surrounded the Colossus, Jason wondered at first if it was all silverstone plundered and hauled here from the Silver Walls. Lords ahorse, distinguished by their plumed helms and fur-lined mantles. Knights athwart barded war horses. Men in coif and mail hung sturdily on their spears and halberds.

There had to be at least ten thousand. At least.

Sunlight glanced off the arrows pointed at Jason and his men from the Colossus's arcades. *These usurpers leave nothing to chance,* he pondered as he made out the archers atop the amphitheater's ledges and battlements.

Jason approached from the other side of the field with his *Hathrimnyr,* their plate armor and chain mail clinking a somber melody. They were closing the distance when trumpets blared from atop the amphitheater.

"No farther, Warchild!"

Sam Gramlore parted from the arrayed forces on a war horse, armored for battle. His eyes danced under his sunlit blond hair as he rode forward.

Beside Jason, the Bull grunted out his contempt, or his pain, more like. They both needed to be in bed, not ahorse. Wexley had insisted on coming out despite his wounds from swords and daggers. Up close, he looked well past his age.

We are no King's Army, hardly an army to begin with. And with archers nested a hundred feet up, Shaddon's lackeys had the clear advantage. He had no way to take the Colossus from this force, not without a proper siege.

Jason had to hope that Shaddon wished to avoid further calamity. He had to hope right now, for Lorana's sake.

Tugging on his horse's ornamented reins, Jason detached from his army with a triangle formation that included Wexley and his knights. The other side's bows tautened. He held up his hand, signaling his men to halt.

"MEN OF THE WORTHY ASSEMBLY!" he shouted. "Is this how

you'd conduct the Kingstrials of our country? You broke ancient laws! Snuck into my camp like thieves while my men and I lay abed! Free my sister, or there shall be more blood."

And our kingdom will fall, shattering like glass on the rocks of your ambition, he thought darkly.

As Gramlore rode out, a white flag in one hand, mounted men accompanied him, silks of cream and violet aswirl over their armor. Darren Thorngale rode with them, his eyes fixed on the man who killed his oldest brother, nephew to the man he accused of killing his father.

Jason beckoned to the Bull, Ulbridge, Wexrenn, and the Wall knights Kyle Urron and Harold Marc, and they detached for a cautious trot forward.

The parties met in the middle of the field of death, horses snorting their discomfort. Gramlore handed off his white flag and pulled out a scroll tucked into his gauntlet.

"We demand the usurper Shaddon Eddenhold," Wexley growled. "Not you."

Gramlore smoothed his flaxen beard. "I've been tasked to parley with you on behalf of King Shaddon."

At the mention of *King Shaddon,* muttered disbelief and calls for blood flew up from Jason's men. Lips curling, Wexley looked like he might just draw his sword and lob off Gramlore's head, his own death be damned. Everyone swore and cursed or bristled but Jason himself, who demanded calm.

The uproar wrung a thin, satisfied smile from Gramlore. He extended the scroll to Jason. "This is for you, my lord." He said *my lord* with infuriating smugness.

Jason flitted from the parchment to Gramlore's laughing eyes. "Should I consider this terms of surrender?"

"This"—Gramlore jabbed the scroll at him—"is far more than you deserve, Warchild."

"Where's my sister?" Jason tensed the reins for a jingle. Mailed hands clenched their spears and sword hafts a little more tightly.

"I'd answer my king, if you value your head," the Bull said, eyes simmering.

Gramlore looked his rival up and down tauntingly. "You don't seem well, Lord Trevor. Maybe you should leave the rule of the Cloudlands to someone stronger."

He added in the same breath, with a cutting look at Jason, "And Jason Warchild *isn't* your king or anyone else's. This scroll tallies the Assembly's votes. They've named Shaddon the victor of these Kingstrials and rightful Lord of Loran."

Ulbridge showed what he thought of that with a cone of spittle. Someone behind Jason laughed in disbelief.

"Shaddon hasn't won a single Trial," Jason said. "He is no king."

Gramlore grinned. "Decamp and leave the Meadows in peace. To ease the sting of defeat, King Shaddon will, after his coronation, grant you Redmount Castle and its estates, along with all their incomes. He knows Hexar loved you, and wishes to honor that love. He'll even seat you in the Wing of Lords, to make laws beside every other rightful lord in the kingdom."

Redmount, Jason thought grimly. *House Eddenhold's family castle . . . and a seat in the Worthy Assembly.*

Jason's hand moved without him thinking, and his horse trotted forward. "You speak of *laws?* You and that zealot have shattered them. By the laws, no claimant can enter another's camp. *You have no right!*"

"*Right?*" Darren Thorngale glared knives into Jason. "You protected my father's killer, and now you've killed my brother. RIGHT?"

"'Three Trials, three Wings,' the peasants say," Gramlore said. "'Only the Worthy crown their king.'" He shrugged. "That's what happened while you slept. You won two Trials, not three. So, the Worthy chose."

"Your cunt must be as big as your mouth," Wexrenn said.

"The Worthy stole," Jason said before Wexrenn finished. "How could I have lost the Third Trial *if there wasn't a Third Trial?*"

Gramlore extended his arms to encompass the ruined field. "Look around. The peasants that you and your traitor uncle sought to seat in our Assembly attacked us. The rebels reaved like Uzmen. Dismembered the High Bishop. Stormed and desecrated the Colossus. The murderous mob freed the griffon while they were at it—so no, *there will be no Third Trial.*"

"The Second Trial was supposed to be a dragon-slaying," Ulbridge said. "The Assembly agreed to a *naumachia* when a dragon didn't show."

"Because someone burned the ships ferrying that dragon to Loran," Gramlore responded curtly. "Much like your beloved peasants burned the new king's ships."

"There *could* be a Third Trial," Ulbridge went on, as if he hadn't heard the objection, "but you and this Assembly of two wings won't allow it."

"That revolt you slept through *was* the last of the Trials," Gramlore said. "Thank the twelve for Shaddon Eddenhold! He rallied our forces! Put down the revolt like a king." He had a self-righteous air. "You should be *on your knees* thanking him. Those peasants you adore—like the ones who killed Hexar—wanted to hold Princess Lorana hostage inside the Colossus, which they briefly *did* hold. Until Shaddon the Protector put a stop to it."

Wexley spat. "Tell the truth, you bastard," he slurred his words. "That twat lord invaded our camp to seize the princess. To take *her* hostage, so that we'd concede the crown."

Gramlore nodded at the field. "The proof of what I say is all around you. Just"—he inhaled contentedly—"smell it."

"If what you say is true," Jason said, "what did the rebels want in exchange for my sister?"

Thorngale laughed. "The Wing of the Commons."

"They want *justice.*" Jason urged his horse closer, drawing looks of warning. "There's still time to undo this treachery," he pressed the lords softly, earnestly. "This injustice."

"*Injustice?*" Thorngale gritted his teeth.

"*How* can you be so foolish?" Jason fired back, his voice imploring, urgent. "Loran teeters on a knife's edge as it is. A temple burning. The revolt in Rosbury. God and gods, they burned the ships your false king sailed on! And now . . . now you *inhale* the reek of death, as if it were a rose blossom?"

Gramlore had a listless, casual boredom.

"The revolt was just the beginning, you fool. If Shaddon steals the crown like this—if the Worthy Assembly aids and abets him—"

"'Just the beginning'?" Gramlore shook his head gravely. "Are you with your own class, Warchild, or the vicious rebels?"

Jason gritted his teeth. *You were right, Evan,* he thought. *They uncork a poison vial, and it spills out on all of our heads. And for all that's happened, they cannot see that their cruelty and contempt uncorked it.*

Gramlore studied the Bull. "How does it feel, Lord Trevor, knowing that you allied with a king of the *scrorn-ner-gaith* who brought death to your own people?"

Wexley didn't seem to register the insult. He didn't seem to register *anything.* He stared down at his mare, sweat lacing his forehead. *He shouldn't have come. No one can see him this way.* Ulbridge muttered to Wexrenn in their native tongue, and the two men clasped their liege's arms, holding him upright in his saddle as the great lord suddenly swayed left.

Thorngale kicked his horse forward. "I want Sinclair," he said through his teeth. "He must answer for his crimes."

"King Shaddon demands Sinclair's immediate surrender," Gramlore added. "If Sinclair doesn't give himself up, the lives of the people he loves will be forfeit. Just like your chances of ever being anything more than a warmongering bastard in anyone's eyes."

In one sleight of hand Jason had his sword drawn, and so did Thorngale. The other men unsheathed their blades with a *shiiiiiink.* He glanced wildly about, at archers nested in arcades high above, the mounted knights and men-at-arms yards away.

Wexley merely reached for his sword and fell sideways, toppling to the soil in a singsong rattle of armor that brought laughter from the Assembly's forces. His horse slid out from under him, bolting off.

Gramlore threw back his head, laughing. Jason led his horse on threateningly.

Pffft, a fletched arrow appeared in the soil, and a second, and a third, *pffft, pffft.* The missiles spooked his horse, jerking him. He grunted as his side sutures split open. He felt blood saturating his gambeson, down to his thigh.

Thorngale urged his mount forward. "Come on, bastard. Give me a reason . . . or give me Evan Sinclair." He plucked the scroll from Gramlore's hand and tossed it in front of Jason.

Jason glanced orders at his men, circling to ride back to camp. It took him, Ulbridge, Wexrenn, and Kyle and Harold to heave the Bull over another horse, which buckled unsteadily. They galloped back to the *Hathrimnyr* with laughter in their ears.

Wexley lay strewn across a bed of cushions. Eorl held the back of his hand to his brow. "Hot with fever," the apothecary said. "Just as you were. We need to pour a bath."

Jason helped men haul his iron tub from a corner of the pavilion. He, the lords, and squires went to unfastening the Bull's thick gorget and cuirass and greaves. Wexrenn returned with men hoisting buckets of tepid water they poured into the tub.

Eorl soaked chamomile blossoms and mashed mint leaves in sweet oils, dumping it all into the bath. Together, they eased the hulk of Trevor Wexley inside, water spilling over the edges.

"My assistant is searching for boneset from Wesswood," the apothecary told them. "There's a better weed to heal our lord, but it's in Southland, and—" He stopped short of saying it, but Jason already knew.

But the weed we need is in Southland, where the Assembly forbids us from traveling, he thought bitterly. *They don't want me anywhere near the Silver Walls, my home.*

Jason gathered to set a watch with Ulbridge, Wexrenn, the other nobles, and Rogir Levan. The mood was grim. Someone set a fire outside and boiled onion broth, but no one seemed interested in eating. A rust-colored orb of a sun drifted down his tent wall.

Ulbridge nursed a cup of honey-wine mead thick with froth, passing it to Wexrenn. "What now, my king?" he asked wearily. It was the question no one had the stomach to ask, until now.

Jason eased forward in his chair, minding his freshly sutured wounds.

"I've failed the Bull, and you," he replied. He dismissed their insistent rebuttals, shaking his head. "No, *hear me!* I've played the fool. I allowed my kinslaying uncle to live. I lost the Free Believers by crowning a prieslenne the Virgin of Venas. I entered the Kingstrials thinking if I played honorably, out of a love for country, others would do the same. But they haven't. Because they *don't* love this country. They suckle it like ticks."

The Mumbler Orrin said that, before vanishing, Jason thought. *He said we didn't need any more ticks ruling us . . .*

He rose slowly. "They invaded our camp. Took Lorana hostage. Loran is a cracked vase, and holding all the shards together hasn't helped the Cloudlands, peasants, or us."

Ulbridge smiled a hard smile, as if he read his thoughts.

"Fetch me ink and a quill, and the fastest horsemen in the *Hathrimnyr*," Jason told him. "Along with our best, most loyal scouts. We need the Kingdom of Tesos."

"Tesos won't come."

Jason swiveled at the voice.

Evan Sinclair lurked in the tent flaps, a haggard shell of himself. Dark circles ringed his eyes. He looked in want of a bath, good ale, and perhaps a sword to run someone through with, too.

"Loran is unraveling. Our neighbors want no part in it . . . yet, anyway. To leave here alive, you'll need a hostage." Evan smiled poignantly. "Behold."

CHAPTER 28

Highdaughter

he king's daughter listened as gaolers traveled to and fro through the earthen hall outside, keys jingling. Their Medecian accents hung in her ears as they escorted prisoners in and out.

Executions, Lorana knew. *They're killing the peasants they took prisoner to make an example.* Easing her back against the unforgiving stone wall, she tried to reassure herself that they wouldn't make an example of *her*, too.

She was Hexar's child. Alyse's daughter. A steward. And for all the misery of her dank, windowless cell, for all the rats that woke her brushing her toes with their whiskers, they were feeding her. Daughters of Divna came in to pray with her. *And yet, and yet, and yet . . .*

Her ride to the Colossus had been a hellish blur.

Thrown over a destrier, Lorana had gasped and cried and cursed Shaddon and every Intercessor as every jolt quickened pain in her arm, making it feel as if a giant were ripping it off. She remembered fleeting glimpses of fires leaping off pavilions, mounted knights shouting orders as they thundered past, and all around her the screams of rebels being put to the sword.

More death awaited them inside the Colossus, along with piled wreckage that had once caged a griffon. Shaddon ordered his silver-faced men to cauterize and dress her wound, then off he went, and off she went, through earthen hall, down a flight of cracked steps, into a windowless little hell. The Intercessors slammed her rusted iron door before she could reach it, hands grasping.

Oh, she'd protested. Lorana had banged her fists against the door, shouting at the top of her lungs, demanding someone release her immediately. She was the steward, she declared. When that didn't work, she made threats about a new Long Summer. She promised to lock up traitors, make heads roll.

Most of all, she demanded to know about Anyasha.

In response, her guards laughed at her. At *her*.

They laughed on the first day. They laughed again at her demands on the second day.

The truth of her situation became her miserable friend in the darkness of her cell below the Colossus. She was powerless. Shaddon's forces had put down the revolt and exploited chaos to take power. Her brother lay unconscious, or dead. The lords and priests ruled aboveground. Soon, they'd crown her uncle.

Have Anjan's Walls been taken? Her head swung between anger and paranoia like a wind-whipped branch. Parlisis had dispatched another armada to Southpoint bearing a Medecian host, maybe. But that would've meant a long siege.

One truth burned through her like volcanic ash. Kept her from collapsing in on herself. Filled her with rage.

Edenia had betrayed them.

I should've poisoned them, she raged within. *Edenia, my uncle, all of them. I should've taken Gram's head. Drexan's. Then I'd have Anyasha. I'd have Zuran. The Silver Walls. Why didn't I, Father?* She subsisted not on the bread and jug of water the guards left for her, but on the small solace that at least, *at least* she'd done one right thing by sending her sister to Tesos. *Will King Grisholm intervene on our behalf when he hears of this?*

In her solitude, she wasn't sure news would reach anyone anywhere. Her cell was a cramped one, with a slop bucket and straw matte; it stank of mildew and rat droppings. Torchlight flickering through her door cracks showed walls riven with deep claw marks. She hoped they were claw marks from the beasts ancient Romarians had once held in these cells, anyway, and not fingernails.

Maybe a griffon made these scratches, she wondered one day. *How apropos if so.* They'd at least had the decency to pull out their arrow and dress her wound. It was healing, but her arm burned still, making it hard to sleep consistently. And sleep deprivation was making her feel insane.

Only her rage grounded her. Rage for Edenia.

On her third day alone, the stone maiden reached inward for her weapon of last resort. Huddled against her door, she began to cry, sniffling like a cunt.

"Please," she pled in a brittle voice. "Will you tell me about my servant? About my brother? At least him. I've lost my father already." Tears blinded her. Bitter tears, true ones before long.

No one answered. She clenched her fists, resisting an urge to pound on her door, when the squeal of hinges echoed down the hall. Feet shuffled past outside, chains clattering. Shadows swam in the torchlit cracks of her door.

Prisoners. The princess quickened at Jason's voice, but it soon became apparent that it wasn't him.

". . . fucking bastards, *give me my wife*, I, I want to see her," croaked a man, someone almost wondrously familiar. His voice came to her from what felt like ages ago, on Remembrance Day, before everything fell apart. He sounded uncannily like Jason. "*LET ME SEE MY WIFE!*"

It's Sinclair's ward, she realized. *Rathos Robswell.*

"Shut your mouth," a guard cut off Rathos. "You'll see the Mad Lady . . . after we finish with her." *Leah Sinclair, his wife?* Lorana pondered. His wife was Mina Sinclair, though, not her outlaw sister.

The shadows in her door cracks pitched into a frenzy, as Robswell rose up against his captors. The desperate lurch of an injured animal it was, and short-lived. His captors hammered him with their fists as if he were steel on an anvil.

"I'll, I'll kill you," Rathos slurred. "Everyone . . ."

If only I could help you do it, thought the princess, listing against the door.

"Your Blessedness," a guard said brightly, followed by the other watchmen, each rushing to say it first.

Her. Days of unspoken rage came to a boil inside Lorana.

"I'm here to see the princess," came that sweet voice. "Open the door."

"Your . . . Blessedness. This place is not meet for your holy person. We would escort you back to your pavilion if—"

"I'm to be queen, sir." *You mean queen consort, you cunt.* Loranians would set their kingdom ablaze before enthroning an *actual* queen, as Lorana knew too well. "Open the princess's door for me, or I will have my husband give me your insolent hands as a gift at his coronation."

Her door cracked open. After days in darkness, the light blinded her. Rusted iron chains dangled from her cell wall, she saw. Two guards maneuvered her against the wall and clapped them over her wrists. The manacles were overlarge, meant for thick-wristed gladiators of old, not her. As soon as the guards left, she wriggled one palm halfway through.

In the doorway stood Edenia, angelic in a white sleeveless surcoat that accentuated her shapely body. Torchlight glowed through the nimbus of her hair. Silken-white gloves patterned with silver thread reached her elbows, making her seem regal. The Most-Sought Hand in the Thirteen Kingdoms, indeed.

"Your Blessedness." Robswell was speaking.

Lorana peered past the prieslenne and saw Robswell, a puppet in the strings of his shackles, rising on one knee. She'd underestimated the guards' cruelty. She hardly recognized him through all the bruises, one eye swollen shut, upper lip looking like it'd been split.

"Get them to their cells, *now,*" a guard growled.

His underlings worked fast, dragging Robswell off with a line of shackled peasants from the revolt. "'Daughter of twelve, hands of men and women all,'" Sinclair's ward rattled off.

Robswell had been clever. He'd quoted the motto on the prieslenne's coat of arms, a desperate maneuver that earned him a guard's vicious backhand.

"No, stop." Edenia faced away from Lorana, toward the broken man outside her door. Lorana appreciated the delay. It gave her precious time to think, to plan. "That's the verse of mine office, sir. I'm bound by my duty as high priestess to hear what mercy this one would ask of his prieslenne."

The prieslenne's intercession seemed to mollify Robswell. He quivered on a knee, wincing as a guard yanked on the chain collared around his neck. "Thank you, Your Blessedness. I ask for mercy, just not for myself."

"Good," Edenia said loftily, "because I have none for you. You're a member of Sinclair's Loyal Company, are you not?"

"I am. I am a traitor." *We're all traitors to our own hearts,* Lorana remembered the king telling her. "I . . . I did my treason for good, but I shall not defend it. I only ask mercy of you."

He asks mercy for his wife, Lorana registered. *I'd ask the same if Anyasha's life hung in the balance.*

"The Mad Lady," a guard spat.

"But she *isn't,*" Rathos rasped. "Our castle was sacked. My Mina, she never left the bailey. She's lawful. She's never done any treason with outlaws or Companymen. I swear this on my soul. She's been beaten. Defiled. And she carries our child."

"*Child?*" Edenia held a hand to her chest, taken aback. "Is what this traitor says true?" she asked the guards in a tone of rebuke.

"Your Blessedness," one guard began, "he's been saying so, but this woman he speaks of is accused of being the Mad Lady of the Heretics. Rapists, thieves, and murderers."

"Perhaps she's a heretic, but children are blameless, as is the one she carries. I will have her brought under my care. If it's true she's been defiled, my betrothed will take the defiler's head."

"But . . . Your Blessedness—"

"Do you want to lose your hands?" Edenia said fiercely. "Bring this woman to my pavilion *NOW.* We'll learn the truth." She gazed at Robswell. "This is my mercy. The Head speaks."

Sinclair's ward exhaled suddenly, deeply, as if he'd just been given the breath of life. "The Hands serve," he agreed. He continued to thank

Edenia profusely as his guards forced him back up and down the hall with other shackled prisoners.

Edenia told the turnkey to remain outside. After refusals, insistences, and another imperious threat from her to remove hands, the door clapped shut.

It was just them, the princess and the prieslenne. In the glow of her torchlight, her lover looked like an apparition. She worked the torch into a cobwebbed sconce on the wall.

"Oh, flower," Edenia said softly, her eyes wobbling with concern. "How did this happen?"

The stone maiden's face crumpled at once. She sagged in her chains. "Oh Eden," she said, her voice moist. "It's . . . what's happened . . ." She trailed off, congested.

Edenia looked as if she ached to hug and comfort her. Yet she stayed right where she was. "Oh, my poor flower. I know of your suffering. Things have taken a turn since the revolt."

"The peasants—Eden, they tried to take *me!*"

"I know. You and Jason wanted to do what you felt was right, but peasants are treacherous. They sacked the Colossus, as no one has done in thousands of years. They tore the High Bishop apart like animals. They burned Shaddon's ships." At that, Lorana nearly smiled. *At least the peasants were good for something.* "But things have improved. We're in control." She said *We're in control* with satisfied firmness. "Soon, we'll end the other revolts and restore order to this godless kingdom."

"*We?*" Lorana arched an eyebrow. "You must mean my uncle. Whom Parlisis is forcing you to wed." A slight growl punctuated her voice when she said *forcing.*

Edenia stroked her arm. A nervous tic that Lorana knew well. *You lied,* Lorana knew, *to me, to Jason, to the world.* "I've seen a different side to Shaddon. He's brave, Ana. Honorable. He might make a good king."

Brave. Honorable. She fought down a pang of anger. "Is it king already? We still have a Third Trial, no?"

"In their madness the peasants released the griffon. There can be no Third Trial now. The Kingstrials are over."

Of course. The Assembly could choose another Third Trial, as it had when Gordon Whitecastle's ships burned off the coast and the dragon didn't make it. But they wouldn't.

Edenia ventured closer. "Try to be grateful, Ana. He saved you from that vicious rabble. What would've happened had he not ridden into your camp with all his men? Jason . . . he's *alive* because of him."

That struck something vulnerable in the princess. For days, she'd teetered on the edge of madness, believing that Shaddon or the peasants had killed Jason. "Did Shaddon take him, too?" *As he took Erick. As he's taken me.*

The ghost of a smile passed over Edenia's lips. "No."

That means I have a chance. Jason had woken to defend himself against Vayne Adrias; he was alive. Her circumstances were improving quickly. "Then the Kingstrials are not over," Lorana said. "Not while Jason Warchild lives."

The look of pity on Edenia's face made her want to do things to it. "Ana . . ."

"Shaddon lost the First and Second Trials."

"He had a champion in the Second—"

"A champion the Assembly ruled can't win a Trial."

Edenia rolled her eyes at the ceiling, smiling, as if Lorana had said something ridiculous. "Sweet flower. Oh, sweet flower. What is the Worthy Assembly? Just a council of old bones. Bald fools who sit and talk and scheme to thwart the man who sits Anjan's Silver Walls. What matters is courage. A king's courage. Your father knew that. Shaddon proved himself worthy of the Silver Throne by putting down the revolt. Now your father's brother succeeds him. Thank the twelve."

Lorana pictured coiling her fingers about the prieslenne's supple neck. She wanted to strangle her, crying and screaming as she choked the life out of her. "The Worthy rule Loran with the king," she reminded her.

"The Worthy crown the king. And soon, they will."

The princess tugged on one chain. "If my *honorable* uncle saved me, why was I whisked into a black cell and chained like a traitor?"

Edenia wore a cold, affronted dignity. "Sir Vayne Adrias was found murdered in the Warchild's camp."

Warchild. Lorana resisted the urge to remind her of her marriage to Jason. An insult would come to her easy enough, but it'd spin Edenia into a whirlwind of angry denials that the guard outside would hear.

"Loran is a sovereign kingdom—"

"The seal of my father's protection knows no borders. You know this."

A little closer. "Eden, why was Sir Vayne in our camp to begin with?" she asked.

Edenia shifted. "My betrothed dispatched Sir Vayne to negotiate with Jason."

He was a messenger of death, and you sent him to kill Jason, your own husband, as he lay comatose, Lorana knew, knew with absolute certainty as she observed the woman she knew like the back of her hand. *As you paid Rose Guild assassins to deliver terms to my brother, giving them your silverstone wedding ring as a line of twisted poetry.*

"Then Shaddon broke Trial rules," Lorana said adamantly. "The laws are clear. No matter what the Worthy does, *he is no king.* And he's a fool to think a realm on fire will let him within one mile of the Silver Walls."

Dressed half in shadow, half in torchlight, the prieslenne's pretty face said what her lips would not. Edenia glanced at the door. She crossed the cell, coming within inches of the princess. Intoxicating lavender fragrances wafted up from her bosom.

The prieslenne leaned in, close enough for a kiss. "Listen to me, Ana," she said softly. "Shaddon will be king, and I, his . . ." She paused. "Nothing will stop it. But it doesn't have to go ill for Jason . . . or for us."

Their lips met. It was a lover's kiss, slow, trusting, vulnerable. *She loves me,* she knew, *not Jason. Eden always loved me more, as much as I loved her.*

By the time the turnkey heard the rattle of metal and barged in, Lorana had her chain looped around the prieslenne's delicate neck. She tightened the chain as the guard came near, taking pleasure in how iron links chewed into her soft skin.

"Alert someone, and I'll break her windpipe," she growled low, past Edenia's ear. Lorana tautened the chain, drawing a painful, gurgled sound from her hostage. "Inside. The door." Nervous-eyed, the man did as told, closing the door quietly. "Your sword. Lay it on the floor."

The guard was uncinching his sword-belt when Edenia flung herself against her, hurling her into the wall. She slipped out of her chain and punched Lorana's bandaged arm.

Lorana gave a short scream. She fell, clutching her arm as blood saturated her bandage and trickled down, and suddenly the guard was on her, kicking her repeatedly in her belly until Edenia had him stop. Her scream issued silently, along with her tears and the crimson droplets off her bottom lip.

Edenia swung her foot into her side. Lorana curled up in agony, sputtering. "Why . . .?" she managed. "Why, Eden?"

Edenia towered over her, eyes aboil. "*WHY?*" She landed a foot in her stomach. "You ask me that? YOU?" She kicked her in her flank. "I was a *hostage.* Taken from my parents."

The king's daughter crawled on her stomach to a corner of her cell. Edenia followed her, all her attention bent on her.

"One of us," Lorana said through her tears. "You were . . ."

Lorana couldn't recognize the woman she'd been friends with, made love to. Her eyes screamed disdain, fury, and, above all, the sweet satisfaction that comes from turning the tables.

"One of *YOU?*" Her pale arms trembled down to their fists. "I was *never* one of you. I am a *prieslenne!* Daughter of the White Citadel. Priestess of the one true faith. Venas sculpted me from blood and clay in my mother's womb. Maetha breathed air into my lungs, Helsar forged my soul, and Divna gave me my sacred charge."

Lorana glared up through a blackened eye. "Dracar made you a traitor, and Gourda gave your cunt that fishy flavor."

The guard's boot flashed in her face, and her cell turned white. A high-pitched ringing was all she heard. She clutched at her nose, wondering if it were in pieces, with the blood pooling in her palms. *Father, what has become of me?*

". . . always were clever," Edenia's voice found her as the ringing subsided. "That's why I tolerated you, Ana."

She reached for the slack chain, as if she could still choke her. "You . . . you killed my father," Lorana wheezed.

Edenia chuckled. "Me? I *wish* it'd been me. I hated that old, fat, stupid king, him and you and all his disgusting sons. The crown prince who called me a whore and snuck into my chambers late at night." *Garrett, you're a monster . . . and I wish you'd done worse.* "The bastard who actually thought I loved him. Me, the Most-Sought Hand in the Thirteen Kingdoms!" She laughed. "When the throne is mine, I'll tear out your family root and stem. I'll find where you sent Heather and have the little bitch's head mounted on Traitor's Gate."

"I'll kill you," Lorana vowed. *I've never believed in gods, but I will. I will swear by the god who gives me Edenia's head.*

Edenia traded a smirking look with her guard, as if they were in on some joke. "No, actually. You'll help me."

Lorana spat blood onto her elaborately laced white boot.

Edenia took something from the guard, a wad of cloth. Kneeling, she unfolded the cloth as carefully as if there were lemon cake crumbling inside. "You once gave a lonely hostage a flower. It bound her to you. Consider the favor returned."

She overturned the cloth, and out fell a finger. It'd been mangled by the blade that had severed it, but Lorana could see its rose-vine tattoo.

CHAPTER 29

Vestments of Many Colors

he luster of the forest that couldn't burn held Zur nearly as captive as the ropes about his wrists and ankles. Bound with his back to a large oak tree, he shifted posture now and again, fascinated by how Graywood's riven surfaces reflected sunlight like a mirror.

Too long, he warned himself inwardly. *I'm gazing too long.* He cringed from the throbbing that beat anew in his temples.

Some yards off, Bill cackled. His oily hair and wrinkly, bloodstained clothes made him look a haggard mess. "*Look there!* Tom tol' you."

"I told you," agreed his hog of a companion, chuckling.

"Yes," Zur said, "you're quite observant."

At that, Bill soured. He pushed himself erect, clutching at his bandaged thigh. "What's that, eh? You want a beatin' like you got from Jacob?"

The opportunity was too tempting to pass up. "Like the *beatin'* you gave the peasant who bled you in the Rotwood?" Zur mocked his Southland accent.

Bill lurched forward; Tom and Devan restrained him. "Just you wait, you lil' bastard." He smiled coldly. "Just you wait for Summer Solstice. Then we see who bleeds."

Or maybe you'll lose that other eye first, and bleed a little more, Zur thought darkly. *When Drexan King's Crow finds me . . . and deals with you and your friends.*

He had to hope. He had to. Uther had acknowledged the truth of his situation in the Rotwood: he was to serve as a Gift, and Drexan had told him what that meant.

In a few days' time, they'd kill him in a blood ritual to open the door a little wider for the Nagarthessi to enter his world.

But he had reason to hope. He'd last sighted Furos in the skies three days ago, after Flint Way had surrendered to waist-high grass. After arriving at Graywood's borders days earlier, Uther had departed with Orthos, Owen, and Jacob. He'd shared nothing of their plans, of course. Zur couldn't resist savoring the chance that maybe—just maybe—Drexan had killed them. Today he detected a growing fear among his three watchmen; Bill's outburst only fed his suspicion.

The very notion that Uther and his men might've met an end at his lord's hands eased the pounding in his skull. *They'd be no match for you, Drexan,* he thought with wild promise and wild hope.

On some level, it still troubled to think that Drexan had killed Hexar. Did that make him a kingkiller by association? If he was . . . was his capture by the Nagarthessi's servants his own penance in the Kingkiller's Curse?

He'd have to parse it out later, after he found a way out of this. *These men serve demons. A kingkiller my lord may be, but* at least *he doesn't serve Asha-Ra and Pathazar.*

Losing interest in Zur, the watchers returned to gambling. Furos was nowhere to be seen in the wide blue sky. *I am to die in a few days' time, to resurrect evil, and it's a nice day.*

Graywood helped take his mind off his terror. As the sun traveled to noon, he noticed that he wasn't alone in distracting himself with the swordwood. Devan often stared at the mirror forest while the other two played. He called the boy's name when he passed by to find privacy for a piss.

"Water, please?" Zur eyed Devan's waterskin longingly.

The boy stalled. Overhearing, Tom stopped a dice throw, hand suspended midair.

"He donna need water," Bill told Devan in a bullying tone.

"He's Elzura's Child, ain't he?" Tom couldn't resist. "He'll piss water for himself if we let him." His big belly shook as he giggled.

"You haven't given me any water since the little I had this morning, and it's past noon," Zur said with pretend hoarseness. "What good am I to Uther or the Nagarthessi if I die from thirst before Summer Solstice?"

"There's a brook nearby," Devan intoned softly. "I can fill the skin there."

Bill worked his jaw silently, annoyed by his defiance. Tom said something under his breath, gave a shrug, and hurled his dice. Losing, he tossed his hands up in despair, which lured Bill back to the game. Devan padded over, unslinging his waterskin cagily.

Zur *was* thirsty, that much was true; he squeezed the skin with both hands, gulping down water. In his periphery he saw Devan watching Bill as he clapped his hands for another win. Tom cursed and hung his head.

"I don't serve them," the boy said faintly, for his ears only. "The ones you mention. I don't."

Zur held the boy's waterskin to his lips to play like he was still quenching a thirst. "Uther does," he returned. "Why do you accompany him?"

"You don't know. You haven't *seen* him."

Uther Brune has some power over Devan, he deduced. He decided he needed to use this chance to gain other information, something that could help him. "This isn't the first time you've been to Graywood, is it, Devan?"

Something between fear and sorrow passed over Devan's face. The boy looked at his feet. "I think you've had your fill." He snatched the waterskin away so quickly he dribbled water.

"I wasn't lying before," Zur told him. "About my friends. I have powerful allies. Princess Lorana calls me brother. I serve Hexar's Crow." *The people who lie to me,* he knew in the back of his mind, but it wasn't a priority. "If you can help—"

Devan looked like to piss himself. "You don't understand. You haven't seen . . ."

"Seen what?"

"Seen the truth," came the old man's voice.

Devan bowed his head, as for nobility. Out from the forest stepped Uther, Jacob, and Owen. Seeing them, Bill caught Tom's wrist to halt a dice-throw.

"Fuck, Owen, your *arm*," Bill blurted out.

So consumed was he with the priest, Zur had overlooked the walking misery that was Owen. A sleeve of leaves crusted his arm, oil-black around their edges. The skin beneath looked pink and tender, singed like boarflesh. Owen walked with a pronounced limp. He wore grief in his face.

Tom and Devan hastened over to Owen, doing what they could to help their companion lay down with Bill by the fire.

"Orthos?" Bill asked with a searching look.

Uther sighed. "Give thanks to the true gods, my friends," he said. "They've called Orthos home to them."

A whimper escaped Owen's lips. He collapsed to a knee beside Bill, shuddering with tears he wouldn't let anyone see. Bill, Tom, and Devan looked on, shocked. Terrified. Spittlelip glared at Zur as he readjusted the sling of Drexan's travelsack, *shrriping*.

"Those we serve will welcome him," the priest added.

At that, Owen stood abruptly, wiped his face, and hobbled off, limping back into the Rotwood. Tom jiggled after him like a quibbling wet nurse.

Drexan, Zur knew immediately.

"Jacob." Uther had a commanding tone. "Untie the lad." He regarded Zur disinterestedly. "Let's show him."

Dazzling from outside, Graywood had a sinister quality within that would give even the bravest men pause. Nothing made its home here. No birds sang. There were no woodland animals. Save for their footsteps and Jacob's irritated slurping, the swordwood was silent as a crypt.

Zur minded his feet and hands as he walked past steel-enameled logs and trees. *At least I'm free from my bonds,* the hostage thought, rubbing wrists patterned from hempen rope.

It occurred to him that he could run. Maybe he could reach the Rotwood; maybe Drexan would find him there.

But the priest had no fear of him running. Zur understood why. The barest misstep in this deadly place could cost one an appendage, even his life.

Passing by trees with his reflection, he spotted a face he hardly knew, lumpy with the hills of purple bruises, one eye puffy and a bottom lip cracked. A scrape from Spittlelip's blade scabbed his cheek. Unruly curls spilled off his head in every direction. He seemed older. *I only recently had a fourteenth birthday,* he thought emptily.

Staring too long, he winced from the throb in his temples.

Uther seemed to notice his discomfort. "Watch your feet," he said. "You'll keep the feet and suffer fewer headaches."

The hostage sidestepped a tree stump needled with fierce briars, hundreds of them, a torture device better suited to the Red Tower than the wilderness. "What do you care if I suffer?"

"A great deal, as it turns out." Without warning, the priest arrested Spittlelip by his shoulder, stopping him in his tracks just before he stepped over a shiny log. Walking by, Zur peered past the log and saw a steep slope razored with glinting leaves.

He did that as if he knew he'd fall, Zur thought. "'A great deal.' You mean to sacrifice me for your Nagarthessi tomorrow."

With a long stride, the false priest stepped over a pile of steel leaves. Zur and Spittlelip walked around it. "Things must be set to rights, but that doesn't mean I want you to suffer."

"You'd serve the enemy of mankind, and you'd call what you're doing setting things to rights?"

Uther halted to give him a look up and down. "Tell me, Elzura's Child, would those peasants you sought help from in the Rotwood have saved you from us?" Zur made no reply. "No," he said for him, "they would've hacked off your head, stolen your clothes, and called themselves godly men for it."

"Whereas you mean to set me free with a wineskin."

Looking up, Uther meditated on blue sky visible through pockets of steel canopy. "Do you think our boy, Devan, evil?"

Zur remembered how the boy nearly slipped his truth earlier. He contemplated outing Devan's own apprehensions about Uther and the Nagarthessi, but winning an argument with his captor wouldn't help Drexan, or himself.

"Any who serve the Nagarthessi," Zur said instead, "share in their evil."

"Ideas planted in you by your Crow." He thought he saw a smile play along the priest's lips. "The Nagarthessi *are* the true gods, Zur."

Zur couldn't help himself. He smirked. "Mumbler. Priest. Sylvanian. Servant of evil. You wear many-colored vestments. How many gods do you keep, Uther?"

"Evan Sinclair caught me in the same lie." Zur searched his eyes, looking for another lie. "I was a priest, collared by Parlisis himself. But the Nagarthessi are the *real* gods. They have shown me their power, and I am their priest. Those who serve them will share in the riches of their new world.

"Think you any man in my service fights with a desire for evil?" Uther went on, ducking beneath a fierce-looking branch. "We came to Pathazar and Asha-Ra as men broken by a world we did not choose for ourselves."

"No one chooses this world," Zur countered.

"But some of us are born to higher stations." The priest swiveled on him. "Take you, for instance. You were seized from Casaan but raised behind the Silver Walls, castle of Anjan Half-Elf, with wine and bread at a king's table, and with nearly every chance at life that a high-born has."

Zur laughed bitterly. That netted a dark look from Jacob Spittlelip.

"Devan?" Uther continued, as if he hadn't heard the laugh. "Before Lord Uthron rescued him, he was in Peshar Grathos's vile hands. Bill? Before Rosbury, he killed a partridge of your late king's to feed his child, and for the crime suffered both his eye and time in a cell that forced his wife to remarry, to keep that child. Tom fled to Rosbury after being falsely accused of theft by a sheriff who desired his land. Orthos and Owen were the last members of a family loyal to Lord Stoddard Trambar—a crime that King Hexar repaid with a king's crime. Now Owen *is* the last of that family." He smoldered.

"And Jacob. Poor Jacob." Uther reached for the peasant's porous cheek with almost fatherly tenderness. "He fell in love with one of your kin and married her secretly, unaware that her lord lusted after her. When the nobleman found out, he summoned them to court. He commanded Jacob's wife to pull out his tongue with hot pincers, or lose her head. Blinded by tears, she made a botch of it. Lord Eric Sundry beheaded the Casaanite woman, anyway." Spittlelip shut his eyes, moist lips quivering, as if he were reliving his trauma.

Zur wanted to roll his eyes. *Eric the Tall. Another lie.*

"A disfigured face attracts few friends, so Jacob spends his time with horses and goats—and *for that*," Uther added thickly, his anger plain, "his neighbors heap despicable calumnies upon him, accusing him of *lying with beasts*."

"So," Zur said caustically, "because you've all endured terrible wrongs, you'll kill me?"

"By making you a Gift we give your life meaning." Uther spoke with the firmness of a devout believer. "Yours is the lie that Drexan Lorrain foisted upon you—the lie upon which all priestkings and readers founded their two fraudulent faiths. Pathazar and Asha-Ra were sealed away in hell because they threatened the order of things. When they reunite on Odma, there will be no more suffering. No more kings, no more lords, no more Commons. Only a grateful world living in harmony. *You* should feel grateful for the important role we give you in righting the world." He turned and strode on, as if offended.

Feel . . . grateful? Zur choked on his spite and incredulity. *And I'm the transparent one,* he thought. Uther had clothed his tortured reasoning in the Ascendant King myth. *No, not a myth,* he reminded himself, thinking on the giant clothed in faces. *My god is as real as theirs . . . and more powerful.*

"I would rather live." As the words left his mouth, Zur fell asprawl on hands and knees. He gasped from the points of steel needles. Fire lashed his palms and shins.

Spittlelip stopped to haul him up.

"I told you to show care," Uther said with a distant look.

The lip-sucking cretin looked him up and down, *shrrip*ing with contempt. He tugged on Drexan's travelsack and strode on with the false priest. When neither was looking, Zur balanced the needle in his pocket so it didn't tear through the fabric.

He glanced at his pinpricked palms, wiping them on his tunic, ignoring the shoots of pain. Onward he trudged through the lifeless forest. They walked for another ten minutes before Zur saw a devil among the trees.

Polished as the swordwood, the God Who Rebelled and Died had the form of a seated man, hands upon his knees, with a wolf's snout and the curled horns of a ram. Wings shaped like kite shields fanned out from his backside. He was monstrous.

Zur observed his surroundings, noticing a slope to his left. Below lay the spears of steel branches. He'd seen them at Rorn Abeth, in the mirror with the knight groping for a wooden idol. A chill spread through him. *Terrible things have happened here.*

Uther padded over to the statue, admiring the craftsmanship of its ridged snout. "You asked me how many gods I kept. Did you know this isn't Dracar?" He walked about the statue. "Sylvanians built this to honor a goddess of fertility. A thing of beauty. How they understood to melt swordwood and craft something so exquisite . . . It's beyond me and any man living."

"This *is* Dracar," Zur said flatly.

In Loran, there was no other statue for the God Who Rebelled and Died. But there were pictures. Zur had come across them in the South Tower library's books. Elvarenists portrayed Dracar this way, horned, snouted, and winged.

The old man looked at his feet, as if Zur had made a *faux pas*. "No, it isn't Dracar. At least, not originally. The Sylvanians who came to this altar sacrificed goats. Infertile women prayed that with her long snout, the goddess would sniff out whatever malady they suffered like a truffle pig. With these wings, the goddess fluttered over their houses like a butterfly, protecting newborns. She was a fierce, albeit fictional deity."

"Fascinating," Zur muttered.

Uther had an icy expression. "To Loran's first priests, she was an opportunity. A clever Elvarenist etched this likeness into a wood block. Called it Dracar, his fallen god. The lie was a deliberate one. He wanted Sylvanian converts to associate the goddess with evil. To spread the word, until everyone came to see the Old Ways as evil. So a goddess of life was profaned in the eyes of Loran. For power. For dominion."

The puzzle pieces finally fell into place. Zur harrumphed. "But no one spun lies about Dracar and his demon sons, Uther. They *are* evil. As evil as you."

Uther walked toward him, hands clutched behind his back. "And yet you and I both serve their cause."

He spat, as if expelling spoiled fruit. "We're nothing—"

"Alike?" The Nagarthessi's servant raised a questioning eyebrow. "Try again. Different sides of the same coin. Drexan lied to you. Barefoot Knights and the Nagarthessi have always seen a world ruled by men for what it is—chaotic, destructive, and doomed. Desperately in need of divine intervention."

As he ventured closer, Zur backed away. "I'm no Barefoot Knight . . ." *I killed no king.*

"But we have the same power in our blood. We *both* descend from Anjan Half-Elf's Windriders. The gods have called you home to this place so that your blood will open doors." He made a fist, as if he'd snatched something long pursued. "*All so that we can end man's suffering.*"

"You lie to yourself as much as your followers, Uther. The Nagarthessi will destroy us all." Zuran's heart hammered in his throat as his hand neared his pocket. "The readers and priests were right. One of the demon brothers lay buried here. This swordwood contains the door the First King closed on him."

"And closed it remained," Uther agreed. "For ages."

"Until recently." Zur stepped forward. "Until you killed Uthron's knight at this altar and cracked the door open."

The false priest smiled. "I suppose your King's Crow put it together. Yes, my cousin sent us here to make a Gift that would open the tomb of a god." His smiling lips became a hard line. "My cousin . . . whom you and your lord murdered."

"Uthron wasn't the last," Zur said defiantly. "The Barefoot Knight who killed Uthron and Orthos is hunting you."

"Was."

Spittlelip unslung his travelsack, flipped it upside-down. Out tumbled a familiar helm, rolling to Zur's feet. Tears slid off his cheeks, pelting a charred skullcap.

A smear of dried blood blinded the Eye of Guldan.

"He died fighting bravely, for you, if it's any consolation," Uther said. "Laid a clever trap that killed our man. Kindled fire from his sacred blood and—"

Zur leapt at the old man, clenching the swordwood needle in his fist like a dagger. Adrenaline overrode the fearsome pain pumping his palm as he stabbed at Uther's heart.

In a blur he was on his knees, the false priest's hand tight about his throat. The needle pierced nothing but his own flesh.

Uther grimaced. He held Zur in place, on his knees, while Spittlelip pried one finger free after another, removing the thin deadly needle by force.

"So close." Uther tightened his grip around his throat. "It would've gone better for you and Drexan if you'd let Uthron seize you in Sarah's Forest. My cousin would've taken you here directly, sparing you much pain. Now . . . tomorrow . . . on a day holy before even the priests arrived . . . your ancient blood will bring forth another god. *And you will help us set things right.*"

A pillar of smoke churned up from Uther's feet, engulfing him, as if hell had opened up beneath his feet.

Not smoke. Black mist. Living shadow that expanded and contracted pulsingly, like a heartbeat given dark form. A frost colder than the fiercest winter wind benumbed Zur's throat.

Beside the shadowking, Jacob Spittlelip grinned wetly.

CHAPTER 30

The Kingmakers

athos plodded into the Colossus ahead of nine peasants, chains clacking from shackled wrists to feet. Sunlight blinded. A single cry echoed across the arena—"*TRAITORS!*"—and suddenly stones, rotten fruit, and all manner of foulness rained down from every direction. Intercessors forced the ten men to file by the lowest wall, through wet sand that slowed their feet, giving throwers ample opportunity to hit them.

Everyone's eyes must've adjusted at nearly the same time, a wrenching coincidence. One prisoner behind Rathos called on Maetha's godface. Others, all grown men, wept.

Rorin's amphitheater had been remade into a forest of horrors. Thousands of spears littered the sand arena, each a skewer for three or more tousled-haired heads.

The faces were old. They were middle-aged. They were Rathos's age. Many were younger.

They were peasants who'd rebelled and died.

They weren't tarred. Black flies carpeted heads, lances, sand, whirring noisily; Rathos gagged when one dove into his mouth. His horrified sputtering gave the guards a good laugh. Assemblymen spilled over the walls, jostling for space to find the best throwing position; a rock welted Rathos in his temple. An Intercessor forced him up, swearing to mount his head if he fell again, and he pointed to just the spear he had in mind.

More than fifty yards separated the canopied dais erected at the arena's center from the vast circle of mounted heads and flies. Upon the dais resided two chairs, griffons soaring on their velvety cushions. Banners of cream and violet surrounded the dais, lest anyone doubt which religion held dominion today.

A king and his queen consort would soon sit in the chairs, but only a fool would think Hexar's brother a true sovereign. Unseen puppet strings would drape any chair to suffer the zealot. *To Parlisis a throne,* Rathos thought darkly.

Yet he clung to hope, held onto it as if it were driftwood keeping him afloat. Locked in his cell, forgotten, he'd had no word about Evan or Jason Warchild. Were they alive? Even if they were, even with their *Hathrimnyr,* they couldn't hope to mount a rescue. Shaddon and Sothos and their forces held the high-walled Colossus at least three to one.

So he'd petition the new king for mercy. Kings had to hear their subjects' requests, especially at their coronations.

He was no fool. He had no faith in the Assembly's honor, but he trusted in Sothos's need to keep up appearances. Over this masquerade lurked the cloud of violent peasant uprisings and scrapped Kingstrials. Like smart procurers, Sothos and his men would sell an undesirable whore in rouge and finery—in pomp and ritual and lanced heads, in this case, so the kingdom would buy her.

Mercy would buy life for Rathos and Mina. Just like his father, they'd flee Loran for the Free Kingdoms, only on foot, in rags. He knew not whether Karl and Dana had found safety, but if so, they wouldn't meet them again, not while Shaddon ruled. In his mind he tended sprouts of hope, possibilities for action from behind another kingdom's walls.

But a king's forgiveness came at a price. Especially for a child and ward of Evan Sinclair. Rathos knew what he had to offer. And he'd betray his adopted noble house. His oath to the Company. The Fourth Wing.

He'd betray Evan himself.

Shaddon will hear my petition because his coronation must seem legitimate, Rathos knew. *May you forgive me when I speak, Evan. But I won't betray you for my life alone.*

She'd suffered. They both had. Under threat from the lash, beatings, and steel, they'd marched across a kingdom, east on broken Romarian roads and north through Barbara's Gorge. Walked and walked until their feet gave out, and then up again, stumbling. Suffered mockery and thrashings, for days.

His wife had been raped.

He thought he'd die from the beating he took for savaging the rapist. After that, Mina had made him swear on Sir Matthus that he wouldn't die for her honor. "Follow the star of reason," she'd demanded through tears. "Do it for our child."

A prieslenne had saved Mina, ironically. In the dungeons, Edenia Highdaughter had sworn on her twelve gods to take his pregnant wife under her care and treat her gently. Weeks ago, he'd cursed Parlisis's daughter. Now he might kiss her feet.

A few days past, the prieslenne had sent Rathos word of Mina's condition. "Take hope," her foreign handmaiden had whispered in broken Common through his cell door. "Your wife, safe. She and baby well." She repeated that twice: she well, baby well.

Then another handmaiden, the next night, with news that felt like salve for his wounds. "She eat," the thick-accented girl had reported. He asked what. "Apples," she'd replied. For the first night since Caerdon's sacking, he'd slept.

Let it not be said that only spoilt fruit grows on the Lonely Isle. Perhaps I misjudged you when you laid laurels on her head, Warchild. Perhaps you love Edenia Highdaughter with reason.

The Intercessors made their prisoners sit yards from the spitted heads. A sweaty, hellish wait it was in the damp sand. Flies nettled them incessantly and stones pelted the ground around them off and on, for hours. Lost in misery, Rathos craned up at the benches from which peasants had once made laws alongside lords. He scanned the Wing of Clergy, a sea of off-white cassocks.

Not one gray-robed Free Believer sat in the Colossus.

He knew the truth immediately. Jacob Sulley had taken his Free Believers and left. A brilliant maneuver. By departing with his readers, the Master Reader had sawed off one of the more load-bearing legs from the chair of the new king's claim. Rathos counted missing some half of the Wing of Clergy. The Wing of Knights seemed sparser, too.

Two Trials, two and a half Wings, Rathos mused bitterly. This Assembly was worthy in name only . . . but not as vile as it'd been while Peshar Grathos had spoken for the clergy.

He'd learned about the High Bishop's grisly fate from the gossip his watchers shared outside his door. Grathos had been found disrobed, unburdened of his head, arms, legs, and loins. The more gruesome the rumors, the better. He couldn't decide which he liked better: Commoners pulling the emissary's teeth to sell like griff talons, or the tale about how they'd paraded his head before them like a sacred relic during the revolt.

The pederast had deserved his death and Rathos did not mourn him. How many families had been dismembered by the cleric's child-theft laws, how many innocent children delivered into his wrinkly, repulsive hands?

But all this death could've been avoided. Evan had warned the kingdom, for years. Rezlan had warned them. The Worthy had turned a deaf ear to them, called them traitors. *Now our foes entrench their positions, foisting upon us a king beloved by no one but lords and priests who'll profit under his rule.*

One lord stood to profit more than anyone. One lord had done more than anyone to enthrone Shaddon, to dismantle the Company. He'd orchestrated Caerdon's sacking, had Savan and his pets thrash and march Rathos and his wife across Loran. He'd incinerated Rathos's father and killed Sarah Sinclair.

Surveying the benches, Rathos spotted Jon Redoak and many of Lordsbane's lackeys, but not Sothos himself. *Does he control this ceremony from the Red Tower?*

Trumpets blared suddenly from the Colossus's ramparts. The northern portcullis clanked open. Out swept the royals-to-be in a chariot drawn by white, silky-maned stallions worthy of great songs.

Gilded leaves engulfed the chariot, flame-like, as if Shaddon were Sacreis himself, earthbound with sunlight's gift. Behind them wound a serpent of a procession, men in striped cream-and-indigo uniforms, feathered morions, and the collars of starchy white ruffs. They rested halberds on their shoulders.

By their drawn looks, Rathos knew the prisoners felt as he did. *This isn't a coronation; it's an invasion.* Loran belonged to the Lonely Isle now. Lords and priests rustled to their feet, crying *"Shaddon and Edenia!"* and *"Scourge of Peasants!"* Men hugged each other and kissed cheeks, as if they'd won Hexar's wars in Uzland and the Brace and reclaimed the Cloudlands.

Their jubilation was lost on the man who would be king. What an awkward coupling. Where Hexar's solemn, unsmiling brother deigned not to acknowledge the fanfare, his betrothed waved at their kingmakers, beaming, as if this coronation were hers. Rathos saw how otherworldly her excitement seemed to those within earshot of riotous flies.

The chariot circled the dais twelve times before stopping. Shaddon exited and ascended the dais, Sons of Sacreis dutifully carrying the train of his ermine-trimmed mantle. All of his life, Rathos had heard about this eastern menace, Hexar's brother, said to disembark carriages on the neatly filed steps of peasant necks. He'd always pictured someone plainly corrupt. Beneath the panoply of shiny foreign armor he saw only a paler, fatter Hexar with sunken, beady eyes.

The queen consort sashayed out of the chariot as if she'd been born to the moment, silky golden hair swirling down her backside. Edenia outshone the sun king in a sumptuous dark-blue satin gown, a thousand pendant diamonds twinkling like stars in its folds. White rose petals wreathed her neckline and calendared bosom. Daughters of Divna followed her like blue ghosts, hefting her train. Peasants trained their gazes on the prieslenne, awed by the sheer amount of wealth she wore.

To sew such a gown would've taken months. Months and months of planning, with all the expectation of victory.

Rathos recalled Rezlan's warning at the Last Elflord. *A game tilted against us. We played by their rules for the noblest reasons, Evan. But what peace did we buy for this realm . . . for ourselves?*

Linking hands at the dais, Shaddon and Edenia faced the Assembly. To a man, every Assemblyman chanted, *"TWELVE GODS FOREVER! TWELVE GODS FOREVER!"* Rocks pelted the sand about Rathos and the prisoners like hail.

A Daughter of Divna handed Edenia a smoking chained censer. She wafted incense about Shaddon, praying in First Tongue. An Intercessor forced Rathos to bow his head out of respect.

Edenia finished her prayers. She strode to the dais's edge, basking in the applause. "There once lived a little foreign girl at an ancient, powerful stronghold," she said in a timorous voice the Colossus's acoustics carried. "You knew her as King Hexar's hostage, someone who ate beside Casaanites. Now she will sit beside his brother—a righteous king. Our protector."

She waited until the cheering subsided. "And yet I am not the one who should be speaking. A coronation begins with the High Bishop speaking, not a prieslenne." *She offends no one by failing to mention that the Master Reader traditionally speaks with him,* he mused. "I address you because there is no one else." She made fists. "Because someone gentler and more pious than any born in the last century was taken from us by an evil unseen since shadowkings walked the earth."

Were Mina not in the prieslenne's care, Rathos would've spat. And Edenia scowled in his direction, as if he had. "Peshar Grathos had one better among you," she said, "and *he'd* be the one speaking to you this day but for a foe who groomed that evil patiently."

Everywhere, shouts for Evan the Traitor's head loudened.

"Maetha cries with us," Edenia said, "and Justar vows his vengeance, as does our king. Thousands of years ago, Willard the Wise bequeathed to Loran three Trials to choose a king. But Shaddon Eddenhold didn't prove his worth in some tourney or sea battle. He did it by defending Loran." She swept her hand at the skewered heads. "And yes, before anyone asks, I prefer *this* gift to laurels."

Everyone had a good laugh. The man to be king registered a fleeting smile.

"Now show me your worth," added the prieslenne, hands lifted heavenward, *"and help me crown a king for the new age."*

Hot, muggy, and awhir with flies, the ceremony observed all the rituals at a rushed clip. Heralds played the King's Grace on their trumpets without dwelling on the most rousing notes. Singing hymns, the chorus of Edenia's handmaidens would've sounded angelic, were it not for the Colossus's acoustics, which amplified the sounds of them gasping to catch their breath.

Rathos understood their haste perfectly. Every ritual had to play out, just not for a second longer than necessary. *They're afraid . . . as they should be.* The longer the king remained north with his armies, the more tenuous his claim to the Silver Walls. A revolt in Rosbury had incited a string of others, not least the one that had slain Grathos and placed in Shaddon's lap the gift of an excuse needed to take power. Southpoint was vulnerable, and the king had need of towering walls.

Silence settled on the amphitheater when Edenia called the Worthy to pay homage. Rathos expected lords and priests jealous of their power to protest . . . but he expected too much. Like obedient chattel, the unworthy one by one left their seats to queue up and kiss Shaddon's ring. A lord recognized Rathos from Remembrance Day and urged everyone to spit on him as they returned to their benches.

Traitor, they cursed him. *The only traitors here are rulers who kneel before a tyrant like simpering whores,* he thought.

Trumpets blared the King's Grace, and out strode the one lord speaker uninjured or alive. Garbed in a padded doublet, a cape fluttering from his shoulders, Frederick Midliche balanced on his pillow a crown as dazzling as Edenia's gown. Arches of beaten gold and silver enveloped the indigo cap, encrusted so thickly with diamonds the crown looked as if it were clutched by a glittery octopus. An obscene crown required an equally gaudy centerpiece jewel, a fist-sized chunk of silverstone that gave the crown a halo-like aura. Rathos wondered how many starving Midlanders that circlet could feed.

Midliche climbed the dais. The Fox was as calculating as the Little King, Evan had held. Sunlight winked in the treasures he wore: a sapphire ring on his finger, gold in his buttons and necklace, golden chains on his shoes. He was no Elvarenist. *At what price were your loyalties bought, Fred?*

Midliche knelt before Edenia, elevating his pillow to her. She lifted the crown to reveal yet another, a circlet agleam with rubies and emeralds.

With befitting gravitas, the prieslenne stepped behind her betrothed's chair and slowly lowered the first crown, soaking in the moment. The king stood to wild applause. He stepped aside for Edenia to seat herself . . . and promptly returned the favor.

Matter-of-factly, as if her crowning were a transaction.

"I will not rule Loran alone," the king began.

Rathos couldn't hear Shaddon finish over the jubilation, but he didn't need to try. He hadn't merely crowned Edenia a queen consort. He'd enthroned a *co-ruler*.

The first queen to rule Loran in a thousand years smiled exultantly, a crown aglimmer in the bed of her golden hair.

He met the eyes of the peasant prisoners. They looked despondent, fearful, dubious, or livid. *These Commoners have more sense than their tone-deaf rulers,* Rathos thought. *A high priestess is her faith. The faith crowns a king, and in return, he queens its high priestess . . . and weds Loran to her religion.*

The queening was artless. Unfathomably foolish. Insane. It only made sense when he remembered that readers weren't the only Assemblymen unseated here today.

Shaddon raised a hand, softening the applause. "To you, the Worthy of Loran, I give a queen as godly as Divna," the king said. Edenia smiled. "But I'll give more to the rest of this realm. Mercy, for the faithful. Justice, for the wronged. And a lance for the head of every rebel, heretic, and traitor against us."

"*TWELVE GODS FOREVER!*" the unworthy boomed. Rathos listened as the king painted a portrait of the Loran that would be. Where Hexar had shattered ties with Priestking Parlisis, his brother vowed to name a new High Bishop to his king's council. Where stood the husks of fire-gutted temples, Shaddon would erect glorious new ones. Narrowing his eyes at Rathos, the king swore to hunt down Evan Sinclair's Companymen like vermin, until traitors plagued the Assembly and land no more.

Shaddon unsheathed his sword and held it high. "AND IF ONE FILTHY PEASANT HAND RISES AGAINST US," he swore, "I'LL TAKE THE NEXT THOUSAND LIKE IT."

The Colossus roared. "The Head speaks," Edenia said.

Through the wall of "The Hands serve" arose a stubborn voice, along with repeated refusals to be quiet. Rathos and the captives twisted about to see the source of the disturbance. Of all people, it was a priest, high in the southeastern section. He muscled through a press of clergy, insisting that he was still an Assemblyman, that he be allowed to speak.

The priest swatted off the handlers angrily. All eyes were upon him, but he was fearless. ". . . a mistake," his voice drifted into hearing, "a grievous mistake! You fools, are you all blind?"

Shaddon scowled. The new queen donned the look of cold disapproval a mother would give her unruly child. "Clearly this one wanted Gelder for his king," she said, to laughter. "Why do you call us blind, when you cannot see? Today your king and I have retaken Loran for . . ."

To audible dismay, the priest spoke over the prieslenne. "I wanted Shaddon for king, but not *you!*" he cried out. "I call you blind because that's what you are. Commoners are in arms! We took their children and gave them to Peshar. They're showing us we must change, or be killed. *For gods' sakes,* they burned the ships our king and queen came on! Now half an Assembly crowns someone who won no Trial. *He* crowns the prieslenne. I'm collared and cassocked. I serve Parlisis. But do you not see the bed you make for us? This kingdom *hates* queens!"

Edenia seamed her perfect brow. "We are the Worthy," she said frostily, "and I *am* your queen."

At a nudging look from Shaddon, Intercessors filed up the benches to arrest the dissenting priest. His protests faded as he vanished with them.

The only Assemblyman here who sees the star of reason wears a cassock,

Rathos mused bleakly. *And no one but the prisoners heard him.*

Their turn finally came.

Intercessors forced prisoners into single file and marched them toward their king and queen for summary judgment.

Rathos found himself fourth in line. The man in front of him anchored his feet and refused to budge. "No queen shall judge me," he growled, and he lost his head on the spot. Assemblymen cheered as the headsman impaled his prize on a lance. Rathos took his place, sidestepping corpse and puddled blood.

A scrawny herald by the dais listed out their treasons for the Worthy to hear. The first man had helped lead the Colossus revolt. Jonathan Smith his name was, a Thorngale blacksmith. He'd formed a band of Thorngale deserters and tried to defile Princess Lorana, said the herald, to a wave of jeers.

Shaddon wouldn't even hear his plea. "I condemn you to hell," pronounced the king, and the forest of heads grew.

Their cheering. All Rathos could hear were their cheers, so joyous one would mistake this for a wedding, so deafening he almost couldn't hear himself think. He couldn't discern the third man's words through his nausea, only the whistle of a sword as it sliced the air.

A rough shove pitched him forward, nearly to his knees. Rathos staggered up, trying to hear Mina. "You won't die for my honor, do you hear me, Ray?" On a dusty road, in a tree's shade, she'd shaken him by his bloodied shirt. "Promise me, Rathos. *Fucking promise you'll think.* Follow the star of reason. We need our child to survive this. I want you to promise me . . ."

Dimly, Rathos heard his name, as from a dream. His gaze climbed the dais. Edenia had the airs of a benevolent stranger helping some lost wayfarer find his way again. "Robswell," the queen intoned. "That is your name, sir, no?"

The king scowled. "He's not a sir," he blurted. "His father was. I remember Sinclair's knight. Also a Commoner. A traitor. He fathered Warchild."

Edenia watched Rathos, somewhere between curiosity and a bully's delight. "You're Jason's . . . half-brother?"

It was a lie he'd heard before. He wouldn't argue. *I'd call myself Jason Warchild's grandmother, if it saved Mina and our child.* "I'm not my father, Your Majesty," Rathos said. "Nor am I Sinclair's man."

"Yes, you are." The king pointed at him. "You're Sinclair's ward. A Loyal Companyman. And you were found harboring the vicious outlaw called the Mad Lady. Brave men detained you both at Caerdon Castle, where you were plotting to aid the Heretics."

Jeers rained down with stones. Rathos pressed forward; Intercessors held him fast by his arms. "I won't deny it, Your Majesty," he said. "I am a traitor. I pledged myself to the Loyal Company, not to make war, but peace. But my wife—she's not an outlaw. She's innocent, and with child besides." He leaned against the rails of arms restraining him. "I petition Your Majesty for her release. In return . . . I'll tell you all that I know about Evan Sinclair and his Loyal Company."

Rathos would've given up Karl, Rezlan Ambrose, the Last Elflord Inn, the blackpowder—everything, everyone. Shaddon paid him a weary headshake. "We have more than we need," he said loftily. "I will not grant the petition. You're a traitor. You'll die a traitor."

"MY WIFE," Rathos shouted as they forced him to kneel. A sword was drawn. "Mina's her name. The prieslenne, she—"

He listened to the new king over the explosion of cheers. "Your wife, this Heretic, we'll free, she and her devil child," he said. "Sinclair trades his life for hers."

Rathos searched Edenia's face. "Is it true?" he called out.

Edenia observed him coolly, making no reply.

The king gestured to an Intercessor with an impatient flick of his fingers. Rathos was thrust to his knees, his neck exposed for the sword's stroke. He stared at peasant blood below him and realized he knelt in it.

Their cheering. All around him, the Worthy rejoiced at his imminent execution. *You're my song, Mina.*

Moments passed like hours. Unclenching his eyelids, he risked a shaking glance at the headsman. The Intercessor's sunlit sword wavered over his neck. *They mean to torture me,* he thought. His headsman watched the dais like a trained hound waiting on his master's word.

The queen was speaking to the king. Hard as ice when she rebuffed the priest, Edenia seemed soft as any wife entreating her husband. The king listened intently, his gaze averted from hers. Rathos sensed an unease between the new royals.

Shaddon shot Rathos a wild look. The king stood, waving off the Intercessor urgently. The headsman sheathed his sword and scooped up Rathos by his armpits.

"Take him to Sinclair," the king ordered.

Intercessors led Rathos away. Prisoners begged him with wide-eyed expressions, as if he had the power to save them, to take them with him.

"Wait, WAIT," Rathos cried. He elbowed one guard's face, unmasking a young Medecian. He slogged through the sand, to the dais, one precious second ahead of his captors.

The king looked at him. "I granted your petition," he said.

"I'm petitioning for my wife. For Mina Robswell." Rathos struggled in the ghouls' grip. "If you're freeing me, I thank you, Your Majesty," he added hurriedly. "I wasn't taken here alone. I won't leave alone. I petition for my lady wife's release."

The king seemed almost embarrassed. He gestured for Intercessors to lead Rathos away, and this time, he screamed at Parlisis's daughter, for all to hear.

Something was coiling its fingers about his heart. "*You swore you'd keep her safe,*" Rathos said. "If your vows mean anything, give her and her child safety. Show me her, Your Blessedness!"

The prieslenne clutched at the fronts of her armchairs. "Show me her . . . *Your Majesty,*" she corrected him.

It took him a moment to understand his transgression. He nodded agreeably, hastily. "I ask for forgiveness, Your Majesty," he said. "Let us leave together, Your Majesty. Please." His voice thickened with anxiety. *"I swear, we'll be loyal. Forever.* House Sinclair will never again do treason. I swear it, Your Majesty.*"

Edenia's smile had the warmth of sunlight piercing dark clouds.

"Your love for your wife moves me." She signaled one of the Intercessors. "Show him Lady Robswell. Let man and wife leave together in peace."

Nodding, the Intercessor headed for the lances.

Terms

he *Hathrimnyr* faced some ten thousand men across a field strewn with trampled reeds, headless corpses, and curling smoke. Cavalry, archers, and footmen spilled across the Golden Meadows, massing thickest in front of the Colossus, the teeth of their pikes visible.

It was an impressive display, for a thief.

Jason wrinkled his nose. The sweet fetor of burning flesh made the moment hellish. He patted his horse's neck, thinking of Erick. *Easy, friend. Soon it'll be over.* He glanced at the men at his back, fewer than four thousand in all. A brave, paltry force.

Were that you were with us, Lord Trevor. The Bull had lain abed the past week under Eorl's tender care, forehead moist and hot with infection. Jason and the Bull's nobles had feared loss of limb, or worse. Wexley looked likely to recover, but he couldn't lift a sword, let alone mount his horse.

"He'll need rest," the apothecary had insisted. "Whatever comes in the next day, my lord, you must leave Lord Trevor out of it, or I fear his death."

My lord. That'd been the first time anyone had milorded him since their arrival at the Golden Meadows. Everyone else still called him king, out of habit or stubborn refusal to accept reality. It'd filled him with pride, once; now it filled his mouth with bitterness.

Feet away, Wexrenn stirred anxiously in his saddle. "King Jason, this is a trick," he complained. "They said noon."

"We don't leave without Lady Mina," Jason said sternly.

"Coronations take time, Lord Russell," Evan observed. "Especially when they're illegitimate."

His uncle stood by his side, somber. He'd farewell his firstborn with dignity, in a green doublet cinched with silver buttons, gray-dyed breeches, and polished black boots, parting gifts all from Ulbridge. He looked years younger without his beard. "That was a mistake I made before my first time in the Red Tower," he'd explained to Jason as he shaved the evening before, "giving them more hair to use."

To that, Jason had vowed that his uncle wouldn't see the inside of Shaddon's Red Tower. *Charles, you traitor . . .*

A deadly serious look of rebuke, that had drawn. "You must leave after the exchange, no matter what happens," Evan had said. "Their numbers and defensive position give them advantage, but the blood of a peasant revolt hallows these Golden Meadows. Your strength lies not in arms, but in what others will say when it becomes known that the only Trial victor mustered on that field against a king who won nothing."

What others? Jason thought. More than six hundred of those crisped cadavers had been Cloudlanders, many of them anointed knights. Pavilion stakes littered the field, a reminder of the noble lords slain and their houses fled, of Free Believers long vanished. The Loyal Company had proven the falseness of its name by betraying Evan and him. The bastards had even sacked his mother's castle.

But Gram Sothos was quite possibly dead. He smiled at the almost-divine justice rendered upon one of his mother's killers. *If you're alive, Gram, will you simply be called Pinkflesh?*

With little left to lose, save for his child, Evan would trade himself and his secrets in return for her release, but Mina was the one captive they'd gain in this twisted arrangement. Of his half-sister, Jason had no news, merely assurances that the king would treat Alyse's daughter as gently as if she were his, as if his word were strong as swordwood, as if he hadn't trespassed into his rival's camp and stolen the Kingstrials.

Nor had they any word about Anyasha. Nor any about Sinclair's ward, who'd secured the Loyal Company. *What else can be done?* Jason asked himself inwardly. He was tired from ruminating, lightheaded from pain in his left flank and limbs, bitter, and furious with his enemies as much as himself. *What else can we do but allow the theft of Hexar's crown, my wife and the people we love with it?*

As he'd recovered in his pavilion, coming to terms with his role in the rape of Loran, Jason wondered if he could ever forgive himself. *You called me a fool, Ana, and you were right. I wanted to save Loran from bloodshed, but bloodshed came, from the peasants I would've seated in the Colossus. I've endangered us all. Because I wanted to win my crown like Father won his.*

Jason balked when Evan volunteered himself as hostage. He'd told his lords to draw up siege plans. But sieges required catapults. Supplies. A siege could last months or years, even for a well-provisioned army. The king and his Assembly had more men, more food. They had the Colossus.

Above all, they had four hostages. Jason had none.

Inevitably, the star of reason illuminated his path. Leaving under these circumstances would forfeit the crown and reward Shaddon for stealing it in plain sight . . . but it was the only way.

Squealing winches drew their attention north. Shaddon's forces parted along a rutted dirt road. Out rode Sam Gramlore in flashy armor, tugging Mina Robswell by a rope. Peeling off a contingent of Intercessors, Thorngale accompanied the Bull's rival at an unhurried pace, a king's banner rippling in his grip.

Ulbridge patted Evan warmly on his shoulder. "Tonight my *scrorn-ner-gaith* will make pea soup for your Mina," he said.

Wexrenn squinted through Evan's skyglass. He recoiled sharply, as if the eyepiece had scalded. "Jason," he ventured.

Evan snatched the skyglass before Jason could. Pressing into the eyepiece, he rotated a center pipe to maximize what he saw. His breathing rattled in his chest. His lord uncle slackened as if pierced by an arrow, wailing raggedly. As Ulbridge caught the fainting nobleman in his arms, Jason grabbed the skyglass.

He didn't need it.

Gramlore crested a slope, a victor aswagger on his mount, Thorngale and Intercessors alongside him. Gramlore tugged his rope surprisingly gently. Behind his horse lurched a specter of a man, wrists tethered. Hair bedraggled his face like moss.

It was Sinclair's ward. He cradled something.

Something vaguely purple.

Jason kicked his courser's flanks, closing the distance in a blustery charge through low fires and billowing smoke. Hooves pummeled the earth behind him as Wall knights scrambled to keep pace. He shuddered to a halt yards away from the lords, his horse rearing.

Gramlore raised the flat of his hand. "Keep a distance, my lord."

Up close, Rathos Robswell looked ghastly, his once-lean face puffy and distorted with purplish-gray welts. Blood traced his cheeks and the seams of his mouth. His pale lips quivered ceaselessly, as if he were on the verge of uttering something.

Jason would never forget his gaze. Pink grief wreathed his swollen eyes.

In his hands Rathos clutched his wife's head. Her mouth gaped unnaturally, as if brittle thread held her jaw, like to snap any moment. Black blood congealed in the orifice of her scalp, matted with violet hair.

"*SAVAGES!*" Jason exploded.

Thorngale urged his destrier forward, to Eddenwood's unease. "You'll know savagery when I kill you slowly, for my brother," he seethed.

Five blades emerged beside Jason. A grin played along Thorngale's lips. The remaining Wall knights drew closer on their horses, warily.

"Six on one. I knew worse odds in Uzland." Thorngale had his palm on the stag pommel at his side as he sized them up.

"Try two on one." Ulbridge thundered up in a cloud of dust, alongside Wexrenn and a ring of others. "Those are the odds all Loran will offer your evil king, when the Cloudlands join everyone else against him!"

Pride mingled in him, with bitterness. *Is this what it will take to unite a kingdom?*

Sam Gramlore rushed to placate them. "*NO,* Darren, do nothing," he said breathlessly. "We come in peace. Despite the gravity of Sinclair's crimes, we come here seeking peace. Truly, Lord Jason."

Jason couldn't restrain his laughter. "*PEACE?*" he barked. "My uncle invaded mine camp while I lay unconscious. Seized my sister. Conspired with traitors in the Assembly to end the Kingstrials. I would've decamped today, you idiot. For peace."

"You'll decamp because we outnumber you," Thorngale said.

Gramlore rounded on the young lord. *"Darren. Please."*

Evan was right, Jason thought. Sweat glistened on Sam's brow. *The whole realm is watching, and this nobleman is one of the few smart enough to be nervous.*

"If Shaddon desired a peaceful withdrawal," Ulbridge said with a nod at Rathos, "he wouldn't have done . . . this."

"It was a mistake." Gramlore sighed. "Queen Edenia, she wanted to make an example of the Mad Lady. She didn't know."

Queen Edenia? Gramlore could've declared war on the Cloudlands. Before he could finish, cries of dismay erupted from Jason's men. His, no one heard. *My love . . .*

Gramlore glanced behind him, at Shaddon's approaching reinforcements. "Please, have your men withdraw at once, and we'll avoid further tragedy," he said. "We don't have Sinclair's daughter to trade, but we have Matthus's son. And you, you can still be legitimate. Hexar's ancestral castle can be yours."

Jason brandished his sword. "I want my sister," he said. *"WHERE IS SHE?"*

The Lord of Eddenwood was explaining that she was safe, perfectly safe, when Thorngale loudened his voice over his, "A bleeder like this one, she was, Lord Warchild." He gestured at the Colossus. "Shall I fetch her head for you to hold, too?"

Amid the uproar, Jason's gaze sauntered left, to the pale visage lumbering past his horse. Sarah Sinclair's brother had earlier shaven and looked a decade younger. Now he seemed well past his years, on the verge of collapse, barely able to set one foot before another.

"Uncle," Jason breathed with a catch in his throat, but Evan either didn't hear him, or did, and paid him no mind.

Thorngale sat forward in his saddle, a gleam in his eye. "If you long to see your Mina whole again, Sinclair, say the word."

Evan made no acknowledgement. It was as if no one else existed but Matthus's son. As his warder came nearer, Rathos lifted his anguished gaze. He resisted grief's pull, lips squirming together.

Since Southpoint, his uncle had lived up to his reputation as a courtier with rough elbows, by turns diplomatic, earnest, and agreeable, but secretive, opportunistic, and ruthless above all. "An eel's eel," Hexar had maligned his brother-by-law. Jason had seen Evan shed his mask just a little, only once, when he'd shared how Sarah Sinclair had died.

Clutching his child's head, Evan Sinclair shambled toward Jason, utterly maskless, shoulders bowed. He thrust Mina up at him, lips twisted in the snarl of someone straining to hold all the shattered pieces together. "*Bury her at Caerdon,*" he rasped through his teeth, eyes screaming. "*Leave with Rathos and bury her beside her mother.*"

"Your castle belongs to King Shaddon now, you old fool," interjected Thorngale, "not to Lord Warchild."

Jason scowled past his uncle. "You changed the terms," he said. "I demand new terms. We'll give you Sinclair and decamp, in return for Robswell, my sister, and her servant."

Gramlore was unsmiling. "You know that's impossible."

"Then my *Hathrimnyr* will decide how this ends."

"Lord Jason. Please. It'll end in more needless death, yours included. The king loves Alyse still. He holds you responsible for embroiling her daughter in your treason. He'd sooner have the men behind us butcher you than forsake her."

"Let me bring him her head," said the Stormsword. "He should hold his sister's head."

Hexar's fury overpowered reason. Jason coiled his fingers about his haft. Then he saw Evan. Looking upon his distraught uncle, remembering the words of their discord and their final, weary agreement, he relented. *Very well, uncle . . .*

"My cousin," Jason instructed Ulbridge hoarsely.

Dismounting, the Cloudlander collected Mina with utmost reverence, lifting hair from her line of sight, as if she needed to see. And thank goodness, Jason thought, with Rathos following every brush of his fingers. With Ulbridge covering her head in his cape, Gramlore stayed the reinforcements.

"Sinclair for his ward, Lord Jason," Gramlore insisted.

Passing Rathos, Evan embraced him, whispered in his ear, and kissed his forehead. As Rathos trudged past Jason's lines, Gramlore beckoned the Intercessors, and Evan Sinclair donned chains like old familiar clothes.

"You're saving lives today, Lord Jason," Gramlore said.

"You risk yours by fucking speaking," Wexrenn hissed.

"Very well then." Gramlore rode up, handing Jason a scroll pinched by ribbons of cream and violet. A kingly signature bled through the parchment.

With Evan clinking between them, Intercessors withdrew. Thorngale stayed a second longer. "I must congratulate you, Lord Warchild," he said. "A castle, title, and seat in the Wing of Lords. What would your whore mother say?"

The Stormsword dug his heels into his horse and rode off in a whirl of cape, the new king's banner smacking in the wind.

Jason withdrew behind the lines of the *Hathrimnyr* with the Wall knights, his lords, and Rathos, back to relative safety. Gates squealed shut in the distance. Glancing over his shoulder, Jason saw Shaddon's forces converge again over the dirt path like silver seawater. *Be you god or gods, please protect my uncle.*

Hunched over, Ulbridge gazed alongside him. "What now, my king?"

"I'm not king." Jason gave him Shaddon's decree. "Burn that."

He nodded. "Your cousin. Shall I have her head tarred?"

"I defer to her husband. Tell your men to decamp. We've lost the Kingstrials."

At Ulbridge's cry, lesser lords and commanders barked orders to the *scrorn-ner-gaith*. Jason lost sight of Robswell in the migration. After a brief, frantic search, he found him on a slope, facing the Colossus, hair ruffling in a breeze.

A word is needed. He'd spoken to Rathos only once, on the day he headed west to win the Loyal Company. Climbing down from his horse, he went to stand beside his cousin's widower. He wondered if Rathos knew he was there.

"I swear to you," said Jason, "Shaddon will not reach the Silver Walls. We won't forsake Evan and my sister." *Nor you, Eden. No matter what lies my enemies spread.* "And Mina will have justice when Shaddon hangs. I swear it on my mother."

A silence lay between them. Rathos turned about, face twisted with an agony Jason hoped to never know. Tears glistened on his bruised cheeks. "The king didn't crown himself," he said thickly.

He lingered on Jason before stalking off.

CHAPTER 32

The Stone Maiden

It was a nauseating sight, the forest of spears and rotted heads, aswirl with flies. The stench was something from hell. Looking on from the shadows, the prisoner would've thrown up, if her belly had anything in it. Lorana hadn't eaten anything in a week.

The grisly display didn't seem to unsettle Loran's lords and priests. Seated on their benches, they looked like satisfied conquerors. Spotting her, some laughed in asides like children in on a joke about her.

And why not? These Elvarenists were celebrating a long-sought conquest, and the princess who'd fought them was now in chains.

Conversation dwindled as Lorana emerged from the northern portcullis. It was a long, slow, silent trudge through the damp sand, in the heat, to the arena's center. She stood tall before the dais that seated a king and queen.

If the revolt had given Shaddon pause, he didn't show it. The illegitimate king wore a crown with diamond-encrusted bands that clutched at it like tentacles. Among all the wealth in that diadem nestled the biggest chunk of silverstone she'd ever seen outside the Silver Walls. Pulsing gently, the crown's glow should've lent Shaddon an otherworldly aura, but the frumpy sovereign dispelled all that with his squinting. It was difficult to see through silverstone light, after all.

Lorana knew it was the silverstone of Blackstaff's rod . . . seized as he'd seized Loran. *That obscenity is apropos as a jewel in his crown.*

Beside her unworthy uncle sat the first queen to rule Loran in a thousand years, unworthier still. The gems in her silver crown glimmered in the luster of pilfered silverstone.

Edenia had never looked more beautiful, dressed in a rich dark-blue gown, her skin soft and fresh-scrubbed. She stared at Lorana, the hint of a smile teasing her rouged lips. This was her moment in the sun, the famous hostage who'd betrayed House Eddenhold to become queen. She was exultant.

Lorana hated herself for ever loving her. Cursed all her pining for her while she was away. She was a cauldron aboil with grief, fear, a desire for vengeance . . . and envy.

Yes, envy. *I was born to rule, more so than my brothers,* she thought. It was because of Loran's great hatred for women with crowns that the Kingstrials had been fought. Yet here this queen sat, the picture of feminine authority. *May they add your blood to King Lathros's,* she thought.

Lorana clutched at the dignity remaining to her. For this humiliation, her captors had insisted on a gown of sky-blue, dagged sleeves that drooped from her wrists and a girdle of beaten silver. Her brown hair had been washed and cascaded down her backside.

They wanted her to look and sound like a princess. Like a steward, not a parakeet trained to repeat her masters' words.

"As a judge of the Kingstrials," she said, her clarion voice carrying around the amphitheater, "I am uniquely positioned to declare the victor. I am steward, princess, and daughter to King Hexar. Every ear in the kingdom shall hear my words and take what I say as lawful and true."

Shaddon nodded slowly, squinting through silverstone light. He was nervous.

Hexar's daughter. If I were anything like him, I'd seize two of these head-laden spears and hurl them through their bellies.

There was Anyasha to think on. They'd taken her during the revolt, she'd learned. How bitter her tears had been, alone in the dark, after Edenia had unwrapped the stump of a bloody, tattooed finger and left it on her cell floor.

Lorana wanted to believe that her love wept in a cell belowground. But . . .

In her heart, she knew the odds were that Anyasha was already dead, her head among all the other heads perched atop spears. She'd wailed for them to show her the girl, pounded on her cell door until she scraped her knuckles raw.

They never gave her proof. Only empty threats of more flesh.

She was under no illusions. Elvarenists despised Elzura's Children. It would've been wiser to keep her alive, to force her cooperation, but Loran's conquerors were zealots. *I committed treason against my heart, Father. All I have now is vengeance . . . all because we tried to rule Loran better than you had.*

Sinclair had been right all along. The peasants had been like boiling water, and the fire beneath had needed guttering before the cauldron's contents frothed down its sides.

Peasants had needed their seats. A voice in their rule.

The nobleman had been right again on the night of the revolt: Jason had exemplified nobility. Together, they'd tried to save Loran from itself, use it like a shield against the covetous priestking and his seven servile kings . . .

But for what? Lorana looked around her, at the heads on spears, the Elvarenists watching raptly from their benches. For Parlisis, Jason's noble aims had been a door to Loran, and he'd simply opened it and walked through. The priestking and all his allies—and his daughter— had conspired to raze Hexar's house, scattering it like dust in the wind.

They wanted the Silver Walls. They wanted Loran back in the fold. They wanted to crush the Free Beliefs that threatened their faith's dominion over millions.

They'd been utterly ruthless in their designs, and out of hope, House Eddenhold and its allies had believed that most of their coun- trymen would put their country before religion.

They'd been wrong. Damnably wrong.

You're dead because we chose the Kingstrials, Yasha. Zuran is lost to us. All because we tried to stop a war we didn't think we could win. We tried to rule responsibly. Decency blinded us, and our enemies happily exploited it.

Lorana seared Edenia with her gaze. In exchange for her lover's freedom, she was to call them king and queen. Rightful. Lawful. Ordained by a High God and his twelve gods.

She turned her steely gaze to her soft, fat uncle. "Uncle, I am indebted to you for saving me during the peasant revolt—something I never wished to see in our kingdom," she said for all ears. *Never mind that your silver-masked ghouls shot me with an arrow. That you killed Anyasha.* "For this . . . I am sorry that I cannot find that you won the Kingstrials. You are not the king."

Shaddon squinted at her through his crown's aura. Edenia twisted her lips. All around her rose the scorn of Assemblymen. Scanning the sand around her, she saw pebbles, decay-bronzed fruit and lettuce, and other hurled spoil. *I am not who came before me,* she thought. *I am Hexar's daughter, and they will not disgrace me by throwing refuse.*

Her uncle's grimace made him resemble her father more than she liked. "Frederick Midliche named *me* the king-victor," he said, his insistent tone like that of a child denied dessert.

"The Fox is entitled to his verdict, but he is a merchant, and merchants serve their purses first. I am a steward of the Silver Walls. I serve this country first."

Edenia sat forward, clutching the fronts of her armchairs. "You owe your rightful king your life, Your Highness," she said, the edge in her voice belying her formalness.

"I'm grateful, Your Blessedness," Lorana responded coolly. "But his victory was out there"—she pointed to the southern portcullis—"not within the Colossus." *And because you come to power through marriage, your crown is worthless, you evil cunt.*

"He saved you from a revolt you, Sinclair, and Warchild whipped up against us. While your claimant lay abed, a small, sleepy boy, my betrothed rallied the land against the rebels."

"He won no Trials, Your Blessedness."

The prieslenne's fair, perfect cheeks turned a noticeable shade of pink. "*Your Majesty,*" she insisted lividly. "You shall call me . . . *Your Majesty.*"

If not for the need for appearances, Lorana would've laughed. Wide-eyed with fury, Edenia Highdaughter brought to mind her tantrum-prone little sister. She was small, petty, and pathetic—a fair face elevated by privilege, nothing more. *I traded the golden loren of my true love for you, a copper penny.* Her half-brother deserved better.

Lorana hadn't deserved Anyasha of Nuur.

Watching Shaddon nod, she realized he was granting speaking rights, and not to her. Jon Redoak rose from a lower-level bench, seething. A splint held his right arm in place, and a jagged scar on his right cheek vastly improved his appearance. *So Peshar Grathos wasn't the only lord speaker to suffer during the revolt,* she thought with dark pleasure.

"I was there when King Shaddon mustered his forces," he barked. "On the night Evan the Traitor burned Lord Sothos, on the night your peasants tore Speaker Grathos apart like rabid dogs, I was there."

Burned Sothos? I wish I'd been there to witness it. "As was I, my lord."

Redoak spun on the other Assemblymen. "WHAT DOES IT MATTER THAT OUR KING DIDN'T WIN SOME STUPID GAME?" he bellowed, looking rabid himself. "Willard's rules are clear—a king must have blood on his sword, and he must lead men in battle. KING SHADDON DID THIS!"

The Assembly clamored with wild applause, until the steward's voice triumphed over them. Rorin's amphitheater amplified sound from the sand arena more than it would any voice in the benches. Sinclair had taught her that.

"Only kings can ride griffons," Lorana said without raising her voice. Everyone heard her. "In the Kingstrials, they *must* ride griffons to be king. My father did this. His brother did not."

"YOUR PEASANTS FREED THE DAMN BEAST!"

"They're my subjects as much as yours. And even if they hadn't, Shaddon still wouldn't have won a Trial you agreed to."

Redoak waved her off with his one free hand. Swaths of the Assembly surged to their feet, galvanizing other benches. Lords and priests raged at her in a storm of voices—"*TWELVE GODS FOREVER! TWELVE GODS FOREVER!*"

Twisting, Lorana saw her stuffy uncle looking proud, as if vindicated by the crowing of his fanatics. Edenia grinned down devilishly.

The steward's voice drowned out their chants. "IS THIS WHAT IT MEANS TO BE WORTHY?" she cried out, her voice bounding from wall to wall. "Chanting! Throwing pebbles like fatherless children! Lauding ill-gotten power, in violation of your own laws. Wars have been fought to protect the Worthy Assembly's independence from the crown. Oceans of blood spilled." She shook her head in disgust. "How cheaply you trade your mighty seats for a pair of crowns."

May every peasant in the land hear my words, she thought. *From Rosbury and South Farcombe to Hexwaite and Peacefield, may they hear me, and burn this kingdom to the ground.*

Shouts and curses flew from every direction. Her uncle cradled his head in his hand, eyes low and averted with shame.

His wife-to-be was less inclined to speechlessness. "Says the woman who whips up mobs against the Assembly and beds Casaanite women," Edenia said with a cruel smile.

Laughter filled the Colossus. Lorana circled about slowly, her steely gaze fixed on Edenia, and it was then, just then, that she saw regret in the false queen's eyes. Regret, and realization that she'd led herself onto dangerous ground. *You always were an idiot, Eden.*

Lorana waited until her sentimental uncle, who'd so loved Alyse Jannus, who wouldn't stand for the Assembly humiliating his niece by her, finished his grating calls for silence.

Which timed just perfectly with her last arrow loosed.

"Yes, I took to bed a Casaanite woman, and loved her," she admitted to stunned silence. "But you deflowered me first." An avalanche of jeers and threats cascaded down to Lorana. "It was after my father left to find Garrett and Jason in that storm. You came to my bed. You crawled under my sheets and licked me between my legs."

Edenia veiled her discomfort with a thin, nervous smile anyone could see through. "*Lies,*" Lorana read her lips saying.

"'I have you, my flower,' you told me, that night and every night you crawled beneath my sheets," Lorana proceeded. "'I'll always have you,' you promised me—"

White-hot pain seared her temple and flared behind her eyes, disorienting her. She saw the stone at her feet, touched her forehead, pulled away two fingers smeared with her blood. *Fatherless children.*

As the ringing began to subside, she heard her uncle demanding the arrest of the stone-thrower, and silence.

"You say you serve your country," Edenia said stonily. She made a dismissive flick of her hand at the Intercessors lined up at the eastern wall. "And so you shall, steward."

It took a second gesture from the false queen before the Intercessors heeded her, Lorana noticed. Despite the throb of her temple and her spinning world, that delay, and its implied loss of respect, wrung a smile from her.

Crossing the arena, silver-masked shadows surrounded her on all sides. They had no need for force. Lorana staggered ahead of them, ahead of the relentless jeers, her bloody head held high.

CHAPTER 33

Outnumbered

haddon knows he's unloved. Illegitimate. With revolts spreading like pox, Assemblymen want him protected behind the Silver Walls as soon as possible. Their ships are gone, so they'll take the path of least resistance." Wexrenn traced the vein of a road down the crinkled map, north to south. "Scythe Road is that path."

Jason hovered over the table, studying the map of Loran with Wexrenn, Ulbridge, and his lesser Cloudlands lords. He sweltered in his gambeson. But for braziers aflicker around the pavilion, there was little light.

More light wasn't needed to assess the war map. Jason knew the odds. *The path of least resistance is right*, he thought. Vile, annoying, and too proud by half for someone called the Lord of Sheep Hills, Wexrenn nonetheless uttered a hard truth.

They were outnumbered. Wooden game pieces littered the map, horse-heads all, confiscated from a squire's game set and recently painted: crimson for Jason, violet for the new king, his queen, and their forces. Violet pieces dominated the north, bearing down on the Midlands like a towering wave. Scattered across map and table, red horse-heads accounted for less than a fourth of all pieces placed.

This wasn't your plan, Evan, but it's the best we can do.

It'd been Evan's idea to trade himself as a hostage. It was for more than his daughter's life. "I'm the one Shaddon wants, not you," he'd told Jason at the Golden Meadows. "The Loyal Company betrayed us, but I'm the only man here who can give up the names of its members.

Take me anywhere with you, and he'll set the dogs on you. But trade me for hostages—while the kingdom watches—and he'll feel pressured to abide by terms of peace. He'll let you and the Cloudlanders withdraw."

Shaddon had been treacherous, *even then*, striking off his cousin's head. But the ploy had worked. Jason retreated west with his *Hathrimnyr*, hoping to sell his enemies on the illusion that he planned to lick his wounds at Eddenloxley Castle. They changed course in Westland, riding south into midge-infested hill country Cloudlanders knew like the backs of their hands.

There, they'd made camp.

They'd make war on this false king. They'd rally any lords who'd supported Jason, Tomas Fawkes, or Sam Wuthers in the Kingstrials— or, at least, any lord with a grievance against the false king and his Unworthy men.

They'd intercept Shaddon on his ride south. Exploit the element of surprise to rescue Evan, Lorana, Anyasha, and any other member of House Eddenhold swept up in the revolt. *And you, Eden,* Jason thought. *The idea was to save you . . . if saving was what you wanted.* If they could capture or kill Shaddon . . .

Evan had urged him to do more than rally the houses of slain lords. *If we were to adopt your plan, uncle, the Bull and his army would abandon me, and there'd be even less hope than there is of saving you, Lorana, and Anyasha.*

It was a fool's plan already, teetering on the knife's edge, all but dashed yesterday when Sam Hornby barreled into camp with ill tidings. The knight reported seeing a formidable force streaming north— thousands more footmen, cavalry, carriages. He'd reported seeing banners from nearly every house seated in the Wing of Lords . . . even the ones Jason had hoped would ally with his *Hathrimnyr*.

Even House Wuthers. No one wanted to be on the losing side— whoever did?—but this left Jason and the Bull's lords crestfallen. *Lords want peace for their noble houses, even if it means shaking hands with a devil who orchestrated the deaths of their own heads of household.*

The bastard prince toyed with game pieces. He aligned this one with that, trying to eke out battle formations that'd make this battle remotely winnable. But the numbers weren't there. *Just like in the Trials.* Despairing, he slapped a regiment of crimson horses off the table. His lords looked on in silence.

"I hadn't counted on the cowardice of so many lords." Jason slicked sweaty raven hair out of his vision. "Present company excluded."

"'Twas why we Cloudlanders exited the Wing of Lords in the first place," Ulbridge said with a halfhearted smile.

"No, it wasn't." Hitherto silent, Wexley lay abed, one leg dangling, hair and beard tousled like he'd just woken from a drunken stupor. He lurched off. In his knee-length tunic, the Bull resembled a boy. A large, intimidating one.

Wexrenn approached him. "Lord, you're recovering—"

Wexley swatted his vassal aside with a wave of his huge hand. "We left the Assembly and this kingdom," he said in his baritone voice, "because Charles Burke *is a liar.* Because his fucking lies *killed* my brother."

Jason glanced at the pommel of his sword, in its scabbard, propped against a barrel. They'd somehow avoided this topic since leaving Northland. *And now we know the truth a trial by sword did not illuminate.* "I thought we settled this, my lord," he said.

The Bull clutched the stripe of a bandage swaddling his belly. Sweat sheened his face. "He betrayed your house. Now he's betrayed your house again. As I betrayed the Cloudlands for you and your rabble wing." He spat in disgust.

"I think you should lie down, Lord Trevor."

Wexley shoved past his lords, fist drawn back, as if he planned to strike the man he'd called king. Everyone heard the *snap,* the stitching in his flank. He doubled over. "Hanorr," he said as he staggered down to a knee, then to his side. Crimson sopped his bandage like spilt wine. "Hanorrrrr . . ."

One of the lesser lords dashed out of the pavilion, crying for an apothecary. Jason retrieved a rag from the bowl of tepid water on the table, applying it to the Bull's moist forehead.

"He shouldn't have come to this meeting, not like this." Kneeling, Ulbridge began the impossible task of lifting his liege. Wexrenn joined in to help him, and Wexley tottered out on his lords' shoulders, just as an apothecary reached them.

Jason remained in the pavilion, feeling more alone than he had before. *God and gods,* he thought hopelessly. *Shaddon has Lorana, Evan, Anyasha . . . my wife. Near all the Assembly's lords and their forces at the Colossus for his escort. And here we are, in the hills, bickering like children.*

Furious, he swept more pieces off the table. "I should've accepted your forgery, Ana," he said aloud, as if she could hear him. "I've been a fool." Kneeling, he gathered horse pieces from the floor. He arranged them again on the map.

"If it's any solace, you weren't the only one."

Jason swiveled. A noon sun bled through the tent flaps, silhouetting the intruder. He could tell it was Evan's ward by his slender build, his rumpled hair. An unsightly bruise bulged the left side of his cheek like a tumor. His wrinkled tunic and breeches draped him loosely, like to slide off his thin figure.

So my cousin's widower lives. Grief had made a recluse of Robswell. Jason hadn't seen him since leaving Northland. Day or night, no one saw him. Around their cookfires, men spread rumors about the mysterious tagalong, coining a name for him in their native tongue: *spucar,* or ghost. *Spucar* looked like he hadn't slept for days.

Jason didn't know Rathos. He'd never even met Mina while she lived. But his heart ached for him. To comfort him, he'd had meals delivered outside his quarters daily, up until men complained about all the flies lured by uneaten spoil.

Rathos ventured a step inside. "Had you been the only fool," he added, "your assassins could've saved us much trouble that day they met you on the Street of Kings."

Jason chuckled grimly. "Yes, they could have. A good thing my lords just left. With the mood they're in, they might've just taken your tongue, for your discourtesy."

"Like I said, you haven't been the only fool." Fidgeting firelight showed dark circles under his eyes, the plum-purple bruises fading to yellow on his face. "Your half-sister was one, thinking she could out-play zealots. She fancied herself a king, crown, cock, and all."

"You're under my protection, Robswell, but you'll watch that tongue."

His cracked lips tensed with the hint of a smile. "Evan was a fool. He believed that if we swung the Loyal Company for you, their power would swing the Assembly, too. Let's not forget the Cloudlanders. But I was the *great* fool. The nemesis of justice."

Evan's ward was trying Jason's patience, and fast wearing out his welcome. "Do tell." Truthfully, he spoiled for a fight.

"I believed petitions and processes could save Loran from the lords and priests raping her. In fact, I aided and abetted the rape. My wife . . . my child . . . paid the price for my foolishness. My naivete."

Child? "I'm sorry, Robswell."

Bending low, Rathos retrieved two crimson horse pieces and plopped them in the other's hands. "You missed these." He studied the map. "But you'll need more than a ragtag army and painted game pieces to save Evan Sinclair's life."

Jason disliked his tone. He assumed a royal's aloofness as he returned the pieces to the table. "You know, it's a crime for lowborn men to eavesdrop on their lords."

Rathos hacked loudly, as if from coughing. Jason realized that awful choking sound was the wretch's attempt at *laughter*. The bastards had beaten him so severely that he couldn't laugh properly. "You're the second man in a few months to confuse my station. And I haven't been eavesdropping. One need only listen to the sounds of your camp to know something's afoot."

He twirled a finger about, indicating the clamor outside that to Jason's ears had become background noise: whetstones scraping swords, iron pounding iron, groups of men trudging by. Rathos looked at the map. "I don't sit on your war council, my lord, so perhaps I misunderstand this map, but—"

"It doesn't look good," Jason admitted softly.

"No, it doesn't. We're outnumbered. Four to one."

We're? At least I'm not as alone as I thought.

Rathos studied the horse-head pieces that represented the *Hathrimnyr*, tidily organized into columns across a sprawl of elegant script, *The Midlands*. His puffy right eyelid fluttered. "You plan to intercept the king and queen on Scythe Road."

Jason bristled at that word, *queen*. "It's something we've considered."

At least in war, he kept his secrets. In the Brace, he and Garrett only brought their estranged half-brother into council after months together. He knew his uncle's ward half as well as he knew Evan, which wasn't much. But he couldn't deny what Rathos saw plainly for himself.

Rathos didn't seem to buy it. "You'd ambush them. Save Evan, your half-sister. Perhaps even capture or kill your other uncle. It's brave. Some might say desperate."

It's the best we have. "Or clever."

"Desperate," Rathos insisted. "You'll fail. You'll die on that parched road, or suffer capture and die in agony later."

"I thought it was 'we,' Robswell?"

Unaffected, Rathos narrowed on crow-footed marks on the map. "What makes you so sure they'll take Scythe Road?"

"It's the fastest, most direct route to Southpoint."

Rathos shook his head. "Shaddon's been away for years, but the lords with him will know that road leaves them wide open to ambush. It's too risky for them."

"Then their only other path is Barbara's Gorge," Jason said as he followed Rathos's line of sight. "The canyon would expose them to worse. Archers will line those cliffs and rain death."

"If there are trained archers, they'll be yours. Shaddon's escort wagers you won't risk your flesh and blood in a storm of arrows. He and his escort would make it out safely—because they'd be right. Love matters more to you than power."

"Peasants would resist them." Jason tapped the area of the map that read *Rosbury* and *South Farcombe.* "That's why they'll take Scythe Road. Barbara's Gorge feeds into Midway Road, where revolts spring up every day. Shaddon's lords would be fools to lead his host through the heart of Loran's uprisings."

Rathos smiled wanly, thickening the sallow pulp of his cheek. "Which is why I've left the comfort of my quarters to speak with you, my lord. I know how to find you more men. Which is what you'll need if you want to save Evan, your half-sister, and anyone else—and arrest the false king and queen."

I know what he means. "Evan convinced me that he knew where to find men, too. He traded himself to save you—"

"To save Mina," Rathos interjected.

"—but he—*we*—planned for battle. He thought the lords would flock to us. He didn't know Houses Wuthers and Fawkes, even lords in your own Company, supported Shaddon—"

"*I'M NOT TALKING ABOUT THE BLOODY LORDS.*" Rathos seemed as shaken by his outburst as Jason. There was a pause in his sleep-deprived eyes, as if he expected a rebuke, or for a knight to barge in and haul him off to a pillory.

"I know what you're thinking, but I want to hear you explain it yourself—softly, and with some courtesy," Jason cautioned him, "or I'll have you whipped."

Rathos composed himself with a look of contrition. "While you lay abed, after the Second Trial, the ground shifted beneath you," he said more measuredly. "Every person in Loran felt this earthquake when Commoners stormed Rorin's Colossus"—he swept a hand over the black ring in the map's north—"*to take back what was theirs.*"

He gathered all the crimson pieces off the map, one by one, adding to the columns until they spilled across Scythe Road. When he finished, a crimson wall awaited that violet wave surging southward. "You need men. As it turns out, you have an embarrassment of riches."

Jason stared at him. "Evan thought much the same as you. He suggested rallying Commoners to our side."

His uncle had also intimated something . . . troubling. He hadn't entirely been truthful, he'd told Jason. "My hands are on these revolts." His hands had taken to shaking as he'd watched them. "They're red as

Gram's, but I bloodied them in the light of the star of reason. Nothing has been for nothing. Everything is laid before you, Jason. You need only reach out"—he'd closed a fist in the air—"and take it. Rally your countrymen—peasants and lords alike—*and lead this kingdom to salvation.*"

I'll rescue you, uncle, Jason thought grimly. *And then you'll answer for any part you played in this madness.*

"Evan was right," Rathos said. "Rallying peasants is the only way you'll stop these tyrants from seizing the Silver Walls for themselves. You must do this."

"I'm trying to free people I love, not fan these revolts."

"What a luxury." Rathos gave him the most biting look. "I was chained like an animal when your Virgin of Venas had me shown Mina's head."

A silence lay between them. "You propose conscripting Commoners," he said after a long moment. "After they killed my men in the revolt—*tried to kidnap my sister—handed my uncle the excuse he needed to take power?*"

"Shaddon would've seized power with or without a revolt. And neither Evan nor I would propose conscripting them."

As if the Bull needed another reason to question our pact. The irony of it made him chuckle. "Only a lord can call his little folk to war. Only a king can summon all his lords' Commoners. I have neither a castle nor a crown. Why would they follow me?"

"Because men follow leaders. Not titles."

Jason had a pointed look. "Would they follow someone who crowned a prieslenne the Virgin of Venas?"

Rathos pressed his lips firm together, as if trying to spare Jason a volley of angry words. "The laurels offended many, but Edenia's *actual* crowning angers far more. Luckily, we have a proxy leader. This man commands more respect from Loran's peasants than a false king, his harlot queen—or you, frankly."

"You mean the Master Reader." Jason was tired of hearing allies suggest finding this impossible-to-find man called Jacob Sulley.

"Listen to me." Rathos stepped closer. "Tens of thousands of Commoners inhabit the shires between here and Eastland. If Sulley and his readers raised the alarm in even a fifth of those, you could have the army you need. If thousands of peasants organized on their own to swarm the Colossus for the Wing of the Commons—if they burned Shaddon's ships on their own—how many would rise up against the zealot to stop him and his queen from taking the First King's castle?"

Jason laughed witheringly. "Assuming that Jacob Sulley is anywhere near us. Neither he nor his readers have been seen since leaving the Kingstrials." *Because of me, Eden*, he thought. "No one knows his whereabouts. Believe me—I've sent scouts in every direction searching for him."

"Someone knows Sulley's whereabouts. I know who."

"Is he within half a day's ride?"

"Try an hour's ride. And *she* is."

Jason regarded him skeptically. *My other cousin, and the real Mad Lady,* he understood. Evan had shared the truth about his daughter at the Golden Meadows. Jason would celebrate her for burning his mother's murderer, but the Cloudlanders would sooner slit her throat—and his—than see him clink cups with a reviled outlaw.

"Leah Sinclair," Jason said. "Of all people, why would *she* know of the Master Reader's whereabouts?"

"They're allies. She and the Heretics have been secretly escorting peasant children to safety for months, eluding the justices and priests with Sulley's support." Seeing his reaction, Rathos smiled derisively. "Are a Master Reader and Mad Lady such strange bedfellows, to someone who allied himself with Cloudlanders to seat the Fourth Wing?"

Jason looked at the map. "Tell me where she is. My Wall knights will gain the truth from her."

"No. The steward was fond of sending Wall knights to kill Leah and her men. If they saw your men coming, they'd flee, and you'd never find her." Rathos leaned over the table, hands sprawled on either side of Scythe Road. "Lend me your fastest horse. I'll find her . . . and deliver you *a Common army*."

Jason took his measure with a long look. "No."

Rathos looked to be somewhere between disappointment and rage. "How do you mean . . . no?"

"Your freedom was bought at a steep price. You haven't slept in days. Evan would curse and kill me if I sent you into harm's way."

"Harm's . . . way?" Rathos was in Jason's personal space in two strides, seizing him by his gambeson collar. "I've already been in harm's way. *My wife! My child! My home!* Everything's been taken! *EVERYTHING!* All I've got is Evan." Tears streaked his bruised cheeks.

And vengeance, Jason surmised. *What man wouldn't want it after being forced to carry his wife's head?*

Any other man, and Jason would've thrashed him worse than any of Shaddon's henchmen. But the truth was sinking in. "Even if you or Leah could find Sulley," he said as he pried free of Rathos's fingers, "why would he rally the peasants for me?"

"Because you aren't the only person in this kingdom who had the Kingstrials stolen from him."

Sunlight sliced through the pavilion's gloom. Rogir Levan stepped through the flaps, arrested by what he saw. The ward unlaced his hands from Jason's collar guiltily.

"My king?" the knight asked Jason, shaken. He looked as if he'd run Robswell through with his sword that instant.

Jason straightened his gambeson. "Sir Rogir, please escort Sinclair's ward outside." Rathos flickered to his feet, defeated. "He'll wait for Sir Sam Hornby, whom you'll summon. Tell Sir Sam that I need him to dress lightly—mail under a tunic and breeches. Tell him to bring our two fastest horses. He leaves with Robswell in twenty minutes."

He eyed Rathos. "Two days, Robswell. Scythe Road."

He expected surprise or gratitude, but Rathos had an air of satisfaction, as if he'd known Jason would reach this decision all along. "Until then, Lord Jason." He left in quick strides, brushing Rogir on the way out.

CHAPTER 34

Furos

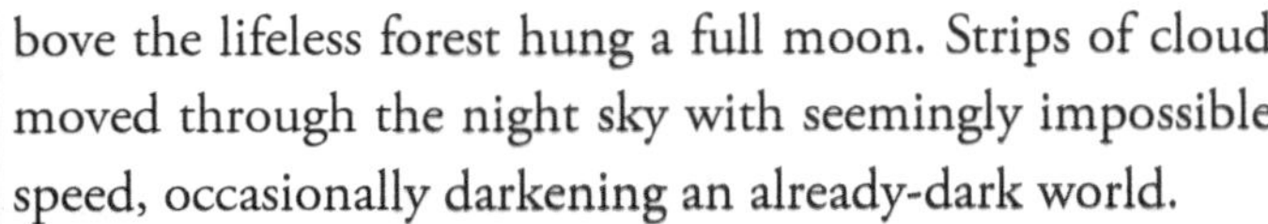bove the lifeless forest hung a full moon. Strips of cloud moved through the night sky with seemingly impossible speed, occasionally darkening an already-dark world.

Zur sat tied to an oak tree, hands bound behind the trunk. He stared at the helm at his feet. By starlight, the blood caking the Eye of Guldan looked like dried mud. As the shadows of his captors drank and gambled by a fire in the distance, he allowed himself to grieve . . . and curse himself bitterly.

I failed you, Drexan, the boy thought. *I should've gone with you to the Great Tree. To the Oracle, to safety. Because of me, the most miraculous man I've ever known is dead. But I'm soon to follow.*

A terrible solace that was. Summer Solstice was on the morrow. Self-pity turned to madness that dressed itself up as fearlessness. He shrugged off his life before tonight as a dream, a dream never his again, one he'd always taken for granted. Against all sanity, against all hope, he pushed himself to look forward to death . . .

Until he remembered that his Windrider's blood would open the doors for the next Nagarthessi to cross into reality.

He recognized the Lame King constellation among the stars. Gods had raised heroes to the heavens, there to dwell forever. *You died for my sake, Drexan,* he thought. *A Casaanite's sake. You belong in the skies. Not me. Never me. I wasn't even fit to clean your inkpots.*

A bush rustled nearby.

Something chirped. *I know that sound.* He turned his head to stare at the bush. Leaves stirred, and out leapt Furos. *Furos!* The griff padded through grass, flexing his wings, his tail aswirl in the air.

Zur followed the animal's line of sight to the crackling fire ringed by shadows. Save for Uther, they'd been toasting their fallen comrade all night. Now and then, someone would look in his direction. Right now, Tom consoled Owen, while Devan and Bill threw dice and the others slept.

Do shadowkings sleep? Zur wondered grimly. *I suppose I'm about to find out . . .*

A Windrider's blood coursed through his veins; it needed to be released. On the way back from Graywood, Spittlelip had dragged Zur by the scruff of his neck, through a crucible of bits of leaf and fern. Zur had cursed the man all the way, but now, inwardly, he thanked him.

A speck of steel a tenth the size of Zur's pinkie nail glinted in the ruts of his tender flesh. That wrung a smile from him.

Hands tied behind the tree, Zur slid his ankle along the soil, back and forth, until he flushed from telltale pain. On his ankle glimmered a bead of his potent blood, a blood that could light fires and allow him to see as the griff sees.

"Furos," he whispered loud as he dared. "*Come, come.*"

The griff twisted his head curiously. *Do you blame me for your master's death, as I blame myself?* Zur wondered guiltily. *Are we not friends . . .?*

"Close your eyes," he remembered Drexan saying. "Do you hear his heartbeat?"

Zur closed his eyes. Bowed his head. Sought a fortress of calmness within himself. He imagined himself as a caterpillar, woven in his cocoon's protective silk, fastened to a formidable bough of the Great Tree of Loran.

The voices around the fire faded in his ears, becoming muffled . . . then distant . . . and . . .

He heard a single heartbeat. Then a forest of heartbeats.

Opening his eyes, he beheld *himself.* His world grew huge, and in the thick of bewildering noises and sights he saw Zuran of Tribe Nuur bound to the tree, unseeing, head low. As Furos, he unsheathed talons from his feline paws.

He'd never controlled Furos at night. His fear surrendered to awe for a symphony of cricket wings as deafening as a king's horns, for the countless nocturnal creatures trampling the soil like elephants. The griff's belly rumbled and it took all Zur had to keep him from bolting after a hedgehog.

A giant's laugh ricocheted from the fire, so slow, loud, and distorted that Zur wondered if a griff could drink wine, and if Furos might've siphoned a wineskin somewhere. *Be careful,* he and the griff thought as one. *Do this thing now.*

Circling the tree as Furos, he picked at the ropes binding the boy with his front talons, thread by little thread. By himself, the griff might've made quick work of the bindings, but the boy possessing him was clumsy. Frustration billowing into panic, Zur went with his first instinct and buried his sharp beak deep into hempen, chewing until the ropes finally, *finally* unraveled.

Reentering the familiar world of man, Zur stretched his arms and smiled wearily as his ropes slid off. He stood, rubbing his wrists, wincing as he spotted a nick in his skin from the griff's beak. Furos poked his head out from behind the tree, giving no indication that he'd minded the leash of Zur's mind.

Zur looked south to Graywood, catching his reflection in a moonlit steel tree just as migrating clouds immersed his world in darkness again.

He slipped back into Furos and flew skyward with a burst of energy, wings flapping through warm summer air. The griff scoped out what lay north, the Rotwood, and what was south. *Uther Shadowking will track me in the Rotwood, even by night,* he knew. *Where then do I go? Where is safety?*

From within Furos, he detected movement near his own shiftless body on the ground. He slipped out of the griff before Devan's rope slipped around his neck. He fronted toward the squire, pumping his palms for a pause between them.

"Devan, I've seen Uther, what he is," Zur rasped above a whisper.

He wanted to reason with him. "You don't have to serve him or his demons. Come with me. We'll escape tonight."

The boy's eyes trembled, then went still. "Then you know you cannot escape him," the squire said. "Uther's gods are real." Twisting to the fire, he cried at the top of his lungs, "*HE'S ES—!*"

Zur slammed into the squire. They fell to struggle in the dirt, rolling toward the glittery death of Graywood. He gasped as Devan sank his teeth into his arm like a rabid thing. Boiling up, he kicked the little fiend right in his belly.

The blow pushed Devan off balance and onto the point of a moonlit branch that slipped through his chest as effortlessly as steel through silk.

Zur trembled as he watched the boy's mouth froth with blood that rolled down his neck. He wanted to throw up. *I've never killed before.*

Feet gathered in the distance. When the shadowking's men halted in a huff, they found their Gift twenty feet inside Graywood, on the other side of a pathway crosshatched with luminous reeds and branches that could open arteries.

Bill stared at the dying boy, heaving. "*Murderer!*" He tried for Zur and recoiled sharply, holding the part of his arm that'd scraped against a particularly menacing-looking branch.

Owen held his head, sighing. "He's inside Graywood, you idiot," he muttered.

Moonlight silvered the curved dagger that Tom drew. "Think you'll be safe in there?"

"Well." From behind razor-sharp limbs, Zur beckoned him closer. "Come and find out."

Overhearing footsteps, the men parted for their leader, the shadowking.

Uther gazed at Devan's twitching body. He sighed. "This will only prolong your pain," he told Zur gravely.

He seemed at a loss, as if a wall stood erected between them. In a way, a wall *was* between them, between Zur and a changeling as vulnerable to swordwood as anyone else.

Zur steeled himself against fear. "You seemed fine in here the other day, creature," he baited him.

The priest touched his emerald ring. "I am a man of faith," Uther said. "How's your faith, Zuran? You'll need it in a forest like this at night. If some root catches your foot, we'll find you on the morrow in sunlight. Then, we'll remove the foot."

"Better if you get out of there," Tom warned him.

The shadowking's companions watched Zur intently, hands curled about the hilts at their waists, waiting. *There's only one way forward,* Zur thought as Spittlelip joined their ranks, staring malevolently.

He'd have to do the impossible. He'd have to navigate Graywood by night.

Turning, he began to maneuver through the swordwood, ignoring his enemies' dark words and halfhearted entreaties. He tried to block out Spittlelip's irritated *shrriping* entirely.

He'd need to lose Uther and his men fast. Moonlight and starlight illuminated everything unobscured by steel canopy—roots, branches, leaves, needles. *Be with me, Drexan . . . be with me, Ascendant King. And you, Furos.* He sensed the griff gliding above him. *I need you most of all right now.*

Walking cautiously, he ducked beneath serrated leaves and fierce-grooved branches. He walked on, until he couldn't hear Spittlelip's *shrriping* anymore.

Turning, he realized he couldn't see Uther or his men. *They're choosing another way to get me. They know this place better than I do . . . but I have Furos.* Zur slowed his heartbeat, his breathing. *Forward. Only forward now.*

Using moonlight and starlight as his guides, he identified a makeshift path through the tangle of sharpness and kept to it, avoiding jagged limbs, stepping over twinkling roots.

Inching through a press of low-lying branches, Zur sliced his arm on a leaf. He applied pressure to his cut, smiling grimly. *So long as I don't nick an artery, or open my neck,* he pondered, *every drop of blood I lose will keep the power of my blood fresh and sustain my connection with Furos.*

Shutting his eyes, Zur slipped into the griff as he'd don a shirt. Reopening Furos's eyes, his world curved like the surface of a vast marble. The moon shone through the clouds, illuminating a wreath of green around the unnatural shimmer of swordwood. The forest of the Rotwood surrounded Graywood. Safety was near.

Still, he couldn't exit Graywood in just any direction. Moonlight danced off the swordwood's borders intensely, showing boy and griff that steel branches pressed together thickly north, south, and east, nearly as thick as walls. Zur judged it difficult to walk through those areas unscathed.

There! the boy and griff thought as one. *Safety is west.*

Something enormous slammed into the griff, wresting control from the boy below. Zur fell as he'd plunge off a cliff, back into his flesh. He gazed up and around wildly, panting, checking himself and his swordwood surroundings. *What in hell was that? Wind?*

He was groping about for the griff, eyes closed, when he heard angry cursing behind him. His pursuers had found a way into the swordwood. They were near, and in as much danger as he was right now.

Zur bolted west. Trees lashed out with claws, slicing up his cheeks and ribboning his tunic. He dizzied trying to watch his feet and blurring swordwood at the same time, all while taking the shrapnel of bits of leaves in his legs. He constantly checked the sky for Furos, following his dark, fluttering shape west.

He suddenly realized the shape was *enormous.* He wasn't following Furos at all. *Whatever that is,* he thought, *it knocked a fearsome wind into my griff, and I don't want it any closer.*

He halted behind a steel tree, drenched with sweat and breathing hard. He closed his eyes and gloved Furos, with no trace of whatever he'd been chasing after.

"*I GOT 'IM!*"

Scrawny arms hooked around his chest, and he tumbled out of Furos and into a wrestling match in the dirt. Moonlight showed him the white of Bill's eye. He stabbed it with a single finger, and Bill flew off him, right into a pile of glinting leaves.

Bill's screams in his ears, Zur ran as fast as his feet could carry him, as fast as his eyes could track moving soil and night surroundings blurring past. He stopped at the lip of a hill that cratered into darkness, teetering dangerously.

No, he thought as he lost balance.

He tumbled head over feet downhill, grunting through dark, until his rolling descent landed him in . . . leaves. Pliable, crinkly leaves. Leaves that ripped easily and smelled of rain. Sitting forward, he mashed up some in his hand, remembering that most leaves couldn't, in fact, maim or kill.

He rose unsteadily. To his left, he saw trees, green trees blessedly free of steel coating, and navigable spaces between their wooden trunks. Nearby, a brook prattled. *The Rotwood.* Glancing behind him, he saw the swordwood, shimmering like a hall guarded by armored men.

He was out of the swordwood, not out of mortal danger.

I need you, Furos. He returned to the skies above in a rush of wind, stretching his wings and searching woodland below.

Something was wrong in the Rotwood. Something fanned out from Graywood, a pestilence that slew whatever it touched. Decaying everything in its path, it barreled straight toward Zur where he stood. *Uther Shadowking.*

Blinding pain severed Zur from his griff. He was on the ground and couldn't breathe. Hands throttled his neck as the beginnings of a light rain pelted his face.

Not rain. Spittlelip was strangling him, spittle oozing out and onto Zuran. He sucked at his skin holes, *shrrip, shrrip.* He was too strong.

I'll give you new spittle holes. Zur closed his eyes, and out of the night darted Furos, talons grasping for Spittlelip's face.

A pain worse than anything he'd felt gutted Zur through his stomach and severed their connection. Screeching, Furos tumbled to the ground, Tom's dagger lodged in his dark belly.

FUROS! Zur wept as Spittlelip tightened his grip on his throat. Tom emerged off to the side, a satisfied smile curving his plump lips.

He plucked his dagger from the dying animal, cleaned it on the fur, and twirled it skillfully about his fingers.

"That'll be breakfast." Tom kicked Furos over with a foot, inspecting his work. "Get off 'im, Jacob. C'mon, Uther told us—"

Tom screamed wildly. Spittlelip whirled to see his companion levitating midair, flailing his arms frantically. Eyes wet, he flew backward into the forest, as if hurled by a giant invisible hand.

Precious air surged into Zur's lungs as the mutilated peasant released him. Spittlelip scooped up Tom's blade. He took a small step right, a small step left, searching for danger.

Something thick and black sprang out, roping Spittlelip's ankles. Night threw Jacob to his stomach and began reeling him into the forest. Zur looked on in horror as the man slithered off, screaming-eyed and clawing feebly at dirt.

He stumbled to his feet, bewildered and panting.

Thunder growled through the forest. *Uther,* he thought, preparing to run.

A forearm lurched out of the forest, thick as a branch, and with it the nemesis of dragons. Moonlight etched his black feathers, the dark fur of his muscled hind legs, the horns of his ruffled ears, his leaf-flecked mane. The beast arced wings thirty feet in length, tip to tip. Blood spattered a huge mustard beak.

The eyes. Zur remembered his huge eyes, pools of gold slivered with black irises. *The griffon from the Walls. The one meant for the Third Trial.* He flew in the brook's direction.

Zur collided with something, and a dagger met his neck.

"Now you lose a foot," Owen whispered in his ear.

A blur and a wind freed Zur. He spun around to see his attacker panicking as the griffon's tail wrapped him as snugly as a python. Face to face with the king of the skies, the peasant began crying out, not for his gods but for Uther. A snap of the monstrous beak ripped Owen at the waist, and with an unceremonious fling of his tail the griffon catapulted legs and intestines into the woods.

It was just Zur now. The griffon advanced on him, throat working to swallow the rest of Owen. The boy staggered back into a tree trunk.

I wish I'd known something more about you, Mother, he thought as he shut his eyes.

Nothing happened.

Slowly, Zur opened his eyes. The griffon crouched before him like an enormous feline, his wings folded down. He tilted his head, side-eyeing Zur curiously, as Furos had so often.

You don't mean me harm, Zur realized with astonishment.

From the night came a calamity of noise, bushes rustling, branches snapping. The winged beast crouched low like a wild cat, growling so deeply Zur heard the vibrations in his bones.

He comes, Zur heard his heart say. Somewhere in the wilderness, *out there,* trees thrashed apart, snapping and falling, as if they were merely bushes in something's way.

The griffon lowered himself to the ground, on forearms and haunches. He slanted his wing at Zur, almost deferentially.

The wing looked almost . . . scalable.

Zur fortified himself with a little breath. Up the wing, over the flank, he climbed the animal. Close to the wingbone, he lost his grip, sliding down a slick wall of oily feathers. The griffon's tail coiled snugly about his waist. He panicked as the thick tail lifted him up . . . until he found himself astride the backside, lowered as gently as if he were the creature's cub. His world lurched as his mount rose on all four giant paws, snorting out a challenge.

The nearest tree barreled down suddenly, filling the air with soot and leaves and splintered wood.

From the ruin gleamed the stars of little white eyes.

The griffon wheeled about, the bulk of his muscled body shifting as the shadowking rushed to deal death. Mist fumed over the soil in its wake, blackening grass. With a terrifying hiss, the griffon sickled out talons as long as dirks.

Time slowed.

Zur felt it before he saw the clash unfold, felt himself fall from the griffon as the dance began. Talons sheared through mist, and *did nothing*. He saw Uther rip into the mighty griffon as if he were cooked meat, beheld the ruin, the puddled blood and snakes of pink intestines slathered about the forest floor.

He saw himself dead in Graywood, a Gift for Uther's gods, as clearly as he saw a wide forest path slashed with moonlight ahead of them.

"Go now," Zur urged his mount breathlessly. "*RUN, RUN!*"

The griffon sprinted into the dark. The world was wind and leaves, a chaotic blur. Clutching fistfuls of feathers, he lay flat across the furry backside. The shadowking frighteningly kept pace, a relentless vapor just feet from the flank, sickle-shaped claws reaching for Zur. Over the pounding paws and snapping leaves, he heard a shrill scream. A scream of rage.

The air cracked like thunder under the griffon's wings. Suddenly Zur no longer felt the heave and pitch of earth. The forest slid away as a starry sky rushed up to meet them. Wind roared in his ears and would've thrown him, if not for the tail hugging his waist, pinning him to his mount. Peering down a flank of wind-ruffled fur, Zur saw Graywood shrinking into a gemstone no bigger than the palm of his hand.

They soared over the world. Through wisps of clouds, Zur recognized the Lame King, and beside it, a gathering of stars he did not know, all shining brilliantly.

Answered Prayer

aded wheat stalks shivered against the sides of gilded carriages. Shod hooves and spoked wheels crushed the crops spilling across the road. Horses rode by hastily, their muscular hind legs materializing in slivers through the stalks. Thousands of boots marched together, drumming cobbles.

Jason huddled beside his Wall knights in the wheatfield, sweat bullets running off his forehead and cheeks. It'd be a hellish day. He gestured to Ulbridge, who signaled the archers.

Hell was loosed on the king and queen's caravan. The whistles of arrows mingled with terrible screams. Dozens of men collapsed all at once, clutching at their wounds. Knights wheeled their horses about clumsily, tails lashing air.

A third volley sang out before the enemy quite literally returned fire, showering them with flaming arrows. Within seconds, the driest part of the kingdom snarled with wildfire, filling the air with heat and smoke. They couldn't stay hidden in the wheatfield any longer without roasting alive.

Jason stood and unsheathed his sword. "*FOR LORAN!*" he cried. Thousands of voices echoed him.

The bastard prince flew out of the crops, plunging his sword through the visor of a knight's helm. At his side, Rogir Levan shoved his blade up a Hexbrook man's armpit. Erick Seam and Kyle Urron blew through four wounded footmen, slashing viciously. Sam Hornby slew a man and leapt onto his steed; Harold Marc bounded onto a destrier.

Thousands of Cloudlanders, knights and *scrorn-ner-gaith*, surged past Jason, fighting for the realm on a dusty road only recently crowded with starving, malnourished Commoners. Shaddon and Edenia had given orders to clear out the rabble. To ward off any trap laid for them.

Only so much could be cleared in a desiccated wheatfield that went on for miles. The Assemblymen allied with the two monarchs had known this, and they'd come anyway. It was the height of arrogance.

All of this depends on you, Robswell, Jason thought. Sam Hornby had loped back to camp the same day he'd left, sharing that Rathos and the Mad Lady had gone east to find Sulley and rally an army. *If you fail, we'll live only in songs about the short-lived treason of a bastard prince and his Cloudlanders.*

The *Hathrimnyr* didn't have the numbers, but the Bull's men fought savagely, piercing mail with their steel, caving in armor with blows from their hammers. All around them, King Hexar's silver griffon soared in banners aflutter. Through the smoke, Jason spotted the sigils of eagles, two-headed dragons, thrice-crowned harts, of crossed black axes and motley archers and stout towers. Songs of steel and his own pounding heart filled his ears.

Shield strapped to his left arm, Jason staggered over a horse fluted with arrows and swung his blade at a Redoak footman, cleaving through chain links. Whirling, he ran through another in a tabard with Wess Dyvar's crossed axes. Through his helm's visor, he saw banners of flame rippling in the dead wheat.

Hell, Jason thought. *I've led my men to hell once more.*

Chaos reigned. Arrows showered them like desperately needed rain, *thwip thwip thwip,* clattering off armor, downing men of all sigils, thudding against the corpses. Knights ahorse thundered past, crashing through shield walls, impaling men on spears that shattered like tourney lances. Fire rippled the air with heat; smoke made it hard to breathe. Men called out orders or begged for mercy, or for their mothers. Jason saw a road glutted with mangled corpses. A Cloudlands man crawled over the gore, clutching his severed right arm, as if thread and needle would do.

I didn't want this war, Jason thought, arm shuddering as he cleaved through a Sothos footman's shoulder. Warm blood splashed his face. *But at least this isn't a game. And the Worthy called me Warchild, after all . . .*

There were no rules here. No mealy-mouthed men jeering or cheering or exploiting rules. The only rule that counted was that you kill the man before you, the one flanking you, the one behind you, and any who replaced them.

At his feet, a Cloudlander struggled in the dirt with a Greathall man, gritting his bloodied teeth as he put all his weight into carving a hole in his foe's cuirass with a stiletto dagger. A herald's horn blew as a mounted knight sighted Hexar's bastard prince and threw his heels into his steed's flanks, charging through the chaos, his sword aglimmer in firelight.

Arching his heel, Jason waited until the knight loomed a foot out before swinging his sword into the horse's neck. The animal screamed as it careened from the blow, throwing the rider. Jason beheaded the man before he could find his footing.

Through the din of carnage, a familiar voice cried for his attention.

Levan pointed south, shouting something. Down the way, the fighting thickened impenetrably. A shield wall ran from one crackling side of the road to the other, manned by Assembly knights and ghoul-faced Intercessors. Cloudlanders slammed against the barricade, slipping in muck or on the piled bodies. Spears snaked through from both sides.

The carriages, Jason understood. He'd positioned Ulbridge and Wexrenn half a mile down the road to light fires of their own, to keep Shaddon and Edenia from reaching Southland—from reaching safety. But they were a failsafe that could fail.

"*TO ME!*" Jason cried through the calls of war horns. He found a riderless white courser and clambered up, clutching the reins, willing obedience. "*BREAK THE WALL! THE WALL!*"

His Wall knights heard him. Streaked with blood, Hornby and Marc kicked their stolen steeds into a charge. Cloudlanders fell in with them as Jason barreled through the churn of smoke. To his left Levan and Seam scrambled over corpse hills, trying to keep pace.

Jason dug his feet into his horse's flanks and vaulted over the shield wall and spears. He stabbed an Intercessor in his belly, wrenched it free, and clanged swords with the knight who took his place. His presence seemed to embolden his men. The shield wall strained under the flurry of swords, spears, and pummeling hooves.

The glint of a spear was what Jason saw, and suddenly his smoky, burning world toppled sideways. He wriggled his foot free of his injured courser's stirrups before it dragged him off. He slipped under the world, prey for the scrambling, trampling feet of men trying to obey him and smash the shield wall. Feet flew from every direction, bludgeoning his helmless face. The air was oven-hot. He was drowning in pain and heat.

A hand gripped his and tugged him out of the chaos. Jaw throbbing like it might fall off, he squinted through smoke and pain, trying to make out his savior.

A Thorngale knight had saved him. He was a knight par excellence, striking in his gleaming armor and the silvery fish scales of chain mail. A cobalt cloak fluttered off his shoulders. Steel antlers webbed the sides of his helm. *Not a knight . . .*

Darren Thorngale stood statue-still amid the chaos. "YOU KILLED MY BROTHER." A Cloudlands man charged him and fell, his belly ripped by an effortless arc of the Stormsword's sword. "NO ONE KILLS YOU BUT ME, LORD WARCHILD."

Jason realized he'd lost his sword and shield in the pit of feet. He was naked.

As men ran past, others filed beside him. Four of the Silver Walls's greatest knights, in fact.

Rogir Levan and Kyle Urron leapt at Thorngale, swords ringing against his. Erick Seam handed Jason a sword. Harold Marc joined them to drive the Stormsword back as other men fought and fell and died around them, as fires breathed hot air at their backsides.

Five against one would've been unbeatable odds, but this was the lord who'd single-handedly killed thirty-nine Uzmen. He fought like his brother, but he was much faster. Inhumanly fast. Jason flew right and left, drawing on every instinct he had as a swordsman, but Thorngale parried his strokes and those of his men. A Cloudlands knight ahorse galloped by, the twirl of his spiked flail nearly smashing Jason's head.

There was no lull in their fighting, even when Thorngale stuck his sword through Erick Seam's face. It was four against one, and then a

Lamporean footman leapt out of the fires and skewered Kyle Urron, so it was three. Rogir Levan avenged the knight by lopping off his killer's head, leaving Jason's flank unprotected, and the Stormsword exploited it by slicing him open like ham.

It was a poetic gesture, reopening a sutured wound made by Gavin Thorngale. Jason detected a smile on Thorngale's lips. A smile. *He's toying with us,* he understood. *These are my best men, and we're like mice fighting a cat . . .*

In one stroke the Stormsword beheaded Levan and Marc in lurid founts of blood. Jason had known Rogir all his life, and Marc and the others nearly as long. As their slackening bodies fell, he let fly his sword, beating Thorngale back with reckless, furious strokes. The Stormsword wasn't smiling anymore. The song of their blades rang in his ears.

Suddenly, Jason heard much less. Battle raged all around them, men screaming, flames snapping, and listening to it was like listening while underwater. *He cut off my right ear,* Jason realized. Adrenaline deadened his pain. Blood sheeted down his right shoulder.

Thorngale raised his sword for a killing stroke, changing course midway to cut down someone who rushed him. He was a red-haired peasant boy in a studded jerkin. The Stormsword pulled free his sword, looking confused.

Jason didn't need a right ear to hear the blasts of enemy war horns, or to know what was happening. Out of towering flames poured a Common army, deluging the road, peasant men and women and boys, even girls. They wore all manner of armor, nasal helms, dented pauldrons, cuirasses, jerkins. Ill-fitting, knee-length hauberks made some look like scaly fish with legs. They wielded the tools of their trades and filched weapons. Swords. Dirks. Hammers. Scythes.

Thorngale raised his sword and vanished beneath a mob of peasants. A dozen men and women surrounded Jason, threw him to the ground, kicking and beating him with clubs and the butts of scythes. He cried out, shouting that he was with them, *he was with them.*

In fits and starts, the mauling stopped. Commoners who'd attacked Jason helped him to his feet with great care. His head pounded painfully, as if someone had struck the bloody ribbon of his right ear with a mallet; someone had probably done just that.

Amid all the peasants, Jacob Sulley sat athwart a piebald horse, Willard Potter reborn a mace-wielding Free Believer. A leather cap covered his head. His voice carried over the din as he commanded peasants like a general. Though Jason heard but little, he understood what the Master Reader told them: this was Jason Warchild. He was not their enemy. Anyone with a mountain sewn on their surcoats was not their enemy.

Sulley pointed them at their enemy—at the shield wall, and the Intercessors holding those shields.

Peasants within earshot changed direction, and anyone who saw them fell in line. Countless people trampled knights on foot, overwhelming frightened war horses, cutting down footmen with eagles and dragons and harts for sigils. There had to be thousands of Commoners. Tens of thousands.

Not just Commoners. With the peasants rode a merman ahorse, the helm of a beaked skull bouncing on his shoulders, violet hair fluttering behind him. Heads burst like melon fruit as he swung his morning star with a warrior's precision.

Not him—her, Jason thought. He marveled at his cousin, the Mad Lady. *Her sister's vengeance.* What could only be the Heretics gave chase with Leah Sinclair, among them a pale-skinned Uzman slashing his axe and a gangly fellow gutting men with his sword and flapping his free arm as if he were a chicken.

Once again, you deliver allies for me, Rathos Robswell. He couldn't see Robswell amid the thousands charging south.

Of the peasants charging south, a number peeled off and concentrated their strength on a brawl on the road. Circling, Jason saw them swing all their steel at a single foe, but their numbers counted for nothing against sheer indomitable talent.

With every swing of his blade, the Stormsword cut down two to three peasants, their armless, legless, headless corpses piling up at his feet. *Not one blade,* Jason realized with a start.

Two swords flew like the wind in Thorngale's hands. He hacked off a peasant's arm with one blade and buried the other in a boy's heart. The last remaining Commoners fled from the ambidextrous killer. Locking eyes with Jason, the Stormsword waded through a mountain of gore. Of all the blood drenching his armor, it was possible that not one drop belonged to him.

A god, Jason thought. *The best the Silver Walls had to offer lost their lives to a god who fought them with one hand behind his back. He's right: no one else kills me but him.*

Thorngale trudged through the road's flotsam of death, a haunting sight. He'd lost his antlered helm. Blood-soaked hair ran down his shoulders like red rivers. "I underestimated you, Lord Warchild," Jason heard him say very faintly.

"And I, you," Jason confessed.

"You're nothing." Thorngale spat blood to his side. Jason realized he *had* been wounded. A fletched arrow stuck out of his side. "No king. Not even a man. A traitor to your class." He pointed a sword. "I'll take that other ear. Then, everything else. Until you're nothing."

An arrow sprouted in Thorngale's backside. A second *thunked* into his pauldron. He spun around.

Astride his black courser, Robswell pulled a third arrow from his quiver and nocked it, flames billowing behind him. The Stormsword ducked the next arrow. He reached the Companyman in four quick strides, startling his courser so that it tossed its rider to the dirt. Robswell raised his arms shakily over his head as Thorngale arched his swords for a finishing blow.

And that's the last time you underestimate me.

Jason ran into Thorngale with all speed left to him, his arms shuddering as he plunged his sword through his back, chewing through mail. Wrenching his blade free, he caught a final, smoldering look from the realm's greatest swordsman before he sent his head whirling into flames.

He offered Rathos his left hand, hauling him up. Rathos smiled gratefully, a strange sight amid the carnage. "I never was a good shot," he said. His olive-green eyes flitted to the bastard prince's monstrous head wound. "Lord Jason . . ."

The Mad Lady rode up in a cloud of dust. Shorn her griffon skull, Leah Sinclair seemed an otherworldly vision, violet hair erupting about her blood-smattered face.

She said something. Rathos threw a leg over his courser. Knowing what was happening, Jason climbed up with him.

The way was clear. Shaddon and Edenia were still in the Midlands. And they were trapped.

With Jason holding on behind him, Rathos kicked the horse into a furious charge, Leah outpacing them on hers. Plumes of smoke wafted over the road south, a road clear of shield walls, writhing with Loranians, whipped by flames.

On this humble road, thousands lay dead. *This was what I didn't want,* he thought as a man covered in flames bolted past.

The fires fell away on the blustery gallop south. Sulley's Common army lined Scythe Road, taking spoils of war, pulling off bloody cuirass plates and gathering castle-forged swords.

A crackling flame wall loomed over the carriages near the road's end. Zarold Ulbridge and Russell Wexrenn helped Jason dismount, their faces drawn in worry. He realized there was an arrow in his shoulder. He didn't know when it'd struck him.

Jason flew to open carriage doors, checking each vehicle with Rathos and Leah. At the third carriage, he fell to his knees.

The People

moke blackened the eastern sky, flowing westward like a storm. *Perhaps it is a storm,* Rathos thought. Looking up from a forested hilltop, he saw the pinhole of a red sun in the smoke drifts. Slivers of blue sky reminded him that not all the world burned.

Glancing at the sprawl of striped pavilions below him, at the ants of Cloudlanders and peasants, he wondered whether it'd do to move camp. The wildfire set by the king and queen's men wouldn't abate. Even now, flames consumed the Midlands like locusts, fanning out in every direction, including theirs on the edges of Sylvanwood.

As the wildfire spread, it burned shires and villages, and that was causing problems of another sort. Displaced peasants wandered west in droves, toting whatever they could carry on their heads, under arms, or on skinny mules, trusting Warchild or the Master Reader would shelter and feed them.

New arrivals weren't received warmly.

Rathos watched as haggard people streamed out of the trees, into camp, flanked by children and mules. A welcoming party of Cloudlanders immediately rushed them, telling them what they'd told everyone else—no, go back, turn around, we don't have supplies, you're fleas and we can't support more of you. It was a heartbreaking scene. Men beat already-beaten peasants, cursed in their faces, shoved them back toward the forest. Soot-faced children wept as if the world were ending.

Before Rathos finished spooning broth into his mouth, the scene played out like before. Wary-eyed peasants and readers who *had* fought in the battle leapt up from their cookfire seats. They ran full speed at the agitators, battering them with filched bucklers and pots and pans, whatever wouldn't lead to nooses. With fights spreading like wildfire, some stragglers did, in fact, turn around tiredly.

"It's hard to believe these people were fighting *together* just days ago," Leah Sinclair remarked behind him, appalled.

Rathos sipped more broth. It was painful to swallow, but he was making himself. He owed that to Mina. "It's Cloudlands knights who start the fights," he said.

"It's no fault of those Commoners their villages burned," she added. "Someone ought to stop this madness."

"Who?" Rathos set his broth bowl on a large rock that had served him as a chair. To say that he was annoyed wouldn't do his mood justice. "The Master Reader? Trevor Wexley? No one is in charge here."

Turning, he felt hollow. *Is this how it will be now, between us?* Leah looked *just* like her. Just like his Mina, if slightly taller, her arms laced with sutured battle scars. She sleeked her violet hair back in a ponytail, as if trying to downplay Mina's likeness. In place of her pauldrons and leather she wore a white blouse and gown, and it didn't help with his remembered pain.

She watched him with vulnerable hazel eyes, seeking something he couldn't give her. Not yet, at least. He turned back to the scuffle between Cloudlanders and peasants, and was surprised to find the man who would've been king down below, escorting refugees past boiling-eyed knights. *Perhaps someone still leads here, after all,* he thought.

Flanking him, Leah watched Jason lead people to shelter and dwindling food stores. "He's kindhearted, but a fool, doing that. The Bull is already wroth with him for sending us to rally peasants."

Rathos snorted. "Every Cloudlander would've been put to the sword without the Commoners. Trevor's as much a witless tyrant over his people as Shaddon and Edenia will be over us."

"My men tell me he plans to decamp with his people and return to Eddenloxley tomorrow."

Yes, Leah, that's well-known, Rathos thought irritably. The Battle of Scythe Road, some were calling the attempt to arrest Shaddon and Edenia, to rescue Evan and Lorana. Others, like the Bull's men, lamented the battle as the Warchild's Folly.

Rathos had warned Jason, and Jason hadn't listened. Wise to an ambush, the Assembly had shuttled a regal decoy through the Midlands, carriages filled with Edenia's fine gowns, nothing more. To lend the procession a convincing appearance, they'd sent the Stormsword and thousands of men to protect it, to die for it, while Shaddon and Edenia had ridden through Barbara's Gorge unchallenged.

Their ploy had been utterly ruthless. As ruthless as they'd been in sabotaging and stealing the Kingstrials.

As ruthless as the Warchild should've been in dispatching archers to the canyon's heights. Now, the king and queen were safe behind impregnable walls of brick and silverstone, their hostages in dire peril. The kingdom was theirs.

Jason had lost. In a day's time, he'd lose the *Hathrimnyr*.

Why is it that no one ever listens to us, Father? he thought, furious— at Jason, at Evan, with himself. *Only when it's too late, with everyone covered in soot, the country burning, the sky dark as night. But then, we never listened to Rezlan Ambrose . . . and Mina paid the price. Our unborn child paid the price. Our child . . .*

Leah was speaking when Rathos asked, abruptly, "How is Creature?"

"He lost an eye, not his voice." She attempted a smirk. "He bleats like a lamb when he's in pain."

"Pretty Phillip?"

Leah stroked her arm listlessly. "Less pretty, now that he's noseless." A wall of silence lay between them. "Do you want to ask after more outlaws . . . or do you want to talk?"

Talk. Talk about his dead wife, the song of his heart, the woman whom their enemies had all too happily misidentified as her violet-haired sister. He'd been uninclined to seek out Leah or grieve with her, and distant when she lurked around. Rathos was furious with her—furious because she, like Jason, hadn't listened to him, furious because his anger had nowhere to go. His grief and fury never left him. Not when he slept, for however long he could. Not when he woke, sweat-drenched and wailing. He'd begun to worry that his rage, like a wildfire, would never, ever abate. That he'd burn eternally.

Tears clustered in her long eyelashes. "It's my fault," she said. "Just please, tell me . . . my hair . . . you warned me . . ." The realm's most feared outlaw wilted to her knees, clutching at his legs. She wanted forgiveness. Begged for it.

Rathos quickly helped her up. "Not here, not here, Leah," he shushed her. "The Mad Lady won't command her Heretics for long if she's seen like this, crying like a babe." He lifted her violet bangs out of her line of sight. "We'll need the Heretics, if Mina Sinclair is to find justice. Won't we?"

Her eyes darted past his shoulder. A string of audible "milords" strayed into hearing. The man of the hour trudged wearily uphill, past trees.

Besides, Leah, he thought, *you're not the only one I blame.*

The bastard prince looked as battered and defeated as Rathos felt, the result of a war they'd tried to prevent. Jason walked stiffly from a healing shoulder. Fresh sutures stapled the cuts to his handsome face and thick arms. He'd lost his right ear to the Stormsword, and with the sling of that bandage draping his right eye looked half-blind, not half-deaf. His raven hair seemed darker. His frayed gambeson sported dried blood, both his and not.

Jason comported himself with princely dignity. He bowed his head despite the pain he surely felt. "Lady Leah." He looked at the ward. "Rathos, a word?"

Leah folded her arms with a surly look, as if she'd planted her feet, and that was that. She resented Jason. He hadn't made time to meet with her or thank her for her invaluable role in the battle—mostly because he'd been wounded. More so, she blamed Jason for her father's capture.

Rathos smiled to defuse the awkwardness. "Lord Jason, without Leah and her Heretics, we wouldn't have rallied the peasants for the battle. They joined Sulley and his readers in visiting every shire we came across for a hundred miles. We exhausted ourselves. If you wish to speak, she should listen."

Jason looked as if he had trouble hearing. "I'm grateful—"

"It was the hooves of my horse that kicked Gram Sothos into the fire," Leah interjected. "While Warchild here lay abed, dreaming of foreign whores with golden hair." She flicked two fingers at him dismissively.

Jason's blue eye flickered from her back to Rathos. He refused her bait. "I *am* grateful. But this is a matter I'd discuss with Rathos, my lady. Alone."

She glanced at Rathos, checking him for signs of dismissal, which he gave with a curt look. She sighed, then strode toward Jason. She swung at his jaw, socking the bastard prince hard.

"I'm no lady, and you're no king, *cousin,*" Leah sneered. "Because of you, my father's head will decorate a spike."

She paid Rathos a look, then stalked off downhill, her violet ponytail swinging.

Jason touched his red bottom lip. "She hits like a man."

"Perhaps it's truth that hits harder." Rathos regarded him coolly. "What is this matter, Lord Jason?"

"Jason will do." His smile showed the blood on his teeth. "We're brothers in arms, now, you and me. Without you, the Stormsword would've skewered me, and we'd all be dead."

There is that. Rathos remembered expecting death, fires at his back and the realm's deadliest swordsman looming over him, before a sword pierced Thorngale's chest. "Edenia called us brothers, you know."

"Edenia's a lying traitor." The bastard prince spat.

Rathos nodded, glad to hear Jason say it in his own words. Before battle, speculation had been rife among peasants about whether the bastard prince meant to save Parlisis's daughter. "I owe you my life, Jason," he said. "Thank you."

Jason glanced away, as if embarrassed. "Don't thank me. Leah's right. It's because of me that we lost Lorana. Evan."

"You're not entirely to blame."

"I should've listened to you about Barbara's Gorge."

And there is that. "Yes, you should've. But we're small men, Jason. This twisted kingdom is bigger than you. Bigger than me. We did our best to deliver peace and justice. Evan tried for twenty years." He shrugged haplessly. "Our enemies care only for power, and they won."

Jason squinted as if he were reading lips. Rathos shook his head wearily, to put the matter to bed. "So what did you want to discuss, Jason?"

The bastard prince watched him dully. Rathos expected to repeat himself. "I need your help to save this kingdom, Rathos," his brother in arms said. "To dethrone these tyrants."

Rathos swung between emotions, from disbelief to grief, from exhaustion to anger. His hand quivered as he made a fist. He settled on a scornful, world-weary laugh.

"You didn't hear me," Rathos began crisply.

"Actually, I heard everything you said."

"Then hear this," Rathos said hotly. "I'm going to bury my wife's tarred head somewhere in this forest. I mean to find my sister, if she's alive. Then we'll leave for Tesos. Unless you want to lose your other ear, or your head, I advise you do the same. Once the Bull leaves, you'll be alone. Shaddon and Edenia won't stop until your head"—he poked his swaddled scalp, to bring his point home—"rots atop Traitor's Gate. Our parents died for the Common cause in an explosion. I'd rather not follow my father, or my wife . . . "

Or you, Evan, he thought darkly. *Will you ever forgive me for abandoning you? Will I ever be able to forgive myself?*

He circled about, reaching for his broth. Ants were busily scaling the bowl's sides, unaware that their comrades paddled their tiny legs fruitlessly on the surface.

"Shaddon and Edenia will kill Evan and trade my sisters," Jason went on. "They will grind to dust everyone in this realm who isn't with them. Then, Parlisis will use Loran to invade the Free Kingdoms. How long will you be safe in Tesos, then?"

"Long enough." Rathos overturned his bowl, watching as ants drained out with broth. "Trevor is abandoning you, Jason."

"We have a Common army."

Rathos scoffed. "Thousands of unarmored peasants can turn the tide of battle on a stretch of road. But in a siege? You won't have catapults, *and don't tell me that you'll go begging noble houses.*" He sliced the air with a wave of his hand. "Not a goddamn lord fought with us. Not even the ones with cause."

Jason stood firm. "I'm not talking about the bloody lords," he said.

"Before Evan exchanged himself, he told me that he'd had a hand in the revolts. Everything had been laid out before me, he'd said, and all I needed do was reach out"—he closed a fist, as if he clutched Evan Sinclair's elusive prize—"and take it." He came closer. "Rathos, *he told me about Barley Tower.*"

The charred lance of Blackfinger cut through him the way it sliced through crowded treetops, cut through doubt and fear and layered grief, everything hidden from him after Edenia had forced him to walk to freedom with his wife's cold, damp head in his hands. The head of the song of his heart, and it'd weighed less than a pumpkin . . .

Rathos denied himself hope, uneager to hope again, ever again. He measured the look in Jason's eyes with disdain and rage. *You fool, the lords and priests stole everything from you, and will take more, and . . . oh, Father . . . I could never . . .*

"Rathos," Jason said again, louder, as if *Rathos* were hard of hearing. "The tower. Is it true?"

"I don't . . ." Rathos suddenly felt lightheaded. "Evan told me he thought so. There was a parchment Evan said he found in the crypts. Years ago." He smiled grimly. "He said your king father lied to him about selling the blackpowder."

The bastard prince returned the smile. "He told lies when it came to love." He waxed serious. "Five hundred barrels, Evan told me. One was enough to blow Sunder Way to hell and scald Gram Sothos, even though he was inside a house."

Jason clasped his shoulder. "We won't have the Bull. But *Rathos . . .* if we have House Sinclair's great weapon . . ."

The man known as Silvertongue shook the hand off his shoulder. "You *will* need the Bull," he said. "And you'll need to address everyone. Tonight. Do everything I tell you. Can you do that, Jason, son of Hexar?"

The bastard smiled. There was hope in that smile. "I will."

"One more thing." Rathos unslung the bandage from his face, peeling off crusted blood. Jason shouted in pain.

Night fell over the forest, and with it a blanket of smoke, obscuring stars. Scythe Road's veterans crowded around the forest clearing. Those who couldn't find room on the grassy slopes filled the woodland. A wall of readers and Commoners encircled the space, shoulder to shoulder, looking down.

It made Jason feel as if he were in the Colossus's arena again, surrounded by Assemblymen. *Maybe these men will be Assemblymen,* he thought.

Scanning the clearing, Jason saw a sea of faces between the trees. Word had spread quickly. Several thousand people filled this forest tonight. He headed toward the four braziers aglow in the clearing.

Children followed him from camp like fascinated kittens, tugging at his hands. "King," a brown-haired girl kept prattling, as if the word had some magical enchantment, "king, king, king, king . . ."

The earless side of his head throbbed more intensely when he locked eyes with his champion. Trevor Wexley waited for him on a log like a god sitting in judgment, his thick black armor reflecting the fire's glow. He still looked wan from his wounds, but no less intimidating. Around him sat Ulbridge and Wexrenn, lesser lords, and knights with the mountain on their surcoats. Jason couldn't see any *scrorn-ner-gaith.*

Wexley had ordered his peasants to remain behind, on the grounds that he needed lookouts. The Bull didn't want his peasants mingling with Loran's peasants. There'd been enough of that.

Gently, Jason pried his hands free of the children. He strode into the clearing. His body ached terribly, as if a giant had stepped on him, but when he saw their faces—*all* their faces—he felt stronger. Taller.

Jason searched the faces for them. Rathos would stand with the Master Reader, who had the most important role to play tonight, but where were they? He remembered what his uncle's ward had told him. "Jacob is the key," he'd said on the hill. "If you can win his confidence tonight, you'll have the army we need."

We. He finally found his bruised brother in arms among the trees with Sulley. Rathos observed him intently, as if he were grading a student. *If only Matthus and Sarah could see us, Rathos. If only Evan could . . .*

Faintly, he heard a baby squalling somewhere. The world was quieter, would always be this quiet. Rathos had listened to him pitch his voice, correcting him like a teacher his pupil if he spoke too softly or loudly.

"A kingdom gathers here tonight," Jason said. Furrowed brows and squinting eyes told him that he'd practically rasped his delivery of the first line. He repeated himself. The approval he saw in Rathos's olive-green eyes steadied his confidence. "A war-weary kingdom. A very different realm from the one we knew under my king father."

Everyone's faces veered away, toward Sulley. He realized the Master Reader had interrupted him. Straining to hear, Jason overheard the last part: ". . . not so different at all. The peasants still have no voice in their Assembly."

Jason heard the livid shouts of agreement clearly. "Spoken truly by the man who rallied us all to Scythe Road." He pointed the spearhead of his hand at the religious leader. "Without the Master Reader, we would've certainly faced defeat at the hands of tyrants. The best among us gave their lives, or were never at all found."

Never at all found. His mind's eye drifted to Sam Hornby, the vanished Wall knight. No one had found Sam's body, and it was likely no one ever would as the wildfire spread. *All the men who followed me are dead or missing. You were right to keep the truth about bastard laws from me, Father.*

"I chose the Kingstrials after the king died to prevent war from happening." He spoke with his hands for emphasis. "The Worthy cursed me a Warchild at birth. I wanted to prove them wrong by seating Commoners among them and claiming my crown in the arena, as Willard the Wise wanted."

He allowed a dramatic pause, eyes roaming as he took in a forest of faces. He tapped his chest with his fists. "*I was wrong.* The Worthy may deem me a bastard, but my father raised me to be a prince at the Silver Walls. A silverstone aura obscured the star of reason from me, and I couldn't see its light. Not until now." He checked the smoky skies with a fleeting glance. Stars blinkered through.

"What does the star of reason's light show you now, Lord Jason?" Sulley asked with a critical look. He barely heard him.

Jason let his hands fall to his sides. "We live in a kingdom of wolves." Evan had called Loran that, the day he was traded for his daughter's head and her pulpy-faced husband. "Do we bargain with wolves?" he asked his audience. When he didn't hear an answer, he shouted out, "DO YOU BARGAIN WITH WOLVES THAT WOULD EAT YOU?"

"NO," Rathos cried down. The lash of his voice raised a scatter of noes, some more forceful than others.

"*Do you ask wolves for seats in their den?*" Jason cried out.

"NO!" more peasants cried as one, fervently. The thunder of their voices sent lords like Wexrenn to trembling. Their liege rested iron-hard eyes on Jason, unintimidated.

"*Do you ask the wolves to spare your children,*" Jason went on, exhorting with a hand, "*OR DO YOU KILL THE BEASTS?*"

"WE KILL THE BEASTS," a chorus answered him. Some simply cried, "WE KILL THEM!" *I've lost an ear,* Jason thought, *but I can hear more clearly than I ever have.*

"And so we will." Jason paced between crackling braziers. "A false king and queen sit Anjan Half-Elf's Silver Walls. Rather than play the Kingstrials, or stand and fight, these cowards of the Lonely Isle seized power and ran. They didn't just steal the Trials from me." He pointed at the myriad faces.

Before he could even finish, a thousand peasants and men of cloth shouted as one, "*THEY STOLE THEM FROM US!*" "*Turel e'sartha!*" men chanted the Worthy Assembly's ancient motto. "*Turan e'sparta!*" many more finished full-throatedly. "Sara of Rosbury!" a woman's ragged scream summited the clamor, as if she honored the martyr with her final breath.

"We will take back what is yours," Jason swore to them. "We shall surround the city of light and shadow. We shall lay siege to the First King's castle and starve out usurpers. And if you deem me worthy of my father's seat, my countrymen, I'll decree you Worthy of yours."

Amid the roars of approval, Rathos stepped into the light, uncurling his hand at Jason like a gargoyle on his perch. "We've heard promises before," he called out. "From Lord Evan's Loyal Company. From Lord Tomas Fawkes . . . from you, Lord Jason."

Jason flushed slightly. Rathos had told him to anticipate unfriendly queries as he steered the people like a ship rudder, but he hadn't expected to feel undermined. *Evan said the Loyal Company called you Silvertongue, and I see why*, he mused.

Rathos eyed the Cloudlanders. "But what of the lord who followed you east? Will *he* fight for the Wing of the Commons?"

The din of an excited crowd dwindled to murmurs. The peasants riveted their gazes to the great bearded lord known for treating his own folk like shit crusted to his heel.

Trevor Wexley sat hunched over, huge hands clasped together. He watched Jason as warily as a wolf. His vassals stiffened expectantly. The world was quiet for Jason, but he imagined that with two ears he'd only hear embers popping.

Jason took a step toward Wexley. "The Worthy named me a bastard, and the Kingstrials' law against bastards was clear," he said. "I needed a champion. I fought a trial by sword for this lord before you. I am indebted to Lord Trevor for mustering his *Hathrimnyr*. For shedding his own blood for my claim." Rathos had told him to pepper his address with pauses, and he did so now. "Yet there is a mistrust between lords of the Cloudlands and their Commoners."

"*Scrorn-ner-gaith!*" someone's voice carried. It sounded like a boast, as if *scrorn-ner-gaith* were a noble title, a war cry.

"Centuries of mistrust," Jason said again, speaking with his hands. *A mistrust deepened by the Grand Inquisitor, a traitor.* "Centuries of mistrust that I can't heal or resolve, even if I were king. I've spoken with Lord Trevor. The Cloudlands will never be part of a realm where peasants law-make with their lords."

The forest snarled with curses and jeers, with the fury of a people done with hateful lords. "*Go back,*" they said, "*make them go back!*" Jason pumped his palms at the woods, urging calm in all directions.

"And they will," he vowed, "after they've helped us tear down these tyrants. Cloudlanders will not be our countrymen, but our allies. Our not-so-silent friends." Jason lingered on his father's Bull. "Trevor Wexley, help me take my father's crown and seat the Commons. I would not name you Lord Paramount of Eddenloxley, the Cloudlands, and Eddenwood, but see you on your own great throne. I'd have the Cloudlands rise as the fourteenth kingdom, with you as its king. *Will you fight for the Kingdom of Loran, Trevor the First, King of the Cloudlands?*"

The great lord lumbered up. He walked toward Jason, fixing him with his stare. "Only if you swear that Charles Burke will hang," his growl resonated through his chest.

Jason allowed a small, grim smile. "A Warchild's word is stronger than swordwood."

The first king of the Cloudlands in millennia reached for the hilt at his side and drew his massive sword. "We shall be kings, you and I," Wexley said in his thick rhotic accent. He spun on the faces in the forest, his sword held high, gleaming in firelight. "*The Cloudlands will see Loran freed from tyranny!*"

There was scattered applause, and almost entirely from Wexley's vassal lords. Peasants themselves had no love of the north's tyrant. Yet all Loranians had wanted the Cloudlands to return to the fold, for the kingdom to become whole again. It was bittersweet to formalize Hexar's Folly . . .

But it was necessary. Coupled with the revolt, rallying peasants and outlaws to the battle had strained their alliance to the breaking point. Jason and Rathos needed Wexley for his *Hathrimnyr* and his friendship with Barley Tower's castellan, without whom they wouldn't recover the blackpowder. They didn't need an icy, mountainous land, however beautiful.

Jacob Sulley and the men in gray linen lining the slopes stared down icily. Rathos had told him they'd receive Wexley's kingship like a defeat. Many readers present had served in the Loyal Company as Reubenites, and they'd seen Jason's alliance with Wexley as a betrayal of the *scrorn-ner-gaith*. Which it was. With the Cloudlands securing independence, that betrayal was set in stone, and Jason would have to live with it.

That wasn't even the hardest part about tonight.

Sulley navigated down a shrub-strewn slope. With his stubbled scalp and gaunt, pale appearance, the Master Reader seemed a specter, floating toward Jason. Dressed in the rags of gray linen, a belt of rope around his waist, that specter looked like just another threadbare reader . . . not the most important man in the forest tonight.

The man on spiritual footing with priestkings regarded Jason stonily. "Lord Jason, you were not my first choice in the Kingstrials," he said. "That was Tomas Fawkes, may the One True God bless and keep him. Many readers were sworn to you, but we would've rallied for any man who lifted his sword against the Lonely Isle's tyrant. The tyrant who pilfered Loran like a cheap bauble for his twelve false gods."

Jason felt the weight of the forest's stares.

A line creased the Master Reader's forehead. "You lifted not a sword but laurels, and you set them on the head of the priestking's daughter," he said with an edge to his voice. "The high priestess who calls herself queen of a kingdom, equal to the false king himself." He tilted his shaven head slightly. "We stood with you in the battle, Lord Jason, but we will not suffer Shaddon, nor anyone who claims to love Edenia Highdaughter. Do you understand?"

"Yes," Jason replied.

"Have you ever loved the priestking's daughter?"

In the periphery of his eyes, he saw Rathos, watching. "As a friend, years ago, but that time is past," Jason answered. *That time is past,* he reaffirmed to himself. *You betrayed me, Edenia. You betrayed us all. And for that, I will not save you.*

Sulley arched his eyebrows. "Do you love her?"

Jason spat. "No. I despise her. I regret having ever named her the

Virgin of Venas, this priestess who married a kingkiller. I'd see her head on Traitor's Gate."

The night erupted with applause and bellowed chants, "*TRAITOR'S GATE! TRAITOR'S GATE!*"

Sulley could've well been as deaf as Jason. He remained cool and collected, waiting until the shouts died down. "Do you reject and renounce the false queen Edenia Highdaughter," he asked in a hard, rising voice, "her father the priestking, the false king Shaddon, and any claim by their evil religion on this kingdom?"

"By the Wing of the Commons and the One True God, I do," Jason said as jubilation mounted. He strode past Sulley to address the faces in the forest. "Twenty-one years ago, lords and priests marched on Southpoint with an Army of the Gods. *I WILL MARCH WITH AN ARMY OF THE PEOPLE!*"

Jason didn't need perfect hearing. He listened to the night roar its excitement, felt the cries rip through his chest like fire. "*The Army of the People!*" hundreds cried over each other. "*THE ARMY OF THE PEOPLE!*" Hundreds more echoed them, until the entire forest chanted the name for his army, waves on waves of voices, repeating it as one.

The king of the Cloudlands and his lords drew fire-gleamed swords. "*Jason, king of Loran!*" the Bull bellowed. Ulbridge, Wexrenn, and the lords shouted for King Trevor.

On the surround, Jason saw the Mad Lady and her men, and Rathos himself, traversing the slope. He handed a thistle-twined circlet of sticks and leaves to Sulley, and Jason knelt for the Master Reader to lay it on his head.

Jason couldn't hear Rathos over the clamor, but he read his lips. "A crown for the people's protector," he said, serious-eyed and smiling.

CHAPTER 37

A Name

I remember this fondly, Sinclair. You and me, working on questions together. This time's no different. Give me a name—one name—and I'll stop this."

Stop this. The Grand Inquisitor's offer of mercy unraveled in Evan Sinclair's head like a spool of thread. Sweat pelted his chapped lips, tasting acidic.

"We'll have you down, washed and fed, returned to your chamber, I promise. Just one name, Sinclair. One sign of good faith for me to show your king."

Washed and fed. His cold, rat-infested chamber sounded as wonderful as a plush feathered bed. *The world would stop spinning, at least.* Gods of his fathers, he needed the spinning done with. Every spasm sent uncontrollable shudders through his body, twisting the chain so that he revolved like a trussed-up goose in a butcher's stall. A fire burned below him, scalding his feet. He'd remember then, after the throbbing lessened in his calves and arms, after the crushing dull emptiness vacated his skull, after the searing pain faded from his spine, only then, that there wasn't a fire below him at all.

The question of whether there was drove him to the edge of madness. Why else could he smell singed flesh, and why the unbearable burning in his legs? *I can't lose my reason, I can't, I can't, not like her,* he thought in desperate ruminations. *A star, Gram Reuben called it the star of reason. Dumas said my star never truly shone alone.* But he felt alone. Truly alone.

"How much more can a man of your age endure?"

Evan unclenched his eyes. He dangled above a blood-red floor by a length that felt like miles. *Where am I? Oh, yes . . .* He remembered again. *The Dread Chamber.*

He hung suspended from a chain hook by a rope binding his wrists behind his back. If he receded from consciousness, an Intercessor would tug on a pulley, and he'd surface from delirium, screaming.

How long he'd been in the Dread Chamber, he couldn't be sure. Hours? Days? *No, not days, it couldn't have been that long.* He couldn't feel his arms anymore. Nor his swollen, purple feet. A giant pressed his knee into his back, crushing his spine. Each breath scalded his lungs like fire. But it was the loss of feeling in his hands that hurt most. With his hands he'd labored on his atelier, his Moon Tower and Sun Tower.

He'd never build anything again.

But the delirium . . . the visions. Those were almost as painful as the dangling.

"Are you still with us, Sinclair?" Burke asked raptly. He enjoyed this. "Is your star of reason guiding you?"

The pain felt excruciating, but Evan understood what was happening. It helped to consider consequences abstractly. The pulley system worked by dislocating his shoulders, breaking his arms, stretching what wasn't meant to stretch. If he lived—*if* being the key word—he'd never eat or dress himself again without assistance.

Let my death come quickly, he pled to any god or gods listening. *Let me go to the ones I love and beg forgiveness . . .*

The Grand Inquisitor sipped mulled wine. He wiped wine from the tuft of his beard and returned his cup to a table piled with nightmarish devices.

"Do you hear me, Evan?" Burke asked. "Give me a name. One name. I'll loosen the chain, and we'll have you down and ask these questions gently."

There is no gentleness in you, Burke. You worked with Gram Sothos to kill the king. He struggled to speak. Burke leaned in close, pressing his ear forward with a finger.

"Sunox," Evan said.

"Dumas will join you here soon, Evan. Give me a name that would shock me. Petor Ellsby? Sam Gramlore?"

Evan spat on his face.

Burke mopped the blood off with a cloth. Evan reeled round the edges of sanity as his torturer called for iron balls—no, not the ones weighing one stone, the ones weighing two. *Sarah,* he thought as his world spun, *oh, Sarah . . .*

He awoke to Intercessors clasping iron weights around his ankles, faded again, and then fell so sharply he thought the Red Tower was collapsing. He'd never imagined pain like this existed. Twisting, Evan screamed silently. *Kill me. Kill me.*

"A name," Burke said. "I want a Companyman. Refuse me, and we'll add more weights. This time, four stone."

"L . . . eah," Evan rasped. "You . . . killed . . ."

No, the Mad Lady lives. 'Twas Mina they took from me. My firstborn. The child I left as steward. The flame of resistance, of hatred for all the rulers of this realm, burned through him. He cursed Burke and Shaddon and the prieslenne, Gram Sothos most of all. He named as saints every man and woman who'd burn this kingdom with revolts. It was what Evan had wanted. *Give them what they bloody deserve, the king, the lords, the—*

A white-hot flash of pain wiped his mind. He slid back in time, eyelids fluttering uncontrollably.

Evan opened his eyes. He stood in the Sun Tower. Faye reclined in a rocking chair by the window, singing a lullaby as she suckled their infant daughter on her breast. Her dark hair turned lavender in sunlight.

"Isn't she beautiful?" Faye smiled serenely as she cradled their cooing newborn, the picture of a new mother. A good one. "Dana. I want to call her Dana."

Evan sighed the sigh of a husband conceding. "Mina, Leah, Dana. All our girls have names that end with an *ah* sound."

"A name, Sinclair," Burke said.

He inhaled sharply, sputtering. "Daugh . . . t-ter."

The Grand Inquisitor raised himself on his toes, close to Evan's right ear. "If it were up to me, I would've done more to your purple-haired daughter than behead her. It isn't right for people of land and sea to mix." He shrugged. "But a mistake was made. An honest mistake. The king sought to behead Sir Matthus's son, but Queen Edenia, well—she wanted to make an example of someone said to lead Heretics. She didn't know she had the wrong daughter."

Evan choked on grief. *A mistake. They killed my daughter mistakenly.* Rage shook his body. Spittle flecked his lips.

"Give me a name for the king," Burke said, "and I'll give you reprieve from these weights." He placed a foot on an iron ball, splitting Evan asunder.

Reopening his eyes, Evan discovered himself at the helm of a jostling carriage. He heard laughter from inside. *Thick as thieves, those two.* His father had tolerated Matthus on account of his friendship with Evan, but he'd never liked him. "Once a thief, always a thief," his father often told him, ignoring Evan's complaints. "So it is with peasants."

But the truth was that the elder Lord of Caerdon disliked how easily Sarah laughed around Matthus.

Sarah leaned out of the window, tangles of her raven hair frolicking. "Matt would give you reprieve, brother," she said with a mischievous smile. "Let him take the reins. You must save me from him—*oh!*" She giggled as two burly arms swept her inside.

You've never wanted saving, least of all from him, Evan thought contentedly. *But I'll stop it when we see Southpoint's walls. Matthus will understand.* She was the object of Hexar's desire now, not the queen consort.

A jerk on the pulley, and he reemerged from an ocean of memory, drenched in sickly sweat. He sucked in air, as much as his lungs could take.

"Speak a name, Sinclair. Your Loyal Company proved that it wasn't loyal. Why protect them? What has it earned you?"

Fire fumed up his torso. His eyelids fluttered.

Evan swung open the carriage door, his sister's protests in his ears. The sun hung brightly in the sky, catching on the roofs of houses and stalls along the dusty, crowded road. He wanted nothing more than to return to Caerdon, but that was impossible now. It was life in another kingdom, or death.

The other carriage door clapped shut. Steaming toward him, his best friend jerked him close by the front of his silken shirt. Lord and knight had dressed as merchants to blend in on Sunder Way. This wasn't helping.

". . . donna get to walk away," Matthus Robswell snarled in his face. The peasant knight was a handsome fellow, lean and strong-jawed. He was a hard sight when angry, as he was now, his mouth a grave line under his moustache. "Nah from me . . . nah from her. I know your moods. Face me, you fuckin' snake."

Evan was in no mood. For three days, they'd simmered in silence, mostly, with occasional flare-ups, and only Sarah there to keep the peace. He shoved his knight off. They were drawing troubled looks and asides.

"Get. Back. Inside." The young lord pointed a finger in his face. At Caerdon Castle, the menace in his voice would've sent a knight or servant scurrying. At Caerdon, he had power.

Matthus had a left hand that flew like the wind, and its blur sent Evan tumbling down. The silver leaves of Matthus's ring had cut his jaw, and he pulled away red fingers. Evan had given him that ring.

Matthus shook his head wearily. "You made a devil's bargain. You risked her life. *Our* lives. What has it earned us?"

"It was her choice as much as mine," Evan said.

"Everything's a game piece to you, isn't it, Evan?" Matthus cracked his knuckles. "Do you even know what love is?"

On the roadside opposite them was a rustic house. The glint of something lured Evan's gaze to its open window. *No.*

"A name, Sinclair," Burke insisted presently. "Just one."

Evan shut and opened his eyes. There it was again, the reek of burned skin. The spicy smell of blackpowder. A black tower of smoke fumed the skies over Sunder Way. Believing them dead, he took the lives of any surviving archers.

Then, he heard his sister.

Nameless Commoners helped him sift through the smoldering black ruin. Matthus's hand protruded from the burning woodpile, the ring with two snakes still on his finger. Traces of blood from Evan's jaw gleamed in its elegant silver leaves.

The moments that followed had blurred together, and so they did now, the memory he had of carrying the black ruin of her flesh on a makeshift litter. Without even knowing who he was, an older peasant named Jason had offered to take them to his hut.

"My wife's a midwife," Jason, of Sunder Way, stammered out as they stumbled through Eastland's weedy flatlands. Every twist of the fabric nearly toppled his poor sister. "She might be able to save the child. Maybe your sister, too . . ."

At the hut, they splayed her out on a bed of hay. His sister, a noble lady, the Most-Sought Hand in the Thirteen Kingdoms, writhed as the peasant and his midwife wife applied damp rags to the tatters of her raw, black skin. As her breaths slipped out raggedly, Evan began to understand. He'd lose her tonight. He'd lose her and the child both.

Pus oozed from the burns that festered on her arms and legs, her unobtrusive chin and slender cheeks. The raven-black hair men loved to run their fingers through, so thick, clung to her mottled scalp in strands. Hexar would've only recognized Sarah Sinclair by her blue eyes.

God forgive me. And may you forgive me, Sarah . . .

"Milord, I fear for her soul," he remembered hearing from one of the tagalong peasants, a gentle, well-meaning person. "A reader woulda read her the rites. I know Reader Harold—"

Evan didn't remember what he growled then, only that it was enough to make the tagalong leave immediately. Until that moment, he'd been lukewarm with religion. After this night, he'd know no faith, and inwardly scoff at priests and readers.

Sarah's chest fluttered rapidly, and the midwife had no remedies, nothing but half a skin of bitter wine. Evan snatched it from her, supported his sister's neck as he tilted her head, dribbled wine between the pulp of her lips. Absent its sheath, the dagger he'd used to avenge his knight nicked his thigh; he cast belt and blade to the ground.

"A name."

Kneeling, Evan clutched his sister's hand, urged her to push, *push for his sake,* as the midwife reported seeing the bulge of a wispy head. He expected a stillborn, but they had to try. *Nothing can have been for nothing.* Sarah cried in agony. She cried his name, the name of her beloved.

The child came into the world screaming. A boy he was, toes wriggling, splotched with blood, his scalp matted with his father's brittle hair, squinty eyes green like olives. Such a voice he had. The midwife used Evan's dagger to sever the umbilical cord, then whisked the infant into her arms, swaddling him.

Now for the hard part, Evan thought. "I'd be alone with her," he commanded Jason with glassy eyes. "Give us space."

He heard no response. His anger quickened when he saw the peasant still kneeling, gawking at his sister's sex. After the day's horrors, the noble confused his silence with perversion. In that moment, everyone seemed a possible enemy.

"We're nah done here yet," Jason said, eyes widening. He stood briskly and swept the babe from his wife, who resumed her position on hard-packed earth, as startled as her husband. Evan stared like an idiot, unbelieving.

"A name, Sinclair. Just one, and we'll free you tonight."

Eyes opening, Evan turned on his rope. Ghouls added four more stone to his already-strained ankles. *Free . . .*

Night had fallen on the hut in the wilderness. All the world seemed populated by nothing but screeching crickets. Jason had exited through the door of their spotted deerskins. The midwife—he couldn't recall her name, then or any day since, regrettably—stayed to help. She had to.

Evan couldn't hold them both.

He stroked the patch of raven-black hair on the second one's head. His eyes were also hers, sea-blue. The first babe had squalled a storm, up until his brother's birth.

But this one, the one in his arms, perked with a smile that reminded Evan that love still existed.

I love them both, Evan thought, grief and joy swirling inside him. The babe curled a pudgy little finger about his thumb. *But if I was forced to choose one . . .*

He raised his eyes from the babe. His sister's chest had a racing flutter now. She wasn't her, wasn't Sarah Sinclair, just a tender pink shell patterned with tar-black splotches, strings of hair glued to her scalp. Yet when her eyes opened, she was his sister, the sister he'd known before the war.

"Brother." She had a surprisingly calm voice. She sounded . . . alert. Self-aware, even. It was remarkable. It was *her.*

"Sarah?" Evan told the midwife to fetch her husband, to hand off the second babe. She'd live, his sister would live. It'd be a miracle. *The miracle of Sunder Way,* he thought.

Sarah propped herself up on her hands, seemingly oblivious to pain. "I'd hold him," she said.

Evan traded looks with the peasants. "Sarah . . . sister . . . please, lie down—"

"*Please.* Evan." She spoke with the confidence of someone with days ahead yet, without laboring her breaths. "My son."

"Which . . . which one?" He chuckled as tears spilled down his cheeks. "The gods gave you twins, sister."

In the mask of her dark, crusty face, blue eyes darted from one infant to the other. "The one with his eyes."

"A name," his tormentor demanded.

Tears should've gathered in her eyelashes, but shorn them, they fell instantly, dabbing her scalded chest as she rocked the first child gently, to and fro.

Sarah lightened with a smile. "He's him," she told Evan.

She squeezed the child against her bosom, as snugly as if he were his father. Still smiling, she handed him off. Seconds later, Evan lowered the other child, the one with her sapphire eyes.

"A name."

It happened fast, his sister snatching his dagger, arching it over her head for a thrust at the infant's belly. The midwife had enough wits about, and she paid for her quickness with a stab wound, and yet still made safe the screaming babe.

Sarah fought her, then Evan, cursing him, cursing them all to hell. He wrenched away their father's silver-hilted blade, its eight-pointed star spotted with blood. Somehow, the husband balanced both infants in his arms as his woman stanched the blood sheeting down her arm. The infants wailed hysterically, drowning out the noise of crickets.

Sarah wasn't Sarah. She stared at the second babe as if he were an intruder. A stranger. A threat. The rage contorting the black pork of her face made her seem a demon, not his sister. That was what Jason began to accuse her of being—a demon.

Ignoring the peasant, Evan went to her side, tears on his cheeks as he tried to ease her down. This moment was horror atop horror. *She's in pain, she can't see reason,* he thought.

She shoved him away, weeping and twisting her lips with a snarl. "They spoke to me in the fire," she said, chest heaving, as if from panic. "The brothers. They will bring ruin and death to our kingdom. To the world. Until everything we love burns."

Evan couldn't recall her every word after that, the drivel of a woman wracked by pain and dying.

What he remembered of her madness would chase him into his nightmares, burning images into his retinas that he saw again on waking. Tongues of flame leaping from the First King's castle, liquefying forests of steel. Crowned men who fell screaming into the throats of white-eyed giants so enormous they dwarfed mountains.

And above all, her final words. "The brothers," she said, eyes wide at her sons. "*The brothers.*"

"Give me a name, Sinclair, or you risk dying tonight."

But I'm dead already, Evan thought. *I died when she died.*

Evan cradled his sister close to his chest, listening as she begged forgiveness. She pled to kiss the infant she had sought to bleed. She begged forgiveness from her newborn sons.

The young nobleman denied his dying sister. He had to. He wept and cursed gods he could no longer say existed for this . . . this final horror.

Still in his arms, Sarah beckoned him close. "I'm a coward, a wicked and evil mother, I can't do what I was asked, I—I love him too much," she whimpered. Her eyes had begun to mist.

Sunlight found the nobleman still clutching his sister. The light glistened on her black brow like a crown. She hadn't been able to wear a crown as consort to a king . . . but a wild thought took root in his grief.

One day, one of her line *could*.

"Give me a name," Burke said, "and I will end your pain."

Evan gave him two.

CHAPTER 38

Home

ircling lower and lower, the griffon touched down on a bald dusty hilltop crowned with pine trees, scattering leaves with stormwind from his wings.

The creature was the size of a carriage, and yet landed as gracefully as any bird. His less nimble rider would've tumbled off if not for the muscled tail snug about his waist. One second, he clenched oily feathers as tightly as if they were reins, gluing himself to the beast's backside. He moved weightlessly through the air, suddenly, to blessed earth, where the tail uncoiled and left him lurching on his feet.

Zuran fell to his knees in the dirt, retching. He wanted to kiss the ground. He rolled onto his back, squinting through the sunlight, warm sunlight that had never felt so welcome on his skin. He flexed fingers stiff from hours of exposure to bone-chilling wind. He picked at a mask of snot crusted over what felt like his entire face. His head pounded like an anvil under a hammer's blows.

He was cold, groggy, miserable, terrified . . .

Yet he would ride again, if his majestic mount wished it.

The griffon did not seem to wish it. After some preening, the king of the skies scanned their surroundings, folded his wings, and descended downhill, wearily.

Zur could barely stand, and he walked so bowlegged he wondered if he'd ever walk normally again. He craved sleep. Yet he couldn't lose sight of the griffon. He half-ran to catch up with his mount as his bulk sauntered through woodland.

Where are we? He looked out on an endless forest. There was nothing north, south, east, or west but woodland sloping with green hills. A grassy mountain ruled the horizon, covered in mist.

As much as was possible with his face buried in oily fur and feathers, he'd tracked their journey through the night sky by following the Lame King's brightest star, as Drexan had taught him. They'd flown north, that was all he knew for sure.

Could we be in the Cloudlands? Zur fought down a feeling of unease. The Cloudlands lords had a bleak reputation when it came to dealing with men from Loran proper. *But Cloudlanders are better than shadowkings,* he thought, *and they hate peasants more than they would Casaanites.*

The griffon advanced sluggishly, head low and grunting. Occasionally, he halted to suck at shallow puddles, or, more curiously to Zur, to gnaw on tree trunks and rake his beak against the bark. Like vassals paying homage, all life gave wide berth: squirrels skittered up trees, a family of deer loped off, and jays and thrushes scattered.

If the skies have a king, you truly are him, Zur thought as he studied his savior. It'd been a disservice to view the griffon by moonlight. The animal was magnificent. Rich, dark, brown fur bushed his muscular forearms, hind legs, thick tail, and backside; black feathers coated everything else. *And I am in your debt.*

The ground swelled into a sprawling hillside the griffon scaled easily. Zur followed with shins and calves that burned ceaselessly. At times he halted to rest his back against a tree, intaking air like an old man, but the beast continued his ascent, merciless, as if they had an appointment to keep. Nervous that his protector could desert him, Zur hastened to keep pace.

On and on went the agonizing climb. Waning sunlight cast the sky in lavender and light pink. An intoxicatingly sweet, rich smell perfumed the air, thickening with every step. Zur fell into a ten-minute sneezing fit that kept his eyes watery. He rubbed his temple, wondering if he sensed a headache coming.

He might've admired the beauty around him, were it not for the sneezing . . .

If he didn't fear nightfall, and what could come with it.

Uther Brune was still out there somewhere. It chilled him to remember the shadowking's shrill, inhuman scream.

You rescued me from danger once, he thought with a look at the griffon's golden eye. *How long will you stay with me?*

He was pondering his options when they finally crested the hill. Here, he had a commanding view of the wilderness.

Specks of birds swirled around the summit of the grass-covered mountain, and it took a moment, a heady one, before Zur realized that all those specks were griffons, and that the mountain he'd been eyeing all day was no mountain at all but the crown of a tree.

A Great Tree.

Neither that name nor a name like the Mother of Trees did her any justice.

From the forest floor rose a vast, fluted trunk feathered in the colors of a rainbow. It resembled the cone of an evergreen tree, only a thousand feet high and rippled in leaves of autumn gold and red, spring green, and rich lavender. Up its immense boughs climbed a cavalry of pale and mottled griffons, sinking the ice axes of their talons into the bark, and past and all about them fluttered tens of thousands of birds. Below, massive roots snaked through a spindly woodland starved of sunlight.

The Great Tree had stoked his allergies. Everything smelled of magnolia blooms and wildflowers and, faintly, mangoes.

It was a beautiful, life-affirming sight. Sacred.

Tears blurred his vision, from the almost insufferable sweetness of the smell as much as from joy. *I'm here, Drexan,* he thought. *I'm here, just as you wanted.* He rubbed his eyes with his forearms.

Eyes adjusting, Zur found himself deserted.

He stumbled downhill, catching sight of the griffon as the beast worked up to a thunderous run. The animal opened his wings and took flight, soaring into the gloom of the Great Tree's canopy.

Zur ran after him. "*Wait!*" he cried. "Don't leave—"

Something whistled past his head.

Whirling about, Zur discovered an arrowhead pointed in his face.

He backed off, tripped on a rock, and fell, landing crab-like on his hands and feet.

He'd feared Uther Brune, but this was a boy—a *Casaanite*. He had an archer's lean, muscular build. That jagged scar down his right cheek made him look wild, and a few years his senior. He wore a scarlet tunic over breeches of roughspun. Zur's eyes traveled from the quiver of arrows at his shoulder to the sword and dagger cinched at his waist.

The boy tightened his grip on his longbow. "Whom do you serve?" he demanded. "Kings, mobs, or the Nagarthessi?"

"I serve but one king," Zur said after a pause. "And if you saw who led me here, you'd be wise to lower that arrow."

A crooked smile worked across the boy's face. "Please. Slytail won't harm me."

"Sir Femi, you're being a rude little shit," shot a voice. "He's expected and you know it."

Sir? Femi lowered his longbow with a long eye-roll. Zur glanced in the voice's direction, at their kinswoman, where she stood in the shadow of one of the Great Tree's towering roots. Wide in the hips and lean, she had a pretty oval face drizzled in braids dyed red as the morning sun. She dressed like a boy, in grass-stained breeches and a leather jerkin laced up the middle that teased a generous look at her cleavage. Zur burned under her caramel gaze.

"You spoil everything, Abeba." Femi sighed. "This one said Slytail would save him. I wanted to test that theory." He slung his bow over his chest, pulled his arrow from the tree it'd hit, and helped Zur up.

Zur flickered from the boy to the girl. "Are you . . . are you of Tribe Nuur? Are you like me?"

"They are of Tribe Chandiwe," came another voice, from his left. A voice from a dream. "And *no one* is like you, Zuran."

He turned to face the only Casaanite in Loran whom a king and his Assemblymen treated with fear and respect, the woman whom Drexan told him had known his mother.

Lady Orella looked exactly as she'd appeared to him at Rorn Abeth, an older, stout woman, stooped in her shoulders and draped in a hooded cloak. Freckles dappled her nose and thick cheeks.

She pulled back her hood, releasing black ringlets of hair edged in silver. Warm, cunning brown eyes met his—eyes that could guide boys like him out of nightmares.

"Under the stars he comes," she said with a warm smile.

She speaks as Drexan and Eric the Tall spoke to each other. "You . . . You spoke to me at Rorn Abeth." Zur bowed his head belatedly. "*You're the Oracle.*"

Orella nodded. "And you are Zuran of the Silver Walls, of the Tribe Nuur. I saw you in the old cave, from my own dreams. We have been expecting you . . . kingfinder."

Kingfinder. His eyes moistened with the remembrance of his unwelcome tidings. "My lady, Lord Drexan Lorrain, he was leading me here and . . . and . . ."

"Drexan Lorrain gave his life so that you could reach us," she interrupted him, "and it was not in vain." She spread her arms, as if to encompass the withered forest behind her, the Great Tree looming above. "Here you shall be safe, as safe as anyone can be now that the foe of elves and men walks the earth again. Yet we are not alone in our fight against the dark brothers."

She pointed her finger up, at the Great Tree's sprawling canopy. Griffons ambled along its gigantic limbs. Larger than his brethren, Slytail navigated a limb with catlike grace, his distant golden eyes fixed in Zur's direction.

"You . . . you sent the griffon for me," Zur understood.

"More like I nudged him," the Oracle admitted. "Away from the madness of revolution, south to the metal forest, where a boy taken from his people and raised at a foreign castle needed his strength."

It dawned on him that she wasn't pointing at the Great Tree at all, but at early evening sky—at the Lame King and a scatter of stars he'd first seen above Graywood.

"Be glad, Zuran," Orella said. "The Repentant Huntsman comes—and so have you."

Today is Summer Solstice, the day of gifts, he realized. For Zur, his gift was this very moment, the one he'd wanted all his life.

"I rode like a Windrider," Zur said with slow realization. "I'm a Barefoot Knight." *Just as you wanted, Drexan.*

Femi burst into laughter. Abeba covered her smile, as if embarrassed.

The old woman clasped his shoulder. "Not yet, Zuran of Nuur. First, we must teach you the power of our blood. Then, you will help us find the Ascendant King. You will ride beside him through clouds like a mounted knight through field. And together," she added with a look full of promise, of expectation, "you will liberate our people."

Zur gazed up at the constellations. *I'm home.*

Epilogue

outhpoint was silent.

David Renworth stood perfectly still in the putrid dark of the catacombs, a shadow among torchlit shadows, listening. The mayor was taking his city's pulse.

Any other summer day, he'd catch the rumor of muffled voices, wheels clacking on cobbles, the laughter of children. He'd hear parish and temple bells tolling.

David heard nothing aboveground. No bells. No wagon wheels. No shuffling feet. No voices bellowing prices. None of the familiar, restless, comforting chaos. Southpoint had no pulse.

He heard only the torch spitting from its sconce, the gurgling of water at his feet. *It's like before,* thought the mayor. *The last time the city was this quiet, an army was marching on us . . . and I had a choice before me.* He held the portcullis of his livery collar, waxing his thumb over its dimpled ironwork. *Amath, give me a better choice today.*

He waited on someone. By his count, he'd been waiting at least three hours underground. They called him Little King, and it bothered him immensely that he had to idle in the muck of the catacombs. Even Lorana Eddenhold wouldn't have tried the peasant mayor's patience like this.

But he'd wait on his friend, his ally, as he had for twenty years.

His life now rested in this man's hands.

You were right, Your Highness, he thought, as if they were talking, and she wasn't a captive somewhere. *I should've closed the city to your uncle and the prieslenne. But I had my orders . . . for I learned the price of betrayal when your mother lost her head. Choices, you see.*

His decision twenty years ago to shut Southpoint to the Army of the Gods, to condemn Alyse Jannus to Hexar's mercy, had saddled him with an unpayable debt. It'd cost the mayor a priestking's favor, barred him from his religion's temples, and enslaved him to a dangerous cult that could sneak a dagger past his handpicked city guard.

Now Alyse Jannus's beheading looks like to cost me my office, or my life, David mused grimly, glancing in an echo's direction. *Whichever King Shaddon desires more.*

One week past, David had gathered with his city guard to greet the new king and his pretty young queen outside East Gate. Ahorse, thousands of the Worthy Assembly's men-at-arms had swarmed out of Sarah's Forest, accompanied by Intercessors.

All smiles and bows, the Little King had signed the diamond and oozed with every courtesy payable to a new monarch, rightful or not. He'd even told him that the city—*his* city—was his.

David might as well have not existed. With a truly singular air of contempt, Shaddon had looked away, refusing to make eye contact. His stony gaze had settled on a city guardsman. "Is there anyone in this rat's nest of a city with the courtesy to greet his rightful king?" he'd demanded of the milk-pale guard, a man suddenly forced to choose between two kings.

One snub hadn't been enough, naturally. It was traditional for Southpoint's mayor to ride behind the new king when he entered the capital. But as the procession began, Their Majesties clarified through that lickspittle Sam Gramlore that David would walk on foot with the servants, at the rear, as befitting his low birth.

Passing through East Gate, he'd meditated on the source of his power, which encircled this rat's nest.

Six gates of oak and shod iron eight inches thick. Three miles of ashlar-rubbled wall, thirty-five feet tall and as deep as five men laid out hands to feet. Forty-three rounded towers from which defenders could hurl boiling oil and hot sand. He knew Rorin's city walls by heart, down to the number of their murder holes, underminable sections, and secret entrances. It was with good reason that Stod Trambar and

Will Potter had aborted their siege, a fact lost on Shaddon and Edenia.

Kings come and go, Shaddon, he'd thought. *Think on your brother.*

A bold thought, an empty threat. The royals had assumed control of the Silver Walls with little resistance, courtesy of Charles Burke, who opened the Great Gates. Some of the late king's household staff had refused to swear fealty, up until the most defiant holdout, Sir Connor Tomas, had his neck snipped. Jon Applewood had been hauled off to the Red Tower, accused of furnishing Lorana with poison to murder Shaddon.

After that, silence fell over the city. Thousands of men-at-arms now patrolled Southpoint, relegating David's city guard to wall duty and harassing peasants out on errand. At curfew, Intercessors haunted the streets like black phantoms.

Shaddon hadn't deigned to meet the mayor's gaze, but the king's attention was unsparing. Three days ago, the new Chancellor of the Chancery, Jon Redoak, had upbraided him for Silver Street's river of refuse, so runny that it'd caused men to slip and injure themselves. Two days ago, Shaddon had demanded David's arrest. He'd relented only when the city's guild masters pointed out that a change of guard at their defensive walls might not be helpful during a time of war.

David was grateful at least for the incompetence of the new monarchs, oblivious as they seemed to what it meant to run this cesspool of a city. They needed him, and that bought time.

Still, he was under no illusion. Shaddon wanted to avenge Alyse Jannus, and he was impatient. War or no war, he wanted David's head.

Kings come and go, thought the mayor. A black rat paddled past his ankle, then reversed course and swam away from the orange hue filling the catacombs like hell's fiery glow.

Holding his torch aloft, Charles Burke waded around a corner. The Grand Inquisitor had traded his crimson robes for a patchy tunic and roughspun breeches that hung off his frail frame.

Stopping, he offered the mayor a gesture that would've stunned anyone familiar with the gossip of Hexar's court.

It was a handshake.

Men like them didn't secure their posts without learning how to mask their intentions effortlessly. Such was how the two spymasters had misled Hexar, his court, and the world for decades, masquerading as rivals bent on destroying each other when, in fact, they worked together.

Allies since the end of the Long Summer, they shared information with each other. Killed together, by ways and means. Even facilitated kidnappings and assassination attempts together.

David shook his ally's hand firmly. "I was starting to worry that you'd become a prisoner of your own Tower."

Charles hacked something between a cough and laugh into his sleeve. *You've never done well in these catacombs,* he thought. *But I played here as a boy. Dumped my first corpse here. I love this city as if it were my mother . . . and I'm abandoning it.*

"His Majesty has a kingdom to quell," Charles said as he cleared his throat. "New revolts by the day, everywhere."

That'll happen when you steal the Kingstrials. "Starting with those on our doorstep. Connor Bagman's peasants surround castles outside Rosbury and South Farcombe."

Charles scoffed. "Serfs armed with pitchforks. Warchild's the threat."

"But together, Warchild and Bagman control everything west of Barbara's Gorge."

"Only most of Southland."

"'Only.' Last I checked, Southpoint is in Southland." David studied the lost sleep under his ally's eyes. His gray hair looked as frayed as hay. "My eyes and ears report that Lord—or is it now *King?*—Trevor has anointed knights training Warchild's peasant army in combat and siege tactics."

A talented chameleon was Loran's Grand Inquisitor, challenging even David's skills of observation, but subtlety wasn't needed to know Charles's mood. He was boiling livid.

It was the Cloudlands' secession. Warchild had made a spectacle of crowning Trevor Wexley king of a not-insignificant swath of Loran. The decision was as unexpected as it was strategically brilliant, compounding the chaos gripping Loran and weakening Shaddon's already-weak claim. Upon hearing the news, His Majesty was said to have hurled his glowing crown at a cupbearer.

David, never fond of Hexar's bastard, had to admit that he was impressed. *Who has your remaining ear, Lord Warchild?*

He understood Charles's fury. Warchild had done nothing less than fling the Grand Inquisitor's great blunder in the kingdom's face. Hexar's Folly wouldn't have happened without Sir Hanorr Wexley's false confession, which they'd needed to throw the king off their scents in Erick Eddenhold's snatching.

But the torturer's reaction had another impetus. *And I'm one of the few souls who know it.*

Charles Burke served more than Loran's king. Like David himself, he took his orders from faceless powers whose aims transcended the continental rivalry between Elvarenists and Free Believers. These powers did not want a divided Loran. They wanted the kingdom of the Silver Walls whole for ends only they seemed to fully comprehend.

The Grand Inquisitor sneered. "Calling yourself a king and your mob an army won't make it so."

"Perhaps. But this 'Army of the People' numbers twenty-five thousand men and counting—"

"Including women and children—"

"—and catapults and trebuchets from the Cloudlands."

The Grand Inquisitor smiled wearily. He'd likely heard the same intelligence from numerous sources today. "Our men have everything in hand, David."

Our men. Shorthand for the order. For their faceless masters.

For the Barefoot Knights of the Northern Vine.

Of the Solemn Order's treacherous, convoluted history, David Renworth, a peasant, knew little. Commoners in Loran held that the Barefoot Knights had scuttled underground like roaches after their destruction centuries ago. But sometime after the Army of the Gods's withdrawal, with Alyse Jannus decapitated and Sarah Sinclair blown to bits, a still-young mayor heard a different account.

One night he'd awoken to a dagger pricking his throat. A dagger held by a Rose Guildsman.

That assassin, the one who'd offered him an ultimatum—his life, or lifelong service—would later disabuse him of his notions. After their ruin, the Barefoot Knights, like any faction of men trying to make sense of disaster, fell into infighting. Cleaving to dark visions, some proselytized a heresy that King Eduard's half-elven brood had not only survived Elzura's witchcraft but fled overseas, and that from their line would ascend the promised king.

Others charted a more practical path back to power. Over ages, these men infiltrated Elvarenism and courts and fortified their position with fantastic wealth. Work quietly, rise slowly, and return to mission: that was the way. So arose the Northern Vine, to which the assassin and Charles Burke both belonged.

Over time, David learned that Charles wasn't the only Barefoot Knight at the Silver Walls. The late Drexan Lorrain had been sworn to his rival branch, the heretical Southern Vine.

Repulsively, Charles and Drexan had shared more than a cause. They'd been lovers.

And in service to the shared interests of their clandestine orders, they'd killed King Hexar.

Not the six peasants who confessed under torture. Certainly not Shaddon. Not even Justen Sothos, although Pinkhands had played his part.

The Barefoot Knights had risen from the ashes to put an end to kings. *And I have no plans to follow Hexar,* thought the Little King.

David could've saved Hexar. He'd had every opportunity. But he'd already betrayed his religion once, and the Rose Guildsman's warning had been clear: David could either serve a holy cause unwaveringly, or he could serve crows.

The mayor stiffened. "Charles, I didn't ask to meet so we could share intelligence."

"Of course not." The Red Tower lord stroked the strip of black hair hanging off his chin that peasants considered his actual, tarred tongue.

"Tomorrow. An hour before sunrise. Wright's Pier."

"Is it Medecia, old friend?"

"For both of us." Charles shook his head. "Before he took Prince Erick, we could reason with Shaddon. He's not cooperating."

Not cooperating, David pondered. *And what do the other Barefoot Knights of the Northern Vine make of that?*

"You've shared Sinclair's confession with him?"

"He knows the truth about Sarah Sinclair's bastards. But our parts here are done." Charles extended his liver-spotted hand. "You earned Medecia, along with the lordship and manor that I understand await you. I'll have our crew prepare breakfast. How do boiled eggs sound?"

"Like a hearty start."

"Tomorrow, then, my friend."

David gripped his ally's hand. He caught the Barefoot Knight's glinting gaze just briefly as he circled and sloshed back the way he came. His torchlight cast shadows that transformed the pale roots creeping out of dirt walls into writhing snakes.

The mayor's smile faded with Charles's torchlight. Turning, he unhitched his sconced torch and handed it to the guardsman in boiled leather emerging from behind a brick column. *You've had your Shadow to protect you, Charles,* he thought, *and I've had Lotho.*

Lotho illuminated the waterlogged path back to the ladder, but David didn't require torchlight. He knew his city. Up the mayor climbed, the ladder squeaking complaint as his guardsman followed.

Inwardly, with every step, he recited the facts about Southpoint's walls. His walls. *Six gates,* he thought, *three miles of wall, forty-three towers.* Repetition felt soothing, like running prayer beads through his hands.

Reaching a wooden hatch door, David timed his knocks, and it slid open in a rush of sunlight and dust mites. A red-headed page no older than ten poked his head inside. He helped the mayor clamber up, then Lotho.

Eyes adjusting, David took in the Free Parish of God's reading hall. He wondered if he was the first Elvarenist mayor to hide in a parish.

I earned Medecia, he pondered as he slipped off refuse-caked boots for a pair of sandals the boy handed him. *A lordship, a manor . . . and the knife to open my throat tomorrow and leave me bobbing in the Shimmering Bay. The Northern Vine's way of thanking me for twenty years of service.*

David knew Charles Burke like his city. That last, fleeting look had told him he'd never reach Medecia if he ventured out to Wright's Pier. He'd outlived his usefulness.

The mayor instructed the page to fetch him ink, quill, calfskin, and a cup topped with squeezed lemon juice. Lotho, he told to unhobble his horse outside.

"Dress lightly and pack bread." David sat at a table, dabbing his quill in ink. "I need you to deliver a message to King Jason. Tonight."

Follow Me for Updates About the Sequel

Please follow me on social media for updates about *A Cavalry of Griffons,* the next book in this multi-volume epic fantasy series:

- Facebook: @authorryans
- Instagram: @asftrabble
- Threads: @schuette.ryan
- Twitter: @RyanMarcS
- Newsletter: RyanSchuette.com

APPENDIX

A GUIDE TO HISTORICAL EVENTS

THE CONFERRAL

Forty thousand years ago, the First King, Anjan Half-Elf, found himself and his army cornered on a mountain. According to the legends, Anjan's elven priest called down a lightning bolt that broke the mountain, entered the First King, and transmitted his power to twelve human champions.

THE END OF KING ANJAN'S LINE

Ten thousand years ago, King Eduard, a descendant of Anjan Half-Elf and an Ansaran, received a Casaanite queen named Elzura at his court. Religious texts hold that Elzura, a witch, cast a spell on Eduard. He vowed to kill his sister-wife, Tretha, and their half-elven children.

The king gave Tretha and his children a ten-minute start before riding out to kill them. A huntsman loyal to the House of Anjan followed on their heels, killing the wanton king and his party, but he was too late to save Tretha and the children.

This ended the House of Anjan and half-elven dominion. Bereft of a powerful king, ambitious men divided Ansara, hitherto one realm ruled from the Silver Walls, into thirteen kingdoms.

Ever since, Casaanites have been called Elzura's Children.

THE AWAKENING

Three centuries ago, a cultural, intellectual, and philosophical revolution spread through the Free Kingdoms. Started by Lord Gram Reuben of Tesos and other freethinkers, this movement taught men to question tradition and follow reason. This led to a schism in Elvarenism, yielding a new faith called the Free Beliefs.

THE INTERREGNUM

Two centuries ago, Sir Bradley Durhurst, along with twelve other knights, killed Loran's king, Lathros Dejoy. Petitioners from the Wing of the Commons helped them storm the throne room. This led to the Interregnum, a period of chaos in which Loran had no king. After Durhurst's ignoble end, Assemblymen restored the crown and expelled two classes from their ranks. Anointed men were driven from the Wing of Knights; the Wing of the Commons was abolished entirely.

THE LONG SUMMER REBELLION

Twenty years ago, a civil war erupted in Loran. King Hexar wanted to divorce his wife, Alyse Jannus, an Elvarenist, and marry Sarah Sinclair, a Free Believer. The Worthy Assembly mustered an Army of the Gods and marched on Southpoint to save Alyse and arrest the Sinclairs. Before they could, Hexar beheaded Alyse, and a blackpowder explosion killed Sarah. Lord Greg Thorngale made a fragile peace between king and Assembly, ending the war.

LORAN'S GOVERNMENT

The Kingdom of Loran is ruled by a king and Worthy Assembly.

THE MONARCHY

The king rules from the Silver Walls, a castle in Southpoint. He executes the laws and wages wars. A queen hasn't ruled Loran since Queen Barbara's reign a thousand years ago.

THE WORTHY ASSEMBLY

The Worthy Assembly is a congress of the kingdom's classes. This body makes laws and raises money for war. Governing from the Colossus in Loran's north, its three chambers include:

- THE WING OF LORDS, which seats Loran's noblemen;
- THE WING OF CLERGY, almost evenly divided between Elvarenist priests and readers of the Free Beliefs; and
- THE WING OF KNIGHTS, which only seats merchants, despite its name.

The Worthy Assembly once seated peasants in THE WING OF THE COMMONS, also known as THE FOURTH WING.

Each wing, or chamber, elects a speaker from its own ranks.

THE KINGSTRIALS

If a king dies without a legitimate heir, his Worthy Assembly must call the Kingstrials, a tournament designed to choose a new monarch. To become king, a lord must win three contests outright, or the Assembly will choose a king by consensus.

LORAN'S RELIGIONS

ELVARENISM

Elvarenists believe in a pantheon of twelve gods. Traditionally, they follow a religious leader called the priestking, who rules from the Lonely Isle off the coast of Eastern Ansara. Of Ansara's thirteen kingdoms, seven are Elvarenist.

THE FREE BELIEFS

Free Believers believe the Elvarenists' twelve gods are faces of One True God. A leader called the Master Reader oversees Free Believers in Loran. The Free Beliefs hold sway in Loran and the Free Kingdoms.

THE OLD WAYS

Although Elvarenists and Free Believers dominate Loran, many in the kingdom still follow the Old Ways—pagan beliefs in gods of field and forest. They call themselves Sylvanians, and they're known for practicing blood sacrifice.

ORGANIZATIONS

THE ORDER OF SIX SIGHTS

An academy based in Anjoun, THE ORDER OF SIX SIGHTS trains royal advisors in letters, philosophy, and statecraft for use across Ansara. Their alumni wear a distinctive steel helm debossed with their insignia—a lidless, all-seeing eye known as the Eye of Guldan.

THE ROSE GUILD

Headquartered in Medecia, THE ROSE GUILD is an ancient military order. Formerly a religious brotherhood, the guild is known these days as a lender, mercenary for hire, and—as rumor has it—a school for assassins. Its motto is *The Body Is Proof,* and its insignia depicts a thorny vine with three black roses.

THE SOLEMN ORDER

For millennia, THE BAREFOOT KNIGHTS OF THE SOLEMN ORDER existed for one purpose: to overthrow Ansaran kings and consolidate all lands and peoples under THE ASCENDANT KING, Anjan Half-Elf's last true descendant.

To this end, THE BAREFOOT KNIGHTS launched numerous unfruitful wars. Wrongly believed to have been destroyed during the Third Halfcrown War, THE BAREFOOT KNIGHTS split into two rival organizations—the NORTHERN VINE and SOUTHERN VINE.

HOUSE EDDENHOLD

KING HEXAR, Lord of Loran, four times married and widowed
The king's children, by their respective mothers:

- GARRETT EDDENHOLD, the crown prince, son
  of HARRIET
- LORANA EDDENHOLD, or ANA, steward, daughter
  of ALYSE
- ERICK EDDENHOLD, the deceased prince, son of ALYSE
- JASON WARCHILD, the bastard prince, son of SARAH
- HEATHER EDDENHOLD, the princess, daughter
  of ROMARA

The king's estranged brother, LORD SHADDON EDDENHOLD, exiled for his role in kidnapping a young ERICK EDDENHOLD

The king's advisors:
- JON APPLEWOOD, an apothecary
- CHARLES BURKE, the Grand Inquisitor and Lord of the
  Red Tower
- HANOR GRAXHOLD, a Tessian, Chancellor of
  the Exchequer
- DREXAN LORRAIN, known as the KING'S CROW,
  Chancellor of the Chancery

The king's knights, including:
- SIR CONNOR TOMAS, master-of-arms
- SIR DAVID BRIDGE
- SIR HORTUS GALLIVAR
- SIR ASTIBAN HOARD
- SIR SAM HORNBY
- SIR JEREMY HUNT
- SIR ROGIR LEVAN
- SIR HAROLD MARC
- SIR BLAKE OXLEY
- SIR ERICK SEAM
- SIR KYLE URRON
- SIR ANDREW WINDKIN

The king's Casaanite hostages, including:

- NAMONI of Tribe Chandiwe, who oversees the Casaanites
- ANYASHA of Tribe Nuur, or YASHA
- JHAZAR of Tribe Groth, also known as the INQUISITOR'S SHADOW
- MUSA and SAAN, brothers, both of Tribe Chandiwe
- ZURAN of Tribe Nuur, or ZUR

LORANA'S lady-in-waiting, LORNA DURROS

LOYAL COMPANYMEN

LORD EVAN SINCLAIR, Speaker of the LOYAL COMPANY, an underground political movement divided into two factions

SINCLAIR'S faction, the PETITIONERS, include:

- GEOFF DONOVAN, also known as the Whore Lord, a brothel owner and Assemblyman
- LORN GRANGER, a merchant and Assemblyman
- DREXYN LAUPHREY, a merchant and Assemblyman
- TRISTAN LOX, a fur trader and Assemblyman
- RATHOS ROBSWELL, also known as SILVERTONGUE, his deputy speaker
- TOM WEBB, a merchant and Assemblyman

REZLAN AMBROSE, a coal hand mockingly called the LORD OF SHOALTOWN, founded the LOYAL COMPANY with SINCLAIR

AMBROSE leads a faction called the REUBENITES, who include:

- LORD JACOB FARRYLL, a nobleman and Assemblyman
- LORD SAMUEL IRONKEEP, a nobleman and Assemblyman
- LORD JEFF MOHR, a nobleman and Assemblyman
- KARL REDMORE, a freeholder
- JON WATLEY, also known as FIREMOUTH, a rabble-rousing reader of the Free Beliefs

The PIGEONS, armed spies and messengers in service to the LOYAL COMPANY, help Companymen stay ahead of the men who want to apprehend or kill them. Their regiments include:

- The SOOTHSAYERS, composed of TOM GOODFIELD, JACOB, REED, VARN, and YULE
- The WATERFOWL

MASON GREXON, a co-conspirator, owns the Last Elford Inn

NOBLE HOUSES, THEIR FAMILIES, AND SWORN MEN

HOUSE DURROS

LORD ALAN DURROS, Lord of Linwick Castle and Lord Warden of South Farcombe

DURROS'S child, LORNA DURROS, a lady-in-waiting

HOUSE FAWKES

LORD TOMAS FAWKES, Lord of Westerliche

FAWKES'S sworn vassal lords include:

- SHANNEN FOWL, Lord of Wesswood
- VENN LAMPOREAN, Lord of Ethelwood
- ORRENN SILVERSPEAR, Lord of Copper Grove

HOUSE GELDER

LORD TOM GELDER, Lord of Major Sunder, an Elvarenist

HOUSE MORLEY

LORD UTHRON MORLEY, Lord of Thorn's Keep and Lord Warden of Rosbury Village, husband to LADY CATHREEN MORLEY, a Magnesian noblewoman

Their children:
* SAM MORLEY
* BARBARA MORLEY
* HARRIET MORLEY
* MAEDA MORLEY

The lord's cousin, UTHER BRUNE, an Elvarenist priest

The lord's knights:
* SIR BARDO LYM
* SIR LUC TOLOS

The lord's officers:
* SIR WILLARD RITTMAN, justice of the peace
* GEFFREY CHAFFER, a justice's deputy
* TOMAS LEER, also known as SWEET TOM, a justice's deputy

The lord's servant, MANNI

HOUSE SINCLAIR

LORD EVAN SINCLAIR, Lord of Caerdon Castle and Speaker of the Loyal Company, a band of traitors, once widowed

The lord's children by the late LADY FAYE HALIFAX:
* MINA SINCLAIR, lady and steward in her father's absence
* LEAH SINCLAIR, the so-called MAD LADY OF THE HERETICS

The lord's late sister, LADY SARAH SINCLAIR, the illegitimate third wife of KING HEXAR and mother of JASON WARCHILD

The lord's wards, sired by the late SIR MATTHUS ROBSWELL and his wife, ANNA, a castle laundress:
* RATHOS ROBSWELL, also known as SILVERTONGUE, a member of the Loyal Company
* DANA ROBSWELL

HOUSE SOTHOS

LORD GRAM SOTHOS, also called THE HAMMER OF THE COMMONS, LORDSBANE, and PINKHANDS, Lord of Saxhold Castle, Speaker of the Worthy Assembly's Wing of Lords. SOTHOS is husband to LADY TESS SOTHOS. Their children include LORD JUSTEN SOTHOS, their firstborn son.

SOTHOS'S sworn vassal lords include:
- PETOR ELLSBY, Lord of Odoro
- DOMIN GREATHALL, Lord of Ivanton
- JACOB HEXBROOK, Lord of Redforge
- JON REDOAK, Lord of Fordham
- DUMAS SUNOX, Lord of Ramsport
- ARON TULLER, Lord of Savon

SOTHOS'S sworn knights include SIR GORDON WHITECASTLE, a trapper

HOUSE THORNGALE

LORD GREG THORNGALE, also known as the OLD OAK, Lord of Thessela, a moderate Elvarenist famed for negotiating the end of the Long Summer Rebellion

THORNGALE'S children:
- DARREN THORNGALE, also known as the STORMSWORD, a hero famous for killing thirty-nine Uzmen single-handedly
- GAVIN THORNGALE, the eldest
- LUC THORNGALE, lastborn

HOUSE WEXLEY

LORD TREVOR WEXLEY, also known as the BULL, Lord of Eddenloxley Castle and unrecognized ruler of the Cloudlands, husband to LADY UTHRA WEXLEY. They have nine daughters.

WEXLEY is warder to the children and wife of his late brother SIR HANORR WEXLEY, a traitor:

- YOSAR WEXLEY, SIR HANORR'S widow, an Orranese woman
- HANORR THE YOUNGER
- TREVOR WEXLEY, named after his warder
- YASMEEN WEXLEY

WEXLEY'S sworn vassal lords include:

- DEREK CLABBARD, Lord of Whitecape
- ZAROLD ULBRIDGE, Lord of Hapry Springs
- RUSSELL WEXRENN, Lord of Sheep Hills

WEXLEY'S other sworn men include:

- SIR HALFORD IRONKEEP, a knight
- EORL, an apothecary

HOUSE WUTHERS

LORD SAM WUTHERS, Lord of Minor Sunder

OUTLAWS AND OTHERS

The HERETICS, a band of outlaws led by LEAH SINCLAIR, the so-called MAD LADY, and which includes:

- CREATURE, a madman
- DUSTIN, her paramour
- GOOSE
- JEFF THE GIANT, a dwarf
- LETHABO, a Casaanite
- LISHA, a Sylvanian
- MURG, an Uzman
- PRETTY PHILLIP
- STONEHANDS
- VENN

MERMAN JARROD, captain of *The Drunken Adventure*

FREDERICK MIDLICHE, known as the FOX, a merchant and Speaker of the Worthy Assembly's Wing of Knights

The LADY ORELLA, known as the ORACLE or LADY AT THE TREE, a mysterious griffon-tamer at the Great Tree of Loran, and those with her, including:
- SIR FEMI
- ABEBA

OTHER REALMS' LEADERS

HIGHLORD KAR KRAVACK, chieftain of the tribes of UZLAND, whose denizens include:
- DUNG, the highlord's dragoman

GRISHOLM OLISTAIR, king of TESOS

PRIESTKING PARLISIS, leader of the Elvarenist faith, rules from the LONELY ISLE, a kingdom in Eastern Ansara

VHIZADYN SKULLTOWERS, a Muhregite general in THE BRACE

THE PEASANTS

Loran's peasants, also known collectively as THE COMMONS, or COMMONERS, the lowest social class

ROSBURY VILLAGE

- SIR DAMIEN SOTHRON, a knight of House Morley
- ROSE SOTHRON, his wife
- SARA SOTHRON, his daughter
- DEVAN, his squire

Other villagers:
- LUC ALMSMAN
- CONNOR BAGMAN

- CALEB BARD
- ELFRED, a priest
- SETH BRIARFIELD
- FARMER GREY and his wife
- DESSA GORD
- ALFORD HEMLOCK
- GARY HENLEY, a reader
- CLYDE HOBBS
- HEXAAR OLMSTEAD
- FORD ROUNSEY
- CAM SUFFREY
- ASHLEY VAULD
- JACLYN WEBSTER
- PRAISE WHORESON

The villagers' children:
- ALFRID
- BRAM HOBBS
- FROGFACE JENNY
- PESH, or PESH THE PRINCE

Rumored Sylvanians:
- BILL
- ORTHOS and OWEN, brothers
- TOM
- JACOB WEESLAW, or SPITTLELIP

PEASANTS AT THE COLOSSUS

- RORYN COOK
- SHANNON IRONKEEP
- JAINA NADLEY
- TYLER ROLFE of South Farcombe
- JONATHAN SMITH
- SHREVE

SOUTHPOINT

LORD DAVID RENWORTH, also known as the LITTLE KING, mayor of Southpoint

LOTHO, a trusted city guard

Kitchen help at the Silver Walls:
- DORIAN FIELDER, friend to TYLER ROLFE
- ERIN, the baker's wife
- SEAN, a butcher, and his sons DONLEY and GAMLEN

RELIGIOUS LEADERS

MASTER READER JACOB SULLEY, the leader of Loran's Free Beliefs, member of the Worthy Assembly's Wing of Clergy

PRIESTKING PARLISIS, leader of the Elvarenist faith, rules from the LONELY ISLE, a kingdom in Eastern Ansara

The priestking's only child, EDENIA HIGHDAUGHTER, prieslenne and high priestess of their faith

The priestking's emissary in Loran:
- PESHAR GRATHOS, High Bishop, Speaker of the Worthy Assembly's Wing of Clergy

Warriors of the Elvarenist faith:
- VAYNE ADRIAS, captain of the prieslenne's personal guard
- TERYLL QUATHOR, an Intercessor

Acknowledgements

Writing a fantasy novel of this size is a lot like illustrating in pen and ink. You may outline a great plot, as you may create a terrific drawing . . . but it all comes down to execution.

I had help from a lot of amazing people to execute this dream. I'm grateful to my editor, Leigh Grossman, for tearing up my first two drafts. Sean Mallen, Mark Eckert, and Cassandra Shuptar critiqued early versions. Ryan Engen and Victor McDonald read the third draft, giving me invaluable feedback and helping me remember why I wrote it. Jason Niehaus went above and beyond, reviewing the third draft twice and returning annotated copies. A special friend encouraged me to finish this work and celebrated it by organizing a fabulous reading in Johannesburg, South Africa, and I'm grateful to her.

Western political theories informed this novel about inclusion, representation, and the dangers of denying others a seat at the decision-making table. I'm grateful to my professor, Richard Ruderman, for exposing me to the philosophers who inspired this work. Brendan Millan introduced me to new dead guys and read several chapters, evaluating the philosophically grounded ones with care. Sam Meddis, another friend and professor, taught me that everything in politics is deliberate.

I also want to thank Nyiia Ricks, my first fan, who read my earliest attempts at writing in high school and called me gifted.

Ted Nasmith's illustrations attracted me to the fantasy genre early on, and it was another dream realized to work with him on two glorious covers.

Finally, I want to thank my mother, Pat Schuette, for believing in me, supporting me, and making the earliest drafts possible.

My love and gratitude to you all.

About the Author

Ryan Schuette is the author of *A Seat for the Rabble*, *An End to Kings*, and *The Art of the Big Lie: Political Cartoons About the Fight for America's Soul*. He's also authored a romance novel under his pseudonym.

Ryan wore a few hats before returning to fantasy fiction and art. He's both illustrated and reported for National Public Radio and various trade publications, including *DS News* and *MReport*. He's also freelanced for Al Jazeera America. He lived and worked in Uganda as a 2008-2009 Rotary Ambassadorial Scholar and holds a master's degree from American University in Washington, D.C.

Somewhere along the way, he also started a nonprofit and fair-trade lingerie company that operated in West and Central Africa, respectively. Many of his friends still wear safari-print boxers.

Ryan lives in Texas, where he looks after his cat, Rusty.

To learn more about Ryan or his epic fantasy series, *A King Without a Crown*, visit RyanSchuette.com.

A *Cavalry* of *Griffons*

The Miracle

he big man shuddered awake to the distant ring of steel.

Praise was still pawing about his cell when a monstrous sound erupted outside the dungeon. Wondering if Thorn's Keep itself was collapsing, he wailed.

A slap upside his head shocked him into silence.

Praise turned about to see Geffrey withdrawing his hand. The new sheriff glared menacingly through the iron bars. "Shut your mouth, you hear me? You'll shut it *now,* you stupid fuck."

His growly voice, the rage in his eyes, all made him feel as small and scared as he'd always felt. Praise wept miserably.

"Stop it, Geffrey, you'll only make it worse," Tolos chided him.

Geffrey spun on the knight, his shoulders stiff. "That's *Sir* Geffrey to you, knight. I'm in charge, not you!"

"Lord Sam had need of a sheriff 'cause Commoners tore Will Rittman apart like mutton." That came from Cam Suffrey, another peasant imprisoned in the dank, sparsely lit dungeon. "You're a useful idiot."

The sheriff clanged his sword on Cam's iron bars, nearly catching fingers. "*SHUT YOUR MOUTH!*" he cried.

Feet across, Alford Hemlock poked his stubbly face through his iron bars. "Your title wonna stop Connor or Firemouth from hanging you, *sheriff,*" he said with relish.

Whirling, the sheriff stabbed at Alford through the bars.

Alford stayed clear of his thrusts, grinning mischievously. "Do you feel the noose tightening yet, Geff? Maybe you could speak up again, Praise? Let Connor know where to find us."

A thread of snot dangled from the idiot's nose. He sucked it up wetly. "Round, round it spins," Praise crooned, rocking to console himself, "until off it rolls again."

Sometimes his rhyme was all that gave him joy. He sang it upon waking every morning, sang it before he fell asleep on his straw. He and the other Rosbury peasants had been locked up beneath Thorn's Keep since Sir Willard Rittman's wedding, and singing gave him comfort.

Praise couldn't say why he'd been beaten and taken. On the wedding day, he'd come across the other men of Rosbury talking excitedly in the forest. They'd told him they meant to attend Sir Willard's wedding, and wouldn't it be fun if he came with them?

It was fun, briefly. Oh, he'd laughed when Alford made a game of throwing refuse at Lord Morley's son. But after that, the wedding went to bits and pieces, the peasants and knights ripping at each other like rabid dogs.

It'd been a terrible stay in the dungeon and often boring, up until last week. Strange-sounding horns had blared outside, exciting the imprisoned peasants and worrying Tolos and Lym, Geffrey most of all. Every day there was talk about "revults."

He didn't know what revults meant, but they spread like the pox, or like wildfire, as Geffrey was fond of saying when he paced back and forth agitatedly. Every day they heard of a new revult. One in Rosbury, another in Southfar, a third in a village near Grayport. Nothing had caused alarm among the turnkeys like word of the revult in Northland.

Whatever a revult was, it made an already-miserable stay here more miserable.

Then, some days ago, the Morley servant, Manni, entered the dungeon to share that Rosbury's peasants now completely encircled Thorn's Keep. After that, they'd begun rationing food. The brown pea soup and soggy bread had been tolerable, but at least that'd been *something*. Now they only had stone-hard heels of bread.

His groaning belly reminded him of his fearsome hunger. He rocked himself, singing the rhyme a little louder.

Twisting, Geffrey glared at him through the cell bars. "So help me," the sheriff began, "if you keep on—"

"You'll *what?*" Alford broke in tauntingly. "Kill another Commoner? Just before our friend breaks down those gates outside—repays you for your betrayal?"

"I done nothin'," Geffrey muttered.

The dungeon erupted with mocking laughter.

Near the dungeon door, Clyde Hobbs grabbed two of his bar cells, as if he meant to rattle them free. "Sweet Tom raped Ford Rounsey's wife," he said through clenched teeth.

Geffrey cocked his thumb at his chest. "Am *I* Tom?" he shot back. "I raped no one, you ask anyone—"

"You and Willard whipped Farmer Grey near to death."

The sheriff spun about on the second accuser with balled fists, as if he'd been struck. "That was *Willard!*"

"Willard murdered Sara Sothron." Reader Gary's voice issued rich and fierce through the dungeon hall, as it always had at Twelve Mercies.

Praise rubbed his thick wrists, remembering how sore they'd felt after the reader had pinned them between pillory boards. He hadn't broken any bell. Hadn't done anything to deserve that.

"You were Willard's deputy," Reader Gary added.

Geffrey flared pink as his stained teeth. "*How many fuckin' times do I have to—?*" He trembled. "I—WAS—NAH—THERE!"

"You might's well have been," Alford fired back. "You were three o' a kind, you, Tom, and Will. It's why Connor and Jon Watley and all their men have Thorn's Keep surrounded."

Geffrey shook his head solemnly. "I was paid to do a job," he said. "And I donna care what you or anyone says about poor Sir Willard. That mad horse killed Sara, not Will. He saw her as his own daughter—"

A deafening clap of thunder silenced them all at once . . . only, it wasn't raining. The sunken dungeon shook as from an earthquake. The narrow chamber ran orange, almost as bright as day, and then darkened again.

Tolos crossed the dungeon as if he were lost in a dream. He stared unblinking through the window as shouts filled the bailey outside. "They're in."

Bardo Lym paled. "*How?*" his whisper eked out. "How can peasants besiege a castle . . . *without* siege engines?"

"Maybe Firemouth found some blackpowder," Alford said with a daring grin, eyeing Geffrey.

"*Lies,*" the sheriff spat. "Hexar got rid of blackpowder."

"Why donna we ask Connor what that was?" Alford raised his voice to a shout, crying for his friend. "*Connor, Connooor!*"

Up and down their dimly lit dungeon corridor, the lost men of Rosbury clamored for rescue. Clyde rattled his bucket against his iron bars. Reader Gary shouted for Connor through the window bars. Trembling, Geffrey strayed to the dungeon's rear wall, to the cobwebbed rack lined with halberds and axes.

The excitement lifted even Praise out of his hunger spell. He jumped about and clapped excitedly, more loudly as other peasants urged him on. Drunk on the liquor of encouragement, he began shaking his iron bars, then hurling himself against them, giggling at the game. Alford and Clyde cheered him on, telling him to hurl himself harder—no, harder, Praise, *harder!*

The relief from weeks of boredom and terror, of Geffrey's bullying, all of it overwhelmed Praise. "Round, ROUND it spins, until OFF IT ROLLS AGAIN." He felt tension in one of the iron bars as he pulled on them and thought it might give. "Round, ROUND—"

Fire lanced through his arm. The great man staggered down, grabbing at the crimson streak on his forearm. Geffrey tried to stab him again, forcing Praise back to his straw bed as he bawled hysterically.

"Who's next, then?" Circling about, the sheriff swung his sword at Clyde, whacking the bars. Ignoring the other guards, he swiped at Alford through his cell bars. Evading strokes, Alford snatched his pail by its handle and splattered his attacker with his own slop.

Geffrey mopped refuse off his face. "*I'LL KILL YOU!*" He searched frantically through the hoop of keys on his belt for the one to unlock Alford's cell.

Alford beckoned him with a finger. "Come on, then, you pink-toothed cunt. If a little girl could lame you with a scratch of her stick"—he raised his fists—"then I can send you to hell with not but what the god o' twelve faces gave me."

"SHE HAD SWORDWOOD!"

"I donna fucking care."

Geffrey didn't see Tolos coming. The knight struck the sheriff's bandaged thigh with the flat side of his sword, and Geffrey fell, screaming as blood streamed down his leg. Tolos didn't relent. He kicked him repeatedly in his belly, again and again, stopping only when the official ceased moving.

Tolos panted heavily. He wiped sweat off his forehead with a greasy forearm. "All right then," the young knight said softly. Fire's glow illuminated the dungeon again, sharpening the blades of flaxen hair on his chin. "All right."

Alford looked on, smiling lopsided. "'Bout fuckin' time."

Everyone applauded Tolos, chanting his name, everyone but Praise and Bardo Lym. The portly knight stared at Geffrey in horror. "Luc . . . Luc—*what have you done?*"

"What I should've done when the siege started," the lean one muttered. "We're in this because of him, Bardo, are we not? He and Sir Willard and their Sweet Tom. They terrorized the peasants—our neighbors, our friends. You lads, you shoulda never been locked away, none of you."

Reader Gary nodded. "If it were nah for Will, Sara Sothron would still be alive, and we might have peace."

Sara. Praise remembered the girl who'd refused to hurl pebbles at him outside Twelve Mercies. *Sara . . .*

"What about your vows?" Seth Briarfield asked of Tolos from the cell beside Clyde's. "Not that I'm whingein', sir."

The knight jerked back his coif. Sweat-soaked brown hair drizzled his forehead in bangs. "I swore to serve Lord Uthron—not his white-haired witch, and the One True God knows *she's* had a hand in all this." He kicked at Geffrey again. "I *certainly* never swore to serve this piece of shit."

"But House Morley . . ." Bardo said nervously.

"Is done and over, no thanks to Lord Uthron himself," the knight said. "It's no use fighting, Bardo." He mopped sweat off his forehead. "We're surrendering. I'd rather wed my steel to Connor Bagman and Firemouth and their cause."

"The Common cause," said Alford, his eyes reflecting the fire outside their dungeon windows. "Should you wish to join us, sir, you'd be welcome. You were more than fair to us here, and that's what I'll tell Connor. He'll treat you well, Luc, I know he will. Connor knows you."

"And I, him." Tolos unhooked his hoop keys and chucked them at Reader Gary, who caught them deftly through his bars. "First you, Gary, then everyone else. Can you vouch for us?"

"Yes, you have my word, Luc." The reader rattled a key in his lock. "Which is mine?" he asked.

"And . . . me, Alford?" Bardo looked as lost as Praise felt. The big man felt sorry for him.

"Depends. Can you be useful, Bardo?" The others laughed.

"This is treason, Luc, you comin' with us," Clyde warned. "I known you all your life. Your mum wouldna care for this."

Tolos smirked. "Nah, she wouldna care for it. Not one bit."

"Round, round it spins," Praise sang under his breath. Outside, steel rang against steel. Peering through his window bars, he saw shadows running up flights of stairs and across battlements. "Until off it rolls again . . ."

"Shaddon is king now, remember," Clyde Hobbs reminded Tolos. "His prieslenne whore's *queen,* if Manni told us true."

"Their Intercessors will burn any peasants in arms," Cam chimed. "Just like they did the Barefoot Knights of old."

The knight scooped a torch free of its sconce on the wall. He held it up. "Then I suppose the king, his queen, and their ghouls'll need more wood and oil." The peasants clapped and cheered him on lustily.

A rustle of cloth drew Praise's attention to the grounds outside his window. Two shadows shuffled by, one clinking with armor. Dagged flames trailed after them, as if they had burning chains lashed to their ankles. The flames rose into walls, preventing him from seeing anything beyond. *Beautiful,* he thought.

His joyous clapping alerted Stram Doling. "Someone lit a fire outside," he said urgently. "We need to go. Not sure Connor can do us much good if we all roast like pigs down here."

Out of his cell, Reader Gary hastened to free the others. Kneeling, Tolos snatched the hoop of keys still tied to Geffrey's belt. Clyde Hobbs told Cam how much he looked forward to seeing his boy again, if he hadn't been taken, that was.

The dungeon door creaked open on its hinges.

Tolos glanced at Reader Gary. "That you, Connor?" he called out. "It's . . . it's Luc. I'm armed, but I'll surrender my weapon." He lowered his sword to his feet, as if it were a prize.

"Now or never, knight," Alford goaded Bardo, smiling.

The fat knight wrestled with his scabbard, tongue slipping across his lips as he worked to uncinch it.

Reader Gary plucked another torch from its sconce. He stepped closer to the door. "Sir Luc speaks the truth, whoever you are. He freed us. He's with us. And we're with Connor Bagman."

The door opened fully, revealing a knight in coif and boiled leather. Beside him stood what looked like a child draped in a short, gray, hooded cloak.

The reader's torch snarled to the floor. "*Damien?*"

Praise peered at Rosbury's lost knight through his cell bars. Sir Damien Sothron looked terrible. His face looked like it'd been scratched to ribbons by a mountain cat, and his skin had a sallow sheen. A mist grayed his eyes.

"It can't be." Clyde stared through his bars.

"*Damien?*" Alford pumped the air with his fists. "Now we have everyone. All the men of Rosbury!"

Even Geffrey slithered up. Tears glistened on his purpled cheeks like morning dew. "*Sara.*"

The knight's daughter stepped into shifting torchlight. Praise didn't know why everyone looked at Sara so strangely. She seemed exactly the same as he remembered her at the pillories. Only, her eyes were white. White as snow.

"Sara," Reader Gary murmured.

Clyde shook his head in disbelief. "No, we *buried* her," he said between quick breaths. "I built the girl's oricus with mine hands." He stared at his hands as if they'd suddenly vanished.

"Sir Damien, what's wrong with your chest?" Cam asked, stunned. "He's been injured."

The knight's chest had as many holes as Jacob Weeslaw's lips. Praise could see *right through them,* straight to the flame wall throwing light outside the door. The trick amused him; he clapped his hands once, delighted.

Reader Gary raised his hands reverently, his long sleeves bunching up at his elbows. "Praise the One True God!" Praise smiled at the sound of his name. "Praise him! Donna you see, lads? God is with Loran's peasants. *It's . . . it's a miracle!*"

As he finished saying *miracle,* Damien opened his mouth. In the dark of his throat whirled the fireflies of orange embers, and then out spewed a jet of flame. Reader Gary screamed as fire engulfed him in waves. He ran this way and that, hysterical, a huge living torch.

Everyone screamed or called on god. They demanded the keys, only to realize that Reader Gary still had them. Praise felt the heat from the reader's crackling corpse as it finally fell. It was terrible. He shut his eyes tight. Tears leaked through.

"Mother, stop it," he wept brokenly.

And for the first time since his mother shut her eyes and went away forever, the big man heard her respond. *Watch,* the loveliest voice in all the world said in his head.

Calmly, Damien began walking past the row of cells on his right, his gait halting and wooden, as if his knees had stopped working.

Inside, Cam Suffrey pled and begged—please, no, no, *please*, Damien. The knight blew out a cone of dragonflame, then approached the next cell. Stram Doling begged for his life, called on the godface of Maetha, and burned. Pillars of smoke rose from the smoldering bodies.

Sara smiled as if she were pleased.

Alford grasped desperately at Geffrey through the bars. "The keys, *Geff!* Open the bloody cell! *OPEN IT!*"

The sheriff didn't hear him. Tears streaked his cheeks. He backtracked on all fours, crablike, until he bumped into the rack of weapons, knocking an axe to the floor.

Clyde screamed at Tolos and Bardo to *do something, do something,* as flame swept his cage. The chubbier guard shook, chin crumpled up like calfskin as he wept.

Sir Luc Tolos recovered his sword. With a fierce cry he embedded his steel in Damen's shoulder, cutting down to white bone.

Dark blood founted from the knight's shoulder, down his front. Damien didn't seem to even notice. He took Luc Tolos's head with both hands. There was a loud *crack*, and the young man dropped to the floor, unmoving.

Damien lumbered on, the sword in his shoulder swaying. Bardo vanished inside a funnel of flame.

Mother, stop it, Praise pled inwardly.

Watch, that lovely voice whispered back.

Half a dozen prisoners remained. Alford was shrieking at Geffrey, who slumped against the wall, mesmerized. The knight inundated another cell with his flame. Smoke and a rancid reek filled the narrow prison, making it hard to see or breathe.

"*I'VE GOT IT!*" Alford jammed a key into his lock and hurled open his door. He went from cell to cell, freeing the remaining peasants, then helped Geffrey up.

Praise was rocking back and forth when Alford flung open his own cell door. "Praise, we need you." He offered his hand . . . and barely withdrew it in time before the cell door slammed shut with such force it left the big man's ears ringing.

Sara walked in front of Sir Damien. Around her and her father, the shiftless bodies of Reader Gary and Clyde and Cam and Stram and Bardo crackled and popped like pigs sweating grease. Their fires flooded the dungeon with orange light.

By now Alford had led the peasants to arm themselves with axes and halberds from the rack. He rallied them to his side. Geffrey remained curled up, crying. The armed peasants faced Sara and Damien from the opposite end of the corridor.

"*HELP ME KILL THESE DEVILS!*" Alford cried. All but the sheriff fell in with him, charging the girl and her father with their weapons pointed.

The white-eyed girl held her scarred palms parallel. She drew her arms apart, as if she were opening a cupboard . . . and the earth trembled.

A hole opened at her feet, spreading with a jagged crevice line that forked lightning-quick toward the peasants. Dust and rocks flowed off the edges into a smoky abyss slashed with the glow of fire.

Frightening sounds drifted up from the chasm. Sounds Praise could never, ever forget. Beasts snarling. Screams for mercy that echoed up.

Alford and the Rosbury men halted at the brink, teetering, trying to back up. The pit swallowed them all, first Alford, who clawed at a root dangling from the soil, then Seth and everyone else, screams fading. Geffrey slid flailing into the abyss.

Moments passed. It was only when he listened to the fire crackling that Praise realized he'd closed his eyes, against his mother's wishes. He peeked through his trembling fingers.

Mended soil showed no trace of hell. Yet Reader Gary, Clyde, Cam, Stram, and the knights remained asprawl on the floor, crackling in fires that licked and charred stone ceiling.

The hooded girl walked ahead of her father, unrushed. Praise's cell door groaned open with a will of its own.

The big man convulsed pathetically, weeping. Piss dampened his breeches.

Look, she said inside his head. He looked hesitantly at his arm. The scar Geffrey had given him was miraculously gone, as if it'd never been there at all. "Mother?" Praise asked hesitantly.

Sara's white eyes twinkled like stars. *Follow her west,* came his mother's sweet voice. *Follow her to me.*

"I will," he told her.

Praise rose slowly. He exited his cell uncertainly, fearing Geffrey's wrath. *But Geffrey is gone,* he remembered.

He paid the dungeon a final look, then followed Sara and her father past the fires, out into the night.

www.ingramcontent.com/pod-product-compliance
Lightning Source LLC
Chambersburg PA
CBHW032102310726
48972CB00001B/71